WHITE TRASH
ZOMBIE
APOCALYPSE

DIANA ROWLAND

DAW BOOKS, INC.
DONALD A. WOLLHEIM, FOUNDER
375 Hudson Street, New York, NY 10014

ELIZABETH R. WOLLHEIM
SHEILA E. GILBERT
PUBLISHERS
http://www.dawbooks.com

First Printing, July 2013

3   4   5   6   7   8   9

For Jack and Anna

ACKNOWLEDGMENTS

This book would not be possible without a great deal of help and support.

Therefore, enormous thanks go out to Sherry Rowland, Kat Johnson, Dr. Kristi Charish, Robert J. Durand, Myke Cole, Mary Robinette Kowal, Dr. Michael Defatta, Catherine Rathbun, Tara Sullivan Palmer, Tricia Borne, Deborah Jack, Lindsay Ribar, Matt Bialer, Dan Dos Santos, Marylou Capes-Platt, Joshua Starr, Betsy Wollheim, everyone at DAW, the internet hivemind, and all of my wonderful readers.

Chapter 1

Rain. Lots of it. Not yet, but soon. I hadn't heard a forecast, and I sure as hell wasn't psychic, but I'd lived in southeastern Louisiana all my life and felt the coming downpour in my bones. Of course, the really dark, ominous clouds helped a bit too.

But that was nothing. Not with zombies roaming the streets of Tucker Point.

Several shuffled along the sidewalk, and a dozen or so huddled together, gruesome and shabby, in front of the Sundown Café, one taking a drag from a cigarette through cracked and bloody lips. Apart from the nearby movie crew, the cigarette was a sure sign these were zombie wannabes and not the real thing.

No self-respecting zombie would be caught dead smoking.

Caught dead. I snorted. But the truth was that zombies were some of the cleanest-living people I knew. Had to be since anything bad for you, like cigarette smoke, drugs, or alcohol, used up precious brains to detoxify the body. And if you didn't get more brains quickly, you'd start to rot. Not fun. I'd been a pill-popping alcoholic smoker before I was turned. Now the most toxic substance I consumed was coffee.

Well, mostly. Every now and then I still took a quick drag for old times sake.

I drove slowly, watching with roll-my-eyes amusement as the crew filmed a couple of fake zombies shambling after a shotgun-wielding woman. No stereotypes here. No sirree.

The majority of the movie-related activity seemed to be taking place at the back of Tucker Point High School, where school had let out for the summer a week earlier. A couple of eighteen-wheelers were pulled up in the lot on the side, and I saw movie people and equipment all over the blocked-off street ahead as well as on the school grounds to the left.

The cop at the end of the street pulled the barricade aside without my having to flash my badge. My Coroner's Office van was plain black with no markings, but he'd probably been on enough death scenes to know the routine well enough to expect me. His face registered recognition, and he gave me a friendly wave as I passed through. I gave a polite hand lift in response but had no clue if I'd ever seen him before. It was probably a lot easier for cops to remember the scrawny little blond chick who worked as a bodysnatcher for the Coroner's Office than for me to remember one cop's face in a sea of identical uniforms.

I proceeded slowly, trying to get a good look at the movie hoopla without obviously gawking or running into anything. Parked against the curb about a half block down was a white SUV with *St. Edwards Parish Sheriff's Office Crime Scene* emblazoned across the side, and right behind it the black Dodge Durango that belonged to Derrel Cusimano, the death investigator I was partnered with.

As I parked behind the Durango, a tall woman with

brunette hair bound up in a severe bun and wearing a sheriff's office t-shirt walked up to the SUV. Maria, a crime scene tech. As I climbed out of the van, she gave me a smile and a thumbs up to let me know she was finished with her work. I returned the smile and gave an acknowledging wave. With rare exceptions, a crime scene tech had to take photos and process any death scene in case there was a need later on to review the specifics. The actual removal of the body came last, after the techs did their stuff and the detectives had a good look at everything. I'd been collecting bodies from all sorts of death scenes for a while now, so I was pretty used to the routine. The techs appreciated that I stayed out of their way while they worked, and in return they let me know the instant I could get on with my own business.

I moved to the back of the van, pulled the stretcher out, and lumped a body bag and a couple of sheets on top, then looked around for my hard-to-miss partner, a big, bald, black guy with muscle to spare. He'd been an LSU linebacker ten or so years back and still looked every bit the part.

I spied him striding across the street toward me with a notepad in his hand. He'd probably been here a while already, gathering information, taking notes, and speaking to detectives and witnesses.

"Perfect timing," he said after he reached me. "Maria finished processing the scene only a couple of minutes ago."

"Yep, she gave me the go-ahead," I replied, then swept my gaze around the area with its bustling activity. Crew members carted fancy equipment here and there, men and women scrambled over set pieces, painting, nailing, clamping, and cutting. A man with deep lines of stress around his eyes consulted the stack of papers on his clipboard and gave instructions—accompanied by a lot of arm waving—to the crew. Apart from the one

scene with the shotgun, there wasn't any actual filming
going on in the blocked-off street, but the behind-the-
scenes stuff made up for it. And there were fake zombies
everywhere. Only about ten or so wore full makeup, but
the rest sported the equivalent of spray-on tan, except
instead of Sun Kissed Bronze it was Decay Grey.

"This is too cool," I said.

Derrel's mouth twitched. He knew perfectly well I
wasn't talking about the body I'd come to pick up.

"So whatcha got?" I asked.

A grimace flashed over his face. "Freak accident. Support pole on some scaffolding fell as our Mr. Brent Stewart was walking by, and he got beaned right in the skull."
He gestured with his head toward a cluster of trailers
and headed that way. I followed, towing the stretcher in
my wake as we passed through the trailer area, then toward a sidewalk that ran in front of a stucco building at
the back of the school grounds.

Near the corner of the building, the body of a white,
middle-aged man lay sprawled face down on the ground
beside a structure of pipes and plywood about twenty
feet long and at least that tall. Part of a set, I realized,
upon seeing the painted façade—a cleverly rendered
perspective of one side of the school but looking far
nicer than the school appeared in reality. A two-inch di-
ameter pipe lay beside the man, along the length of his
body and with a few feet to spare. Blood and hair clung
to it in a pattern that perfectly and morbidly matched
the large dent in the back of his skull.

"Well, hell." I wrinkled my nose at the mess the pole
had made of his head, then peered back up at the set
piece. Now I saw the twisted clamp near the top.

"Yeah," Derrel said with a shake of his head. "Looks
like he was in the totally wrong place. The clamp broke,
the pole fell, and *smack*. Probably never felt a thing. Not
even time for an *oh shit*."

I made an appropriately sympathetic wince. A part of me thought that was probably a good way to go—never feeling a thing and never knowing. Yet at the same time, he never had a chance to say goodbye to his family and friends, even in his head. Death was really goddamn unfair sometimes.

I crouched by the body, taking it all in, then looked around. We were behind a half dozen trailers, probably for makeup and such, and away from the general activity I'd encountered near the street. A few crew members carrying fake body parts passed us as though nothing had happened and headed toward the high school, and several extras in fresh-from-the-grave clothing but no makeup clustered at the back of the furthest trailer, casting anxious glances our way.

"A zombie movie," I muttered. "That's too weird."

Derrel nodded. "Shambling, braaains, the whole thing," he replied, holding back a chuckle. Laughing and joking weren't considered cool on a death scene. "Saw a segment on the news about it last night. *High School Zombie Apocalypse!!*" he said, showing as much smile as he dared. "With *two* exclamations points!"

"Too weird," I repeated with a roll of my eyes as I pulled on gloves. This certainly wasn't the first time a movie had been filmed in the area, but as far as I knew it was the first one with zombies, and my first time anywhere near the action. In the past few years Louisiana had been dubbed "Hollywood South" because of the growing film industry in the state. Movies and TV shows filmed here benefited from generous tax credits and were great for the local economy. And it was always a kick to see local sights show up on the big screen. It somehow made the people here feel as if they were really part of something bigger.

I retrieved a sheet from the stretcher and wrapped up the poor guy's sadly smushed head. Though I'd eaten brains only a few hours earlier, I still had to use a good dose of willpower to keep from giving in to the delicious scent and digging a glob of brain out of the cracks in the skull to stuff into my mouth. That would *probably* go over even worse than laughing.

Close to ten months as a morgue tech/van driver for the St. Edwards Parish Coroner's Office, and I actually felt like I knew what I was doing. That was also the same length of time that I'd been a zombie, but I had a feeling it would take me a lot longer to really get a handle on that lifestyle.

I'd been an unemployed, pill head loser—with "felon" and "high school dropout" to pad out my resume—when I woke up in the ER after a night of drinking and drugs. Even though I had a fairly clear memory of being horribly injured in a car accident, I didn't have a mark on me—or a stitch of clothing, for that matter. Waiting for me had been a six-pack of weird brown, sludgy drinks, and an anonymous note about a job waiting for me at the Coroner's Office, along with the threat of jail time if I didn't take the job. Took me a few weeks to figure out the truth: that not only would I rot and fall apart if I didn't eat brains, but also that if I hadn't been turned into a zombie the night of the accident, I would've died on the spot from the combination of drug overdose and injuries.

Though I'd only taken the job with the Coroner's Office because it was better than going to jail, I quickly grew to enjoy it, and not simply because it gave me easy access to the brains I needed. It was interesting, challenging without being a pain in the ass, and paid better than any job I'd ever had. Ever. Plus, I had some pretty awesome coworkers.

With Derrel's help I got the dead guy wrestled into the body bag and onto the stretcher. Once I had him in the van and the doors closed, I decided to take a few minutes to gawk some more at the movie stuff. What the hell. It wasn't every day I had the chance to see something like this.

I locked the van, then crossed the street to get a better view as a stunt zombie practiced a fall from a third story window to the airbag cushion below. Further down the street several zombie extras mauled an actor in a cop uniform, then backed up and started over, repeatedly. *Gotta get those shambling horde subtleties down for the camera.* I smiled and shook my head. Though I'd watched several zombie movies and TV episodes after I was turned, I couldn't manage much love for most of them since the majority were about escaping from or killing mindless zombies. Needless to say, I had a hard time getting into that sort of thing.

A white van marked "Midnight Productions" pulled up to the curb, and a too-perky red-haired guy wearing an electric blue track suit climbed out of the passenger side carrying a clipboard and plastic grocery bag. He tooted a whistle then proceeded to call names and pass out white-wrapped snack bars to the extras who came out of the woodwork. Roll call and check marks on the clipboard. I figured some fine print contract clause said the movie people had to provide mid-morning protein or granola or some crap like that.

Hell, maybe I can go hungry a few days and get cast as an extra, I thought with amusement. It was beside the point that if I was falling apart enough to *look* like a zombie, I'd be so hungry I'd crack open the head of the first person who walked by in order to get my fill of braaaaiiiiins. Now *that* would be a realistic movie.

Only a few months ago I'd learned that it was a parasite that made a real zombie a zombie, and that parasite depended on brains to survive. Along with survival, it used brains to keep its host, like me, alive and in top physical condition in order to be a strong, ideal home.

Without enough of the food it needed—human brains and the prions within them—the primary need took over, breaking down and using host tissue in a way that closely resembled corpse rot. A hungry zombie looked and behaved a helluva lot like the stereotype and would do anything to get brains.

Hungry Zombie: instant movie extra with a Really Bad Attitude.

"I missed breakfast and now I've lost my appetite for lunch."

I looked over at the speaker to see Detective Ben Roth sweep a gaze over the faux-zombie action, a grimace of distaste twisting his features. He'd shaved off his scraggly mustache a couple of weeks ago, and I still wasn't used to it, though I definitely thought it had been the right decision. Ben was a homicide detective with the St. Edwards Parish Sheriff's office, and even though Mr. Brent Stewart's death was most likely the accident it appeared to be, procedure stated that a detective still had to investigate.

I liked working with Ben on scenes—he was friendly, easy-going, and took his job seriously without being uptight. Working with his partner, Mike Abadie, wasn't nearly as enjoyable. Abadie and I had pretty much agreed to disagree on, well, just about everything.

"What, rotting flesh doesn't get your appetite going?" I teased.

Ben gave a mock shudder. "I can't get into the zombie thing. Freaks me out."

That surprised me. Tall and stocky, he didn't look like someone who'd be easy to freak out. "But I've seen you on gory and disgusting crime scenes, and you never even bat an eyelash."

"I never said it made sense," he replied with a laugh. "It's like those horrible lifelike dolls. I know they're fake, but they still give me the heebie-jeebies."

"Well, lifelike dolls *are* creepy as hell," I agreed.

"My niece has one of those," he said, shuddering again. "I'll take a fake zombie over that plastic monstrosity." Then he shook his head. "Hell, I'll take a *real* zombie over that thing."

I laughed, though I knew he had no idea why I found it so funny. He opened his mouth to speak then frowned as a breeze brought a scattering of rain drops.

"I think that was a warning shot from the coming weather," he said. "Or maybe a sign I need to get started on my paperwork." With a parting smile, he turned and headed back to his unmarked car.

The drizzle stopped as quickly as it had begun, but I knew Ben was right. The black clouds to the west rolled steadily closer. Heading back across the street, I pulled out my phone and started texting, *Did you know a zombie movie was being filmed here?* to my cop not-quite boyfriend and fellow zombie, Marcus.

At least that's what I tried to do. I barely had "Did you know" thumbed in when I caught movement out of the corner of my eye—a helluva lot of very fast movement headed straight for me in the form of a dark silver pickup. The useless thought flashed through my head that nobody should be driving over five miles an hour beyond the barricade, and a glimpse of the driver's pissed, distracted face told me he didn't give a shit. I wasn't tanked up enough with brains to have zombie super speed, and spent a precious split second coming to that conclusion.

This is really gonna hurt, I thought as my body finally shifted into get-the-hell-out-of-the-way mode far too late.

I reflexively braced for the impact of the truck, but something else slammed into me from the side, tackling me out of the path of the oncoming vehicle and to the pavement. My right shoulder popped with a sharp pain as I landed hard with about two hundred pounds of someone on top of me. Distantly, I heard a screech of tires and the crunch of metal as Mr. Scowly's joyride abruptly ended.

For an instant, I assumed Derrel had been the one to save my butt from becoming a temporary speed bump, except that he was closer to three hundred pounds and would have squished little old me like a bug on a windshield.

I shifted to see who my savior was and froze. Blue eyes set in a rugged face framed with short blond hair. I'd never forget those eyes, that face. *Ever*.

It was Philip, the soldier I'd been forced to turn into a zombie six months ago when creepy Dr. Kristi Charish held me captive in her secret lab. Part of her super-zombie-soldier "Zoldiers" project. The last time I'd seen him was when I attempted to escape through duct work, the day after I turned him. He'd hauled me out and thrown me about a dozen feet. He'd been strong even for a zombie. And he had *looked* like a movie zombie then, one eye clouded over, his ear hanging off, and lips cracked away from his teeth, coupled with the unmistakable rotting zombie stench. That had been really Bad News since he'd eaten plenty of brains the day before and shouldn't have rotted that quickly. I'd spent the last half year wondering what the hell had gone wrong with him. More of Dr. Charish's messed up experiments, no doubt.

I took in the sight of him in a flash. He looked a lot better now, almost normal except for a faint grey cast to his skin.

"Philip," I managed to gasp out, right before he scrambled up and off me. I clutched at him, but my fingers closed on air as he turned and sprinted away. Before I could do more than sit up, he ducked between two trailers and was gone.

What. The. Hell.

Chapter 2

"Angel!"

That was Derrel. I struggled to my feet, biting back the hiss of pain as I moved my shoulder. Something was seriously messed up with it, but the pain faded, replaced by a dull stab of hunger—and not for regular food. Yep, definitely broken or torn up somehow.

Derrel's face was a mask of shock and concern as he helped steady me, thankfully on my good side. "Jesus Christ, are you okay?"

"Yeah," I said, with a wince. I hated to do the cliché thing and ask what the hell happened, but . . . "What the hell happened?" My gaze swept the area, taking in the activity around the out-of-control-pickup-meets-parked-car mess down the street, but I was more interested in seeing if I could catch a glimpse of Philip anywhere. No sign of him, but I did see a tall blond woman on the other side of the street pointing a nice-looking camera at me and obviously taking pictures. I guess it *had* been a pretty spectacular moment.

I looked back to Derrel. "Did you see who knocked me out of the way?"

"I only saw the back of his head," Derrel said with a frown. "Dunno why he took off like that. Dude saved your life." His brows drew together in a dark glower. "I'd have been seriously pissed if that stupid driver had creamed you."

"Aw, I almost think you like me," I teased, managing a shaky smile.

Derrel snorted. "Paperwork. Oh my god, the paperwork," he replied, but his eyes shone with relief that I was all right.

I looked around for my phone, saw it about a dozen feet away, apparently still in one piece. And still working, I found to my relief. The screen had a bit of fuzz to it, but a hard shake took care of that.

"You sure you're okay?" Derrel asked, hovering over me like a mother hen. A very large and intimidating mother hen.

I nodded and did my best not to do anything that would require me to move my right arm. That shoulder was trashed. "I'm good. Promise." I gave him a quick tight smile. "Lemme get something out of the van real quick."

I managed to extricate myself from his hovering long enough to get back to the van and snag my cooler out of the front seat. Hunger gnawed at me. I needed brains and I needed them *now*. The parasite dulled the pain, but that meant resources were being depleted for healing. Fortunately, as long as brains were available, my zombie parasite did a speedy job of making repairs to physical damage. Without them, the damage would remain, and rot and brain-seeking desperation would soon follow.

I pulled a water bottle containing a thick sludgy drink from the cooler. Though I always told people it was a protein drink, in reality it was a delicious-to-me smoothie of chocolate milk and pureed brains. I chugged it like a frat boy at a kegger, then sighed in relief as my shoulder pulled itself back together with a familiar sensation of shifting and tingling. My senses remained muted and dull—another way the parasite conserved resources when I was low on brains—which told me I could have used another bottle. Fortunately, the one I had was enough to get me by until I could obtain more. I wasn't starving and nowhere near losing it to the point of cracking open heads.

Of course, I then had to deal with the crazy driver aftermath. First I had to give a statement to the cop who'd been manning the barricade—who'd also narrowly avoided being run over. Then I had to reassure both Ben and Derrel that I was fine and no, I did not need to go to the hospital to get checked out. After that, a bit of shameless gawking on my part as I watched the belligerent driver get handcuffed and stuffed into the back of a police car.

Finally, with all the bullshit out of the way, and Ben and Derrel reassured for the billionth time that I didn't need to go to the ER, I escaped to my van and headed toward the morgue.

First thing I did once I got on the road was call Marcus since, as my not-quite-boyfriend, I knew he'd want to know what had happened. "Hey," I said as soon as he answered. "Did you know there's a zombie movie being filmed in town?"

"Sure did. *High School Zombie Apocalypse!!* Two exclamation points. Bunch of our guys are working security details there."

I chuckled at the "two exclamation points" business. If it ever came out in 3-D would it get a third? "Yeah, I got called out for a death on the set this morning, and then almost got my own body bag when some idjit who wasn't paying attention to the whole 'road closed' thing tried to run me over."

"Wait, what?" he asked, alarm in his voice. "Are you all right?"

"Yeah, but only because *Philip* tackled me out of the way."

"Who?"

"Philip. My zombie-baby. Remember?" I'd filled him in on everything that had happened to me in that goddamn lab, but months down the road there was no reason for him to remember the guy's name.

I heard his intake of breath. "Shit. But . . . wait. I don't understand. Was he attacking you?"

"No!" I said. "I mean, I'm pretty sure he wasn't. It sure as hell seemed like he was trying to keep me from being plowed by that car. And then he jumped up and ran the hell off."

"That is seriously weird."

"No kidding!"

"How are you doing? Hungry? You have anything with you?" I knew he meant brains, not burgers.

"I just sucked down a smoothie to fix up my shoulder, so I'm okay for now."

"I'll bring more for you when I pick you up this afternoon." We had a casual date set for when I got off work today, though he had yet to tell me what he had planned. "Can't have you falling to pieces on me, now can I?"

"That would suck," I said with a laugh.

"Yeah, I kinda like your bits right where they are, y'know?"

I grinned. "You like my bits?"

"Pretty much, yep."

"Cool," I said. "Bring me something to eat and maybe later I'll let you touch my bits."

"Now there's an incentive not to be late," he said.

"You'd better not be!" I said with a laugh. "My bits and I will see you at four." I hung up without giving him a chance to reply. It served him right for not telling me where he was taking me this afternoon.

The rain began in earnest as I pulled up to the rear entrance of the Coroner's Office building, but I managed to get myself and the body inside without getting too wet, thanks to the recently installed new awning.

No one else decided to die for the rest of my shift, which was damn nice since I really didn't want to pick up a body in the rain. When Jerry came in at five minutes 'til four to relieve me on bodysnatcher duty, I gladly turned the van keys over to him, grabbed my stuff, and headed outside to wait for Marcus.

Rain drummed on the awning in a heavy staccato, and barely a minute later Marcus pulled up in his bright blue Ford F-150 pickup.

I gave him a broad smile as I climbed in. "Right on time."

"You know it," he said with a grin as he passed me a bottle. "Now let's get those bits stable."

I took a long drink, then watched him as he drove. Ruggedly handsome with dark hair and eyes, and a great smile, he was a damned good guy who happened to be the one who'd saved my life by turning me into a zombie. He'd also anonymously secured me a job at the Coroner's Office, so I'd have a supply of brains, and helped me establish myself in my new life as a zombie. Later, we had a few hot and heavy weeks as a couple before I backed off to get perspective and space.

It was the whole business about zombifying me and extorting me into taking the morgue job that I'd needed the most perspective about. Pair that with some over-the-top protective bullshit and general treating me like a child, and I'd been damn close to washing my hands of him completely. But the truth was, Marcus had some really great qualities, and I did enjoy him. Therefore, after a number of Very Serious Talks, I'd decided to mentally wipe the slate clean and start over. No point in holding a grudge for shit in the past, especially when his actions *had* totally saved my life and forced me to get my act together. Marcus had promised to try harder and actually get my input on things from now on, and I tried not to overthink anything and simply have fun.

I finished off the bottle, exhaling in relief as the last tugs of hunger faded and the world came back into proper focus. "Yeah, that's the good stuff."

Marcus pulled a baggie of what looked like ugly grey banana chips out of the console and passed it to me. "Now try these."

I replaced the top on the bottle and stuck it in the drink holder, then gave the contents of the baggie a dubious sniff. I liked what I smelled, but they sure looked nasty.

"What are these?" I asked, taking a cautious nibble.

"Brain chips," he said. "I got a dehydrator and thought I'd give it a try. Slice thin and let 'em dry." He shrugged. "Only about half of the brainpower they'd have if they were fresh or frozen, but no cooler needed and they satisfy that crunch craving."

I took a bigger bite. "I like."

Marcus smiled, obviously pleased. "Keep those. I have more at home."

"Cool!" I ate another brain chip and then stuffed the bag down into my purse. "Man, I feel sorry for those fake zombies who have to wear that makeup all day. Wonder how much it costs to pay all those people and stuff?"

"Dunno," Marcus replied, "but I heard that these extras are making a hundred to a hundred and fifty bucks a day, and that they gave first hiring priority to people who were laid off after Saberton Corp bought the farm machinery factory last fall."

"Oh, wow," I said. "That's pretty cool of them." The bigwigs at Saberton had sworn up, down, and sideways that the layoffs were temporary, and that everyone would be rehired as soon as the company nailed down a major defense contract. But the contract had yet to come through, and several hundred people were either still out of a job or making do with whatever work they could scrounge.

Marcus glanced my way. "Well, Uncle Pietro said that State Senator Jane Pennington really pushed for that."

"Even cooler." Then I grinned. "Is it wrong that I want to go hungry for a bit and then sneak in as an extra?"

"Probably, but who cares?" he replied with a laugh.

He turned down the street that ran alongside the high school, not far from where I'd picked up the body, then pulled into the deserted back lot of the football stadium. I used to think *my* high school took their football seriously, but Tucker Point High supporters took it to a whole new level of absurd. After a ridiculously successful, high-profile fund-raising campaign a few years back, the alumni had built a sleek monstrosity that had to be the biggest, glitziest high school stadium in the southeast.

"We're here," he announced as he parked close to the entrance and shut off the engine.

The look I gave him was plenty dubious. "Um. Why are we here?"

He grabbed a thick blanket from behind the seat. "Come on, I'll show you," he said. And with no further hint, he climbed out and headed toward the darkened entrance.

Okkaaaay. I hurried to follow. Behind me, the truck horn beeped as Marcus hit the remote lock.

"Dude, this is kinda creepy," I said with a laugh.

He reached back and took my hand. "In a few minutes you won't be thinking about creepy."

"Well that can be taken a bunch of different ways," I replied.

Marcus broke into a run as the light rain abruptly increased in intensity, then pulled me close as soon as we were under shelter. "So can you," he murmured.

A thrill shot through me. Marcus and I had our ups and downs, but we had some serious chemistry in the bedroom. "Oh wow," I said with an unsteady grin.

His mouth nuzzled my neck. "You're in trouble now. I'm primed."

"So that's why you wanted me to eat the chips!" I rolled my eyes but I couldn't help but laugh. Back at his house he had a brain-pudding that he'd nicknamed "foreplay." Never a good idea to risk falling apart during zombie-sex. Ew.

Marcus chuckled as he took my hand again and headed down a passageway. "I'm no fool."

I peered around as we walked. "Are we allowed to be here?"

"Uh, sure," he said in a very unconvincing tone of voice. "Didn't have to climb any fences did we?"

We wound our way through a dim passageway beneath the seating, then up a set of concrete stairs and onto a covered walkway that ran around the perimeter of the stadium. "This sure is, um, romantic," I said, casting him a dubious look.

"Didn't know you were looking for romance," he said, still grinning as we stepped out onto the bleachers. "Come on," he urged as he began to climb.

"You're so weird," I said, but I went with him.

"You mean besides being a zombie?" he said, shooting me an amused glance over his shoulder.

"Well, yeah," I said, grinning. "That zombie shit's old hat now."

We reached the top of the stairs, and I allowed Marcus to lead me behind the scoreboard and then up a narrow ladder to a hidden alcove above the walkway. He let go of my hand and spread out the thick blanket. I looked out over the empty stadium from our lofty vantage. State of the art, no doubt about that. From the swanky all-glass press box to the perfect grass on the field with Tucker Point emblazoned in the end zones it screamed, *We obsess way too hard over high school football, and don't you forget it!*

"Okay," I said. "This is kinda cool."

His gaze went out to the view "Not so creepy up here."

I sat down on the blanket. "Well, you *are* a zombie, so automatically creepy."

"Wait," he protested. "A few seconds ago the zombie aspect was old hat." He stripped off his damp shirt and dropped it to the concrete. "I think you just say stuff that's convenient in the moment."

"Yeah? You don't seem to mind too much." I leaned back on my elbows and admired the view. And not the one out in the stadium. "For a sorta-dead guy, you're pretty hot."

Marcus flexed his right bicep. "I eat my Brainies." He unbuttoned his jeans then struck a deliberately ridiculous muscle pose.

"Oh my god." I laughed. "Cut that out and come show my bits what your Brainies do for you."

He proceeded to show me in great detail exactly what his Brainies could do for my bits, paying special attention to certain bits, to my great delight. No matter what else I might have been unsure about with the two of us, there was no denying that the sex rocked. Marcus was attentive, fun, creative, and always made sure I got off.

And he was even great about doing the whole cuddling after stuff too.

"You like that?" he murmured as he held me close.

I gave him the smile of a very sexually satisfied woman. "My bits are happy."

He chuckled low and gave me a light squeeze. I rested my head on his chest and listened to the thump of his heart. "I think I kinda like this date-adventure thing," I said.

Marcus was quiet for a moment. "I think I kinda miss waking up next to you in the mornings."

The statement brought a warm rush of pleasure, along with a chaser of guilt and a splash of frustration. We'd been dating—really actually *dating*—for about six months now. I wanted to keep the pace super slow, and he wanted us to be, well, an actual honest-to-god couple. But after the long slogging mess of my previous relationship with Randy-the-loser, I wanted to be sure everything was right before getting too caught up in things like spending the night, and moving in together, and whatever else might come after that. I also wanted to be sure we were together because we were actually compatible, and not simply because we were both zombies.

I slid a hand over his chest. It was a damn nice chest. "Yeah, but I like that we're taking the time to really get to know each other."

"And you don't think that can happen the other way?" he asked. To his credit there was only the faintest whisper of disappointment in his voice.

"Marcus, it's . . . different, okay?" I said with a low sigh. Tilting my head back, I looked up into his face. "Yeah, we'd get to know each other if I spent the night with you or lived with you, but . . ." I trailed off with a grimace, wishing I could explain it better. "I just think it's too soon."

He couldn't completely mask the letdown, but he smiled and kissed me. "Okay, I can take a hint. Or a two by four," he added with a slightly forced chuckle.

Damn it. "Marcus. I'm not saying it'll never happen." Why couldn't he understand? Sure, six months was a long time. But we were both . . . well, we had the potential to live a damn long time. And I didn't want to screw this up.

"It's all right, babe," he said, and for a moment I could almost believe that it was. "One day at a time," he continued. "I can do that."

I snuggled close, and he tightened his arm around me. The warm air and the drumming of rain on the metal roof lulled us both into boneless relaxation. Safe and content for the moment, I closed my eyes and allowed myself to drift into a doze.

"It doesn't make sense."

Footsteps and a man's low voice penetrated my light snooze. I opened my eyes, heart pounding, as I got my bearings. For a moment I was certain that someone had discovered us in our little sex nook, but the only person in sight was Marcus, eyes closed and clearly in a far deeper sleep.

"No way that support fell on its own," the speaker continued, sounding frustrated and annoyed. He was below us, I realized, on the walkway. "I was on that scaffold yesterday. Everything was solid."

"Forget it," another man said. "Doesn't matter now. Sucks to lose Stewart, but be glad it happened before everything else got going. Can you imagine cops crawling around later this week?"

The first man replied, but they'd moved off and I couldn't hear it.

"Marcus," I said softly as I gently shook him.

He blinked awake, focused on my face and smiled. "Hey, babe. Sorry, didn't mean to fall asleep. I guess I was too comfy cuddled up with you."

"There are people here," I said. "I mean, down on the walkway. I think they're from the movie."

He kissed me, then sat up and reached for his shirt. "Not surprised. The big finale zombie attack scene is going to be filmed down on the field in a few days." His voice was briefly muffled as he tugged his shirt over his head. "They're probably figuring out lighting and cameras and stuff."

My jeans and undies were close by, and I began to tug them on. "They were talking about the guy who died," I told him. "It sounded like they didn't think it was an accident, that the pipe shouldn't have fallen the way it did."

He stood and pulled on underwear and pants. "Probably want to be sure they don't get blamed for it." He glanced my way. "Insurance company will check it all out, I'm sure. And Ben's thorough," he added, referring to Detective Roth.

I slipped my shirt over my head, ran my fingers through my hair. "Okay, but then one of them said it was good it happened now before 'everything else' started so there wouldn't be cops around." I leveled a frown at Marcus. "Explain that."

Marcus grinned. "Filming," he stated. "They're in rehearsals and preproduction now. They actually begin filming with the leads in the morning. I suppose it would be a pain in the butt to try and film with a police investigation going on."

"Damn you for making sense," I said, lightly smacking him on the chest.

He pulled me close for a kiss. "I always make perfect sense," he said with a chuckle, then glanced out at the sky. "Rain's letting up. We should probably get going."

Taking his hand, I let him lead the way back down and out of the stadium, then together we dashed through the lingering drizzle to his truck.

I fought back a yawn as he drove me back to the morgue and my car. As nice as the date had been—even with the slight strangeness at the end—I couldn't deny I was ready to get home and chill for a while before bed.

He pulled up next to my car, and I was about to say my goodbyes when Marcus reached into the console and pulled out an envelope. "I have a surprise for you," he said with a smile. "Compliments of Uncle Pietro."

I took the envelope he offered and pulled out two tickets to the Gourmet Gala, a swanky annual charity event I'd never even dreamed of attending. Damn near every restaurant in the parish participated, each with a booth or table where they gave out free samples of all sorts of fine cuisine. Tickets were expensive as hell, which meant that all the movers and shakers and rich people made sure to be seen there. I didn't give a crap about being seen—I just wanted the food.

I stared at the tickets. "You're serious? Your uncle simply gave these to you?"

"Umm, yeah. Sure," he said, lifting his shoulders in a shrug. "He passes stuff like this my way now and then."

"You've gone to this before?"

He smiled. "A couple of times in the past few years."

"And we're really going? Tomorrow night?"

Marcus snorted, pretty obviously amused by my enthusiasm. "That's the plan, if you want to. And judging by the gleam in your eyes, I'd say it was a yes."

Okay, it's possible that I gave a squeal of excitement worthy of a teen girl at a Justin Bieber concert. "Oh my god. I have to find something to wear!"

Marcus laughed. "You have time. Don't sweat it."

I gaped at him in horror. "Easy for you to say! You have a closet full of clothes, and you're a *guy*."

"Okay, okay," he said, grinning. "Just make sure you get something with elastic in the waistband. Lots and lots of food."

"I'll undo the top button. Not a problem."

"Sounds good to me." He leaned over and gave me a

kiss which I didn't mind returning. "Go veg out and I'll talk to you tomorrow."

"Sure thing," I said, giving him a smile as I climbed out of the truck. He waited until I had my car started before driving off. Good dude.

Yet on the way home, my thoughts went back to the weirdness on the movie set this morning. What the hell was Philip doing there? And why save me from a world of hurt and then run away? He was tied in with Dr. Kristi Charish, which left me more than a little unsettled. I didn't want that psycho bitch anywhere near me. There was only one person I could think of who might have some answers—Pietro Ivanov.

He'd thrown me to the wolves a few months ago when he'd allowed Charish to kidnap me, but had since admitted he'd screwed up and had done a lot to try to make up for it. Like the pardon. About two years ago I'd been arrested for possession of stolen property—while driving a car my loser-ex-boyfriend had insisted was a totally legit purchase—and ended up with probation and suspended sentence, and a felony on my record. But shortly after I managed to pull off my escape from Charish's secret lab, my probation officer let me know that I wasn't on probation anymore because I'd been pardoned. Totally clean record. Fresh start. And I had no doubt Pietro was responsible. As well as being the head of the local "zombie mafia," he was rich as hell and had a zillion political connections. No one else who gave a shit about me had the power to pull off a full pardon from the frickin' governor. No way did I trust Pietro yet—or forgive him, for that matter—but there was certainly a truce and potential to rebuild.

There was no sign of my dad when I got home, but since it was barely seven p.m. I figured I could hold off worrying that he was out drinking. He never drank at the house anymore—probably because he knew I sure as hell didn't approve—and to his credit he was pretty damn careful about not drinking and driving.

Unfortunately, that was primarily because a few months ago Mr. Jimmy Crawford got stopped for driving while intoxicated. Fortunately, it was Marcus who had pulled him over. And even though Marcus bent rules like crazy and called me to come get my dad—saving us a ton of hassle and thousands of dollars—the incident pretty much shattered the shaky peace the two men had made, and my dad had gone right back to an active dislike of "that cop."

Scowling in annoyance and frustration with the whole situation, I slugged down about half a bottle of brain smoothie to make up for what I'd burned off in my exertions with Marcus, then flopped onto the sagging couch to watch TV.

I woke later to screeching laughter on some nighttime talk show. A glance at the clock told me I'd crashed for a solid four hours.

Which meant that *now* I could worry about my dad's drinking.

Not that worrying did a damn bit of good. Or arguing, or lecturing, or yelling. I knew that. I could wait for him, brace myself for an argument or worse when he finally came through the door. And for what? It wouldn't accomplish a damn thing.

I shut off the TV and went on to bed, unsure whether to be upset or relieved that he still wasn't home.

Chapter 3

"Five days and counting," Nick said with a smile.

I could only groan. For the past few months Nick, my oftentimes annoying but basically good-hearted co-worker, had been tutoring me for the GED—the high school equivalency exam. Passing it had been a condition of my probation. But then I'd received my mysterious pardon and suddenly I didn't *have* to pass the GED.

Except that I did, for my own self-respect. Hell, having any self-respect at all was a new experience for me, so why not go full tilt, right? Besides, I'd learned that zombies had the potential to live a very long time. Living a hundred years or so as an uneducated loser wasn't all that appealing to me, therefore the first step was to get my damn high school diploma.

However, being chock full of self-respect didn't mean I wasn't totally intimidated by the whole process.

"I'm not ready," I said, looking with dismay at the pile of workbooks that Nick had forced me to plow through in the past months. "There's no way."

His green eyes narrowed. "You won't be if you keep

saying that. You went through the practice test last week and did pretty well, and you've been studying your ass off since then."

I took a deep breath. "Right. Okay. I *can* do this." But then my self-confidence wilted. "I'm still so damn slow on the reading part though. I'm afraid I'll run out of time."

"And you get slower when you're flustered," he pointed out for about the billionth time. "So you need to keep focused on what's right in front of you and not on what's left to do."

"At least I'm good at the math part," I said. Too bad I had to get passing grades on *all* of it—math, science, reading, writing, and social studies. But it was only the reading part that had me worried sick.

Nick leaned back and gave me a considering look. "Have you ever been tested for dyslexia? I mean, it's not that you aren't smart enough or don't understand the words."

I blinked at him. "Um. Isn't that the thing where you see words backward or something? I don't think I have that."

He shook his head. "It's not always like that. Dyslexia can show up in a lot of ways. Sometimes it's only noticed because reading is slow for no other apparent reason, then testing can be done to determine if that's the cause."

"Well, what difference would it make at this point?" I asked with a slight frown. "I mean, I read slow as molasses. Not sure anything can be done about that."

"Not much to be done about the slow reading right now, but if you get diagnosed you can probably get extra time for the test."

"Oh, wow." I blew out a breath. "Now *that* would make it worthwhile." Even if I didn't end up needing the extra time, it would take my stress level down by a fair amount.

"No kidding," he said. "I don't know how long it takes to get tested and diagnosed and all, but it'd be worth looking into." He tilted his head. "And then you could get tutoring to specifically address whatever issues you have."

"I have *lots* of issues," I said with a laugh.

He grinned. "Yes, you do!"

It was an interesting thought. Could it be that easy? And if it really was something like that, then why hadn't any of my teachers noticed it and done something about it?

Or maybe they did, I realized. A whisper of memory intruded, of being pulled out of class when I was in fourth or fifth grade to go to the school office and do all sorts of reading and comprehension tests for a round-cheeked woman. It was more than possible that the school had contacted my mother to let her know I had a problem, and she'd simply never pursued it. She sure as hell wouldn't have exerted any extra effort for me. And my dad had been working on an offshore oil rig at the time. He wouldn't have known there was a problem.

The pieces fell into place. Damn. Had my mother really done that? It made a sick sense. The testing. All the problems in school. Everything. A wave of anger passed through me. I wouldn't put it past her. If it didn't revolve around her, she had no use for it. And damn it, though she was dead and buried and couldn't hit me anymore, this reading thing still had me in its grip. I needed to know what that testing had been about, and maybe even get a black and white answer about whether or not my mom had blown off the test results.

With a mental sigh, I added "check school records" to my list of things to do.

"Probably too late to get diagnosed or whatever before the test this weekend," I said, trying to throw off the cloud of my mother's neglect. "But after I fail this one, I'll look into it."

I knew I'd said the wrong thing the instant the words left my mouth. For a guy who wasn't much taller than me, Nick could be pretty intimidating when he got angry.

His mouth tightened to a thin line. "If you're so sure you're going to fail, why even bother?" He stood and picked up the workbook, dropped it onto the others with a thud.

I sighed and tugged a hand through my hair. "Okay, okay. I'm not sure I'm gonna fail. I'm just . . ." I winced. "I don't do well on tests like that."

He wasn't appeased. "Well, shit. So far, you've told me you're not ready, you're going to fail, and you don't do well on tests like this. From what I've seen, you were close to ready a week ago, you were within a few points of passing the practice test, and you did perfectly fine taking that one. If you're not careful, you'll talk yourself into being a living, breathing, self-fulfilling prophecy."

The words hung in the air of the morgue. Nick had gone from being a pain in my ass and a pompous jerk to being someone I could actually confess my insecurities to. We weren't quite *friends*—at least not the sort of friend I'd hang out or see a movie with—but I trusted him, and I knew he had my back. It was almost as if he'd decided that since I wasn't a threat to any of his own ambitions, he was going to do his best to help me with my own. And I liked to think that his association with me helped "unprickify" him a bit, which might even have helped him finally score his recent promotion to death investigator.

"I'm scared," I admitted, dropping my head into my hands. "I've worked really hard to not be such a damn loser anymore, y'know?"

Nick moved behind me. A couple of seconds later I felt his hand on my shoulder in an almost hesitant touch. "You don't need to be scared, Angel," he urged. "You don't have to do this for anyone but yourself anymore.

Worst thing that can happen, the absolute *worst,* is that you'll need to retest." He gave my shoulder a light squeeze. "Compare that to all the other bad shit that can happen in one day, and maybe it won't be so scary after all."

I turned my head to look up at him, gave him a smile. "You're right. Thanks." I knew all too well how much bad shit could happen in one day, and failing a test wasn't even on the same scale. "It's really not the end of the world if I fail."

"Nope, it's not." Then he put on a grumpy expression. "Except that you'd have to spend that much more time with me. That should be motivation enough to pass."

I laughed and gave a mock shudder. "Oh, god help me!"

"Yep, you're in trouble." Then he cleared his throat and lifted his hand from my shoulder as if he'd suddenly remembered he was maintaining the contact. "Enough moaning. I've got work to do."

"Yeah, moved up in the world from bodysnatcher to big bad investigator," I said with a smile.

"It's about damn time they recognized my worth," he said, only half kidding as he headed out and back to the main building.

I rolled my eyes and bent my head to continue studying.

About half an hour later Allen Prejean, Chief Investigator for the St. Edwards Parish Sheriff's Office, walked past the door of the office, gave me a sour look and made a point of checking his watch as he passed. Scowling, I deliberately waited another minute before putting all my books away. I still had three minutes before my shift technically started. I wasn't stupid enough to do my tutoring and studying on company time. Or rather, I wasn't stupid enough to do so in front of Allen. I studied in the van or in the morgue late at night all the damn time.

Allen had worked for the coroner, Dr. Duplessis, for
close to fifteen years, long before Duplessis was elected.
As a former paramedic who was studying to be a physi-
cian's assistant, he'd supposedly already been offered a
position with Dr. Duplessis's private cardiology practice
once he graduated, and that day couldn't come soon
enough for me. Allen certainly knew his stuff when it
came to death investigation, and he ran the office well
enough. But he was also a dick. His call schedule seemed
to be set up specifically to inconvenience me as much as
possible, and he made no effort to be discreet about my
drug history when requiring job-related piss tests—
which I somehow ended up "randomly" selected for every damn month. There was no doubt he disliked me
intensely, though I didn't know whether it was a simple
thing of not liking me because of my felony/pill-popping/
loser background or if there was some other, more spe-
cific, reason. I knew he'd love to find an excuse to fire me,
so I did my damndest to keep my nose clean, obey every
goddamn rule, and go the extra mile when needed. And
not simply because I needed this job for the access it
gave me to my brain food supply, but more because there
was no way I was letting Allen Prejean win.

After getting my books and notes packed up, I left my
borrowed study space and headed through the building
to the morgue. The only body scheduled to be autopsied
was head-squished guy from the movie set, and after
garbing myself in scrubs, shoe covers, plastic smock, paper apron over that, hair cover, and latex gloves, I made
quick work of getting him out of the cooler and into the
cutting room. Sometimes it cracked me up to go through
the whole rigmarole of protecting myself from biohaz-
ards. I sure as hell didn't need to worry about Hepatitis
or HIV since my parasite took care of that. There'd been
plenty of times when I'd eaten brains straight from the
body bag, while still protectively garbed—another one

of those things that I did by-the-book, since ignoring safety protocols was a fireable offense.

Blood from Mr. Brent Stewart's smushed head had pooled in a sticky mess inside the bag, and when I pulled him from the stretcher onto the metal table the bag slid as well and poured a gooey stream of blood onto the floor. I let out a bunch of nasty words, sopped up as much as I could with towels which then went straight into the biohazard container, then fetched the mop and bucket to get the rest of it up before Dr. Leblanc arrived. I'd barely finished emptying the bucket out and putting the cleaning stuff away when the pathologist came in.

"Shit, sorry, doc," I said as I hurried back into the cutting room. "Had a blood spill, and I don't have your tools set out. Gimme five minutes and I'll be ready for you."

"Not a problem, Angel."

Dr. Leblanc was in his fifties with thin blond-grey hair, and sharp blue eyes that often sparkled with humor. He was unimposing physically—medium height and build with a bit of flab around the waist—but I knew he was tough as nails when it came to standing up for what he believed in. "You've spoiled me by usually having everything ready half an hour before I've even finished my morning coffee." His eyes crinkled as he smiled at me. "In fact I don't think I've ever seen you running late before. Is everything all right?"

"Yep!" I replied as I set out his implements: scalpels, scissors, saw, forceps, rib shears, syringes. "I was studying in the investigator's office. Had another tutoring session with Nick this morning."

"Ah, of course. Five more days." He pulled smock and apron on, tugged on gloves. "Nick's been helpful?"

"Oh my god, more than helpful," I said fervently. "There's no way I could afford to pay a tutor for the amount of time he's worked with me. And he's actually really good at teaching this stuff. I mean he's not, er, his usual self."

Dr. Leblanc's eyes flashed with amusement. He knew exactly what I meant. There was a good reason why I used to mentally refer to Nick as "Nick the Prick."

"You make him want to be a better person," he said with only a trace of facetiousness.

I responded with a soft snort of derision. "Hardly. I think he simply enjoys the challenge of filling my blank slate." I shook my head. "Anyway, it's pretty amazing he's willing to help. A year ago I'd never have imagined I'd have so many awesome people supporting me."

"You were just waiting for your moment to shine," he replied. He moved to the table and peered down at Mr. Stewart, assessing.

"Helps that I had so many people giving me a hand up along the way," I said with a shrug.

He glanced up at me. "That only works if you have your hand up and reaching."

"Well that's damn near poetic," I said with a laugh.

He gave an answering grin. "I blame the formalin fumes." He picked up a scalpel. "Let's find out if there was anything amiss about Mr. Stewart's death."

Except for the crushed nature of Mr. Stewart's head, he seemed to have been in excellent health. The autopsy went quickly, and I drew and packaged up blood, urine, and vitreous samples for later toxicology testing. The conversation I overheard at the stadium, about the death possibly not being an accident, replayed itself in the back of my mind, and the autopsy didn't help put it to rest. While Dr. Leblanc had no problem listing the blunt force head trauma as the cause of death due to the extent of the crushing damage, he fully admitted there was little way to determine if it had been accidental or intentional.

After he finished and left to go write up his notes, I

returned Mr. Stewart to the cooler. It bothered me that we might never find out if he'd been murdered, though I knew there'd be slim chance the killer would ever be found and prosecuted, even if we knew for sure. Lots of murders went unsolved, and I had no doubt there were plenty of accidental deaths that weren't, or overdoses that had been helped along.

I guess all we can do is the best we can, I decided.

The rest of my shift was busy enough to keep it from being boring, but I was glad to leave when it was over. Lightning flashed through the dark clouds of the late afternoon sky as I slipped out the back exit of the morgue, and I felt a bit of relief that the rain had taken a break for the moment. I started toward my car, then almost had a heart attack as a figure moved from around the corner of the building.

"Angel," the figure said, and it took me a couple of heart pounding seconds to recognize the speaker.

"Jesus Christ! Ed?"

He moved closer. "Yeah, sorry," he said. "Didn't mean to scare you."

"That's cool," I said, taking a deep breath to get my pulse under control. "I know you can't exactly saunter up to the front door in broad daylight." Ed was wanted for multiple murders. Yeah, he'd killed those people—all zombies—but he'd been played and manipulated pretty heavily by the ruthless Dr. Kristi Charish. She'd convinced him that the "zombie menace" needed to be eradicated and that killing known zombies would be a good and noble thing to do. It didn't help that he'd seen a zombie kill his dad about a decade earlier—which Charish knew all about and gleefully exploited. The truly tragic part was that she only manipulated Ed into becoming a serial killer because she wanted zombie heads for her own screwed-up research. Bitch.

I peered at him. When I first met Ed Quinn he looked

like the typical boy next-door—tall and slender, reddish brown hair, scattering of freckles across his nose. After he went on the run he went goth as a disguise—dyed his hair black and spiked it, sported a variety of piercings, and dressed in skull-adorned clothing. Now he looked . . . *ordinary*. Dark brown hair in a conservative and boring style. Khaki pants. Dark blue polo-style shirt. Even the freckles were gone, either bleached away or hidden beneath a layer of makeup. I wouldn't look at him twice, which was probably the point, I realized. "How are you doing?" I asked.

"I'm okay. I mean as okay as I can be while being hunted as a serial killer."

I winced in sympathy. "I guess no one's come up with some brilliant way to get you cleared of all that yet, huh?"

Ed exhaled, shook his head. "Nope. Never will be cleared legally," he said, regret tingeing his voice. "Maybe a little redemption if the heads can be restored."

"Yeah. That would be great, for your peace of mind and for them." After the fiasco with Dr. Charish, I'd insisted that Pietro recover the zombie heads from her lab with the hope that the bodies could someday be regrown. Dr. Charish had done it once, though not with complete success. But I hadn't heard squat about the heads in the past six months. I made a mental note to check on that soon.

Ed gave me a resigned shrug, and I could tell guilt ate at him. "Thankfully, Pietro has kept me well-hidden from the law."

"But you can't stay hidden forever," I pointed out.

To my surprise a slight smile touched his mouth. "Actually, I can," he said. "Not here, though. I'm leaving the country tonight. Pietro's got me set up in Costa Rica. New identity. Fake passport and everything."

"Oh. Wow." A sharp pang of loss went through me. I definitely considered Ed a friend. Sure, he'd tried really hard to kill me, but he then made up for it by helping me out when I was kidnapped by Dr. Charish. "Costa Rica, huh?" I fought for a smile and struggled to be happy for him. It really was the only option that made sense, and Pietro certainly had the resources to make it happen. "That's awesome," I managed, then bit my lower lip, met his eyes. "Will you ever come back? I mean . . . will I ever see you again?"

"I don't know," he said, expression suddenly bleak. "Pietro and I talked about it. I'm going to have some plastic surgery." He grimaced, rubbed his eyes. "I think I need some time away to get my head together. It's been nothing but stress and confusion for a long time."

"Yeah, it's been pretty weird," I agreed, then sighed. "I'm gonna miss you. I mean, I know I've barely seen you these past few months, but I've always known that I *could* see you . . . and now you're going so far away."

"I'll miss you too," Ed said. "That's why I wanted to come say goodbye. I was really hoping you'd come out before I had to go."

A warm fuzzy feeling went through me that he'd waited here. "Thanks," I said. "I'm really glad you came by. Maybe you can write. I mean, using your new name and all." I frowned. "What *is* your new name?"

He chuckled. "James Clement, and no, I'm not used to it."

"James." I laughed. "Yeah, that's weird. You don't seem like a James."

"I know, but I can't complain," he said, shrugging. "Pietro really came through for me."

I made a sour face. "Well, he kinda owed you, big time." *Pietro* had been the zombie who'd killed Ed's father. Of course that was right after Ed's father had killed Ed's mother because Pietro was sleeping with her. Yeah, major zombie soap opera stuff.

"He *does* owe me," Ed agreed. "But owing and paying

are two different things. I'm glad he didn't take the easy road and get rid of me."

"Oh shit," I breathed, shocked at the idea. "I never even thought of that. Yikes." A shudder ran through me. "Damn. Yeah, I guess that would've been a lot easier. Says something about Pietro, I suppose."

"Exactly." He gave me a smile. "Give me a hug. I've got to get out of here or I'll miss my flight."

I wrapped my arms around him, hugged him tightly while I tried not to cry and failed miserably at that. "You be careful," I sniffled. "And you'd better write. I want postcards, dammit."

Ed gave me a squeeze and kissed my cheek. "Don't worry, sweetie. You can't get rid of me."

I finally released him and wiped at my eyes. "You'd better go."

"Yep. And I'm going to be sweating bullets until I get through airport security," he said. "I've been assured that I don't need to worry, but damn." He flashed a grin.

"If you get caught I'll bust you out," I promised, echoing his grin.

He laughed. "Deal. But let's not think about that." He kissed my cheek again. "Gotta run. Take care, Angel."

"Always," I replied softly as he turned and hurried to a waiting car. Was it possible to be happy and sad for someone at the same time?

With a sigh, I headed for my car, happy and sad . . . but mostly sad.

Chapter 4

I raced home, showered and changed, even spent about twenty minutes on my hair and makeup and was mostly pleased with the result. I also made sure to chug down half a smoothie to give that extra glow of "yes, I'm really alive" to my skin. Nothing like grey and rotting flesh to kill a great look.

I'd hit the thrift store before my tutoring date with Nick and totally struck gold in my quest for a properly stylish and dressy outfit to wear to the Gourmet Gala that wouldn't break my pathetic budget. It helped that I was a pro at finding cool stuff for next to nothing. For about thirty bucks I walked out with a cream silk blouse, black dress slacks, and a really striking thigh-length jacket in a dark red velvet. And as rainy as it was, I intended to wear my black boots, and to hell with whether they were appropriate for the event. They had low heels, so would hopefully be dressy enough.

My dad was in his usual spot in front of the TV when I came out to the living room. I plopped down on the other end of the couch and pulled my boots on. His gaze stayed on whatever show he was watching without even the barest acknowledgement of my presence. He had his feet propped on the coffee table, a position he claimed took the pressure off an old back injury he'd sustained a decade ago on an offshore oil rig. Years of hard drinking and smoking had left him looking way older than his actual age of forty-eight. Even though he'd made an effort to clean up his act in the past few months, it couldn't erase the haggard look and sagging jowls that had been long in the making. His light brown eyes were clearer though, and these days he kept his face clean-shaven most of the time, a big change from the scraggly beard he used to keep so he didn't have to bother shaving.

"Have you eaten yet?" I asked.

"If you'd be home sometimes you'd know." He finally looked over at me, eyes narrowing at the sight of me all dressed up. "Where the hell you going now?"

Scowling, I zipped up my boots. "I spend pretty much every night here, Dad. You don't see me 'cause you're not here in the evenings." I gave him a hard look, cocked an eyebrow at him. "What, are you out feeding the poor or something noble like that?"

"What's that supposed to mean?" he demanded. "I can damn well be out if I want to be out."

I stood and pulled on my jacket, reveling in the way it flared out and swirled as I moved. I loved that jacket. Loved the way it felt. Loved everything about it. "You know what I mean. You making the rounds of the bars again?"

His expression darkened. "Well, what if I am?"

My mouth tightened. "Yeah, what if you are." I sighed, shook my head. "Whatever. I'm going out with Marcus tonight. He got tickets to the Gourmet Gala ."

"Well, that's some shit," he said with a small sneer. "Act like you're all worried about whether or not I've eaten anything and then go off with that asshole to stuff your face and leave me here to fend for myself."

"Oh, for fuck's sake, Dad! Y'know what? I won't ever ask how you're doing again." I stomped out of the house and slammed the door behind me, only to hit the steps and realize I'd forgotten my purse. Scowl deepening, I slammed back into the house, grabbed my purse, and then once again stomped out and closed the door hard. Didn't help my mood that I thought I heard my dad give a snort of laughter. Yeah, so much for a dramatic exit.

Plus, Marcus wasn't even there yet, but I wasn't about to go back inside to wait. Fortunately, for my own state of mind, it was only a few minutes before he pulled up. I dashed through the rain to the truck and climbed in as quickly as I could.

"You look great, hon'," Marcus said with an appreciative smile as soon as I had the door closed. He leaned over and gave me a kiss.

"Thanks. Ugh," I said, returning the kiss. "Sorry, the 'ugh' wasn't for you. Let's get out of here. Dad's being a pain again."

"Uh oh," he said as he pulled out onto the road. "I was wondering why you were huddled on the porch. I didn't think I was running *that* late." He slanted a glance my way. "What's he doing now?"

I heaved a sigh. "The usual. Defensive bullshit. Pissed that I'm with you. Whinery and bitchery. Same old same old."

"Crap," he replied, grimacing. "I thought he'd gotten better."

"I thought he had too." I controlled the urge to rub my eyes and smear my makeup all over my face. At least I'd remembered to use waterproof mascara and eyeliner since it was raining and so damn humid. "I don't know what the deal is," I continued. "There's no beer or booze at the house, so I figure he's drinking somewhere else. He knows I'll go ballistic if I find any at home."

"Sounds like you've at least put the fear of Angel into him," he said with a low chuckle. "It's a start."

I gave a bark of laughter. "Yeah, there is that." And it was true. Late last year he'd given me some real bullshit, and I'd used zombie strength to pin him against the wall. He didn't have a clue I was a zombie, but he sure as hell knew he couldn't mess with me like that anymore.

I peered out the window. "When is this damn rain supposed to stop?"

"Never?" Marcus made a pained face. "The forecast says it's supposed to be hard rain like this for at least the next four to five days. And this past winter was wet as hell, which means we're primed for flooding in all the low lying areas." He looked over at me, worry flickering in his eyes. "Like where you live."

"We'll be fine," I reassured him. "I mean, the worst we've ever had is some water across the road."

Marcus nodded, clearly relieved. A wave of warmth went through me at the concern. Damn it, he was nice, sexy, considerate, and we were great in bed together. Why the hell was I holding back?

"Still, five days of rain sucks ass," I said, yanking my thoughts away from my issues. "There's not much worse than picking up a body in the rain."

"You could get lucky," he said. "Maybe no one will die, and there'll be no bodies to pick up for a couple of weeks."

I shook my head. "Nope. Then Allen would convince the coroner to lay off staff, and I'd be the first to go." I made a sour face.

He raised an eyebrow. "But you're the shining star of the Coroner's Office, remember?"

"Election's over," I reminded him. "He can dump me at will. I think I only still have a job 'cause Dr. Leblanc sticks up for me."

"At least you don't give them any real reason to fire

you." He paused, then chuckled. "I mean, any that they know of. Swiping brains would do it."

"Swiping brains would get me *committed* if I ever got caught," I shot back, laughing.

We made it to the fairgrounds and found parking that wasn't too far of a hike, then Marcus and I huddled close beneath a compact umbrella, arms around each other as we headed to the entrance.

The venue itself consisted of a half dozen or so long tents spaced out on either side of a paved walkway. Each tent had about fifteen tables around the perimeter, each table belonging to a local restaurant eager to hand out small samples of their cuisine. The rain had slacked off to a drizzle, yet I still saw quite a few elegantly dressed couples pop open umbrellas to walk the ten feet or so between tents. Maybe it was a bitch to get water marks out of silk? I sure as hell wouldn't know.

As we made our way through the tents, I amused myself with some people-watching. No surprise, there were plenty of folks here who absolutely reeked of wealth. Quite a few trophy wives and even a scattering of trophy husbands. High powered business-types and a generous handful of politicians roamed the event, including the coroner, Dr. Duplessis, who I shamelessly avoided by ducking behind a thick-necked man who turned out to be a former Saints player. Last thing I needed was to annoy my boss by making him feel he had to stop meeting-and-greeting to be sociable with me.

Marcus did his best to murmur names of people he recognized, or point out who he thought I'd get a kick out of seeing in the flesh. "Karla Stanford," he told me with a nod toward the C-level actress—well past her prime but still dressing like a twenty year-old, and not doing it well. "Jerome Leroux," he said, subtly indicating the silver-haired and quite handsome man who owned the high end Leroux Jewelry. That surprised me. Rumor had it that he'd been a recluse since his partner—in more ways than business—had committed suicide last year for no known reason. He sat alone at a table looking so forlorn I wished someone would go sit with him. "Nicole Saber," Marcus said with a nod toward the CEO of Saberton Corporation and daughter of its founder, Richard Saber. A tall woman with honey-blond hair pulled back in an elegant twist, she wore an elegant black pantsuit that managed to be sensible and sexy at the same. She sipped her wine and idly twisted a stray lock of hair around her index finger over and over as she conversed and laughed with table mates, all the while watching the proceedings with a keen eye. "And that's her son, Andrew Saber," Marcus added. He didn't gesture or point, but I had no trouble picking out who Marcus meant. Andrew Saber was a good-looking man in his late-twenties or so, tall and broad-shouldered, with the same honey-blond hair, bright blue eyes, and regal profile as his mother. He stood near her table, faint smile touching his mouth as he idly scanned the area and pretended interest in the eager conversation of a forgettable man beside him.

Yeah, we did some people watching, but mostly, we ate.

"I do so love free food," Marcus said. He took a bite of an oyster-something and let out a small moan. "And good free food is even better."

"Oh my god," I said with a weak laugh. "I should have paced myself better. There are still three tents to go, and I'm about to explode."

"Now you know what I meant about the elastic waist-band," he replied, grinning.

"Yes, next time I'll wear my sweat pants with the designer jacket."

We made our way through the crowd, then paused to get our bearings. One woman, a leggy brunette in a skin tight sheath of a dress and impossible stiletto heels gave me a startled look that slid to one of amusement. Her eyes met mine briefly before she pulled her gaze away. She leaned close to murmur something to the woman by her side, and a second later they both tittered, glancing at me again.

I turned away, face heating, reminded a bit too much of high school and the way the popular girls pointed and laughed at my complete lack of anything that could "fit in."

"Marcus," I murmured. "Is there something on my face? Or a sign stuck to my back?"

To his credit, he actually gave me a solid look-over. "No. Why?"

"Heels over there, the woman behind me in the red and black dress and stupid shoes, keeps looking at me and laughing," I told him, trying very hard not to be as unsettled as I was.

"Snobby bitches all over this place, babe," he said with a reassuring smile. "And it doesn't even matter if you have money or whatever. Someone like that tries to put everyone down they can." He gave me a squeeze. "You look great. She's probably jealous. And her feet have to be killing her, which makes her doubly bitchified."

I laughed. "I never thought I'd hear 'doubly bitchified' coming out of your mouth."

Marcus grinned. "It seemed to fit the moment."

I smiled up at him. "Thanks. I'm probably overreacting."

"Don't sweat it." He made a face. "Really have to have a thick skin around some of these people. I'm here for the food, and they're here for dirt and gossip."

"I hate that crap," I muttered, then caught a glimpse of a familiar face through the crowd. "Isn't that your uncle?" I asked with a lift of my chin.

Marcus's gaze followed mine. "I do believe it is. I wonder if he's as overstuffed as we are?"

"We should thank him for the tickets," I said, remembering my inconsistent manners.

He eyed me. "Can you still walk?"

"Waddle," I replied. "I can most certainly waddle."

Marcus slipped an arm around my waist. "Waddle on, then."

Together we wove through the crowd, murmuring apologies and "excuse mes" as appropriate along the way.

Pietro Ivanov looked over at us as we approached. He was slightly stocky with brown hair touched with grey and dark eyes that glinted with keen intelligence. For all outward appearances he was a hale sixty-something, but I'd seen his eyes go ancient once and had no doubt he was far, far older. I didn't know a damn thing about tailoring or suits, but Pietro looked *really* good in the dark grey one he wore, and it radiated Expensive. Odd as hell, though, was the splint on his left wrist. Being a zombie with no shortage of brains, there was no way he should have an injury. Faking it? Had to be. But why?

A smile crossed his face. "Angel. Marcus. I'm so glad you could use the tickets." He gave Marcus's upper arm a squeeze, then offered me a polite kiss on the cheek, which I managed to accept without appearing as startled as I was.

"Thank you *so* much," I gushed, fully aware that I was gushing and not much caring. "This is awesome!"

His smile widened. "You're more than welcome. Have you been here long?"

"About an hour," I replied. "Long enough to get totally bloated." Crap. Not the most couth thing to say. I fought back a wince.

"Not me," Marcus stated with a smile. "I've barely touched a thing."

Pietro gave a low chuckle. "I don't believe that for a second." He shook his head. "I've been busier than usual this time with little chance to eat yet." He tilted his head at the two of us. "Do you have a minute? I need to get my date a drink, and then I'd like to introduce you both to her."

I assured him we had all the time in the world. He smiled and went off to the refreshments table, and I swept my gaze around the tent area. This one wasn't as crowded as the others, mostly because it held only tables and a couple of serving booths for drinks. People clustered around tables, plates of all sorts of food piled high before them, and filled the air with the hum of conversation and bursts of laughter.

Marcus gave me a quick kiss. "I'm going to find the men's room while Uncle Pietro gets drinks. I'll be right back."

"I'll be here," I told him. "Or stuffing my face."

Chuckling, he strode off through the crowd. I allowed my attention to drift across the paved path, to the tent that held a booth we'd bypassed earlier, where wonderfully evil-looking bread pudding was served. I could probably stuff a few more pounds of food into my gut. Surely my parasite would keep me from exploding, right? After all, what the hell good was a zombie parasite if it couldn't help me drastically overeat every now and then?

I felt someone come up behind me. I turned, surprised to see Heels leveling a smirk down at me.

"Well, it looks like my jacket did make it into the Goodwill bag rather than the trash after all," she said in a smooth purr. "Unless, of course, you dug it out of a dumpster." She tilted her head, and I instantly hated how perfectly her hair flowed over her shoulder with the movement. "So, which was it?"

Are you fucking kidding me? I'd seen this kind of scenario in movies, but did this actually happen in real life? "Excuse me?" I managed. I didn't miss that the two women with her had smirks of their own as they eyed me. Perfect noses. Perfect breasts. Perfect bitches.

Heels reached out and tweaked the collar of the jacket with a French-manicured hand. "Simple question," she said. "Goodwill . . . or dumpster?"

I eyed the bitch, then widened my eyes in mock comprehension. "Oh!" I made a show of sweeping my gaze over her. "Now it all makes sense! I was wondering why the pockets were stuffed with condoms." I tilted my head in a mockery of her pose as her eyes narrowed. "So, simple question. Were they yours? Or did men give them to you to keep your skank under control?"

Her mouth tightened then opened in a snarl, but before she could speak I felt an arm tuck through mine. I flicked a glance over, expecting Marcus, and was briefly taken aback when I saw Pietro instead.

"Ah, Jessica Langburn," Pietro said with a pleasant smile. "I haven't seen you since you tried to swim the Kreeger River in nothing but your thong and had to be fished out by the Sheriff's office boat patrol." He chuckled. "That was . . . priceless. Do you plan to amuse the crowd with something equally entertaining today?"

Jessica's eyes went wide in horror. Without another word she spun and fled as quickly as she could in those insane stilettos, her two cronies trailing after her wearing similarly mortified expressions.

I tried not to utterly wilt in relief as Pietro turned a look of amusement on me. "Even though you were doing a marvelous job of cutting that venomous bitch down to size," he said, "I didn't think you'd mind some additional firepower."

I gave a weak laugh. "Not at all. Thanks for the assist."

"I call those types 'piranha,'" he said. "You're okay?"

"Absolutely," I assured him. "Though my next move would have been to slug her, which might not have gone over so well."

Laughter flashed in his eyes. "Probably not. And then she would have been the poor victim of an attack, giving her even more drama to spew," he said. "Not that I would have minded seeing you slug her though," he added.

I grinned. At times he wasn't so bad. "Hey, Pietro, Marcus said he was gonna tell you about what happened with Philip and me the other day at the movie set, but I forgot to ask him if he ever did."

"Yes," he said with a nod. "He did tell me, and I'm looking into it."

Nagging worry surfaced. "But does that mean Dr. Charish might be around as well? What if she's up to more bullshit involving me?"

Pietro's face grew serious and contemplative. "Legitimate concerns indeed, though she would be a fool to act against me again. My people are working on it, but you be sure to let me know if you have any more trouble whatsoever."

"Okay, thanks," I said, relieved. "It's not just me," I added. "I mean, last time she messed with my dad, and that's way over the line."

"She stepped over a lot of lines and burned all of her bridges," he agreed, a whisper of anger tightening his expression. "Keep your eyes and ears open, and you'll be fine." He gave me a genuinely reassuring smile, then lifted what looked like an iced tea in his other hand. "I need to take this to my date. Walk with me?"

At my nod he headed for the back of the tent, keeping his arm tucked through mine. "You and Marcus can sit with us for a few minutes and help keep *her* piranhas at bay."

I shot him a questioning look. "Your date has piranhas?"

"A different breed of piranha, perhaps, but still wanting a piece of her." At my baffled look he explained, "She's Dr. Jane Pennington—State Senator and recently elected to the U.S. House of Representatives. Way too many piranhas, though a little better now that the election is over."

"Oh, wow," I said. Gulping, I swept a glance over myself. Was this jacket stylish or ridiculous? The fact that Heels had owned it wasn't exactly a glowing recommendation in my eyes.

Who the hell do I think I am, pretending to fit in with important, influential people? Yet even as I thought it, Nick's face came to mind as though he'd heard the negative self-talk and was prepared to give me a heap of shit for thinking so little of myself. *Get over it, Nick,* I thought with a stifled snort of amusement. *You're not the one playing Goodwill Girl meets Congresswoman.*

Oblivious to my inner angst, Pietro steered me to a table where a slim, dark haired woman sat, thirtyish or so, and looking perfectly at ease in a sleek navy-blue skirt suit. Under the table, I noted the bulk of an air cast on her right leg and a cane leaning against her chair. *Not a zombie then,* I realized. Not with unhealed injuries. Unless she was faking it too? Whatever the deal was, I had no doubt there was a connection between her possibly-fake injuries and Pietro's definitely-fake one.

"Jane," Pietro said with a warmth in his voice that surprised me. "I'd like you to meet a friend of mine, Angel Crawford. Angel, Dr. Jane Pennington."

My confidence increased as I managed to do the handshake and "pleased to meet you" thing without embarrassing myself.

"And please call me Jane," she insisted with a smile. A moment later, Marcus found us and was duly introduced as well. We all got seated, and I tried not to focus on how very out of my depth I was. Good grief, first name basis with a frickin' congresswoman? Me? What alternate universe had I slipped into?

"And now, with a full table, I can have a few minutes peace," Jane said with a chuckle.

The drumming of rain on the tent eased to a soft hiss of drizzle. Marcus laid his arm across the back of my

chair in a gesture that felt juuuuust right, not too posses-
sive and not too distant. For the next few minutes the
conversation shifted to topics that ranged from neutral
to mildly amusing—nothing that required a great deal of
thought or effort.

A sharp increase in the buzz of the crowd drew our
attention to the outside walkway.

"What on earth?" Jane murmured. She straightened
and peered in the direction of the increasing murmurs
and laughter.

I followed her gaze and drew in a sharp breath. Ten or
so zombies shambled down the sidewalk between the
tents, giving low moans of *"Braaaiiins"* and reaching toward people at tables. I shot a quick look at Pietro, but
he didn't seem the least bit concerned. If anything he
looked indulgently pleased.

Duh, they're the movie zombies! I realized with a wash
of relief. What a perfect place to do some promo and fish
for more investors. Everybody who was anybody was
here. Money. Lots of money.

"Oh my god, Pietro," Jane breathed. "They look
amazing!"

"New makeup people," he commented, eyes on the
lurching actors.

"You're an investor, Uncle Pietro?" Marcus asked.

His uncle nodded. "One of several. Having the movie
here is a nice boost to the local economy. In fact the
other investors are here tonight as well. J. M. Farouche,
Francis Renauld, and Nicole and Andrew Saber." He
gave a nod toward the fake zombies. "I have no doubt
this performance is partly to reassure us that our money
is being well-spent." Pietro's mouth twitched in amusement.

As the hideous group made its way past, a zombie
woman with half a face groaned *"Braaaiiins"* and lifted
a shredded hand toward us. Another zombie with a

bloody face and protruding guts lurched toward Nicole Saber, who took a half-step back, an expression of genuine interest on her face. She peered closely at the extra as if assessing the realism and quality of her investment, then dismissed him with a laugh and wave of her hand. Beside her, Andrew Saber took a sip of his drink and looked on with utter disinterest.

Marcus grinned, leaned close to me. "Weird as hell, right?" he murmured.

I bit back a laugh. "Yes!"

Marcus turned to Pietro. "How many extras did they hire?"

"Close to a hundred," he replied, still watching the zombies as they continued up the path to the cheers and applause of the crowd.

"Yikes. Do they have to do makeup on *all* of them?" I asked.

"Well, yes, but the majority of them have very basic makeup since they'll be in crowds seen at a distance," Pietro explained. "Only a couple dozen or so will get the more detailed makeup like those." He nodded toward the cluster of zombies as they drew out of sight. "Those are the ones who'll get the close camera work."

Jane turned to Pietro, expression aglow with excitement and delight. "You'll get me onto the set for filming, right?" she asked with a smile. "I'd love to see."

"I'll check with Vince and get you in on a good crowd scene," Pietro told her, smiling.

"Oh, it doesn't have to be anything big," she protested, though her eyes brightened at the thought. "I don't want to get in the way, and I certainly don't want to be on camera." She let out a soft snort, then chuckled. "I get enough of that now. I simply want to see how it's done."

Pietro smiled. "Too bad you're a congresswoman-elect. You could get yourself made up."

Jane laughed. "Oh, my goodness, no. I love watching zombies and zombie movies, but I don't ever want to *be* one."

Okay, so not a zombie, which means her injuries are real, I thought, very carefully keeping my expression under control. *But that still doesn't answer the question of whether or not she knows Pietro is a zombie.*

Marcus gave me a light squeeze. "Hey, babe, did you ever get the bread pudding you were lusting after?"

"I wasn't lusting . . ." I stopped, then shrugged. "Okay, I was lusting. It smelled amazing. I would do terrible things to that pudding." I gave him a bright smile. "You offering to go get some for me?"

Jane raised an eyebrow. "Lustworthy bread pudding?"

Pietro chuckled. "Come, Marcus. The ladies want bread pudding, and we should oblige them."

It wasn't until the two went off together that I realized I'd been left alone to talk to a congresswoman. *Okay, I can do this. Now try not to say anything stupid.* Easy, right? "So, um, you and Pietro," I said. "You known him long?"

"A few months now," she replied, a flicker of something I couldn't identify passing quickly over her face. "I met him at a fundraiser."

"I only met him about six months ago or so," I said, then couldn't think of a damn thing to follow that up with. An awkward silence threatened, but Jane saved me.

"I absolutely love your jacket," she said with an appreciative smile. "The color is gorgeous on you, and it's a terrific style."

"Thanks!" I replied, then added, "I actually picked it up for fifteen bucks at Goodwill." Somehow I had the feeling it wouldn't matter to her where I got it. And there was also a small part of me that wanted to establish that I wasn't a snob like Heels.

She didn't disappoint me. Her face lit up in honest appreciation of the find. "What luck!"

"I'm a pro at finding the good bargains," I said with a laugh. But then I sobered. "At the risk of being rude and nosy, what happened to your leg?"

She sucked in her breath with a hiss and shook her head as though it was an ugly memory. "Pietro and I were in a serious car accident a couple of weeks ago. I've been told I'm lucky to be alive."

"Oh, man, I'm sorry to hear that," I said, then hunched my shoulders. "I mean ... not sorry you're alive. Sorry you had the accident ..." I groaned. "Jeez, someone needs to shoot me right about now."

But Jane merely gave a nice laugh. "It's all right. I know what you meant. And I still don't know how Pietro managed to get out with only minor injuries. Moreover, his driver was completely unscathed." She shook her head in amazement. "A real miracle."

"A miracle," I echoed. *She doesn't know we're zombies, and Pietro's pretending to have an injury.* What the heck was he up to? Was he trying to get a congresswoman in his pocket? It certainly wasn't out of the realm of possibility, especially for Pietro. And maybe their relationship had started out that way, but judging by the way he looked at this woman and how his voice seemed to deepen on her name, it was pretty clear he was crazy about her now.

"Pietro told me that you and Marcus are an item," Jane said with a slightly questioning tone, as if wanting to be sure of our status before continuing.

"We're dating," I said, hedging on the whole "item" thing. Was "just dating" an "item"? Or did we have to actually be boyfriend and girlfriend? And if Marcus and I were dating each other exclusively, were we actually boyfriend and girlfriend no matter how hard I tried to deny it? Was I overthinking the hell out of this? "He's a great guy," I finished gamely.

"Hard to find those," she said. Her gaze drifted in the

direction the two men had gone before it returned to me. "Are you from this area?"

"Lived here my whole life," I admitted. "Never been farther away than Talladega, Alabama actually," I added.

"Anywhere you've ever dreamed of going?"

"Oh, wow," I said, exhaling. "Everywhere. Anywhere. New York, L.A., D.C. . . . God, I'd fucking love to see the Smithsonian." I winced. Yes, I'd just dropped an F-bomb on a congresswoman. "Sorry. I mean, I'd love to see it."

The woman leaned forward. "Don't tell the press," she said quietly, then cast a furtive glance around, "but I've been known to say 'fuck' a time or two."

I grinned weakly. "Be pretty boring if you could never cuss, I guess."

Jane laughed. "I don't think I'd make it through my day!"

"What's it like being in Congress?" I asked.

"Well, I don't actually know yet," she answered with a kind smile. "I was elected in a special election, but I won't be sworn in until next week. It's a dream come true, so I'm banking on it not being a nightmare."

"Yeah, I guess that would kinda suck if it was miserable," I said, wrinkling my nose. "But that's still pretty damn cool that you got to reach your dream."

Some emotion briefly darkened her eyes but was gone before I could get a sense of what it was. "Yes, it's very damn cool," she said, smiling. "Do you have a dream, Angel?"

I frowned. "I don't know." I looked around at the soiree surrounding us. "In a way simply being right here is a dream come true. I mean, it wasn't all that long ago that I was a real mess. Didn't care what happened to me." I took a deep breath. "These days I try to take it one step at a time. Right now I'm trying to pass the GED. After that . . ." I shrugged, "don't really know, but whatever it is, I intend to kick its ass."

"That's a good start," she replied. If she was surprised or put off by the fact that I hadn't finished high school she hid it well. "It takes a lot of determination to do something like that," she continued.

I was more than a little pleased that she wasn't doing the pity or disdain thing at all. I definitely saw why Pietro was so gaga over her. Or rather, as gaga as a man like Pietro could be. "I don't know about 'determination,'" I said with a shrug. "I want something better for me and my dad." I gestured at the Gala around us. "The only reason I'm here is because Pietro gave me and Marcus tickets. And don't get me wrong—it's *awesome* that he did that for us. But I'd love to someday be able to do something like this and not have to think, 'Oh, wait, if I buy these tickets then I can't pay the light bill or the water bill.'"

"It seems like you're on the right track," she said. "You said your life was a mess not long ago, but you certainly don't show it now." She smiled. "Are you working?"

"I work at the Coroner's Office," I told her, then grinned. "I wrangle dead bodies."

Jane laughed and made the typical that's-kinda-gross face I was accustomed to. "I'm sorry I asked. Do you . . . like it?"

"Y'know, it's actually really interesting," I replied, then paused. "It, uh, gives you a lot of perspective, that's for sure."

She tilted her head, eyes on mine. "How so?"

I met her gaze easily. For a Congresswoman, she was really easy to talk to. "Well, you get to see that lots of times people don't get a chance to say goodbye. Shit can happen out of nowhere, and then you're gone." I shrugged and spread my hand. "And, well, it doesn't matter how rich or powerful you are. You're still gonna die eventually."

Her expression grew sober in thought, and I grimaced. "Sorry, I'm being a major downer here," I said.

She chuckled. "Not at all, I—" She turned at a sudden commotion in the tent near the walkway.

The sight of another zombie actor stumbling through the tent triggered an odd oh-shit-something's-wrong feeling in my gut. He'd been with the group earlier. I remembered his filthy, sky blue polyester suit. As I watched, he staggered drunkenly between the tables and yelled an incomprehensible word a couple of times that sure as hell wasn't *braaaaiins*.

Some people drew back in alarm but, based on the grins and chatter of the crowd, it was clear that the majority thought it was part of the movie promo.

Jane winced as the zombie grabbed at a patron's plate, snagging a chunk of cake and stuffing it in his mouth. "Oh, dear. That's a bit much, isn't it."

"No kidding," I murmured as the oh-shit feeling grew.

And then the breeze shifted. If I hadn't been fairly well tanked up, I might not have noticed it, but right now there was no mistaking the very faint stench of zombie rot.

Alarm shot through me. *That's a real zombie.* I quickly swept my gaze around, but Marcus and Pietro were nowhere to be seen. Something needed to be done before this zombie started smashing heads.

Something needed to be done. By someone.

Shit.

Why did I have the feeling that someone was going to be me?

Chapter 5

I quickly dug the bag of brain chips out of my purse and stuffed them into my jacket pocket, then did my best to put on an exasperated expression. "Well, hell, he must be drunk or something, and everyone's frickin' watching him," I said. "I'm gonna try to get him the hell away from the crowd and see what's wrong with him."

Jane shot me a startled look, and I suddenly realized how ludicrous it no doubt seemed to her that I—all barely-one-hundred pounds of me—was planning on confronting what she assumed to be a rowdy drunk. "Angel! Are you mad? We should wait for Pietro and Marcus. You could get hurt!"

"I won't get too close," I hurried to reassure her, though she didn't look at all reassured. "They aren't far, right? Just call Pietro and tell him what's going on." And with that I stood and headed off through the crowd before she could make any more extremely sensible protests.

Being skinny had its advantages when it came to slipping through a crowd. I ducked between a couple of gawkers and came face to face with the zombie. Close up I smelled the undertone of rot better, but his appearance confused the hell out of me. Movie makeup . . . and chocolate cake. A gruesome fake eye hung out of its prosthetic socket on one side of his face, but latex gaped on the other where he'd clawed at it, exposing the real grey, peeling skin beneath. This was a hungry real zombie made up as an extra, but he sure wasn't acting right. I'd been starving more than once and there was no way I would've confused cake with what I really needed.

I yanked the bag of brain chips out of my pocket and opened it. "Hey!" I waved the tasty morsels in front of him, hoping the scent of the brains would get through to his zombieness. "Here zombie zombie zombie!" In my peripheral vision I saw the crowd had stopped and was watching me. Great, they probably thought I was part of the stunt now.

The zombie swung toward me, his one clear eye focused on the bag. "Braaaaaiins," he rasped and reached clumsily for the bag. I pulled it out of his reach and backed away from the crowd toward the exit. He followed to the sound of scattered applause. I figured if I could get him outside, there'd be less chance he would hurt someone plus more room to take him down if it came to that, once Marcus showed up.

He staggered toward me and grabbed for the bag again, but I easily dodged. "Braaaaaaiins!" he bellowed as I backed away. Light rain spattered me as we left the shelter of the tent, but I didn't stop. We weren't far enough from the people yet—people who applauded and cheered their rescue from the zombie. Give me a break.

"Here!" I pulled a few chips from the bag and dropped them onto the sidewalk. I felt a little bad making him eat off the ground, but I didn't want to get close enough for him to grab hold of me.

He didn't seem to mind though. He crouched, snatched them up and stuffed them into his mouth, then lurched toward me again. "More . . . braaaaains . . ." He'd picked up a bit of speed, a side effect of getting some brains into him. Even at half-strength, the chips would be like the nectar of the gods for a hungry zombie. I moved away more quickly as he shuffled toward me and continued to drop chips, leading him like a cat with tuna. The rain began to pick up again, but I wasn't about to stop now that I had his attention.

We'd made it about a hundred yards from the tents when he abruptly swiveled his head to the right, head lifting as if he scented something. I shot a quick glance that way, and cold knifed through me at the sight of a bus stop and a woman waiting there. The zombie took a staggering step in that direction, a tortured moan coming from his throat as if he was fighting an inner battle to keep from going after the woman. I knew what that battle was like. I'd been hungry before, ready to club down the first person with a non-zombified brain to cross my path.

"No!" I waved the bag at him. "This way. C'mon. Don't go over there. I'll get you more brains, I promise."

He stopped in the glow of a streetlamp, swaying as he looked back at me. His lips curled back in a snarl, but I got the sense it was more pain and confusion than menace.

"Here," I said, making a quick decision. "Have the rest of these." I held the bag out, hoping that there was enough brain power in them to counter his desire for fresh brains.

The zombie looked to the bus shelter, then back to me. His breath rasped as he turned and made a sluggish grope for the bag. I let it drop to the sidewalk, but to my shock he ignored the bag and made a lightning-fast grab of my wrist.

Shit! I sucked in a gasp. He was way stronger than I expected a zombie that shambly to be.

A menacing growl shuddered from him as his lips twisted back in a wicked tooth-baring snarl. "Aaannn-gggellll." The word—my freaking *name*—came out in an ugly wet croak.

"What the hell?" The initial shock of getting grabbed melted into get-the-fuck-away-from-me. I made a strong twist of my arm in an attempt to free it and landed a solid kick in the bastard's zombie balls.

To my dismay, he only grunted and snarled with the impact, then clamped harder on my wrist with bone-breaking strength. Excruciating pain shot up my arm, while his other hand swung slow and wide, arcing for my throat.

Okay. I'm in deep, deep shit. Yeah, I was a little slow getting a clue. But with that extra jolt of fear I turned into a punching, struggling, kicking, psycho redneck zombie bitch.

Bad Zombie clamped his free hand on my shoulder and lunged in for a bite. I threw myself backward enough to shake the shoulder hold and avoid anything to do with teeth. A sickening wave of zombie rot stench struck me, and his grip on my wrist slipped as skin sloughed from his fingers. This was Not Good on a whole bunch of levels. No way should he be rotting this fast. And now I had zombie ooze on my jacket on top of everything else.

"Let GO!" I snarled. I made a savage punch at the arm that held me, heart pounding from the desperate cocktail of anger and fear.

With the force of the blow, flesh slid from his fingers and my wrist slipped free. But I didn't even get a fraction of a second to celebrate that victory as his other hand knotted into the sleeve of my jacket and yanked my arm up to his open mouth.

I let out a yelp of pain and dismay as he bit down hard on my forearm. "You fucker!" I shouted and punched his eye—well, I punched where his eye was under the dangling eyeball prosthetic.

To my total surprise, he let out a near airless moan and let go, latex dangling from his face and his real eyelid and upper cheek knocked away.

I wanted to allow myself a brief moment of self-congratulation at my badassery, but the abrupt release of my arm sent me staggering backward, and I barely managed to keep my footing. Plus, now another zombie dude loomed a couple of yards behind Bad Zombie.

Time to get the hell out of here. I turned and ran—

—and barreled straight into a wall. A wall that threw an arm around me and pinned me to it. Okay, not a wall, but *another* goddamn zombie pretending to be a zombie. Within about a half a second, Wall Zombie had my back to his chest and his arm locked hard around me. *Shit.*

Bad Zombie shambled toward us with the unsavory declaration of, "Miiiiinnnnne."

Wall Zombie kept an unshakable hold on me and leveled a gun at the advancing zombie. "Tim, NO!" he commanded in a low, raspy voice.

It looked like Wall Zombie intended to shoot Bad Zombie, which meant maybe he was a Good Zombie, but I didn't care. I went right back to struggling like a psycho. All I wanted was to get the hell *away*. "Let me *go*!"

"Hold still!" he ordered me through clenched teeth, then fired the gun. Except it wasn't a normal gun, and it made a *whuuuush* instead of a normal *bang*.

His voice abruptly registered. I craned my head around in shock. "Oh my god," I breathed. Though I couldn't see his face under the makeup, I knew his eyes. *Philip.*

Bad Zombie staggered back with a sound between a

growl and a sob. He pawed at a yellow tufted thing in his shoulder, and I realized Philip had shot him with a tranquilizer dart.

Looming Zombie moved in close behind Bad Zombie, got a hand on his arm as he swayed. I didn't have a clue what was going on, but I knew it would be a lot better if I wasn't right in the middle of it. I ramped my crazy-chick struggles up another notch, but Philip easily kept a solid hold on my scrawny ass. Even through my thrashing, I could feel his whole body tremoring against my back, as if he was shivering from cold or fear. But neither of those reasons made sense. Sure, we were all soaking wet from the rain, but it was the middle of summer. Something else was up.

"Roland, get him out of here. *Now*," Philip ordered. He produced what looked like a candy bar with a white wrapper and tossed it to Looming Zombie, who ripped it open and scarfed it down. The whole thing reminded me of a dog getting a treat.

Bad Zombie collapsed on his back in the pool of light from the streetlamp, thrashed for a moment before subsiding into twitches. Wrecked latex and makeup left what remained of his face exposed, and it only took me a second to recognize him. Square jaw. A nose that had been repeatedly broken. Horror backed by anger slammed through me. I'd carefully memorized the features of the men who'd been my jailers when I was Dr. Charish's unwilling test subject. This guy was one of the assholes who had callously watched me get strip searched.

Which means that he's probably one of the two men who got turned into zombies by Philip right before I escaped Dr. Charish's lab. My gaze snapped up to Looming Zombie—the one Philip called Roland—and met his eyes. Gorgeous blue. *And that's probably the other one.* One of Charish's guards had eyes like that. The makeup couldn't hide those.

Oh, this was all kinds of bad. Philip and his freakin' zombie-spawn. He'd been in bad shape when he made them—mean, near berserk, and rotting too soon— damaged by some experimental shit Charish had done to him. Who the hell knew how screwed up the two he'd turned were.

I landed a hard kick to Philip's shin, but he seemed unfazed by my struggles. I got in a few more solid kicks and foot stomps, and then he tucked away the tranq gun and pulled a knife.

I made a strangled sound pushed out by panic. "No . . . no! Let me go," I managed. "Oh god." It was hard as hell to kill a zombie, but I had no doubt he knew how to do it.

"Shut up, Angel," he said, voice deep and hoarse. He wrestled my bitten arm up and sliced the jacket sleeve. "Have to make sure the goods aren't damaged."

A stupid pang of grief went through me, and I stared in horror at the long rent in the lovely fabric. "You cut my jacket!" Yeah, I was captured by a couple of Evil Zombies, but a girl has her priorities. "You fucking *dick!*" I slammed my boot heel down into the top of his foot. "Get off me!"

Philip hissed and shifted. "God damn it, Angel."

"Let her go," a clear, strong voice commanded from off to my right.

Philip hauled me around with him as he turned to face the approaching man—who, unnervingly, had a very real gun drawn and pointed at us. Fortyish with close-cropped brown hair, the newcomer bore a serious-as-all-hell expression perfectly complemented by a dark suit. I had no clue who the hell he was, but I was pissed and scared and desperate. I thrashed and kicked back hard into Philip's shin. "Yeah. Let me GO!"

Philip tightened his arm around me and looked to the left where Looming Zombie moved away with the tranquilized Bad Zombie slung over his shoulder, then dragged me backward with him into the shadows. "No problem," he snarled, and shoved me roughly forward.

Totally off balance, I went sprawling to the sidewalk. The palm of my right hand grated against the concrete, and white hot agony shot through me as my already broken wrist impacted and shattered.

"*Asshole!*" I shouted as I soon as I could get a full breath, though it came out as more of a pained wheeze. I shifted to sit heavily, cradling my arm to my chest, and caught a glimpse of Philip sprinting away before he was lost to the darkness.

The man holstered his gun and moved toward me. "Ms. Crawford. Are you all right, ma'am?"

The pain faded and my senses dulled as my parasite kicked in. "No, I'm not all right," I growled as I struggled to my feet. "And, goddammit, that motherfucker cut my jacket!"

"Yes, ma'am," he said in a cool, professional tone. No accent to speak of. And no edible brain scent. Yet another zombie. "What are your injuries?"

"I dunno. My wrist is broken." I examined my jacket sleeve with dismay. I felt my lower lip quiver. "Goddammit," I muttered. "He could have at least cut the seam. What a dick." I snapped my eyes to the man, abruptly wary. I'd discovered from Bad Zombie that knowing my name didn't instantly translate to "friend."

"And who the hell are *you*?" I asked. I took a step back, ready to bolt.

"Brian Archer, ma'am. I work for Mr. Ivanov. He called to say you'd lured a zombie out the west exit."

The relief nearly dropped me to the ground again. "Oh. Good." Of course Pietro had some security people around. I'd told Jane to call Pietro, and he must have sent this dude.

Brian reached into his jacket pocket, pulled out a

white plastic tube thing that looked like a yogurt packet for kids and held it out to me. "Here, you need this, Ms. Crawford."

I frowned at the packet without reaching for it. "Why do I need that?" I glanced back over my shoulder toward the distant tent. "Crap. Marcus is gonna come looking for me." And ohmygod would he ever freak the hell out about the fact that I went off on my own and then got in way over my head. I would never hear the end of it. Ever. *Ever.*

"You need it because your wrist is broken," Brian stated, still holding the packet. "You need food."

I took the packet from him. "Oh, wait. This is brains?"

"Yes, ma'am. And you may need a second one."

Jeez, the "ma'am" thing was weird. I sure as hell wasn't used to it. I tore the top of the packet open with one hand and my teeth. One sniff confirmed that it was indeed brains, and I sucked it down quickly as I cast another glance back toward the Gala.

Brian noticed. "I suspect he will be here very shortly, ma'am. Do you need another packet?"

I shuddered as the wrist pulled back together in a familiar but still eerie-as-hell shift of tissue and bone. "Uh, yeah. If you don't mind. And an alibi," I added with a snort.

He took the empty packet from me and tucked it away. "I don't mind at all, ma'am," he said and pressed a second one into my hand.

I gave him a grateful smile, then sucked down the contents of the second one. Nifty way to package brains for sure. "That should do it. Thanks," I said, then let out a sigh. "Damn it. This sure went to hell."

"Yes, ma'am," he said as he took the empty. "I could see that." In a smooth move he pulled a business card from an inner pocket of his suit jacket, pressed it into my hand. "You might want to hold onto this."

I glanced down at it. It simply said "Brian Archer" with a phone number below the name. Nothing else. "Um, thanks." Cool that I had the number of Pietro's security guy, though I wasn't sure if he was giving this to me out of courtesy or because I had a tendency to get myself into trouble.

"Angel!" I heard Marcus call from the direction of the tents. Quickly shoving the card into the front pocket of my pants, I glanced back to see him hurrying our way.

He gave Brian the kind of nod you give to someone you know, then took me by the shoulders. "Are you all right?"

"I am now, but—"

"She's fine, sir," Brian interjected. "A little banged up for a moment. She slipped on some mud on the sidewalk after the extras left."

I closed my mouth and stared at Brian. He was covering for me? *Well, I did say that I needed an alibi.* I hadn't been serious, but it certainly made things easier.

Marcus exhaled, tension in his face easing. He gave a nod to Brian then looked back at me. "You sure you're okay?"

I tore my eyes away from Brian. "Um, yeah. It was no biggie," I said, more than a little thrown off by the totally unexpected ally.

Brian took a step back, his eyes lingering on me. "I'll be going now and will let Mr. Ivanov know exactly what happened," he said with a faint stress on *exactly*. "Have a good evening, sir, ma'am," he added with a nod in our direction.

"Thanks for all your help, Brian," I said with an equally faint stress on the *all*.

He gave me a slight smile. "Anytime, Ms. Crawford." He turned and headed off toward the parking lot, pausing on the way to pick up and pocket the forgotten bag of brain chips.

"What the hell were you thinking?" Marcus asked,

dropping his hands from my shoulders. "Why didn't you call me?"

I bristled. Yep, here it was. "There wasn't time to call," I told him. "And Jane called Pietro, right?"

Marcus blew out an exasperated breath. "Jesus Christ, Angel, you didn't know what you were doing, or who you were going after. Some drunk extra? I know you're strong, but someone else could have handled it." He said it all in a patronizing tone that slid right under my skin. "And what if it had turned out to be something worse?"

I'd planned to tell him about Philip—if not all the details about the broken wrist and such—but holy crap I was so *not* in the mood to get chewed out. Annoyed, I edged back from him. "Who else was gonna handle it? Someone who didn't know it was a zombie and could've ended up a victim? I was the only one there who could do something."

Marcus stared at me for a second. "Wait. It was a *zombie* zombie?"

I glared right back at him. "Yeah. It was a zombie made up like one of the zombie extras. I don't know if he really was an extra or just pretending to be." A zombie pretending to be a zombie pretending to be a zombie. Made me dizzy.

"So you didn't go after a drunk dude ... you went after a crazy, hungry zombie."

"Yeah. And if I didn't do something, someone was gonna get hurt," I said. "And I was tanked." I scowled at him. "C'mon, Marcus, I handled it, didn't I?"

"Sure, this time," he said, eyes dark with worry. "But it could have turned out differently."

"So can walking out to get the damn mail," I shot back. "Marcus, I *handled it*. Can't you give me a little bit of credit for that?"

"Okay, okay," he sighed, then gave me a smile. "You're right. Forget I said it."

Relief pushed back the annoyance. He was trying, and I had to give him props for that. And it was damn important. If we could ever get past this babying crap, we might actually have a chance to make it together. Okay, yeah, this time it had actually been a teensy weensy bit dangerous, but that wasn't the point.

I gave him a smile in return, then wrinkled my nose. "Anyway, I'm pretty soaked now, so I guess that's my sign that I've eaten enough."

He slid an arm around me. "Ready to call it a day and head home? Pietro's going to get Jane out of here as soon as he knows you're okay, which I'm sure Brian has already told him by now."

"Probably best." I gave him a squeeze. "Thanks. I had a really great time. Even with zombie chasing." And lots and lots to think about. Lots.

He chuckled. "I did too. Besides, I think I'd explode if I ate one more thing."

I laughed as we headed for the parking lot. "Body parts everywhere."

"Ewwwww. That would ruin some dinners," he said, grinning.

"Nah," I said. "I'd tell everyone it was part of the movie promo."

"As long as I died for a noble cause."

I gave a solemn nod. "Overeating is the noblest of causes."

Chapter 6

I'd actually planned ahead for once, and swapped part of my eight a.m. to four p.m. shift with Jerry, the other full-time van driver, so that I didn't have to come in so early in the morning after the late night out with Marcus. Jerry was an early riser who hated working nights, which meant he was more than happy to take the first half of my regular shift, and in return I agreed to be on call for him until midnight.

And so, of course, the call for the first body pickup of the day came in at two minutes past noon, and during a downpour like Niagara Falls.

The van's windshield wipers slapped hard at the pouring rain, and I squinted to read street signs through the slight fog on the windows. A silver pickup crossed the intersection ahead, same make and model as the one that almost hit me on the movie set. The one Philip saved me from. I frowned. What the hell was that about? Save me, then be a total asshole like he'd been last night? It made no sense . . .

A piece clicked into place. It made no sense until I

remembered what he said when he cut my jacket. *Have to make sure the goods aren't damaged.* So he hadn't saved me from the truck. He'd saved me *for* someone else. But who? Dr. Charish? Some new bad guy?

Whatever. He'd earned a choice spot on my shitlist.

I finally found the street I needed and made my way down a street lined on both sides by identical duplexes. It could have easily been horrifying in an institutional and *Conform!* sort of way, yet I saw that the residents here found all sorts of ways to add character to the cookie-cutter structures and make their own place unique. Even through the driving rain it was easy to note personal touches, from carefully tended flower beds to small additions like gazebos or rock gardens, to choice of paint colors. I had no doubt that everyone who lived along this street was a renter, and it impressed me that, with rare exceptions, they all seemed to take pride in where they lived. I'd never lived in a rental a day in my life, and right now the biggest "personal touch" I gave my house was to keep the weeds hacked down to something that could resemble a lawn.

Derrel's Dodge Durango and the St. Edwards Parish Sheriff's Office crime scene van were already parked by the curb in front of my destination. I only saw one unmarked unit, which told me that this was the type of death that didn't require a horde of detectives.

I parked behind the unmarked car, then pulled on a raincoat I'd picked up at Goodwill during my Gala shopping. On a normal-sized human it would probably hit mid-calf, which meant it was ankle-length on me. And when I paired it with the white rubber shrimp boots I currently sported, I had every confidence it would keep me awesomely dry. The only drawback was the polka-dots. Lots and lots of polka dots in varying sizes and in eye-searing colors. Fine. I'd be dry *and* visible.

Detective Abadie sat in the front seat of the unmarked car, typing on his laptop. I rapped hard on his window as I passed and gave him a big bright smile when he jerked in surprise. He raked a gaze over the raincoat, rolled his eyes, and gave me a sour look before returning his attention to his laptop in a pointed dismissal. I laughed and continued up to the house with the stretcher and body bag. Abadie didn't like me—though he'd once clarified that he didn't *hate* me, he simply didn't *like* me, which somehow made all the difference in the world and made it particularly fun to harass him in any innocuous way I could.

This duplex had a small but tidy front yard and a utilitarian, no frills look about it. A couple of pieces of white wicker outdoor furniture and nothing else on the porch. Derrel stood there, out of the rain, and looked up from his notepad as I approached. "Nice slicker," he remarked. "Four more days, right?"

I got the stretcher and myself under shelter, pushed my hood back and shook the worst of the water from my raincoat. "Is everyone counting down to my GED test date?" I asked in mock exasperation.

"Sure thing. There's a big calendar down at Double D's Diner." At my shocked look he laughed. "I'm kidding, promise! Figured that might be a bit too much pressure on you."

"Ya think?" I said, then gave a weak laugh. "I'm barely holding it together as it is."

"You'll do great," he stated with such utter conviction that it was hard not to believe it.

"Thanks, Derrel." I slipped my raincoat off and draped it over the back of a chair. "So, whatcha got here?" I asked with a jerk of my head toward the house.

His eyes dropped to his notes. "Brenda Barnes. White female, twenty-eight years old. Roommate found her dead on the bathroom floor about an hour ago. No obvious trauma."

"Y'think it might be drug overdose?" Sadly, the death of someone that young was far too often the result of such a thing. I should know. Hell, it had been an OD that got me turned into a zombie.

But Derrel shrugged, shook his head. "Doubtful. No vomit or pulmonary edema. The roommate, Ginger Nelson, swears the victim wasn't a user, and there were no pill bottles or other evidence of that."

"I guess that's both good and bad," I said with a slight wince. "I mean good in that it wasn't a bullshit way to die."

"Agreed. So for now I'm not inclined to call it a suicide or an OD, though toxicology will show that for sure." He closed his pad. "The roommate said she turned the victim over when she found her, so we don't know what her original position was, but she stated that it looked like the victim simply fell to the floor."

I nodded. Perfectly natural reaction to move the person to see if they were okay or to try and help them. It was only a big deal when it was a murder or anything suspicious, since moving the body could alter or wipe out evidence.

Derrel pulled out his phone and stepped away, no doubt to call Dr. Leblanc and give him the rundown. Pushing the stretcher before me, I headed inside. The décor within echoed the bare, no-nonsense feel of the exterior. Simple furniture: couch, loveseat, and coffee table, with scrapes and dings that spoke of their age. A modest-sized TV. A bookshelf made of cinder blocks and pine boards with an assortment of worn paperbacks, knick knacks, and framed pictures on it. Yet everything was clean and tidy, and I got the impression the "no-frills" look was due more to a careful hoarding of available funds than a lack of creative personality.

In the living room, a young, teary-eyed brunette in jeans and a t-shirt stood with her arms hugged around herself. The roommate, no doubt. Ginger. That's what

Derrel said her name was. I heard the click of a camera shutter, and a peek down the hallway told me that the crime scene tech, Sean, was still working.

The young woman looked over at me where I stood by the stretcher. "This is horrible," she said, voice quavering. "She was *so* happy."

"I'm sorry for your loss," I said, hating how empty the words sounded. But I never knew what to say to the bereaved. I usually didn't *have* to say anything, since Derrel was the one to handle that stuff. He always knew what to say. For that reason alone I wasn't sure I could ever be a death investigator. I'd fumble it and say something inappropriate, or worse, start crying along with the grieving friend or relative.

But apparently my empty phrase of condolence was all right. Ginger let out an unsteady sigh and shook her head. "She'd just gotten a break, and then this. It's like a cruel joke."

"What kinda break?" I asked.

Ginger dabbed at her eyes with the wadded up tissue in her hand. "She'd been unemployed for nearly a year—one of the first to be laid off by the factory. Then she got the call to be an extra in *High School Zombie Apocalypse!!*"

"Two exclamation points," I said, then instantly regretted cracking a joke about the movie.

But a small smile touched Ginger's mouth. "She used to laugh about that too. Pretty silly, I know. Still, the laid off workers were given first dibs. Sure, it's temp work in a goofy movie, but it paid well, and an extra grand or so makes a big difference when you're barely scraping by, y'know? Brenda said it was like winning the lottery for a bunch of folks."

I nodded in understanding. *Barely scraping by* and I were old buddies.

She sighed and crumpled the tissue in her hands.

"And even beyond the money, she was having the time of her life. They'd even talked to her about doing a small part in another production."

"I bet being in a movie totally rocked," I offered.

She smiled a bit again. "Whenever Brenda got home she'd tell me all the cool little details." She reached for a stack of pictures on the coffee table, pulled three out and handed them to me. "Look, here she is with and without makeup."

The first showed a petite redhead, grinning and waving in front of one of the movie set trailers. The second was a smiling zombie with a maggoty gash in the grey, rotting flesh of her cheek, and the third, that same zombie with slack face reaching toward the camera with convincing movie-zombieness.

"That's really cool," I said. "Looks like she was having fun."

"She was one of the featured zombies," Ginger said with a touch of pride in her voice.

I peered at the photo. "Was she at the Gourmet Gala last night? Some of the extras were there for a promo thing."

Ginger nodded. "She sure was. I talked to her when she got home, I guess at about eleven or so. She said it was a blast." Her face fell again. "God, and now she's dead. This is so crazy."

Was Brenda a real zombie like Tim and his friend last night? I wondered. But if so, surely she wouldn't look like a normal dead person now. I itched to get close to the body to find out for sure, and to my relief Sean stepped out and gave me the nod that told me it was okay for me to do my thing.

Luckily, Derrel chose that moment to return inside, so I was saved from having to say something like, "It's been great talking to you, but now it's time for me to put your roomie into a body bag"—but, y'know, less insensitive.

Derrel gently guided Ginger to the couch to get more information about Brenda's next of kin, and I made my escape to the easier company of the dead chick.

There she was, on her back on the bathroom floor, looking as if she was asleep except for the utter stillness and half-open eyes. She definitely wasn't a zombie either. No whiff of rot, and I was barely hungry enough to smell a regular, unzombified brain within her skull.

I made quick work of getting her into the bag and, as she was slender and short, I didn't need Derrel's help to get her onto the stretcher. I draped the dark blue Coroner's Office cover over the body bag, then wheeled the stretcher out while Derrel kept Ginger occupied. Even though it was obvious a body bag lay beneath the sedate cloth, it still offered a bit of shielding from the emotional impact. Derrel and I were pretty good about doing our best to make sure friends and family didn't have to see the body being removed. That was one of those "final" things that tended to hit people pretty hard.

By the time I got outside the rain had slacked off to a sluggish drizzle—still annoying after so many days of rain but better than the earlier deluge. I tugged my raincoat back on, then pushed the stretcher and its burden to where I'd parked.

A flicker of movement down the street caught my eye as I shoved the stretcher into the back of the van. I closed the door and turned, mystified to see a blond woman with a camera aimed in my direction. *That's the same chick who was taking pictures of me on the movie set.* What the hell?

Though I knew damn well she saw me looking at her, she didn't lower the camera and no doubt got some great photos of my scowl. A few seconds later, she turned and strolled casually off in the opposite direction.

Shit. Every muscle in my body screamed at me to chase her down and demand to know why the hell she was taking pictures of me. But leaving a body in the van so that I could run down the street was a sure way to get fired.

As if the universe wanted to help me make up my mind, lightning split the sky, followed immediately by a crash of thunder that shook the van. I jumped and let out a squeal, then dashed for the driver side door and climbed in. Yeah, I could probably survive being struck by lightning, but it would hurt like a sonofabitch.

About two seconds later rain slammed down in a deafening roar on the roof of the van. Fine, I could take a hint. No chasing down mysterious photographers today.

But as soon as this rain let up? All bets were off.

Even with the wipers going at mach ten the visibility remained utter crap. To add to the driving fun, the ditches and drainage systems had obviously thrown up their collective hands and said, "Fuck it, I give up!" which meant that water of varying depths covered half the damn streets. And of course that meant that traffic was a frickin' nightmare, because, apparently, heavy rain and flooding streets were signals for everyone with a car to leave the house and run every non-essential errand they'd been putting off until the weather and road conditions were maximum-shit.

Yeah, I was in a peachy mood.

The rain eased up to slightly less apocalyptic levels by the time I reached Tucker Point. As I drove past the high school I peered over to see if the movie people were trying to shoot in the rain, but while there were plenty of trucks and trailers parked by the main building, there was little sign of activity. Probably doing as many interior shots as possible, I decided. A few people clustered under the overhang at the front of the school. A red-haired man gestured at the downpour in obvious agitation as a slim black woman stood with folded arms and gave a disinterested nod as if she'd heard the rant before. Another man in a suit paced back and forth with a cell phone held to his ear, while a mousy woman in jeans and a t-shirt looked out at the rain with a faint smile on her face, as if enjoying the show nature had put on for her.

I made it to the morgue without further incident, got the body of Ms. Brenda Barnes inside and logged in. As soon as I finished that, two funeral home workers showed up, one right after the other, and I went through the usual rigmarole of releasing the bodies they'd come to pick up. Neither of the funeral home workers were zombies; I smelled quite-edible brains in both of their skulls. In fact I realized—after each departed with his respective cargo—that in the past six months the few zombies I'd met had all been associated with Pietro's organization. I hadn't met any "independent" zombies in that time.

I paused as I set out the scalpels and tools for Dr. Leblanc and pondered that. It was true that Ed had succeeded in killing off close to half a dozen zombies, including Kang, who I'd met not long after I'd been zombified. He was the first zombie to give me the slightest clue about how to survive as a brain-eater. His job at Scott Funeral Home supplied a sideline in dealing brains to a handful of undisclosed local zombies—at least until Dr. Charish put a bounty on his head, literally, and Ed decapitated him. After I escaped her, Pietro's people supposedly recovered Kang's head along with others from her lab, but I hadn't heard a thing about it since. And maybe there was more to Kang than I knew. Hell, I'd only been a zombie a short time before he was killed.

So were the only zombies left in this area ones who worked for Pietro? Or were there still zombies who worked at the various local funeral homes though not in any capacity where I'd come into contact with them?

"Angel?"

I jerked, startled out of my reverie by the voice behind me. "Shit!" I dropped the scalpel in my hand and turned to see Dr. Leblanc. "Jesus, you scared the crap out of me," I said with a shaking laugh.

But instead of giving an answering laugh, his eyes dropped to my left hand, and a look of alarm spread across his face. "Good lord, Angel!"

I looked down to see a deep slice along the lower part of my thumb. *Crap*, I thought as I stared stupidly at the gaping flesh of the inch-long gash and the thick drip of blood onto the floor. *I just mopped that.*

Luckily Dr. Leblanc had no desire to gaze at the pretty patterns my blood made on the tile. With a quick motion he seized one of the towels I'd set out and pressed it to my hand. "I'm sorry I startled you," he said, concern in his eyes as he maintained pressure on the gash. "You were standing so still I thought something might be wrong."

"Sorry," I replied with a weak smile. "I was lost in thought."

He lifted my hand, pulled the towel away enough to allow him to peer at the wound. *Crap*, I thought again. I wasn't tanked enough for it to have healed on its own at all. Then again, that was probably good since it would've been really tough to explain why I'd been bleeding only seconds earlier.

"Ah, damn," he said, wincing. "You're going to need a few stitches in that."

I groaned. "Oh no, is this a workman's comp thing? Will I have to fill out an incident report?" I knew the answer to that. I'd damn well memorized the employee manual to be extra sure I wouldn't accidentally give Allen a reason to write me up or fire me. Any injury requiring medical attention required a metric fuckton of paperwork.

"Sadly, yes," he said, pressing the towel back down over my hand. "But since it was completely my fault I'll write it up for you." He gave me a smile. "Least I can do."

"Can you stitch it up as well?" I asked hopefully. "There's no way I'm gonna go sit in an ER for something this tiny." Especially when a few slugs of brain smoothie would take care of the whole problem. Craaaaap. This meant I couldn't eat until this whole thing was dealt with.

To my dismay, Dr. Leblanc shook his head. "Best that I don't. However, I know someone who can do a fine job on it and save you an ER trip."

With that he led me back to the main building, though he allowed me to hold the towel on my hand myself. I expected him to lead me out and over to Dr. Duplessis's practice which was right across the street, but instead he shocked me by bringing me to Allen Prejean's office.

"Allen. We've had a bit of an accident," Dr. Leblanc said, contrition tingeing his voice. "Completely my fault."

Allen frowned, eyes going to the bloody towel around my hand. "What happened?"

"Angel was setting out equipment, and I jostled her when she had a scalpel in her hand," he said, surprising me with the mild lie. Maybe he figured Allen would still find a way to make it my fault if it came out I'd cut myself because Dr. Leblanc had startled me. Damn, but I loved the pathologist.

Allen opened his bottom desk drawer, pulled gloves out of a box and tugged them on, then stood and moved to me. I let him examine the gash, and even I had to admit it was an ugly wound for a non-zombie to have. The cut extended from the outer edge of my thumb and into the meat of my palm. It gaped open about a quarter of an inch, and I could see the white sheen of a tendon within. Didn't hurt though. That was nice.

"Needs stitches," Allen muttered. "Probably about five, I'd say."

Dr. Leblanc nodded. "I agree. But any chance we can take care of that here and avoid her wasting hours in the ER?"

Allen looked up at Dr. Leblanc. "I could do it since it missed the tendon. I mean, I have a suture kit, but I don't have any lidocaine."

"I don't need it numbed up for just a few stitches," I said quickly. Allen gave me a doubtful look, but I hurried on. "Seriously, if you can stitch it up, that'll be fine."

"I'll get started on the incident report while you take care of Angel," Dr. Leblanc said as if the matter had been decided. After another couple of seconds of hesitation Allen shrugged.

"Okay, but no screaming or crying," he grumbled. "Come on."

I followed him down the hall and into a small, rarely used room that had become more of a catch-all storage space than the consulting room it once was.

"Have a seat there by the desk," he told me as he looked through the cabinet.

I did so, mentally bracing myself against him being a jerk to me, or rougher than necessary, or any crap like that. Hunger poked at me, reminding me how unnecessary all this was, and I bit back a sigh.

Allen turned back to me with suture kit, wound wash, and towels in his hands, set them all on the desk and flicked on the swing-arm lamp. He folded one of the towels into a pad and set it on the desk by me. "Okay, Angel, rest your forearm there and get comfortable."

"Thanks for doing this," I remembered to say as I set my arm on the folded towel. "I really didn't want to have to go to the emergency room."

He unrolled another towel and draped it over my forearm. "Emergency room sucks," he said. "This way you'll be done in fifteen minutes instead of three hours."

"You've done a lot of stitching?" Not that it really

mattered since I wasn't exactly worried about him botching it up. Even if he did, a slug of brains would take care of it.

Allen didn't shift his careful focus from the wound. "I've gone with Dr. Duplessis four times on Doctors Without Borders rotations," he said. "Did quite a few sutures."

I blinked at him in surprise. "Really? Like other countries?" The instant the words left my mouth I realized how stupid they sounded.

But Allen didn't deliver the condescending sneer I expected. "Yes," he replied as he opened the suture kit and began removing items. "Africa, Guatemala, and Haiti twice."

"I never knew that," I said, frowning slightly. "Why don't you ever talk about it?"

"It hasn't come up," he replied with a small shrug. He picked my hand up carefully and sprayed wound wash on it. I wasn't sure if it was supposed to sting, but I figured I'd give a slight wince anyway.

"Wow. Did you like it?" I asked.

"I wouldn't have gone four times if I didn't," Allen replied. He finished cleaning the slice, then replaced the towel beneath my arm with a fresh and dry one. "I'm going again in October, but without Dr. Duplessis this time." He pulled off the latex gloves he had on, then put on fresh sterile gloves from the suture kit.

"That's really cool," I said, meaning it. "Where are you going?"

"Guatemala again to work in a children's services clinic in the highlands," he said. He picked up the needle, then adjusted my hand on the folded towel. "Okay, Angel," he said, speaking calmly and, to my continued surprise, gently. "Take a deep breath and let it out."

I did so, fascinated and a teensy bit weirded out by this completely alien-to-me side of him, then watched as he did the first stitch with smooth efficiency and tied it off. He'd obviously done this a few thousand times.

Allen glanced up at me, a small frown touching the corners of his mouth. "Damn, Angel, you didn't even wince."

Shit. "Oh, um, I was watching you do it, and, uh, kinda forgot it was supposed to hurt." I let out a weak laugh that sounded false even to me.

He pursed his lips, then returned his attention to my hand and began the second stitch. "Watching usually makes it worse."

"I guess working in the morgue has gotten me really used to gore." I shrugged. "Seems less scary to watch and see what's going on."

He knotted the thread. "Actually I'm the same way. I'd rather see it coming than be surprised." He turned my hand slightly. "I think you can get away with only four stitches on this," he stated. "It's really shallow here at this end."

"Okay, cool. Thanks." I said. "I guess it's good the scalpel was really sharp. I mean, I barely even felt it." I winced as he did the next stitch, but when his frown deepened slightly I suspected I'd done so a fraction of a second too late.

"Do you generally have numbness in your hands?" he asked as he tied off the last stitch. "Or lack of sensitivity to touch?"

Double shit. "Nope. Not at all!" I replied brightly. I lifted my right hand and wiggled my fingers. "Totally fine!"

Allen cut the suture thread and set the needle aside. "Even a sharp scalpel hurts like hell. I know."

How the hell was I supposed to explain it in a believable way? "Um, that arm was broken when I was twelve," I said. "Maybe there was nerve damage or something."

He shrugged, cleaned the wound area again, then

taped gauze over the stitched cut. "Could be. You definitely don't have normal pain sensitivity."

"Or just used to it," I said before I could stop myself.

"Used to getting sliced?" he asked, frowning more.

"No, um . . . used to getting hurt." I hesitated, then
gave him a tight and humorless smile. "Mom used to
smack me around. That's how my arm got broke," I explained, even as I wondered why the hell I was telling
him this. "She went to jail for it." *And died there*, I
thought. *Killed herself on my sixteenth birthday.* Luckily
I had enough self-control to keep from sharing that
lovely tidbit of family history.

But he didn't comment on my little revelation. He
wrapped up the suture kit, dropped the needle into a
sharps-disposal container, stripped the gloves and placed
them in a biohazard trash can. "You're all done," he told
me curtly, sounding almost harsh after the gentler tone
of before. "I'll check it in a couple of days, but I don't
anticipate any issues with it. Keep it clean."

"Sure thing," I said. The old Allen was back. "Thanks
for saving me a trip to the ER."

"Don't make a habit of it," he replied, then left the
room without a glance back.

I sat silently for another couple of minutes. Why the
hell had I told him about my mom and her abuse? Because for a short time he'd been almost nice to me?
Great. He treated me like a normal person, so of course
I had to make sure he knew I wasn't normal.

Taking a deep breath, I stood and returned to the
morgue. After pulling gloves on over the gauze, I finished getting everything ready for the autopsy.

Dr. Leblanc returned as I was getting the body of
Brenda Barnes onto the table. I hid a smile as I noted he
was deliberately noisy as he walked.

"Everything go all right?" he asked.

"Went great," I said brightly. "All put back together."

He glanced down at my hand. "Does it bother you? We can postpone until the morning, or I can get someone else to assist if it hurts too much."

"Oh, no, I'm cool," I assured him. "Allen did it in four stitches. Hardly aches at all."

Dr. Leblanc gave an approving nod. "He's good. I know you have your differences, but anything is better than the emergency room for such a minor wound."

I got the body stripped of clothing and shoved the block under her shoulder blades so that her back was arched, making it easier for Dr. Leblanc to do the Y-incision and examine her organs. With her head dropped back I could see remnants of the zombie makeup—green, grey, and beige grease paint along her jawline, and square patches of lingering adhesive on her neck.

I stepped back and looked over at the pathologist.

"Why doesn't he like me?" It bothered me now. It had never bothered me before, at least not like this. But now Allen was someone I could actually respect, and suddenly his opinion of me mattered. And *that* bothered me as well.

A grimace flickered across his face as he shook his head. "I don't know, Angel. It's been like that since day one."

Taking a deep breath, I did my best to throw off the stupid desire to give a shit about Allen's opinion of me. "Oh, well," I said. "Brenda's been waiting long enough. Let's get to cutting."

Chapter 7

The autopsy of Brenda Barnes went quickly, though Dr. Leblanc remained puzzled about the cause of death despite knowing *what* had killed her: hypertrophic cardiomyopathy, which was a condition where the heart muscle got too thick to pump blood properly, he'd explained. What he couldn't figure out was how the heck she could've had that condition, since her medical records showed absolutely no sign of any thickening whatsoever in a full physical she had right before being laid off only a year earlier.

Muttering about misread test results and sloppy record keeping, he returned to the main building in the late afternoon, leaving me free to finally scarf down some brains to appease the insistent waves of hunger. I peeled up the gauze and tugged the sutures out of my healed flesh since they itched like crazy now, then taped the gauze back down. Later I'd figure out how to keep Allen from wanting to check it in a few days. Oh yeah, and figure out some way to explain why it healed without a scar. Maybe I could buy some miracle scar cream and claim it did the trick. I groaned and resisted the urge to beat my head against the cooler wall.

After making absolutely sure I was alone in the morgue, I retrieved an empty container from my cooler and "harvested" the brain of Ms. Barnes. During an autopsy the organs—including the brain—were removed, examined, and samples taken to be stored in formalin. Yet afterward, the organs weren't returned to their former body cavity but instead ended up in a big plastic bag that was set between the body's legs for its trip to the funeral home. Therefore, once the autopsy was complete, I snagged the brains out of the bags for my own consumption.

In fact, that's how I'd met Kang. He'd confronted me after he noticed that the brains were missing from the body bags when they arrived at his funeral home.

I got the container safely tucked away in my cooler and back in my car without incident. The rest of my shift was blissfully dull with only one other body pickup—an apparently natural death of a man with a history of heart disease who showed all the signs of a heart attack. Once he was in the cooler and logged into the system, Derrel and I grabbed a bite to eat at Paco's Tacos, then I returned to the morgue and managed to squeeze in several hours of studying. When midnight finally rolled around, I clocked out, left the van keys in the box by the door, and got the heck out of there.

Lightning followed by a tooth-rattling crash of thunder heralded the start of another goddamn downpour. I dashed to my scrappy little Honda, yanked the door open and clambered in. It sure as hell wasn't worth much on the open market, but it ran—most of the time—and right now it scored points for being dry.

I jammed my keys into the ignition and cranked the car. Hunger—the normal human kind—reminded me that, though I'd gorged on tacos at seven, it was now after midnight. What the hell. A late night snack never hurt anyone. There wasn't a whole lot open at this hour, but the flickering neon of Double D's Diner promised destressifying pie and hot chocolate, plus the parking lot had only three other cars in it. Score.

The rain still pelted down in torrential sheets. I clutched my dorky raincoat around me, pulled down my hood, and made a dash for the slim awning over the door, then scowled blackly as the rain abruptly eased to a mere drizzle.

"Really?" I snarled up at the sky. "You couldn't ease up thirty seconds earlier?"

I shook the worst of the water off and entered the diner, hung my raincoat on a peg beside two normal-yellow ones and a bedraggled umbrella, then headed to the counter. The waitress slid a mug of hot chocolate and a plate full of apple pie to me as soon as I sat down.

"You know me too damn well, Lurline," I said with a laugh.

The rangy, well-worn woman grinned. "I know how you are when you get off work in the middle of the night." She leaned her elbows on the counter. "Anything good today?" she asked with a gleam in her eye.

"Sorry," I told her. "Only one today and there was no mess or yuck of any sort. Very ordinary natural death."

She heaved a disappointed sigh and pushed off the counter. "How'm I supposed to live vay-car-ee-us-lee through you if you don't got any good stories?"

I laughed. "I'll make up something good and gory for the next time I come in here."

"You better!" she announced, then sauntered away to check on another customer.

Grinning, I dug into my pie and allowed the loving embrace of sugar and fat to shield me from my worries. I glanced around idly as I ate. The old, bald guy at the far end of the counter was another regular, and a young couple nestled in a booth, laughing and whispering as they shared a heaping plate of blueberry pancakes.

Through the broad windows of the diner I saw a Jeep pull into the lot and park, angled with the passenger side toward me. But the headlights remained on, and no one made a move to get out for almost a full minute. Finally the driver exited and moved to the back. Though she wore a light jacket with the hood up, I could tell it was a woman by the general build and grace of movement. She opened the hatch, huddling beneath it to stay out of the light drizzle as she rummaged through the contents as if looking for something.

But my heart did a weird little flip when she straightened and pushed the hood back from her face. It was her. The stalker blonde.

She didn't have a camera in her hands, however, and after a few seconds of frantic thought I decided she probably hadn't followed me here. First off, I figured she'd be a little more sneaky about it if she had. Plus, the expression on her face was a far cry from the calm focus I saw earlier today. Even from this distance it was tough to mistake the expression of worry and anxiety.

She'd parked on the other side of the diner from my car, so there was a damn good chance she had no idea I was here. *Perfect time to find out what the hell's going on.* I dropped a ten on the counter to more than cover my coffee and pie, slung my purse across my chest and headed out, grabbing my obnoxious raincoat on the way. Sure, without it I'd probably have an easier time getting close before she realized it was me, but I really didn't want to get wet. Yeah, I was a weenie.

I strode toward the Jeep with my hood up and purpose in my step. With the way she was parked I came up on the driver's side, which was fine with me. Hopefully that would make it easier to stop her if she tried to make a run for it.

She was still doing something in the back, but the sound of crunching gravel beneath my boots alerted her to my approach. She ducked her head around the side of the Jeep, eyes widening in surprise at the sight of me.

"Hey! You! I wanna talk to you!" I snarled.

Alarm flashed across her features, then in a smooth move she stepped from behind the Jeep, pulled a shotgun from the back and brought it up to hip level to point at me.

I jerked to a stop, still about a dozen feet from her. *Well shit*, I thought in surprise and a bit of annoyance. *This escalated quickly.* With the way her Jeep was angled, no one inside the diner could see the shotgun. They'd certainly hear the blast, though that wouldn't do me much good.

"Just back off," the blond woman said, tension roiling through her voice. Yet even though the barrel of the shotgun didn't waver, she really didn't look as if she wanted to shoot me. At all. On the other hand, she also looked scared and freaked and a little desperate, and I knew that sort of emotion-soup could easily overcome any reluctance to pull the trigger. Her left hand steadied the barrel, and my eyes narrowed. She had a splint on that hand that I was pretty damn sure hadn't been there when I saw her earlier today.

I shook my head slowly. "I'm not gonna back off until you tell me what the hell's going on, and why you're following me and taking pictures."

"Because it was my job," she said, voice tight and full of desperate intensity. "But I'm not taking any more pics. I'm leaving." Her grip on the shotgun tightened. "So . . . back off."

I remained exactly where I was. "No. Not backing off." I kept my own voice as calm as I could manage. "What job do you have that includes stalking me?"

She edged toward the driver's side door. "One I quit," she said. "And I have to get out of here."

Watching her carefully, I took a slow step forward. "I'm not afraid of getting shot," I told her. Which wasn't entirely true. Getting shot *hurt*, and I had a feeling getting shot by a shotgun would hurt a *lot*. But I knew damn well something more was going on. "You haven't answered my question."

"Please. I don't want to shoot you!" she said, desperation thickening her voice now. "I have to *go*." Her eyes flicked toward the highway and back to me. Was someone after her?

"Look, are you into something fucked up?" I asked, easing forward another step. Probably a stupid question, now that I thought about it, since she was holding a shotgun on me. "Maybe I can help," I added. Hell, I knew that *I'm so screwed* look on her face. I'd seen it on my own a time or two.

A brief spark of hope flickered in her eyes, but then she shook her head and it died. "Yeah, really a twisted mess," she said. To my relief she lowered the shotgun. "I . . . won't shoot you. But, please, I have to go." Her voice quavered. "The people I worked for, they'll be coming after me. And you don't want to be around when that happens."

Was she concerned for me? Or for what I might see or find out? "First, tell me who you work for," I said.

"*Worked* for," she replied, emphasizing the past tense. She edged closer to the driver's door. I knew damn well she was about to make a break for it, and I tensed in expectation.

"Yeah, fine, who *did* you work for?" I shot back, allowing my annoyance to color my tone.

As expected, she made an absolutely desperate attempt to yank the door open and get into the Jeep. I poured on the speed and closed the distance between us, grabbed the door handle as she slid into the seat, and blocked the door with my own body.

"For fuck's sake!" I snapped. "Would you chill? I want some answers, and I'm not letting you go until you give them!"

· She breathed raggedly, seeming on the verge of tears and, with the fierce strength that burned behind her hazel eyes, it looked utterly unnatural on her. She tugged futilely on the door a few times as if it would somehow convince me to move, then gave up and let her hand drop. "Shit. Shit."

I swept a quick glance around. No one inside the diner seemed to notice our little altercation—helped no doubt by the fact it was all happening on the side away from the broad windows. And the highway remained deserted.

"Can we please talk?" I asked, returning my attention to her.

She sagged. "Sure. Why the hell not."

"Cool. Okay, cool." I glanced around again, then hurried around the front of the Jeep to the passenger side. I fully expected her to start the vehicle and try and take off during those few seconds, but for whatever reason she seemed fairly resigned to my obnoxious desire for information. I slid into the passenger seat, shut the door, then gently pushed aside the barrel of the shotgun that lay across her lap so that it wasn't pointed straight at me.

"All righty, that's better," I said. My gaze dropped to her hand. The pinky and ring finger were heavily splinted, and purplish bruising showed between strips of tape. "Who broke your hand?"

Exhaling, she leaned her head back against the seat. A curious expression of regret and admiration briefly passed over her face. "Brian Archer. Pietro Ivanov's head of security. He caught me trying to get pictures of Ivanov and Jane Pennington."

"Oh, wow," I said, more than a little shocked. Though once I thought about it, I had zero doubt that the ice-calm security guy could break fingers without batting an eyelash.

Her mouth pursed slightly in annoyance, and I got the sense it was at herself. For getting caught? Somehow I could totally believe that would irk this woman. *Irked* looked a lot more natural on her than the verge-of-tears thing. Whatever was going on had to be huge if it pushed her to that point.

"And your bosses are mad you got caught?" I asked, trying to put the pieces together. Yet I figured they'd have to be *really* mad for her to be this freaked. Surely there was more to it.

She gave a low snort. "They don't even know about that. It's . . . other stuff I recently discovered about them." Sighing, she shook her head. "I can't go back." Her eyes went to mine. "Please, I really need to go. And you need to be far away from me."

I stubbornly didn't get out of the Jeep. "What's your name?"

A flicker of exasperation lit her eyes. "Heather," she said, pointedly not giving a last name.

I didn't bother asking for it. "I'm Angel Crawford, but I guess you know that already."

"Yeah. I do." Her gaze dropped from mine.

"Tell me who you work for." I didn't make it a question or request.

She grimaced. "Saberton Corporation."

I didn't expect that answer. "I don't understand. Why the hell would Saberton want pictures of me?" But then my thick-headed brain decided to wake up. "Wait, they do defense contract stuff, don't they?" A chill swept through me. Did this have anything to do with Kristi Charish's Zoldiers project? It had to. "Do you know *why* they wanted pics of me?"

Heather shook her head. "Not just you. Pietro Ivanov and pretty much anyone associated with him."

"What do you know about Pietro...and me?" I asked warily.

She took a deep breath as if clinging to calm by her fingernails. "I know what you are," she said, voice cracking slightly. "And I'm leaving because I don't agree with Saberton's *philosophy*, especially when it comes to using your kind." Her eyes flicked toward me. "Zombies."

Yikes. I knew Dr. Charish had been dealing with some government or corporate group when she had me as a test subject. Was that Saberton? Were they interested in her zombie-soldier idea? "You know a lot of zombies?" I asked, still watching her.

"Met my first a couple of years ago. John Kang," she said to my surprise. Kang, the first zombie who I knew was a zombie. "He was my best friend, hands down," she continued, surprising me even more, especially with the depth of sincerity in her voice. Her mouth tightened. "Saberton wanted him in their pocket because of all his contacts and connections. They wanted me to set him up to, ah, encourage his cooperation."

"Connections like Dr. Sofia Baldwin?" I asked, cocking my eyebrow in her direction. Before her death, Dr. Baldwin had been working to develop fake brains that zombies could survive on instead of human brains.

Heather gave a little nod, confirming my suspicion. This was getting more and more interesting. If interesting meant *holy shit this is seriously messed up*.

"I knew Sofia," I said. "She, uh, did a lot of zombie research." I paused. "They're both dead, you know—Kang and Sofia. Murdered."

Heather's good hand tightened on the barrel of the shotgun. "I know," she said, grief slashing across her face. "God, the only possible good thing that came out of Kang's death was that it happened before Saberton had the chance to get their hooks into him or find out anything he knew."

I struggled to put it all together. From what I'd seen, Kang hadn't held a Pietro-level of power, but he certainly had influence among local zombies, especially those who weren't associated with Pietro. Ed had killed Kang, but I wasn't sure if Charish had specifically ordered that hit or if he'd taken it upon himself. However, she'd openly admitted to killing Sofia. If Charish had been working with Saberton at the time, surely they'd been pissed at her about both losses.

"Were you working with Kristi Charish?" I asked.

Heather twitched, almost as if she was recoiling at the name. She obviously knew who Kristi Charish was. "Not . . . directly," she answered.

I frowned. "What about Philip?" Crap, I didn't even know his last name.

But again she apparently knew who I was talking about. The corners of her mouth turned down, and her brows drew together. "Yeah. Known him about a year. Gung ho company man."

That meant he'd been working for Saberton for at least six months before Charish forced me to turn him into a zombie. That made it pretty evident that Saberton had already been involved with Charish at the time she'd kidnapped me.

"He's a zombie now. An experiment gone bad," she continued with a shake of her head. "Haven't dealt with him much since." Her gaze rested on me as though waiting for me to say something.

Well, I didn't know how much she already knew, but I wasn't about to confirm that I was the one who made Philip a zombie. "Why are you freaked out about leaving?" I asked instead. "Or is this one of those deals where you don't simply walk away?"

Her mouth twisted. "It's one of those things where you know too much, don't like what you know, know they'll kill you over it, so you run and hide and figure they'll find you sooner or later." She shook her head. "And they're on to me, so it's going to be sooner if I don't get out of here."

Silent, I considered her plight. I didn't know a damn thing about this woman except that supposedly she wanted to quit this evil company for somewhat vague reasons. But she knew Kang, and she definitely seemed upset about his death. "What if someone could help you?" I found myself asking.

Heather raised an eyebrow, mouth pursed in skepticism. "You mean like if my fairy godmother came in and waved a wand? It's not going to happen."

"How 'bout a trashy guardian angel?" I said, offering her a slight smile.

She gave me a sigh. "Thanks. But I don't know what you could do."

I forced myself to logically consider why I felt an urge to help her out. It didn't totally make sense—after all, she was working for a company that was probably involved in Charish's Zoldiers, a project which was fucked up on numerous levels. But so far all Heather had done to me was take pictures, as far as I knew. And she didn't want to work for Saberton anymore. Plus the reason she wanted to leave was a damn good one in my eyes. I was cool with helping anyone who was against using zombies.

But mostly it was that expression of "I'm so screwed" that got to me.

"Look, I know what it's like to be in a no-win situation, and Pietro owes me a couple of favors," I said. It would take a lot more than a ticket to the Gourmet Gala to make up for the fact that Pietro allowed Charish to have me kidnapped. "Maybe he could help protect you." I shrugged. "Hell, maybe you could go to work for him instead." Because I totally had that influence, right? I held back the urge to roll my eyes at myself. But, hey, maybe she *could* be an asset to the zombie side of things.

Naked hope and a curious longing brightened her eyes for a brief instant before they shadowed again. "God." Her brow furrowed, and she looked almost wistful. "I don't know. Do you really think he'd help?"

"It's worth a shot, right?" I dug into my purse and pulled out Brian's card. "There you go," I said, setting it on the console. "That's Brian's number." She seemed cool, but I wasn't about to give her Pietro's. Jesus Christ, but I hoped this didn't blow up in my face. What the hell would I do if Heather called Brian, and he told her to fuck off? I didn't know if I could simply walk away from this now if that happened. Yet I also knew I'd put her in a really bad position—I'd slowed down her flight, and now was trying to convince her to turn herself over to the "enemy."

Her eyes dropped to the card, and I could practically *see* her memorizing the number. "You mean now?" she said, glancing back up at me. "It's after midnight."

"Yeah, well, I'm pretty sure he's a robot and doesn't sleep," I said, then shrugged. "Trust me, those fuckers owe me enough that I can wake a few people up." I paused. "Unless you *want* to wait 'til morning and see what happens."

"Shit, no." She pulled a phone out of her pocket.

"Yeah." I reached and put a hand on hers. "And maybe better to use mine. In case yours is, er, tapped or whatever."

She blew out her breath. "You're right. I'm not thinking all that clearly right now. I'm usually good in a tight situation, but this has me clamped down."

"Pretty understandable." I retrieved my phone from the depths of my purse, dialed. "I'm putting it on speakerphone, but I'll talk to him first."

The tinny sound of the ringer filled the car, and a few seconds later: "Archer here." A hint of hoarse slur in his voice suggested he'd likely been asleep.

"Hey, Brian, it's Angel," I said. "Hate to bother you so late, but . . . remember that chick whose fingers you broke today? Well, she's here with me, and she wants to, um, defect."

"The . . . photographer?" he asked, voice still a bit muzzy. "I don't understand."

"Yeah, she works for Saberton and—"

"What?" he demanded, all hint of sleep gone.

Blinking, I quickly put pieces together. "Oh. You just thought she was a reporter or something, didn't you." I flicked a glance at her. She gave me a shrug in return, coupled with a pained grimace. I supposed I couldn't blame her for lying to Brian. If she'd admitted to being some sort of industrial espionage person she probably wouldn't have escaped at all, and certainly not with only a couple of broken fingers.

"Something like that, yes," Brian replied, voice controlled once again.

"Okay, well, she wants to leave. Quit. But figures it's only a matter of time before they find her and, well, y'know."

I could practically hear Brian processing all of this. "All right, Angel," he said with zero hint of the stress he was surely feeling. "What does she want?"

I handed the phone to Heather, though I kept it on speakerphone. "You're up, chick."

She bit her lip and took a deep breath. "Um, hello, Brian. It's me again."

"What do you want, Naomi?" Brian asked. "Or whatever your name is."

Naomi, huh? I realized that Heather probably wasn't her name either. Though truth be told, she looked more like a Naomi than a Heather.

She closed her eyes. "Shit," she breathed. "This was a bad idea."

"Perhaps," Brian said, surprising me by the admission.

"How about you tell me why you want to leave Saberton, and why you're afraid they'll come after you."

A mix of emotions crawled across her face, tight lines of anger, a lip curl of disgust. "I can't deal with it anymore—what they're doing with your kind, with zombies."

A beat of silence while Brian processed that she knew about the zombies, which meant that she had to be in fairly deep with Saberton. I doubted that the info about zombies being totally real was handed out along with Christmas bonuses. "And you're interested in . . . sanctuary with us?" A faintly dubious note crept into his voice for the first time.

She opened her eyes, flicked her gaze toward me. I gave her an encouraging nod. "I . . . yes," she said. "They'll kill me or take me back if they catch me." She paused. "I don't want to go back."

"All right. How long do you suppose you have before they catch up with you?"

"I was on my way out of town when Angel caught me." Her eyes went to the dashboard clock. "Now, I don't know. Not long." The dread in her eyes deepened.

I knew if Brian didn't agree to this, she was completely screwed. *Nice move, Angel.*

"I actually believed you were just paparazzi," Brian commented. I heard a rustling that I figured was him pulling on clothing. "You played me pretty damn well today."

"Yeah, I did." She winced, but at the same time there was a teensy touch of triumph. Probably deservedly so, I decided, if she'd been able to put one over on him.

"I'll meet you in twenty minutes at the corner of Cottonwood Street and Main," he said, to my relief. "Come alone and unarmed," he continued. "You will be searched. Thoroughly. No promises or guarantees. This is a meeting only, and I'll make a decision after that."

Her shoulders straightened, and as I watched, it was as if all the previous desperation fell away. She knew damn well she might be walking into her death, but that was a far cry from being on the run.

"Understood," she said, voice stronger. "I'll be there." She paused as if wanting to say so much more, but all she said was, "Thank you."

"Twenty minutes," Brian repeated and hung up.

I let out a breath. "Hey, that sounds promising, right?" I said.

She continued to look down at the phone for a few more seconds before handing it back to me. "It does. More than I had before."

"You'd better get going," I told her. "It'll take you close to twenty minutes to get to that location, and the roads are really bad tonight with the rain." I dug through my purse and came up with a pen and the back of a receipt. "Here's my number." I scrawled it onto the paper and handed it to her. "Call me if you need anything, okay?"

She took it, and once again I watched her commit it to memory. "Thanks." She gave me a small smile. "Maybe I'll see you around sometime."

"I hope so," I said fervently. I glanced out the window. "Rain's letting up. Lemme get out of here so you can hit the road. Good luck." And with that I snatched up Brian's card, ducked out of her car, shut the door, and raced to mine.

Her headlights came on as she started the Jeep. She didn't move for several seconds, and I had to wonder if she was actually going to go meet with Brian, or if she'd head in the opposite direction. But then she pulled out and turned left onto the highway—heading toward Cottonwood and Main, I sure hoped.

I was half-tempted to follow, but decided that would be going too far. And might make Brian really wonder as well, like if maybe she was coercing me into vouching for her. Instead I behaved, took a right out of the parking lot, and headed toward home.

Chapter 8

The rain came down again in a light but steady fall. I cranked up the defroster and prayed that it actually worked. Even cold air helped keep the window fog at bay, and I hated driving at night without decent visibility.

My phone rang about five minutes later, the caller ID displaying a number I didn't know. I grabbed it off the console and thumbed the answer button. "Hello?"

"It's Heather. Someone's tailing me," she said, only the barest hint of stress in her voice. "Just want you to know . . . well, in case something bad happens. I'm going to call Brian."

"Sonofabitch. You're still headed south?" I couldn't be all that far away.

"That's right. Passing Picayune Street right now," she told me.

I thought quickly as I drove, glad that my job required me to drive all over the damn place, which meant I knew a lot of back road shortcuts. "Okay," I said as I hung a quick right, "take a left at Grover, and then another on Highway 1790. That'll get you headed back toward me."

"Got it," she said, still shockingly cool considering her situation. "Let me call Brian, and then I'll call you back." With that she hung up, and I took the opportunity to hit Marcus on the speed dial and put it on speakerphone. While it rang I grabbed the cooler from behind my seat and snagged a smoothie from it. It didn't take a genius to know it would be a good idea to be tanked up on brains in case shit got crazy.

As soon as I emptied that bottle, I grabbed the other one and downed it as well, muttering a few choice words as the call to Marcus went to voicemail. I hit the "end call" button since I had no idea what to tell him that would make sense in a message.

The excess of brains in my system kicked in, and the world leaped into sharp focus around me, making it a lot easier to drive like a bat out of hell in the rainy dark. The phone rang as I took a sharp right turn onto Highway 1790. Heather's number again, I noted. I suppressed the twinge of disappointment that it wasn't Marcus. He was working tonight, so he was most likely out on a call and couldn't answer his phone. I jabbed at the answer button, keeping it on speaker.

"Hey! Where are you?" I asked.

"Just turned onto 1790." she told me, a teensy bit more stress evident in her voice, though I detected an edge of excitement too. *This* was her true personality. She probably knew damn well she might die tonight, but at least she was *doing* something. "There are two cars following me now. Brian said to get off the road with you and barricade behind the cars until he can get someone to come help us out."

I thought quickly. "Okay, I'm coming toward you—almost to the bridge over Bayou Zaire. I'll pull off the road right past that. D'ya know how many people are in the cars?"

"Only one in the first, I think," she replied. "Don't

know about the second. Oh, and I have my shotgun, so we're not going to be completely helpless."

"I have a shitty attitude," I offered. "That's my best weapon."

She chuckled. "Sounds good. Okay, I'm gonna try and get some distance between me and my buddies. See you in a couple." And with that she hung up.

The rain picked up, forcing me to set my wipers to mega-speed, and I yelled a curse as the right wiper blade flew off into the night. Thank god for the heightened senses of being over-brained. I floored the accelerator, but my poor little Honda shuddered so badly above eighty that I had to back off a bit for fear of dropping the engine out of the damn thing. Still, I managed to catch a bit of air when I went over the Bayou Zaire bridge—noticing rather absently that the water was overflowing the banks—and came down with a cringe-inducing screech of undercarriage on pavement.

I slammed on the brakes and pulled off the road in an impressive shower of gravel, then angled the car so that we could, hopefully, hunker down behind it and still have a view of the road. I thought about turning the lights off but then realized the highway was so damn dark there was a good chance Heather wouldn't see me at all if I did.

The only weapon I had—besides my general zombieness—was a baseball bat in my trunk that had been in there when I bought the stupid car. I'd never played any sort of sport that required it, but back before I was turned I'd pulled it out a time or two when assholes thought the scrawny blond chick was an easy target for harassment. I made quick work of digging it out from under the accumulation of crap back there, then shed my raincoat and stuffed it into the trunk. Yeah, staying dry was nice, but all those bright polka dots would make shooting me a bit too easy for the bad guys.

As I slammed the lid closed, I saw headlights coming

up the highway, and about half a minute later Heather's jeep skidded into an impressive bootlegger turn, sending up a spray of water as she pulled in right behind my car. She climbed out of the Jeep, shotgun tucked under one arm as she fumbled a Bluetooth headset into her ear.

"Sweet driving!" I said.

"Ha! That was one hundred percent accidental," she confessed, eyes bright with adrenaline. "I about shit myself. Thought I was going to go into the bayou." Her gaze shifted to the highway. Two sets of headlights weren't far away. She glanced back to me and pointed to the headset. "I have Brian on the line." Gratification briefly lit her face at the fact that he was willing to provide help even before meeting with her. I was sure she knew damn well that it changed nothing as far as her eventual fate, but it was still cool to see.

Or maybe Brian knows I'm involved and doesn't want me to get too fucked up because of her troubles. That was probably far more likely.

I breathed deeply, taking in everything with my brain-fueled heightened awareness. The tang of adrenaline and nerves from Heather, the fetid odors of the swamp and bayou, the stench of rubber on pavement and the seared-metal aroma of the cooling engines. Every drop of rain stood out in crisp detail. The roar of the approaching cars twined around me like harsh music. God almighty, I was ready for some action.

Heather's mouth pursed as she looked toward the Saberton vehicles. "I'm with Angel about fifty yards south of the Bayou Zaire bridge," she said, and I fumbled mentally in confusion for a few seconds before realizing she was talking to Brian on her headset. "No time to chat, sweetie," she continued. "I'll leave the line open."

I coughed to cover a laugh at the "sweetie." The hard-faced Brian Archer didn't strike me as anyone's "sweetie." I was liking this chick more and more.

My grip on the bat tightened as I peered through the rain at the two cars. They came to a stop about thirty yards away on the opposite side of the road.

"One in the front car and two in the other," I told her. "Can't tell yet if human or zombie, though."

She slicked her wet hair back from her face with her splinted hand as we crouched behind the cover of the two cars. "I'd bank on at least one of them falling into the not-human category."

"Well, this will be fun," I said, eyes on the men exiting the cars. Did they have any idea who I was and that I was a zombie?

No time to ponder that now. I dragged my attention back to the current fiasco. The shotgun under her arm looked like a twelve gauge. "What ammo you got for that?" I asked. "Something better than birdshot, I hope."

Heather put the shotgun to her shoulder. "I have double-aught buckshot in here. Should do some damage," she said. "Too bad someone *broke my fucking hand*," she added in a loud voice as if to be absolutely sure that Brian heard through the open line, forcing me to mask another laugh. But there was no undercurrent of malice or condemnation in her voice. Instead her eyes were bright with an odd mix of humor and eager readiness. I sure hoped she survived this. This was someone who'd probably be fun as hell to go out drinking with. Not that I drank anymore, but, y'know.

The headlights of the other two cars went abruptly dark, and Heather muttered a curse. Our own headlights were angled away, and the steady rain added to the poor visibility.

But my zombie-vision picked up where normal vision left off. "Two coming up on our right," I told her, voice low. "One's crossing the highway to the left. Looks like he's gonna try to flank us." I glanced toward the bayou. "Thank god the water's high. That'll make it tougher for him."

"I'll take whatever advantage we can get at this point," she muttered.

"The two coming at us have guns," I told her, hefting the bat. "You put a couple of shots their way, and then I'll do my part."

The words were barely out of my mouth when she fired the shotgun, and I nearly jumped out of my skin. Recovering after a stunned second, I leaped up from the crouch and vaulted over the hood of the car. As soon as my feet touched the ground, I broke into a dead run toward the oncoming men. The heavy *schick-schick* of Heather pumping the shotgun preceded another blast. A thrill of murderous satisfaction ran through me as one of the men gave a sharp cry of pain and clutched at his right leg.

And then I was right on top of them. I swung hard at the injured one and managed to whack him solidly in the shoulder. Bones crunched and flesh yielded beneath my zombie-strength assault. He screamed and went down hard, while I did my best to nail the other shooter on the backswing.

The second guy wasn't a zombie either, but he was still fast enough to avoid the arc of my bat and get a shot off. Hot fire seared through my gut, with the sharp report of the gun echoing like an afterthought. "Goddammit!" I yelled as I staggered back a step, then I bared my teeth and brought the bat down hard on his arm. His gun clattered to the pavement as he gave a strangled cry of pain. I delivered a devastating blow to his knee, and he let out a harsh scream as he went down.

The blast of the shotgun ripped through the air again, and a second later I heard Heather yell, "*Zombie!*" I spun in time to see her fire again. The man—zombie— loping toward her staggered a bit at the second blast, but in the next breath was on her and slammed her to the ground beneath him, her head thumping hard on the asphalt.

"Shit!" I broke into a run, even as the zombie wrapped his hands in Heather's shirt and hauled her upright. She tried hard to swing a punch at him, but it was clear she was dazed from the head-thump.

I poured on the speed to get back to her. I didn't have training in anything resembling hand to hand fighting, but I'd been in enough scraps and street fights to know that the will to win could turn the tide. I still had the bat in my right hand, and I made a charging swing to clock him in the back right across the kidneys.

He staggered and let out a roar of pain. It didn't drop him, as I'd hoped it would, but he lost his grip on Heather. She stumbled back as he turned on me, his face twisted with fury and hands clenched into fists.

"Batter up, motherfucker!" I cried out as I swung again, this time at his head. Unfortunately, even injured he still had a fair amount of speed. He moved inside my swing, grabbed my arm and took me down to the ground in a foot-sweep thing that probably would've been cool as hell if I hadn't been on the receiving end of it. Twisting frantically, I slammed my booted foot into the side of his knee, which put him off-balance enough that when I swung the bat at his other knee the blow sent him to the ground.

He had some serious fight skills and was on me in a heartbeat, but I had a black belt in dirty-fighting-bitch. Heather had scored a direct hit on him with the shotgun, and holes peppered his torso. Snarling, I forced my hand into a wound in his midsection, widening the hole more, then curled my fingers around anything I could and yanked hard.

"God damn it!" he roared as I did my best to pull zombie-dude's insides out through the hole. He grabbed my wrist and wrenched it hard, but I kept my grip tight on his insides and sunk my teeth into his forearm. I didn't have much skill, but I sure as hell had a lot of will. Unfortunately zombie-dude outweighed me by about a hundred pounds and was a helluva lot stronger. He pried my hand off whatever internal organ now dangled from his abdomen, then brought his fist down hard into my jaw.

I felt and heard bone crunch, and even through the slightly dulled senses that came with burning through brains, it still hurt like a bitch and left me stunned. I tried to struggle and kick, but it was like fighting in fog while wrapped in a giant cotton ball. His eyes narrowed in satisfaction as he drew back his fist again. I thought he was simply going to beat my skull to a shattered pulp, but instead he reached to the small of his back, pulled a gun, and lifted it toward my head.

Well crap.

I caught a flash of movement beside me, and in the next second two things happened: The muzzle of a shotgun made contact with zombie-dude's head, and that same head disappeared in a deafening blast of buckshot, blood, bone, and brains.

The mostly headless zombie slumped heavily to the side. Ears ringing, I lay under him, sucking in air with heavy gasps. A moment later, I shoved him the rest of the way off me, then wiped clumps of flesh and brain from my face.

"Nice job," I said to Heather, or rather, I tried to say. Instead all that came out was, "neh sshov." *Oh yeah, jaw shattered.*

Heather swayed, frowned down at the ex-zombie with what looked like a trace of sadness. "Brain stem," she croaked. "He . . . was going to blow your brain stem."

Oh shit. That would have killed me for sure. I looked over at the zombie corpse. Killed me as dead as he was now.

Heather drew a breath to speak, then jerked and let out a cry as blood sprayed from her left upper arm. I swung my gaze to the two men who I'd thought were out of the action. Wrong.

Heather dove behind the jeep and clutched at her bicep, looking far more pissed than frightened at being shot. Hungry and with breath rasping horribly, I grabbed the bat and staggered back to my feet, lip curling into a snarl as I lurched toward the two men. My head felt unbalanced with my jaw hanging at such a strange angle, and the wound in my gut still seeped blood, but I managed a shambling, inexorable progress toward my foes. The one with a leg full of buckshot and a crushed shoulder got another shot off in my direction, but I had to assume he missed since I didn't feel the punch of lead through my flesh. The second one fumbled with his gun in a desperate attempt to unjam it, but his smashed right arm pretty much ensured failure.

I lurched closer and raised the bat, focused on the one with the ready weapon. "Drop ... gun ... or ... die," I managed to slur through the broken jaw, then jerked and nearly went down as a bullet smacked into my hip. Pain flared, and I swayed for a second, but the hip seemed to be willing to support my weight for a little while longer. With an animal growl, I willed myself to close the distance. A frisson of terror passed through the shooter's eyes right before my bat came down on his head. I didn't have the zombie superpower thing going on right now, but I sure as hell had the really-pissed-off-bitch thing happening, and even a weakling like me could swing a baseball bat to good effect.

"Got one ... rule ..." I gurgled out as I brought the bat down on his head again. "Shoot me ... I ... eat ... you." I dropped heavily to my knees as I smacked him one more time to split the skull open. Growling with a mix of hunger and fury, I grabbed a handful of warm and still-pulsing brain from the shattered head and crammed it into my mouth.

The other man stared at me in horror as he tried to scrabble away, his jammed gun clutched in his good hand. He froze as my eyes locked onto his. I gulped down the brains, and a few seconds later I felt my jaw shift back into place. "Drop the fucking gun," I said, voice an ugly rasp, "or you'll be my goddamn dessert."

He went utterly still, eyes flicking from the gobbets of brains dripping from my fingers, to the blood around my mouth, to his oh-so-very-dead buddy. He tossed the gun away from him, eyes wide in shock and revulsion.

I gave him a slow smile, well aware that it was full of gore. "Yeah, that's more like it." Without taking my eyes from his, I scooped another handful of brain from his partner's skull and stuffed it into my mouth. God damn, but there was nothing better tasting in the whole damn world than warm brain when you were shot the hell up. Like a cold beer after a long hot day of working in the yard.

I scraped out more of the dude's brain, shuddering in relief as everything knit itself back together and normal sensation returned. The rain chose this moment to finally let up, and a chorus of frogs raised their voices as if to celebrate the brief interlude. The harsh breathing of the living man cut through the drip of water and croak of frogs in a strange harmony.

I ran my fingers around the interior of the skull, getting the last few clumps of brain matter, and sucked them from my fingers like icing from a mixing bowl. Deliberately not wiping my mouth, I straightened and moved to the surviving gunman, crouched and did a quick pat down to make sure he didn't have another gun on him. No weapons, but I did find a pack of cigarettes and a lighter in a shirt pocket. Grinning down at him, I pulled a cigarette out, stuck it between my bloody lips and lit it. Even allowed myself one sweet drag. Just one. Didn't want to waste too many brains. But damn, the moment called for it. I was reformed, but I'd never be perfect, and that was okay with me.

Cigarette still in my mouth, I grabbed the front of his shirt and dragged him back toward Heather. He let out a strangled scream as his shattered knee twisted, but I had no trouble ignoring it.

Heather was sitting on the wet ground, leaning up against the tire of her Jeep. At first I thought she was muttering to herself until I realized she was still on the phone with Brian. At least I assumed it was still Brian. If he'd been listening the whole time, he'd sure as hell gotten an earful.

Her face was pale, and blood ran in a slow rivulet down her left arm. Rain-diluted blood dripped from the wet hair behind her ear, probably from when she whacked the back of her head on the pavement when zombie-dude tackled her. I dumped the Saberton guy on the ground and gave him a hard look as I flicked the cigarette into a nearby puddle.

"You can try to escape or cause trouble if you want," I told him. "But when I catch you, I'm eating you. Understand?"

He gulped and jerked his head in a stiff nod. I considered him for a moment, then bent and tore his shirt from him before turning back to Heather. "How bad is it?" I asked as I crouched and wound the torn shirt around her arm in an effort to stop the bleeding.

"I'm okay. Just cold," she murmured, but she looked like she was having trouble focusing on me.

Snorting, I tugged the headset from her ear and stuck it in my own. "Hey, Brian, it's Angel. You got anyone coming? We need help, and calling nine-one-one is probably a bad idea."

"Yes, ma'am. Two cars will be there in about a minute or so," he calmly informed me. "How are you?"

"I'm good for now," I told him. "I stopped for a bit of

a snack. Heather blasted a zombie in the head with her shotgun. She's hit in the arm, got a hard bump on the head, and she says she's cold. May have a concussion. And I need to go pull a corpse off the road. Oh, and I got a live one too. Dunno if you want him or not."

"Most definitely," he stated, approval in his voice.

I tied off the crude bandage on Heather's arm, gave her a wink and smile, then moved back over to my former dinner. "I see headlights," I said to Brian as I grabbed the corpse's arm and pulled him off the road. "Sure hope they're yours. I don't have time to hide this much carnage." Jeez, two mostly-headless corpses, a shirtless guy with a smashed arm and knee, one injured woman and another with bullet holes in her clothing and blood dribbling down her chin, along with various spent casings and shotgun shells . . . no, nothing at all suspicious here.

"First one should be approaching now," Brian replied to my relief. Still, I hurried to pull the corpses and my prisoner behind the cars so that it wasn't quite so obvious that we'd had a little mayhem party here. Relentless hunger set in as I finished—not unmanageable but damn insistent. The one brain had barely been enough to put me back together, and I'd burned up plenty doing my sprint and whack-a-guy bit.

I picked up the baseball bat as the black SUV pulled off the road about thirty feet from where I stood. A black woman in dark pants and shirt climbed out of the car, gun in hand. She swept her gaze over the area in an obvious assessment, then headed my way.

"Okay," I said to Brian. "Someone's here—a woman, tall and black with really awesome braids. And she's not shooting at me, so I'm thinking this is one of yours?"

"That would be Rachel," Brian said. "Dan should be there in another minute or so."

"Gotcha," I said, keeping my eyes on the approaching woman. "What about Heather? She needs help."

"We'll take care of her, ma'am," Brian replied.

I scowled. That could be interpreted several ways.

"Take good care of her," I ordered.

"I understand your meaning," he said. "Angel, Mr. Ivanov requests that you not talk about this incident with *anyone* until deeper investigation is done. Saberton Corporation doesn't play around."

I was tempted to give him the same noncommittal *I understand your meaning* that he'd given me, but instead said, "Okay, got it." I didn't mind an excuse to put off telling Marcus for a while.

I handed the headset back to Heather. She gave me a vague smile and simply held it loosely in her hand instead of putting it back in her ear.

"Ms. Crawford," the woman said as she held a brain packet out to me. "I'm Rachel. Mr. Archer sent me."

"Oh, thanks," I said in thinly veiled relief, then had to hide a surprised start when I realized I couldn't smell her brain. *She's a zombie too!* I quickly tore the packet open and gulped down the contents, mentally rolling my eyes at my reaction. Of course Pietro's security people would be zombies. Duh. Still, it was cool to finally meet another zombie chick.

Rachel crouched by Heather, looking her over and asking questions, like "Do you know what day it is?" and "Who's the President?" She glanced back up at me as I finished the packet. "Need another?" Her cool regard flicked over the obvious bullet holes in my clothing.

"I won't say no if you have a spare," I told her. She silently pulled another from her pocket and handed it to me, then slipped her arms beneath Heather and stood, lifting her easily with zombie-strength.

Yet another SUV pulled up, and a man in a dark sweat suit who I assumed was Dan stepped out. He gave a nod to Rachel as she carried Heather to her SUV, then looked to me. "Mr. Archer advised one dead zombie, one dead human, and two prisoners. Anything else?"

Two prisoners? Shit. Of course Heather would be a prisoner as well. I grimaced as the rain began in earnest again. *Well, at least it'll wash the blood away.* "No, I think that covers it."

Dan gave a crisp nod, close-cropped sandy hair giving him that security-dude look. He was only a few inches taller than me, though, which translated to pretty damn short for a guy. But he was wiry and moved with confident ease. "We'll finish the cleanup here then," he said. "Thanks for the help."

It wasn't a dismissal, but it was obvious there wasn't much more I could do here. Besides, I was soaked to the skin, and my shirt and pants were full of bullet holes. *Looks like I'll be breaking out the mending kit,* I thought with a sigh. No way was I going to throw them out simply because I got shot. Since I seemed to have turned into a bullet magnet, that would get expensive, fast.

"Y'all will let me know about Heather?" I asked Dan.

"I'll make sure someone does," he said with such conviction that I couldn't help but believe him.

"Okay, then, um . . . well, it was nice meeting you," I said.

He smiled. "Be careful getting home." Then he turned away to take care of the mess we'd made.

Chapter 9

It was only a little after one a.m., which seemed weird. So much had happened since I left the morgue at midnight, it felt like it should be at least four in the morning. But apparently a psychotic firefight and zombie fest only took about half an hour from start to finish.

The entire way home I struggled to come up with a story that would explain the pesky bullet holes in my clothing in case my dad was home and still awake. My pants and Coroner's Office shirt were both dark, which meant that the blood didn't show, but after getting shot and beat up and then shot some more—in the pouring rain—I was looking pretty damn bedraggled.

But then my dad wasn't even home. That made hiding the fact that I'd been shot a whole lot easier, but annoyed me anyway because, damn it, why the hell wasn't he home? All too easy answer: he was out drinking.

I shoved my wet clothes into the washing machine, dumped a bunch of other laundry in on top of them, and got the load started.

With that taken care of, I took a quick shower to get

the mud, blood and other grime off, then tugged on a t-shirt and fresh undies and climbed into bed. But once there, I lay awake, listening to the washing machine churn as though it mimicked the agitation of my own thoughts. Six months ago I'd been kidnapped for zombie research and learned that some people didn't have a whole lot of respect for zombies. Based on that experience, I thought I knew how high the stakes were for my kind.

But apparently they were a shitload higher, enough so that Saberton was willing to hunt Heather down to either kill or capture her, simply because she wanted to leave them. At least I sure hoped that was the real story. As much as I already liked her, I knew there was always a chance that this whole thing was a ploy to infiltrate Pietro's organization.

The washing machine finished its cycle with a clunk. Silence ticked through the house, but about a minute later I heard the front door open and shut quietly. Paranoia gripped me. What if it wasn't my dad? What if the Saberton people knew where I lived and were coming after me?

My heart thudded while I ran through escape scenarios in my head. *Out the window would be easiest, then run like hell. No, grab a bottle of brains first . . . except that my fridge is locked, and—*

A muffled curse that was clearly my dad's voice effectively banished my paranoia. Relieved on a number of levels, I listened to his low muttering as he rummaged through the kitchen cabinets, then a few minutes later I heard him go down the hall and open the washing machine. More muttering, then the sound of him transferring my laundry to the dryer, followed by the thumps and creaks of my dad putting a load into the washer and starting both machines.

Mystified about why he felt the need to run a load in

the middle of the night, I remained silent, listening hard, but he did nothing more than go to his own room and shut the door.

I finally fell asleep, lulled by the comfortably familiar vibration of the ancient washer and dryer despite the worries that crowded in my head.

"You have a maggot on your sleeve," Derrel murmured.

Sighing, I flicked it off, watched it sail through the air to land on the wood-paneled wall and slide down to the dull-grey carpet.

My day had begun with a pickup from the hospital, then a hospice death which we only worked because the family was arguing about which funeral home to use. The scene we were on now would normally have been a somewhat ordinary suicide of a terminally ill man— advanced pancreatic cancer. He'd written a careful email to his family explaining his decision and expressing his love for them and detailing his wishes for disposition of his body and funeral arrangements. But in a cruel twist of fate, he'd mistyped the email address, and the family never received it. He wasn't discovered until two weeks after he overdosed on pain meds, by which time he was a yucky, maggot-covered mess.

Which made it impossible to fulfill his desire to have his body donated to science. Poor dude. Couldn't even have this fucked up illness be good for something.

I brought him back to the morgue and got him logged in and stored in the cooler. Dr. Leblanc informed me that he had court and wasn't going to perform any autopsies until the next day, which meant I had nothing to do except wait for another call.

The last thing I wanted was time to reflect and think or anything like that. I didn't want to muse on the incidents of the previous night, or contemplate how right or wrong it was for me to kill and eat that Saberton man. I needed to stay busy and, annoyingly, not enough people were dying to keep me so.

Restless, I went up to the front office and scored points with Rebecca, the secretary, by helping her with filing. That only killed about two hours, and so I went back to the morgue and organized the supply cabinet, made notes of what needed to be ordered and did, essentially, every minor and/or crap job that tended to be put off or avoided.

The grime on the baseboards of the cutting room had been bugging me for a while, and I was down on my knees scrubbing them when I heard the cooler door open.

Frowning, I straightened. "Nick?" I called. "Is that you?" I didn't think he was scheduled to work today, but who else would be going into the cooler?

After a few seconds of no answer, I stood and moved through the cutting room to the hallway. The cooler door stood open, and when I stepped into the doorway, I saw Allen, hands gloved, standing over a body bag on one of the stretchers. The bag was unzipped, and he appeared to be searching through it.

A stab of apprehension went through me. This was the body I'd picked up from the hospital, and it hadn't been autopsied yet. But what if someone at one of the funeral homes had mentioned that brains were missing from the bags of organs? I'd never thought it likely that any non-zombie would notice whether brains were missing or not. After all, no normal human in their right mind would look through the bag of innards to verify that everything was there.

"Allen?"

He glanced over at me, eyes flicking to the rag and scrubber in my gloved hands. "Dr. Leblanc has you doing something useful?"

I bristled, but did my best to hold onto my outward cool. Allen didn't like me, and I didn't like him, and that was that. "No, I decided to do it on my own," I said. "The baseboards have been bugging me."

He gave a snort of what might have been either contempt or disbelief. "Good that you're doing it. No one else would," he said with the clear implication that no one else would lower themselves to crawl around the cutting room floor. He continued to dig through the bag and around the body. "Saves us from having to call in a cleaning crew," he added.

"Yeah, well, I'm all-around useful," I said, biting back a more inappropriate response.

"Job security for now, I suppose." He closed the bag and turned to the one behind him, the maggoty and somewhat decomposed suicide from earlier today. I watched, on edge. The autopsied one—the movie extra from yesterday, whose brain I'd already harvested—was on the shelf to his right.

I couldn't stand it anymore. "What are you doing?" I asked, frowning.

"When things don't end up where they're supposed to be, it's my job to make sure it's not a recurring problem." He unzipped the bag and began to check the dead guy's hands and wrists, ignoring the maggots. "Yesterday there was an issue over a wedding ring that wasn't included in the property of a decedent and had somehow been left loose in the body bag. The family was not amused."

My frown deepened. "I always inventory the property." Hell, it had been my meticulous property inventory procedure that helped me figure out that Dr. Charish was up to some hinky shit late last year.

"This was on Jerry's shift," Allen explained, checking the neck and ears of the maggot-covered body. "Haven't caught you yet with any faults in that area." There was no mistaking the emphasis on *yet*.

"And you won't," I replied stubbornly. "I have a system I use to make sure I catch all the valuables."

Allen looked over at me, lips pressed into a thin line. "I'm not asking you for your system or your proclamation of perfection." He returned his attention to the bag, continuing to check the decomposing body for valuables that I'd already removed. "I'll be doing spot checks, and if everything is where it's supposed to be, you've got nothing to worry about."

"Right," I said. "I got nothing to worry about." Probably good that he didn't ask me what my system was, since it was a slightly altered version of the children's song "Head, shoulders, knees and toes" that I hummed to myself while going over bodies.

My heart continued to thump as I watched him search the bag. I knew that if I continued to stand here it would look weird and suspicious. And what if he decided he wanted to check the non-existent wound on my hand? I still had a gauze bandage over the spot, but there was nothing but smooth skin beneath it. I forced myself to casually turn around and return to the cutting room. My palms were sweating within the gloves, but I didn't change them, simply returned to scrubbing the baseboards, and didn't dare to relax until I finally heard the cooler door close and Allen's footsteps heading toward the main building.

He hadn't found anything out of place, at least I assumed not. He wasn't the sort to put off chewing me out if he caught me screwing up. But what the hell would I say if he ever *did* find out I was stealing brains from the bags? It wouldn't end well. I knew that in my zombified bones. And I had a sick feeling it was only a matter of time before Allen or someone else discovered my horrific larceny.

I gave the sponge a savage twist, wringing it nearly dry, and resumed my scrubbing. If only my unease and worry could be cleaned away as easily as the grime.

Chapter 10

The minute my shift ended I got the hell out of there. I wasn't in an "I need pie" mood, and I sure as hell didn't want to go home yet, so instead I drove somewhat aimlessly for about an hour and scowled at people who didn't know how to drive in the rain. I thought about trying to call Marcus again, but I wasn't sure I wanted to tell him about Allen and his bullshit insinuations that I was a fuckup waiting to happen. Not to mention my fears that Allen would find out about the missing brains, and I'd not only get fired but be without my food source. Marcus would get mad on my behalf—which was all right, but then he'd start giving me suggestions of how to handle it and what to do. And I didn't want any of that. Sometimes all a person needed was to vent and bitch, without having to endure advice which would only serve to drive home the fact that it was a horrible situation. I already knew what I was "supposed" to do. Keep my nose clean. Cover my tracks. Don't give Allen any reason to write me up. Be positive and all that crap.

Problem was, I'd *been* doing that. I actually liked my job

and had no issue going the extra mile and so on. I showed up early and left late—most of the time at least. But all of that wouldn't save me if Allen found out about the brains. And it wasn't as if I could simply stop taking them from the bags—not without dipping heavily into my stash.

Less than twenty-four hours earlier, I'd charged two gunmen to help save Heather's life. And now a stupid encounter at work had me worried I might lose my source of brains at any time. Fuck my life.

I finally drove out to the Tucker Point public boat launch and parked, dismayed to see that the water was well over the dock. Another foot and the whole parking lot would be flooded. *Which means they'll almost certainly open the spillway soon.* I was seven years old the last time the spillway was opened. Mom and Dad and I had gone down to the edge of the bayou that ran behind our house and watched in awe as the normally placid Cole Bayou became a churning rush of mud-brown water. But then the water levels had crept up until the road to our house had several inches of overflowing bayou on it, and I got to listen to my dad bitch and moan about people driving too fast through the water and sending waves lapping over our bottom step. Fond childhood memories, to be sure.

However, right now the high water on the Kreeger River ensured that no one was using the boat launch, which meant it was a perfect place for me to chill and get my head back on straight. Or at least get to the point where I wasn't about to throw something.

Exhaling a gusty sigh, I leaned my seat back and gazed up at the worn headliner of my car. Too damn much going on. Three more days until the damn GED. A pain in the ass boss. The usual angst and uncertainty about Marcus. My dad being his typical ornery self. The bizarre situation with Heather, Saberton's connection with both Philip and Dr. Charish, as well as their disturbing interest in Pietro and others associated with him, including me.

It was a lot to think about and process, but it was that last item that had me frowning the most. Heather had known Kang—been good friends with him even. And Kang and Sofia had been up to something with her fake brains research that caught Saberton's interest. Sofia was dead and gone. But Kang . . .

Kang might have some answers. Pietro had Kang's head, and was supposedly trying to regrow it. Or rather, he had "his people" trying to regrow it. Did he really, or was that just a line of bullshit to string me along? I wouldn't put it past him.

I glanced at my watch. Five thirty-two. Still early enough to make a civilized phone call to Pietro.

Rain began to patter my windshield again as I brought the back of my seat upright and reached for my purse to get my phone. Movement flickered to my left, followed by a startling crash and a shower of broken glass as my side window shattered. I let out a scream and instinctively threw up my arms up to shield my face, even as a hand reached through the busted window to hit the unlock button.

Before I could react, my attacker yanked the door open, fisted his hand in my hair close to my scalp, and dragged me from the seat and onto the wet gravel of the parking lot. I screamed again, this time in pain, and clutched at the hand in my hair. "Let me *go!*"

"Been through this before," my attacker said. *Philip!* My blood ran cold, and I jerked my gaze up to his face. "But Archer's not here to save you this time, darlin'," he continued, voice slightly raspy but with a harsh, uncompromising undertone.

Terror sliced through me as he dragged me farther away from the car. I struggled harder, kicking and clawing for all I was worth.

"Bell!" Philip growled at another man as he tightened the grip in my hair. One glance told me this was the other zombie from the Gala—Tim, the crooked-nosed one who'd bitten me. "Get her goddamn legs!"

Tim Bell. Great, well at least I had the full name of one of my attackers. Didn't do me much good right now, though. Tim made a grab for my legs, but the rain helped me squirm out of his grasp. I kicked savagely at him and landed the heel of my boot solidly in his chest, forcing him to stagger back a step. Philip locked his other hand around my left upper arm while I filled my lungs and let out a scream. Sure, I'd picked the most isolated spot I could think of to do my mopey navel-gazing, but there was still a tiny chance someone would hear, so I had to at least try.

Philip snarled and shoved me to my back on the ground with the grip on my arm and hair. Tim got hold of my right ankle, and I let out another scream while I struggled and twisted and kicked and clawed like a crazy bitch. With the way the two men were handling me, any onlooker would think they were trying to rape me, but of all the possible threats to me right now, I doubted rape was one of them.

Another man stood a few feet away, holding what looked like a walkie-talkie in one hand while he calmly watched the two zombies attempt to subdue me for whatever-the-hell reason. Light-eyed, balding, and ... *non-zombie*, noted the part of me that wasn't fighting for my life, the hungry part that locked onto the closest source of edible brain. The extreme exertion was burning through my brain reserves fast but, with Philip involved, I knew this had to be a Saberton Corp operation, and I didn't dare let up.

Tim got hold of my other ankle and made a move to straddle my legs which I thwarted with violent thrashing. Twisting, I tried to sink my teeth into Philip's arm, but he shifted away before I could do more than graze his skin. He abruptly released my hair, but the instant of relief vanished as he shoved his hand into the center of my chest and pressed down hard.

"No one to hear you," Philip said in a hard, cold voice. I fought to get a full breath, continued to punch at him, but he was smart enough to keep his head pulled back from my crazy-desperate flailing. In my peripheral vision, I saw the Saberton guy pull a gun, but getting shot seemed like a minor threat compared to other possibilities. Like becoming Charish's zombie guinea pig again. That blood-chilling thought inspired a whole new wave of desperate thrashing.

Philip's breath hissed noisily through his teeth as he did his best to pin me down. "This is going to happen," he told me, lip curling. "It'll be a lot easier on you if you cooperate. I can go either way."

"I'm not . . . gonna just . . . let you take me!" I gasped out. Squirming, I managed to get a leg free and landed a hard kick in Tim's face. He bellowed a curse, then threw himself bodily across my legs.

I punched again at Philip but didn't have much power behind it. Growing fatigue weakened my efforts, and the hunger tightened its hold on me. Even as a zombie, I could only maintain this level of resistance for so long.

Beside me, the Saberton man scowled and switched to a different gun. Philip saw it, shot a quelling look at the man.

"Do *not* tranq her yet," he snarled. "You'll ruin it."

Ruin it? Yet? I fought back a sob of frustration as my struggles grew less and less effective. The two zombies simply had to let me tire myself out, and then they'd be able to do whatever the hell they wanted.

Philip shifted to straddle my chest, put his knees heavily on my shoulders and sat back, pinning me solidly. With Tim on my legs and Philip anchoring me shoulder to hip, all I could do was flail my forearms. After a few seconds of that useless waste of energy, I lay still.

"Please . . . don't," I gasped, a sob of frustration welling in my throat. I didn't know what the hell they had planned for me, only that it wasn't likely to be anything I'd find fun and relaxing. Didn't help that it was starting to rain harder, and I couldn't do anything to shield my face. Like goddamn water torture.

"It's going to happen," Philip repeated. "Nothing you can do about it." Though he'd been steady enough before, he'd obviously burned through some brains while wrestling with me, and the results weren't pretty—or normal. His head twitched violently to the side every few seconds, and I felt a tremor shake his whole body. He looked over at the Saberton guy. "It's clear. She can come in."

Saberton guy nodded. "Clear," he said into his radio.

I scrabbled again for a few more seconds, then gave up as I utterly failed to shift the two zombies even a bit, much less off of me. Breathing harshly, I felt my lips curl back in a snarl as I memorized the Saberton man's features, then shifted my attention to Philip. "What's going on? This is all you're good for? Attacking women half your size?"

He gave me a cold smile. "Merely following orders, Angel." Another heavy twitch jerked his head to the side. "I volunteered, remember?"

"Not your best life decision," I managed to sneer, pointedly following the abnormal head movement with my eyes. Even as I did so, my gut clenched at the evidence of pain in his eyes and the severity of the ugly twitching. A weird desire rose to help him, to ease his suffering. What the hell?

Something flickered in his expression but was gone before I could identify it. "I'm not the one pinned on the ground," he retorted.

Asshole had a point.

The scent of a tantalizingly delicious brain teased my nose, and I snapped my gaze to the left as a petite, black woman carrying what looked like a tackle box and wearing a dark blue raincoat approached. My fear spiked again as I tried to determine what the hell these people were up to. She moved cautiously to my left side and knelt out of reach of my hand. My heart gave a sick thud as she removed a rubber tourniquet thing from the box.

"What's going on?" I demanded, hearing the quaver in my voice. I shook my head and blinked to get the damn water out of my eyes. "What are you doing?"

She didn't speak or meet my eyes, simply shifted to try and get the tourniquet on my upper arm. I struggled to twist my arm away, but the Saberton man grabbed my hand and pushed it down to the ground, then planted his foot directly on my upturned palm.

I let out a strangled cry of pain, and he leveled a smirk at me. Obviously he didn't mind using unnecessary force.

"Hold still, or he'll step harder," Philip warned me, twitching erratically.

I glared up at Philip. I despised his sorry ass, but the severity of his condition tweaked something inside me. It was like hearing a puppy crying for its mama—that sound that makes you want to pick it up and cuddle it and make it better. Except that Philip wasn't any sweet puppy, and the ludicrous concern for him that nagged at me made no sense.

"She really messed you up, didn't she?" I said, knowing damn well he'd know that "she" was Dr. Charish.

He looked down at me, pain evident behind his eyes and in the lines of his face, and I had a feeling he had no idea how much it showed. Tremors, the extreme twitching, and what sure as hell looked like terrible pain—and that was only what I'd seen in our short encounters. Asshole or not, that was a crap thing to do to anyone. Fuck Charish. Fuck. That. Bitch.

But Philip merely snorted. "Nothing that's not manageable."

I felt the woman's hands on me as she swiftly tied the tourniquet and palpated for a vein. I bit back a yelp as she shoved something that felt the size of a ball point pen into my arm.

Philip convulsed hard, his weight grinding the gravel into my back. I snapped my eyes back to his, focused, connected with his pain, with the *wrongness* in him. A shuddering moan escaped him, though he clamped his lips tight to try to stop it. With a soft exhalation, I bent my free arm, laid my hand on his hip, desperately seeking a way to comfort him, ease the pain.

Beside me I felt the woman drawing multiple vials of blood. A tiny, distant part of me knew I should be worried about what would happen to me once they got what they wanted—the same part that wondered if I was going batshit insane.

I locked my attention onto Philip. "Let me help you," I murmured, softly enough that he was the only one who could hear me. And I meant it.

Batshit insane! the small part screamed.

Philip leaned down so that his face was about an inch from mine, eyes intense and deadly serious. Rain dripped from his hair onto my cheek. "I'm only going to say this once," he said just as softly, "so listen carefully."

I held his gaze, trembling very slightly in anticipation of . . . something.

His lips pulled back from his teeth. "Fuck . . . you," he rasped, then straightened, a sardonic smile playing on his mouth.

I clenched my teeth as my hatred for him flared white hot, totally burning away the irrational compassionate bullshit. I began to struggle again. It still didn't do any good, and I couldn't sustain it for long, but it felt a helluva lot more sane than the crazy urge to soothe my hateful, asshole zombie-kid.

The woman removed the pipeline from my vein, and I shifted my I-hate-you gaze from Philip to her. She flicked a quick glance at me as she packed the vials of blood into the tackle box, but hurriedly looked away when she saw me glaring at her, then stood and moved back.

In a total dick move, the Saberton dude ground my hand hard into the gravel before stepping off. I felt something break as he did, but managed to choke back any noise of pain. It hurt like a bitch, but with all the energy I'd expended in my useless struggles, the brain-starvation dulled my senses enough to take the worst edge off. I'd already memorized every line of his goddamn face. *Let me find you in a dark alley, you worthless asstard. We'll see who's smirking then.*

He lifted the tranq gun and pointed it at my thigh. I tensed, but Philip whipped his head around. "No," he ordered, rasp in his voice deepening. "Give me a goddamn dart so I can make sure it gets in her properly and doesn't leave as much trace."

Saberton dude only hesitated a second before passing a dart to him. I dared to allow a tiny bit of hope to flare. If he was worried about trace residue, then maybe I wasn't being kidnapped. *Or maybe they're simply going to kill me outright.*

Philip made an adjustment to the dart, then pulled the back end of it off so that he was holding the vial part only. He looked down at me, slight sneer still curving his mouth.

"Night night, Angel," he said, then poked me in the shoulder with the point. Within three seconds my vision began to narrow and his face blurred above me.

"Worst . . . kid . . . ever," I slurred, right before everything went black.

Chapter 11

I woke with a headache, which was weird since I hadn't had a true headache since becoming a zombie. But this was every inch of the real thing. Felt like I had a hangover—and I sure as hell never got those anymore either.

I was sitting in the front seat of my car—driver's side window shattered, rain sheeting in on me. Memory trickled back, and I rubbed at my face, then gasped at the dull flare of pain from my left hand. Swallowing hard, I stared at abrasions and swelling, the odd lump that was most definitely a broken bone. Shakily, I pushed my sleeve up and peered at the crook of my elbow. Bruising there as well, and a large needle mark. Yeah, definitely time to get freaked out.

I shook my head to clear the lingering fog, regretting it instantly as the headache gave an answering throb. *I should be hungry as hell right now*, I thought. After fighting as hard as I did and being injured, I should be starving. I *had* been starving—but now registered only the faintest hint of brain-hunger. *Weird*. A glance at the dashboard clock told me it had only been about twenty minutes since Philip shattered my window.

After hurriedly scanning the parking lot to make sure I was alone, I started the car and peeled out in a spray of gravel. I knew I needed to call someone, but I wanted to get the hell away from this place first.

The lingering dizziness faded a little as I drove, and I managed to reach the relative safety and civilization of the Walmart parking lot without running into anyone or breaking any major laws. I parked halfway out on the lot where I had a clear line of sight all around me. Even though the Saberton bastards were likely through with me for the moment, I figured a little dose of healthy paranoia couldn't hurt. But right now I needed to do something about the damn broken window. Plastic and duct tape would do the trick for now, which I knew Walmart had within. *Then* I could call Marcus and let him have the freakout I didn't have the energy for.

However, when I climbed out of the car a heavy wave of dizziness and fatigue nearly dropped me to the asphalt, forcing me to cling to the open door for support. *Okay, maybe shopping isn't such a good idea since, y'know, the whole swaying-drenched-chick-with-a-broken-hand thing might freak some people out.*

Reluctantly giving up the shopping notion, I collapsed back into the seat with a *squoosh* of water and grating crunch of glass. Too much effort to get out again and move around to the dry, clear passenger side, and too much effort to try to drive anymore. What was the deal with the limp noodle feeling? That hadn't happened when I was tranqed before.

Well, I sure as hell didn't want to sit here until I felt better. I fished my phone out of my purse and dialed Marcus.

"Hey, babe," he answered in the lazy drawl that usually made me melt.

"Marcus, I was attacked," I said, trying to keep my voice nice and calm. Trying hard. Yeah, I'd been in a god-damn firefight just last night and handled myself like a boss, but that was a far cry from being dragged out of my car and held down. I wasn't a zombie superwoman. Not yet at least.

"Where are you?" he asked, all trace of the drawl gone, and I could almost *see* him snapping upright, freaking out in a manly way. "Are you all right?"

"Yeah. I feel kinda weird and shaky, but I'm okay." I said with as much steadiness as I could muster. "I'm in the Walmart parking lot right now."

"Okay. Okay, good," he said, relief evident in his voice. "What happened?"

"I had a bad day at work and went out to the boat launch to think," I said. "I was only there a couple of minutes when Philip smashed my car window and dragged me out, then—"

"Wait, what? Philip?" he asked. In the background I heard the sharp jingle of keys and scuffling noises that were likely him shoving shoes on.

"Yes, Philip" I snapped, muscles tensing as the anger seeped in again. "The asshole zombie I made." *And he was hurting, bad. And I wanted to kiss his goddamn boo-boos and make him better. What the hell was that all about?*

"Right. Sorry. Then what?"

I clenched my unbroken hand. "Oh, then the fun shit happened. He and another zombie held me down for a chick to take my blood. There was another guy there too, human. Motherfucker broke my hand. After they were done, Philip used a tranq dart to knock me out, and I woke up a little bit ago back in my car."

"Jesus Christ," he breathed. "Okay. I'm coming. Just stay put."

"Not going anywhere," I said with a scowl I could feel

down to my core. "Whatever he did made me real weak and shaky. Not safe to drive." I glanced down at my broken hand. "And I need brains. Sorry. I was on my way home and didn't put any in the car."

"No worries, babe," he said, though there was no mistaking the worry in his voice. "Already have some for you." His truck engine roared to life in the background. "I'll be there in five minutes."

"Thanks. See you then," I said, managing a tired smile as I dropped the phone back into my purse. Damned good guy. Yet my smile faded as I remembered my reaction to Philip. *Kiss his booboos and make them better?* I remembered it, but didn't *feel* it anymore. Weird. In the moment I'd sure felt it.

Then it hit me. *Kiss his booboos and make them better.* Like a mother and child. I'd turned him into a zombie, chewed brains and fed them to him like a mother bird, protected him from Charish in his first hours. What the shit? Was the bizarre compassion some sort of parasite-influenced zombie-mama instinct? It sure as hell made more sense than anything else.

An unnatural cold settled in my bones, accompanied by another wave of weakness, and I gave up pondering the weirdness surrounding my horrible zombie-baby. Probably an after effect of the damn tranq, I figured. However, when Marcus's truck screeched to a stop beside my car, I managed to gather enough energy to fling the door open and stagger out. Marcus reached me in a brains-fueled instant, wrapped his arms around me and pulled me close.

"God, you're soaking wet," he murmured. "C'mon, let's get you warmed up." Supporting me, he steered me to his truck, got me in and then tucked a blanket around me. My lips twitched in mild amusement as I saw that it was the blanket we'd had sex on at the stadium. God, that seemed like an eternity ago.

He gave my thigh a comforting squeeze, reached to crank up the heat, then pressed a bottle into my hand. "Drink up," he urged. "You need it." Then he surprised me by pulling a towel, plastic sheeting, and duct tape from behind the seat. "I'll get your window covered."

"You're the best," I told him, totally meaning it.

"You bring it out in me, Angel," he said with a smile and eyes full of a warmth that did more to chase away my chill than the blanket. His gaze dropped to the bottle. "Drink," he repeated, then closed the door and turned away to attend to my car.

I wasn't all that hungry, but I knew my unhealed injuries needed brains. I opened the bottle and lifted it to drink, but my stomach gave an odd lurch at a revolting smell. Frowning, I lowered it without taking a sip. Had to be something wrong with it.

A few minutes later Marcus climbed into the driver's seat, placed my phone and purse on the seat between us. He glanced at the full bottle in my hand and worry darkened his eyes.

"Babe, you need to drink all of that," he said gently with a light touch to the back of my injured hand.

"Can't." I made a face and shook my head. "They don't smell right," I said. "I think they're spoiled."

He frowned and took the bottle from me, sniffed and then sipped. "No, they're good. Your taste must be a little off." He handed the bottle back to me. "Angel, you need to make yourself drink."

I held my breath and forced myself to take a few swallows, then shuddered. "Oh, god, that's really awful."

His gaze dropped to the abrasions on the back of my hand. "Well, you're healing . . . but damn, a lot more slowly than normal."

Frowning, I peered at my hand. "Maybe it's because of whatever knocked me out." My frown deepened as I looked over at him. "I mean, it really knocked me out—

totally unconscious, even though it wasn't for very long."
It was only now hitting me how very odd that was. "When
I got tranqed before it didn't do that." McKinney, Dr.
Charish's muscle, had tranqed me from a distance when
I'd exchanged myself for my dad. "McKinney's tranq
dropped me, and I couldn't move," I continued, "but I
was awake the whole time." Not necessarily coherent
since I was crazed with brain-hunger, but certainly
awake. "And it didn't make me feel weak afterward like
I do now."

Marcus exhaled. "Let's get you back to the house,
then I'll call Uncle Pietro." He glanced my way. "Keep
trying to finish that bottle, if you can. It's doing some
good, even if slowly."

I took slow grimace-laden sips as we drove, but to my
relief the yuck-level began to decrease, and by the time
we reached his house I'd sucked down the last of the
bottle and wanted more. My hand wasn't completely
healed up, but it was well on the way, and the overwhelming weakness had faded to a much more normal
tiredness. What was up with that, along with the brains
being near revolting at first and damn tasty now? It had
to be something to do with the tranquilizer and its effects wearing off.

Marcus got me inside his house and found some vastly
oversized sweats for me to change into since my own
clothes were still wet. After that he shepherded me to
the couch, wrapped a blanket around me, then snuggled
up next to me.

"Thanks, hon'," I said as I nestled close. This was the
protective side of Marcus I adored.

"We need to tell my uncle," Marcus said.

"Yeah." I sighed and leaned my head on his shoulder.
"You do it. I'm too tired to deal with him."

He kissed the top of my head. "Not a problem."

I closed my eyes while he dialed, listened with half an

ear while he told Pietro about the attack, the blood draw, the tranq, my weakness, slow healing and temporary distaste for brains. After that Marcus fell silent, broken only by the occasional "Right" and "Okay" and "I will."

When he finally hung up and set the phone aside, I opened my eyes, gave him a smile. "I'm feeling a lot better," I said. "Thanks."

"You look a lot better," he said, with less of the worry that had tightened his voice before.

"Is it okay if I spend the night here tonight?" I asked.

A smile spread across his face. "You'd have had to wrestle me to get out the door."

I let out a tired laugh. "There's also the fact that my car is still in the Walmart parking lot." I kissed him. "But mostly I'd really like you to hold me for a long time."

He let out a breath of relief, kissed me back. "I can totally do that." He paused. "There's pudding in the fridge, but, ah, only if you're interested."

I smiled. "I think I'm hungry again."

Chapter 12

"Babe."

I mumbled and rolled over.

"Hey, babe," the voice insisted on continuing to speak. Marcus. Waking me up. Damn him. "I'm sorry, but I have to leave in ten minutes," he went on. "I work day shift, and I have roll call at six a.m."

Cracking an eye open, I peered at the clock. Five fifteen. "You're kicking me out?" I mumbled.

Marcus chuckled softly. "Hell, no," he said. "You can stay here all day. But if you want me to give you a ride back to your car, you need to get up."

Crap. Yeah, my car was still in the Walmart parking lot. I briefly debated staying in bed and then finding another way to retrieve the damn thing, but I couldn't think of anyone else I wanted to bug for a ride—or tell what had happened. And I sure as hell didn't want to cough up cash for a taxi.

Reluctantly, I opened both eyes. Marcus was dressed and ready to go in his sheriff's office uniform. It was a somewhat ordinary grey shirt and dark blue pants, but

Marcus had his shirts tailored to better fit the v-taper of his lats, and the polyester pants hugged his firm butt quite nicely. Add the whole duty belt and air of authority, and the man frickin' oozed sexy.

"Fine," I grumbled. I forced myself to roll out of bed, took the clothing that Marcus held out for me. Same clothing I'd had on the day before, but clean and dry now, I noted. Marcus could be pretty damn awesome. Well, except for waking me up at oh-fuck in the morning.

I managed to dress without too many complaints, and then Marcus drove me in his police car to Walmart. To my surprise he got out when I did, opened the trunk of his car and pulled out a hand-held vacuum.

"Don't want you sitting on glass," he said with a smile, and I proceeded to watch in bemused delight as he vacuumed up all the broken glass that littered the interior of my car.

"You just earned yourself some sexual favors," I told him after he finished.

He laughed. "Do you work today?"

"Nope. I think it's gonna be a clean-the-kitchen and study-my-ass off day." I wrinkled my nose. "I know how to party."

"Sounds like fun," he said with a mild shudder. "I'll call you when I get off work."

"You'd better!"

He kissed me, then watched as I started my car and drove off. I glanced back in the rearview mirror as he climbed back into his cruiser. Yeah, maybe it was time for us to officially become boyfriend-girlfriend. Hell, everyone assumed we were already. And he'd sure as hell come through for me last night.

I made it home to a dark house, with only my dad's snoring to break the silence. I'd texted him before going to bed last night to let him know I wouldn't be in and to not worry. He never responded, so he was either annoyed that I spent the night with Marcus or too busy drinking or whatever the hell else he was doing. Screw it. I had a feeling I'd be spending a lot more nights away from home.

For a brief moment I considered going right back to bed, but by this point I was pretty damn awake. Exerting a bit of maturity, I spread my books out on the kitchen table and settled down to work through a practice GED test. That killed a couple of hours, but I managed to pass it by the skin of my teeth and rewarded myself with a mental high-five.

Yet my euphoria faded as the memory of the previous night's fun and games rose again. Hell, this whole week had been weird, with the attack at the boat launch being the shit-flavored ice cream on top of the crazy pie. Though it had been less than thirty-six hours, it seemed like forever since I was out on that rain-soaked highway with Heather and facing down the company men. Was she recovering all right? Was the Saberton Corporation still looking for her?

Jeez, it's corporate espionage on steroids. And brains.

I sat back and considered the various connections, then abruptly remembered that I'd planned to call Pietro about Kang's head. The clock over the stove read nine-oh-five. A more than reasonable hour to call.

Before I could lose my nerve, I pulled my phone from my purse and dialed Pietro's number.

To my surprise he picked up on the first ring. "Hello, Angel. How are you doing this morning? I was just thinking about you."

"Uh, hi, Pietro," I said, trying to recover from the mild shock that he had my number in his contacts. "Better. All the weird weakness is gone, and I feel pretty much my normal self."

"Good. Glad to hear it." He said, sounding like he actually meant it. "How can I help you?"

Crap, I probably should've rehearsed what I was going to say before calling and sounding like a moron. "Um, I was calling to find out if there's been any progress with the heads." It had been six months since his people recovered the zombies' heads from Dr. Charish's lab at NuQuesCor—heads of zombies Ed had killed.

"You mean with regrowth?" he asked, again surprising me by actually knowing what the hell I was talking about. I could be talking about heads of cauliflower for all he knew.

"Well, yeah," I said. "Is anything happening? I haven't heard any news, and, well, Kang was sort of a friend of mine, and I'd really like to be kept in the loop."

"The regrowth itself hasn't been attempted yet," Pietro informed me. "It will be as soon as the right medium is developed."

"Right medium?" I asked, puzzled. "You mean what to grow them back in? Why can't you just put them in a big vat of brains?"

"According to one who knows far more about this than I do," he said, "a big vat of brains wouldn't be sufficient. Coming back from a head alone isn't exactly natural. Kristi Charish was on the right track when using the pseudobrains mix to regrow Zeke Lyons, but she hadn't tested it thoroughly and, as you know, the results were tragic. Finding the right formula is proving challenging, but we're getting closer."

"Oh. All right." Disappointment curled through me, but I also understood. Zeke Lyons was one of Ed's decapitation/murder victims, but when he was regrown he came back all screwed up—appearing at least twenty years older, and with a parasite that couldn't heal the damage from the closed-head injury he sustained after a fall down a flight of stairs.

I resisted the urge to sigh. So much for getting answers from Kang, at least any time soon. "Will you please let me know once you have any news?"

"I will," Pietro said, "but perhaps you'd like to get some direct answers? Maybe even see the heads yourself?"

I sucked in an excited breath. "Seriously?"

"Completely," he replied, and I thought I heard a smile in his voice at my delight. "We did lose one, but the others are relatively stable."

"I would love to see the heads!" Then I bit my lip. "Wait. Which one did you lose? Please don't say it was Kang's."

"No. Kang is stable. It was Peter Pleschia."

I racked my memory for which one that was. Oh yeah, the pizza guy. "Oh, whew. Er, I mean, not great for him, but . . . well, you know." I made a face at my own idiocy. "Anyway. So, when can I go and see them?"

Pietro chuckled. "It's all right. I know what you meant. Do you work today?"

A thrill of anticipation ran through me. "No. I'm off today, work tomorrow, then off again on Saturday, but I have the GED that morning."

"I'll have Brian pick you up at noon today at your place," he said. "Will that work for you?"

Holy crap. Brian Archer, Pietro's hard as nails head of security. "Sure!" I said quickly.

"You'll be meeting with Dr. Ariston Nikas. He heads up all of my research and development operations. He'll be able to answer your questions much more thoroughly than I can."

Oh my god. I was going to get to visit a research lab? A *zombie* research lab?

"That is so cool," I breathed. "Thanks!"

"You're welcome, Angel," he replied warmly. "By the way, apart from your ordeal last night, I heard you were in a pretty serious firefight the night before. Are you doing all right? Do you need anything?"

"Um, no, I'm cool," I said, weirdly touched at the concern. "Your people gave me some stuff on the scene. And I, uh . . ." I gulped. "Well, I ate a bad guy." I killed someone. And *ate his brain*. Sure, he'd been shooting at me, but . . . A shiver ran through me. It shouldn't have been so easy for me to do it. I'd killed McKinney when I was escaping from Charish's damn lab, but that was different. McKinney was a Grade-A bastard asshole and general all-around Bad Person who'd done terrible things to me and to people I cared about. I'd felt zero guilt when I smashed his head and feasted on the contents.

But the guy the other night . . . Just because he was working for the other side didn't necessarily mean he was dipped in sin. Hell, I knew damn well that Pietro's hands weren't clean.

My shoulders hunched forward, and my chest tightened as guilt swept in. What the hell kind of monster was I?

Maybe Pietro sensed my attack of sudden remorse; when he replied his tone was surprisingly mild. "You made a decision in the heat of the moment. I've heard the reports. If you hadn't taken him out and utilized the resources he had to offer, Heather would likely be dead now, and those men would have certainly captured you."

"Right," I said softly. He *was* right. I knew that logically, but I also knew I'd probably never shake that sliver of guilt. And that was probably a good thing. If I didn't feel some guilt and shame, then I really *would* be a monster. "It's kinda hard to get used to. Though I guess you know that."

"Yes, I do," he replied. "But killing him was a matter of survival for you. And as far as eating him goes, you'd have eaten his brain without hesitation had his body been in the morgue, yes? It's simply a different setting."

"Yeah," I said, subdued. "I'm having a little trouble adjusting to the whole being-a-killer thing."

He exhaled. "Maybe we can discuss this more later,

when things settle down a bit," he replied, tone gentle. "My people will be occupied for a few days with the aftermath of your encounters with Saberton, but after that we should talk."

I hesitated. I still didn't fully trust him, not by a long shot. And the quick and efficient response to the highway incident had shown me quite clearly that Pietro was, well . . . when I'd half-joked about him being the head of the zombie mafia, I'd probably been underestimating his power and reach.

But I had no doubt he had a lot more experience with dealing with the aftermath of killing someone. And it wasn't as if I had a whole lot of other people I could spill my guts to. I couldn't exactly go to a therapist and say, "The thing is, I'm having some guilt issues over the fact that I'm a brain-eating murderer."

"That would be great," I heard myself saying.

"Excellent. I'll tell Dr. Nikas you'll be coming by shortly after noon."

"Thanks," I said. "I'll, uh, be ready." I hung up, shaking my head at the awkwardness of my goodbye.

But then I laughed. A year ago I was a drugged-out felon shacking up with my loser boyfriend, Randy. In a couple of hours I was going to see zombie heads in a secret lab owned and operated by the head of the local zombie mafia.

Sometimes life was pretty damn funny.

Chapter 13

I told myself I'd study until eleven which would give me enough time to get ready so I wouldn't be in a frantic rush before Brian picked me up. At least that was the plan. I ended up getting caught up in a practice test, and when I looked up it was eleven-thirty and then, of course, I had a frantic rush to get ready in time.

Fortunately, I was an expert on running late, so by ten 'til noon I was showered, had my hair dried with most of the frizz tamed, and even had a bit of makeup on. I put on the same pants I'd worn to the Gala, but this time paired it with a simple shirt that wasn't at all skanky, and my regular low lace-up boots. I'd briefly considered wearing the same heeled boots that I'd worn the other night, then decided that comfort and sure footing was probably the better choice for a research lab. I wouldn't want to trip and knock something crucial over, land in a bizarre cocktail of chemicals, and end up some sort of freak mutant, right?

I laughed at myself as I dabbed on a touch of lip gloss. I was already freaky enough, thank you very much. *And*

I've also been watching way too many science fiction movies with Marcus!

My dad stumbled out of his bedroom wearing only a pair of ragged boxers while I prowled the kitchen in search of something to eat. He grunted something at me and continued right on past to the bathroom. I rolled my eyes, annoyance winding through me as I stuck a burrito into the microwave.

By the time the microwave dinged, and I had the burrito on a plate, he shuffled back into the kitchen.

"Afternoon, Dad," I said. I figured it was close enough to noon that I could be snarky about the time of day.

He mumbled something that might have been an answer as he scrabbled through the pantry. "Dammit, Angel, we're out of coffee."

"I'll pick some up later," I said around a mouthful of too-chewy tortilla and cheese. "There's some Cokes in there." I shrugged. "At least it's caffeine."

His scowl deepened into familiar lines as he pulled a can of Coke out of the pantry and popped the tab. "You shoulda gotten coffee yesterday." He took a swig of warm soda, gave me an accusing look as if it was my fault that warm Coke sucked compared to coffee.

I took the time to chew and swallow more burrito before answering. "I didn't know we were out," I finally said. "And I was working. Y'know, for the money that buys coffee."

"I buy things around here too, dammit," he growled, then let out a low belch.

I bit back a retort that I knew damn well would start a fight. "So, you going anywhere tonight?" I asked instead.

"Why the hell do I have to get the third degree in my own goddamn house?" He shot back. "I may go out. May not. None of your goddamn business."

So much for not starting a fight. "Jesus, Dad, I'm just

trying to have a fucking conversation," I said. Why the hell did he have to be so goddamn ornery all the time? "You've hardly been home at all most evenings."

He got a cold hotdog out of the fridge, wrapped it in a piece of white bread. "Maybe I have things to do. And you're one to talk after staying out all night." He took a bite, then looked me over as if focusing on me for the first time. His eyes narrowed. "Looks like you're going out again. With that *cop*?"

"No, it's not Marcus," I said, then had to mentally fumble for what the hell to tell him. *Zombie head tour at a secret lab* probably wouldn't go over too well. "I have a meeting, um, sorta job interview," I lied. Badly.

He leaned toward me, frowning. "You get fired?"

"What? No!" I shook my head. "This is mostly a tour, that's all." I jumped at a sudden knock on the door. Crap. Brian was here. And my dad . . .

I groaned under my breath. "Could you maybe put on some pants?"

"Oh, for the love of . . . It's *my* goddamn house." He scowled as he stalked to the window and tweaked the curtain back. I heard him breathe a low curse, and I looked over his shoulder to see a very official-looking black Escalade with heavily tinted windows in the driveway, and on the porch the equally official-looking Brian, dressed in a dark suit, and wearing sunglasses and a Bluetooth headset.

"Who the *fuck* is that, Angel?" He let the curtain drop and rounded on me.

I hissed a whisper, "Jesus, Dad, he can *hear* you!" I swallowed down the last bite of burrito and grabbed my purse. "Hang on!" I called toward the door, then looked back to my dad. "He, um, works at the lab. He's giving me a ride, that's all."

My dad glowered at me as he crossed his spindly arms over his thin, bare chest. "You've sure taken up with some folks that aren't our kind, Angel." Something flickered in his eyes, but I couldn't tell if it was anger or worry. "You better watch yourself."

"I'm *fine*," I muttered, then waved a hand at him to at least get behind the counter so that his underwear wasn't visible. He rolled his eyes and grudgingly complied, but continued to cast dark looks my way as I yanked the door open.

I gave Brian a bright smile. "Hi!"

With the sunglasses over his eyes I couldn't tell if Brian was looking past me and taking in the general state of my house—and my dad—but I had no doubt he was doing exactly that. Though if he found any aspect of it disgusting or amusing, it didn't show at all in his face. Instead he simply gave me a slight nod.

"Good morning, Ms. Crawford," he said, voice as calm and smooth as ever. "Are you ready?"

"Sure am!" I replied, giving him an overly bright smile. I glanced back. "Bye, Dad!"

"Whatever," my dad grumbled.

I kept the smile plastered onto my face as I exited and closed the door. Brian opened the umbrella he carried and held it over me through the light drizzle as we headed for the Escalade, then surprised the hell out of me by opening the passenger door. I climbed in, barely managing to hold back a sigh of pleasure at the buttery-soft feel of the leather seats.

He closed the door and came around to get into the driver's seat. "It's about a half hour drive, ma'am," he told me as he started the engine and began to pull out of the driveway. "Feel free to put on some music you like."

I didn't have the faintest clue how to work the radio or satellite thing or whatever the hell it was. Fortunately it was already playing what appeared to be classic rock at a volume that still allowed conversation. "This is fine,"

I said. If it had been opera or jazz or anything weird, I'd have had to figure the damn thing out for my own sanity.

Brian turned onto the highway, then opened the console and pulled out a packet like the ones he'd given me at the Gourmet Gala. "Can always use a bit more, ma'am," he said with a slight smile, holding it out for me.

"Oh, sure. Thanks," I said, taking it from him. "I tend to hoard and ration out my own stash as much as possible." I tore the top off and did my best to suck the contents down as genteelly as possible. What was the proper etiquette for brain-eating? Pinky up? No slurping sounds? A dainty belch at the end?

"Understandable," he replied. "And you have an adequate stash?"

"As long as nothing goes wrong, I have enough to last me about three months if I lost my job tomorrow," I told him with more than a little pride. It hadn't been easy to build my supply up to that level.

He flicked a glance toward me. "That's impressive planning."

"I've been hungry before," I said softly, looking out at the window. Pine trees and horse farms flicked by as we drove. We seemed to be taking mostly back highways, which made for nicer scenery. "It scared the hell out of me," I continued. "I don't want to hurt anyone." I pushed away the image of the baseball bat splitting open the Saberton man's head.

Brian took a deep breath and released it slowly. "An ever present danger for us." He paused. "Mr. Ivanov told me you had an unpleasant encounter last night."

I swallowed hard. "Yeah, fun times with Philip and a couple of his pals."

"I'm sorry, ma'am," he said with a shake of his head. "It must have been quite traumatic."

I glanced his way. "Look, I really appreciate all the

courtesy stuff, but is there any way you could just call me Angel?" I gave him an apologetic smile. "The ma'am thing sorta feels, well, weird. Sorry."

"No problem with that at all, Angel," Brian replied, slight smile touching his mouth.

I let out a small sigh of relief. "Thanks. And yeah, it was traumatic, but at the same time it was hardly anything compared to some of the other crap I've been through. Pissed me off more than anything." I made a sour face. "Now isn't that some shit? That getting tackled and held down while someone steals my blood isn't the worst thing to happen to me by far."

"More than your share in a very short time," he replied.

"Not quite sure what that says about me," I replied with a low snort. *Shit magnet. That's what it says.*

"Well, you've handled yourself well every time," he said. "I'll give you credit for that. The incident on Highway 1790 was damned impressive."

A warm flush of pride went through me. "Thanks. But speaking of that, is Heather doing all right?"

He seemed to consider the question carefully before answering. "Yes."

That wasn't exactly a super-reassuring response. "She's really all right?" I asked, cocking an eyebrow at him. "I mean, I know she was working for the other side."

"Dr. Nikas has treated her arm and head," Brian stated, features composed in the professional mask. "She's healing fine."

"And then what? What's gonna happen to her?"

"I don't know yet," he replied.

There was a hitch in his voice that unsettled me. "What would she have to do, or prove to you, to get y'all to—" I paused, not quite sure how to say it. "To keep y'all from doing bad stuff to her."

He didn't flinch at the accusation that Heather faced

a very real threat of "enhanced interrogation." Yet worry flashed across his face, briefly cracking the professional façade. "I don't know," he said, and to my surprise he seemed to wilt a smidge. "She's a difficult case."

"She was unhappy enough with Saberton to risk everything to leave them," I reminded him. My own worry grew. "Is she at the lab? Will I be able to see her?"

He hesitated. I braced myself to be told it wasn't possible, and so it was with real surprise that I heard him say, "I'll see if I can arrange it."

"Thanks," I said, relieved that it wasn't a flat out No. I glanced over at him. "How long have you been a zombie?"

"A little over fifteen years," he replied, quickly enough that it sounded like he was glad for the change in subject.

I controlled the desire to ask him how old he was. He looked like he was late thirties or maybe early forties, so did that mean he was that old when he was turned? Did a zombie stay the same physical age they were at when turned, or did the body "stabilize" at some optimum age? Was Pietro actually in his sixties when he became a zombie? And if that was the case, what would happen with a little kid who was turned?

One of these days I would run out of questions about zombies. Sure. "I guess you kinda have the hang of all this then, huh?"

Brian's shoulders lifted in a slight shrug. "For the most part. Fortunately, I'm in a situation where the people I work with know what I am." He paused as he made a turn onto a narrow highway. "Having people around who understand makes it easier."

"I bet it does," I said, then winced as I thought of the scene with my dad this morning. "God, my dad would *freak* if he found out. I can't even imagine." It would be ugly. And messy. And I didn't want to think about that too much. We had enough issues between us without bringing up my weird "medical condition."

"It's hard to get past the ingrained prejudice," Brian said, eyes firmly on the road ahead of us. "A lot of people can only see the monster, and those situations seldom end well." A muscle in his jaw twitched. "Always have to be careful about revealing your nature. It can backfire even when you think they're sure to accept it."

"Well, we *are* monsters," I said with a small sigh. "Hard to sugarcoat that."

Brian gave a sober nod and didn't argue the point.

There wasn't much more conversation after that. I sat back, listened to classic rock, and watched the scenery go by.

Chapter 14

Our route to the lab had been almost entirely back roads and seldom-used highways, though I wasn't sure if that was the only way to get there or if it was on purpose to keep me from finding the place again. If so it worked, since I had no idea where the hell we were, other than in front of an incredibly uninteresting building. It looked nothing like a lab or secret outpost, or even a secret outpost cleverly disguised as a farm house, or anything far less boring than what it was—a cinderblock lump of a structure painted an institutional blue with a small gravel parking lot and only one door that I could see. Scraggly grass scorched brown from summer heat surrounded it, giving way to pine forest after a few hundred yards. Dust hung in the air from the Escalade's passage, and I held back a sneeze, and a little disappointment, with effort.

Brian escorted me to the door and pressed a button beside it. I figured surely there were surveillance cameras, but I still hadn't located them by the time the lock on the door gave a *click*. Brian pulled the door open, and I followed him into a room as massively unexciting as the exterior. Dull tan walls and a tired looking couch. A coffee table with corners that were worn down to the particle-board beneath the veneer. A single door on the far wall. It looked and felt like the waiting room at the public health clinic, right down to a scattered pile of ancient magazines on the table and a faint smell of antiseptic.

I ruthlessly fought back increasing disappointment and crossed mental fingers that the lab itself wouldn't be so crashingly mundane.

Brian took a seat on the couch, snagged a magazine off the table as if expecting a bit of a wait. I went ahead and sat at the other end of the couch and picked up a magazine as well. *Golf Digest* from seven years ago. And a quick scan of the table showed me I had the pick of the lot. What I wouldn't give for some *Highlights* and some good ole Goofus and Gallant. Yeah, that was more my speed.

Fortunately it was only about ten minutes before the door opened and an unimposing man stepped through. His brown, shoulder-blade length hair was pulled back in a ponytail. A hint of grey at his temples added a sense of years to his unwrinkled face. In addition, my failure to smell an edible brain behind that face told me he was a zombie. He wasn't wearing a lab coat, name badge, or anything like that, but I had no doubt at all that he was Dr. Nikas.

He confirmed it when he looked to me with a smile and said, "Hello, Angel. I'm Ariston Nikas." He had an interesting accent, nothing I could identify for sure, but maybe a mix of various European influences.

I dropped the magazine back onto the table, stood and shook his hand. "Nice to meet you, sir."

"A pleasure to meet you," he replied with genuine warmth in his voice. "I've heard a lot about you." He released my hand and turned to the door. "Come this way."

I could only imagine all the stuff that had been said about me lately. I followed him into a short corridor painted in the same drab tan as the waiting room, while Brian fell in behind. Dr. Nikas paused at a door at the end of the corridor, punched in numbers on a keypad, then swiped his thumb on a sensor. A second later the door unlocked with a click.

We entered a barren cubicle of a room that did nothing to raise my hopes for anything beyond boring and mundane. Dr. Nikas gave a smile and wave to the mirrored window of the right wall, where I suspected a security guard or two watched from behind it. He crossed to the single broad door on the far wall and did the keypad-thumb swipe thing again. With a click and hiss, the door, at least three inches thick, slid quietly into the wall on the left.

To my relief and utter delight, we left drab tan behind and stepped into an area that totally looked like a super cool zombie research lab straight out of a science fiction movie. Or rather we weren't actually in the lab yet—I could see that awesomeness through the double glass doors ahead—but it wasn't kill-me-now tan anymore. Corridors led off left and right, painted in graduated shades of rich blue and gold, lit by recessed lighting, and several panels of lights with associated digital readouts twinkled beside the door ahead. And it smelled fresh. Not like fresh-scent dryer sheets or anything fake like that, but more like the air right after a lightning strike.

"I'll meet up with you later, Angel," Brian said. I gave him a smile and nod, and he turned down the corridor to the right while I continued after Dr. Nikas.

"You are interested in the people I have in stasis—John Kang in particular, yes?" he asked as we passed through the auto-sliding glass security doors. *Thick* glass that I had no doubt could stop a bullet.

I liked that Dr. Nikas referred to them as *people* and

not simply *heads*. "That's right," I replied, looking around and taking it all in, utterly fascinated. "Thanks for taking the time to show me around. I really appreciate it."

"Not a problem," he said over his shoulder. "I don't have many visitors. You're a breath of fresh air."

We passed into what felt like the central hub of the complex—and it was definitely a *complex*. This room was large and circular with a high domed ceiling. Several passageways and doors led out, lending to the hub effect, and all sorts of shiny equipment lined the counters and walls. A semicircular central island housed several fancy computer stations and more equipment I couldn't begin to identify.

I wasn't any sort of expert on labs, but it was pretty obvious no expense had been spared, not only on mega-cool equipment, but also on making it a comfortable workspace. Various screens and little flashy lights looked cool as hell, but the whirrs, ticks, and soft pings made the place feel alive. Dr. Nikas ran his hand lightly over a console as we passed it on our way toward a dark corridor on the far side, and I had the feeling he spent a *lot* of time here.

Lights came on automatically as we entered a hallway with walls covered in a tile mosaic of colorful abstract patterns. Dr. Nikas turned and walked backward as he spoke. "While you are here, would you consider giving some blood?"

I almost jerked to a stop and, in fact, stumbled a half step before recovering. "Um. What?" I asked, suddenly *verrrry* wary. "Why?"

He stopped, apparently sensing my alarm. "In general, I try to keep samples of everyone's blood on hand for research or unique individual needs," he said. "And, specifically in your case, to determine the reason Saberton wanted samples so desperately."

It made sense, but still. "Can I say no?"

He seemed surprised by the question, but he didn't hesitate before answering, "Of course."

Dr. Nikas sure seemed nice enough, but right now there was too much of a yikes-factor going on with me to be cool about giving my blood away. "Um, lemme think about it, okay?"

A brief flash of disappointment touched his face, though it didn't seem to be "Crap, I'm not getting my way," and was more like "Darn, it would've been really nice to have that." But he smiled and gave me an understanding nod. "Certainly. Not a problem." He moved to a side door and unlocked it. "Come on in and see Kang."

I followed, relieved that he wasn't pushing the issue.

The chilly temperature and small size of the room reminded me of walking into the morgue cooler, and it took a moment for my eyes to adjust to the dim light. A half dozen vats like oversized stainless steel crock pots lined a counter against the far wall, each with a white index card taped to the front.

Dr. Nikas twisted a knob on the wall near the door and increased the light level a bit. "They do best in low light," he said, moving to the vat second from the left. "This is John Kang. You can look in through the glass lid, but remember that though he looks really bad, his brain is fully encapsulated by the parasite and is stable." He paused, considering. "'Hibernating' might be a way of looking at it. Using minimal resources."

Upon approach, I saw that the index card on the vat read "John Kang" in flowing handwriting that I had no doubt belonged to Dr. Nikas. Something about that personal touch gave me the feeling that he really cared about these heads as individuals and not simply as test subjects. Curiosity burning, I peered through the glass. Sure enough, it was Kang. Despite the head looking like a horror movie prop suspended in some sort of clear gel, I vaguely recognized his features. Like mummy wrappings, strips of cloth bound the stump of his neck, and his skin, though not falling apart in decay, was dark, ugly grey, and shriveled like a raisin.

"That is *so* gross. And cool," I breathed.

Dr. Nikas smiled broadly. "Yes, I wholeheartedly agree on both counts," he said. "I'm currently analyzing research data that may well solve my puzzle of the re-growth medium as well as boost our alternative brains research."

I tore my gaze from the gruesome sight, looked over at him. "Alternative brains? You mean fake brains like Dr. Charish and Sofia were working on?"

"All of their data fed my research," he said, nodding. A shadow of deep concern passed over his face. "I am close—so very close. But in light of some recent information, I am deeply troubled that Saberton may be near as well."

I pushed away from Kang's vat and moved to another. "Well what would be so bad about that?" I asked. "I mean, I know they're assholes," I paused, "serious major fucking assholes, but as long as *someone* develops an alternative, it's all good, right?"

"Oh god, no," Dr. Nikas replied, a hint of alarm in his voice. "*Any* non-zombie group developing them first would be bad. *Saberton* developing them first would be disastrous." He shook his head. "A brains alternative is the holy grail for zombies—a salvation, the freedom to choose not to eat ... people," he continued. "In the hands of those who hold no love for our kind, it would be a means of control and manipulation." He exhaled, ran a hand over his hair. "Saberton could use that to their advantage against us, and if they have a brains alternative, and we don't, we're, well, screwed."

"But wouldn't we still be able to get brains the old-fashioned way?" I asked. "I mean, the way we do now, at morgues and funeral homes?"

His eyes met mine. "Not if, or rather not *when* they go public with what we are—and *who* we are," he said. "We manage to feed our people well with the network in place now. Enough people die to meet our needs." His mouth pursed. "Yet do you think the public would allow any of us to work in the morgues and funeral homes, knowing that the brains of their loved ones would become our dinner? And that's putting aside what the majority reaction would be to the knowledge that there are monsters in their midst."

A shiver ran through me. I'd seen enough redneck prejudice to know *exactly* what the outcome would be. "Well, that sucks."

"Yes, it does," he agreed, then gave me a faint smile. "Come on," he said, heading for the door. "It's freezing in here, and the conversation topic doesn't help."

He dimmed the light before exiting with me into the warmer hallway. "Fortunately I've made some breakthroughs with respect to conducting research on non-zombie test subjects. Which is important since it doesn't risk crippling or disrupting the parasite in a true zombie."

"That's what happened to Philip!" I said, smugly pleased that I'd guessed correctly back when Charish messed him up. I even told Philip so at the time, but he was too busy trying to kill me to listen.

Dr. Nikas nodded. "Experimental food combined with parasite stimulants. A very ugly cocktail for a zombie. Long-term effects on the parasite."

"What does that mean for the two he made?" I asked. "Tim Bell and Roland. I, uh, ran into them at the Gourmet Gala." I made a sour face as I remembered that fun encounter. "Bell was screwed up and confused," I continued. "At one point he grabbed cake instead of brains, and then it got ugly."

"I don't know, Angel," he said, looking sincerely troubled.

"I've never seen a case like it, and I don't have much to go on other than Brian's report of the incident. Bizarre, erratic behavior. I would need to run tests on them."

I bit my lower lip as I thought. "You know, I had to maul the hell out of Philip to turn him," I said, remembering how horribly natural it had felt. "The whole thing took a while—maybe fifteen minutes at least, and Marcus told me that's the way it is supposed to be." Dr. Nikas gave a nod of agreement, and I went on. "But Philip turned those two in a couple of minutes with one or two deep bites. Did it have something to do with the parasite stimulant Charish gave him along with the fake brains?"

Dr. Nikas smiled. "Exactly what I concluded based on what I knew. I am quite certain their parasite is crippled." Then he exhaled, smile fading. "Impulsive creation of zombies, especially *damaged* ones, is not good for our kind. Very risky on many levels. Those two are poster children for why I don't test alternative brains on true zombies."

That reminded me of Dr. Nikas's earlier comment about breakthroughs using non-zombie test subjects. "Wait. You have regular humans eat fake brains?" I made an *eeeeew* face.

"Oh, heavens no," he said, and made just as much of an *eeeeew* face. "At least *I* would never do that. There is a way to cause a regular human to adopt various aspects of the zombie biochemistry, mimicking zombie traits for short periods without actual introduction of the parasite. Quite fascinating really. I have a small number of volunteers from our people with whom I work. Some employees, some family members of zombies."

"That's pretty damn nice of them to volunteer for a study that won't directly benefit them," I said.

"It is," he agreed. "But they all truly believe it's for everyone's benefit to find an acceptable alternate for brains."

Made sense. I could totally see myself volunteering if it was my dad who was the zombie.

"However," he added, "it's important that they be monitored closely, since it can be dangerous to mimic the parasite activity for too long. It limits our work somewhat, but I would have it no other way."

Yep, I definitely liked Dr. Nikas.

We re-entered the main lab area, and I continued to shamelessly gawk at everything. Maybe after I got my GED I could start taking some college classes in biology or something like that? I mean, why the hell not? I needed to start looking beyond the next decade or so.

"Pietro told me you were tranquilized last night, but that it was different from your previous experience of being tranqed," Dr. Nikas said. He peered at me with naked curiosity. "Would you mind sharing your experience?"

"I wouldn't mind at all," I said, then proceeded to tell him everything, including how I'd gone completely unconscious, the brains tasting awful for a while, and the injuries not healing at first.

As I spoke, Dr. Nikas's eyes took on a faraway look as if he either wasn't paying attention or was deeply processing what I'd told him. I was fairly sure it was the latter, and I remained quiet after I finished.

After a moment, his gaze came back to me. "This is new. It seems as though Saberton has found a way to efficiently tranquilize the parasite without damaging it, hence the lack of healing even with brains available, and the temporary revulsion to brains."

"That's bad, huh?" I put the pieces together. "Bad mainly because you can't do it too, and also probably because you don't have an antidote since it's new."

He gave me a sharp look, and I had the feeling he liked that I'd put it together. "Yes. Exactly. The ability to tranquilize the parasite could be extremely useful in research or even ongoing zombie care," he said, expression going grim. "And if Saberton or others have this tranq, and we don't have an antidote, well, it's extremely dangerous."

I pursed my lips. "Would it really help you to have some of my blood?"

Surprised relief shone in his eyes, and he gave me a simple grave nod. "Yes, it would. At the minimum, we are currently at a disadvantage because they have samples of your blood and I don't—and I don't know why they wanted your blood, which puts us at even more of a disadvantage." He exhaled. "Plus, if there is even a trace of the tranq remaining, it could be invaluable."

"All right then," I said. "I'll give you some. Because I really don't want those fuckers to have *any* advantage."

"Angel, I know you don't know me," Dr. Nikas said, face and voice serious, "but I give you my word that I won't use your blood against you in any way."

"I appreciate that," I said.

"Thank you for offering it." He smiled, then looked up as Brian came in.

"Angel, come with me," Brian said, expression locked in *fully-professional*, with an added hint of *grim*.

"Okay, sure thing," I replied. The grimness bothered me, and I had a feeling it didn't mean good things for Heather. I returned my attention to Dr. Nikas, even as Brian pivoted and headed back down the hallway. "Thanks for showing me around," I said. "This has been really neat."

"It was my pleasure, Angel," he replied. "I'll have one of my techs take your blood before you leave."

With a last quick nod, I turned and hurried after Brian.

I caught up with him easily, then followed him into an area that was obviously set up for medical purposes. A crash cart sat against the wall in the corridor, and a glass-doored cabinet containing drugs and various supplies stood beside a long, built-in desk. A pale, thin man with dark hair and wearing faded blue scrubs, sat at a computer workstation making notes from a series of graphs on the screen. An intricate origami dragon perched atop the monitor.

The man lifted his head as we approached. I watched as Brian met his startlingly expressive hazel eyes and gave an almost imperceptible shake of his head before continuing on. A muscle in the other man's jaw leaped, and his lips pressed together before he returned his attention to the computer, typing with greater than necessary force.

"Brian? That guy didn't look very happy," I said as soon as we were further down the hall. "What's going on?"

"I can't say that I've ever seen Jacques look happy, but he has reason today." He opened a door, stepped into a small wood-paneled office, and gestured me in. A compact computer sat on a side countertop with a chair tucked under it. A second chair at the end of the counter gave me the impression that this was a consultation room of some sort. I entered, and he closed the door behind me, still maintaining the stoic and professional air, though I thought I noted a few more cracks in the surface.

Then I saw the hole in the wall with fresh blood on splinters of wood. My gaze went to Brian's hands, and I spied flecks of red on his right cuff. No sign of damage to his hand now, but there were two empty brain packets on the desk. Brian didn't seem at all the type to have wall-punching as part of his normal response to dealing with captives. This situation with Heather really seemed to be messing with him.

"I guess it's not looking so good for her," I said.

Leaning back against the desk, he shook his head.

"No," he said. "She's lying. What info she's given us checks out, but she's sticking to the story that she's just a photographer with the Saberton PR department." Brian's expression went even more grim, though I hadn't thought it was possible. "That matches what's in their official employment records."

"So what's the problem?" I tugged a hand through my hair. If it checked out, why was her being Saberton PR a bad thing? "She was sure as hell taking pictures of me." Then again, for a photographer, she handled herself pretty damn well in the highway fight. "I don't understand. Who do you think she is?"

Brian exhaled forcefully. "All I know for certain right now is that she's not just a PR staffer and she's not coming clean about it." Frustration colored his voice. "I had a talk with her while you were with Dr. Nikas. Played her a bit and found out she knows a little too much about the late Richard Saber." He folded his arms over his chest. "You see, he was a recluse in his last decade. However, Heather let slip about an eye patch the man wore after a bout of cancer. That's something no lower echelon employee would know, and *I* only know of it because of a single photo one of our operatives managed to get of him." He flexed his right hand, mouth tightening. "Damn it, Angel, it's not definitive, but when I put it together with the info she's dribbled and what I smell from her, it's pretty damning."

I could see his point, and my heart sank. "So this whole thing was a ploy to infiltrate Pietro's operation?"

"That's what it's looking like," he said. "She kept her cool after her comment on Saber, but I smelled the fear on her. She knew she'd screwed up."

I had no doubt he'd been tanked on brains when he talked to her, which means he'd be able to smell a flea fart. "What did she say to cover herself?"

Brian shook his head. "She didn't. I walked out to, uh,

do some remodeling," he said with a glance at the hole in the wall, "then went to find you. No more talking for now. I'll let her sweat."

I frowned, remembering my conversation with Heather in the diner parking lot. "It doesn't make sense," I insisted, though I knew that it was more that I didn't want to believe it. "Can I talk to her?"

"I'm sorry. The situation has changed, Angel," he said, voice tight. Frustration tightened the skin around his eyes. He didn't want to believe it any more than I did, but what the hell else was he supposed to think?

"Yeah, I know, but—" I paused, took a deep breath. "She saved my life. And she didn't have to. I'd already taken out the two humans, and she could've waited for the zombie to blow my head off before taking him out. She'd have been home free then. But she didn't." I scowled. "And on a totally personal level, if she's bullshitting us, I'd kinda like to confront her, because I killed a guy for her." I wasn't a wimp when it came to fighting. I'd had to do plenty to survive. But killing took it to another level. "I'm not real happy about that. I just want to know *why*."

"It's not an *if* she's bullshitting," Brian stated. "She *is* and she called you into it." He shook his head. "She's a pro, Angel. I don't know how she did it, but she managed to get personal information from Dr. Nikas, Jacques, Reg—Dr. Nikas's other tech—and me. Stuff we don't talk about, *ever*. But each one of us spilled it in conversation and didn't—" He stopped, exhaled. "Add that to what's stacked in the infiltration corner, and I'm not sending in a visitor right now."

"Brian, there has to be more to it!" I said, not at all willing to leave it like this, despite the evidence against her. "You didn't see her out there." I met his eyes. "Please. Maybe I can get through to her."

His eyes narrowed. "What do you mean by not seeing her out there?"

I hesitated, trying to think how to put it. "It's tough to explain. We were a team. I mean, it wasn't just me helping her out of a fix," I said with a shake of my head. "Brian, I just can't believe she's a bad person. I saw her after she killed the zombie. She looked really torn up about it."

He seemed to be willing to let me keep talking, so I took that as a sign I might be getting somewhere. I tilted my head. "Look, what do you have to lose by letting me in to see her? It's not as if she can ferret out any super secret info from me." I gave him a small smile. "We all know I don't know shit."

He regarded me for a long, silent moment. I braced myself to be all kinds of stubborn when he said No, but when he finally spoke he wore a hint of a smile. "I suppose I have nothing to lose and maybe everything to gain."

"Exactly!" I said brightly as relief flooded in. "Thanks, Brian."

"She's a con artist, and a good one," he said. "I hate to see you getting— " He stopped, visibly rephrased. "I hate to see you waste your time."

I had a feeling he was going to say something about getting more attached to her. "It's my time to waste," I said, then grimaced at the magnitude of the whole thing. This whole deal sucked. "She knows what's at stake, right?"

"I have no doubt." A muscle in his jaw twitched. He couldn't hide his anger at Heather for putting him in a position to have to *deal* with her. "She's playing a big game. If her intention was to infiltrate, or some other scheme, she knows the consequences."

He likes Heather, I realized with a bit of surprise, though at the same time I could totally see it. She was tough and capable and pretty damn likeable. He didn't want to lock her up and do ugly things to extract info. And it was clear he didn't want to kill her.

But I also knew that he wouldn't let that get in the way of whatever he had to do to ensure the security of Pietro's organization.

Brian leveled his impassive, professional gaze on me. "You budge her, Angel, and I'll kiss you."

I gave a surprised bark of laughter. "I'm gonna hold you to that, you know."

"I'm not putting on the ChapStick just yet," he said as he pushed off the desk, "but I hope it comes down to that." He hesitated, then continued with a tightness in his voice that sounded a lot like worry. "Angel, if she doesn't open up, it won't be pretty."

I winced, sighed. "Yeah, I kinda gathered that." And I was the one who'd talked her into coming over to our side. *Or had I?* Anger flashed. If she really was trying to infiltrate, I'd been a convenient patsy. One who opened the damn door and invited her in. That stirred more questions, but there was only one person who could answer them. Whether guilty as all sin or hiding some other reason for her behavior, I wanted to know. I'd killed for it.

For Brian's sake as well as to bolster my fading conviction in her innocence, I said, "Maybe it will all work out."

He gave a slow nod. "See what you can do." He paused. "Please," he added, almost like a prayer.

"Gotcha," I said and flashed him a tight smile. "Lemme at her."

Chapter 15

Brian walked me around the corner and down a hallway. "Remember, she's good at what she does," he told me. "She's, ah, easy to open up to."

"Yeah, I've noticed that," I remarked as he stopped before a windowless door.

"Here's her room," he said. He punched a key code into the obviously locked door. "I'll be monitoring."

I took a deep breath, then entered and closed the door behind me. Heather sat propped in a hospital bed with a rolling table in front of her, pencil in hand, drawing what looked like an intricate swirling abstract. Her left arm sported a bandage and sling to go along with her splint, and traces of bruising showed on her face. A pile of drawings lay on the table beside her hand along with more blank white paper. A dozen or so origami animals of various types clustered on a built-in counter to my right. A doorway led into a small bathroom. No frills and nothing dangerous. Pretty much a secure hospital room.

"Hey, chick," I said with a bright smile. "You look better than the last time I saw you."

Heather set the pencil down and hurriedly shoved her drawing under the others, then stacked the rest of the blank paper on top of them. I let my gaze linger on the drawings and origami. She'd been busy. Or incredibly bored.

She pushed up from the pillows, wincing faintly as if the movement tweaked an existing headache. "Did I look *that* bad?" she asked, still managing a broad smile for me. "I thought it had a street savvy flair about it."

"Right, more like road kill flair," I said with a snort. "Though I don't have much room to talk."

"Nope you had me beat, I think." She let out a low chuckle. "The hanging jaw, the bullet holes. I was definitely outclassed."

"I've had too much practice," I said as I leaned up against the counter next to the origami. "You've been busy." I picked up a little unicorn and peered at the little twisted horn.

She glanced at the animals, then the pile of papers beside her. "Yeah. Otherwise, I'd go stir crazy,"

I set the unicorn next to a paper praying mantis, resisted the urge to play with them and make it look as if the mantis was eating the unicorn. "This is really cool," I said. "About all I can do is an origami baseball."

She smiled, obviously well aware that an origami baseball was nothing more than a wadded up piece of paper. "Paper and pencil were all I could wheedle out of Jacques. And I think I'm still in deep debt for the sharpener."

"You must have done the dragon that's sitting on his computer then, right?" I asked.

Her smile widened with a touched of pleased surprise. "It's on his computer?"

"Perched right on his monitor," I replied.

"Nice," she said, for a brief instant looking relaxed and happy. "Thanks for telling me that."

I lifted my chin toward the pile of papers by her hand, "Whatcha drawing?" She didn't seem to be shy about the origami, so why be that way with the drawings?

She laid her hand on top of the stack of papers. "Oh, just doodles to kill time, that's all."

I sat at the foot of the bed, pulled my legs underneath me. What little I'd seen sure wasn't a simple *doodle*. The girl had some talent. "So, what's gonna happen to you next?" I asked, still keeping my voice light. "How soon you getting out of here?"

Heather shook her head. "No idea. Dr. Nikas says he's keeping me for observation." She shrugged. "Other than this," she gestured to her left arm with the broken fingers and gunshot wound, "I feel okay. A little headachy, that's all."

"Right. I mean after that," I said, watching her carefully. "You gonna come work for Pietro? Is that what you want?"

A whisper of what looked like anxiety tightened the skin around her eyes, but then she gave me a bright smile and it was gone. "Oh, yeah. That would be awesome."

"I mean, that's your whole goal, right?" I continued, all of the lightness leaving my voice. "All of this bullshit. That's what this was all about, right? Get in as one of us?" I cocked my head as her smile faded. "Brian knows you're not just a photographer."

She sank back into the pillows, expression bleak, but not showing surprise. "Damn."

"Brian said I could come in and talk to you," I said. "Maybe get the whole story. He'll probably want to talk to you after I'm done here." My eyes dropped to her broken fingers. "He said Hi to you once already. I don't think you'd like a whole conversation."

Her throat bobbed as she swallowed. "Not that kind of conversation."

"Then talk to me instead," I urged. Damn it. I liked

her, and I really wanted to believe she was for real, but I sure had a bad vibe going on. "What's going on? Was this whole thing a setup so that you could infiltrate?"

She looked away, mouth tightening. "I guess that's what it looks like."

My heart sank. Had I really been duped so thoroughly? "That . . . that's incredibly fucked up," I said, voice shaking a little from the disappointment. "You *used* me?" I shook my head, still trying to make sense of it all. "Were those really Saberton men who were after you? Did you actually kill your own people?"

She gave a tight nod. "They were Saberton."

I stared at her for several seconds before finding my voice. "Wow, that's cold," I managed. "All to get in with us? Did they know? Did they know you were trying to infiltrate?"

Something flashed through her eyes—pain or anger, I couldn't be sure. But when she looked back to me, her expression was hard. "Those guys?" She shook her head. "No. They had orders to capture me. Only way to make it look real." Her mouth twisted. "Problem was, they called in Eggerton, the zombie. He wasn't supposed to be there, and I almost got killed."

I stood, hands clenched. "Only way to make it look real," I echoed. "And so you set me up to *kill* a guy and fuck up another." I took a ragged breath, stomach churning. "I *killed* someone because of you, you heartless bitch!"

"Yeah, and it would've worked if I hadn't gotten hurt," she replied, voice flat and cold. Something flickered briefly in her eyes to disturb the icy façade, but she quickly controlled it before continuing. "I'd have met with Brian under different circumstances, and he'd never have known he was being played. He thought I was," she made air quotes, "'paparazzi' after our first encounter, remember?"

Anger coiled tight in my chest, yet I couldn't ignore the insistent doubts. Parts of her story didn't make complete sense. "How did you know I'd come out and confront you at the diner?"

She twitched a shoulder up in a shrug. "You wanted to come after me before, in front of that dead girl's house. I figured if I walked into the diner you'd take the bait."

Frowning, I cast my memory back over that night. Heather had been wearing a hoodie, and she sure as hell hadn't looked like someone who wanted to be seen or recognized. "Really?" I asked. "You were gonna stroll in and somehow make me believe you were on the run?" My frown deepened as more holes the size of Texas appeared in her version. "And how'd you know I had Brian's number? And that I would even call him?"

Her cool composure cracked, and a bizarre flash of primal fear lit her eyes. She tugged a hand through her hair, wound a lock around one finger.

"That one guy shot you." I was talking as much to help me figure it out as to confront her. "Why would he do that if he was just trying to bring you back?" More and more holes kept appearing in this whole "infiltration" story. I scowled, shook my head. "And godalmighty, if they had to pick someone to infiltrate, surely it would be someone with a better plan."

She viciously wound the lock of hair around her finger, over and over. "My plans haven't worked out so great lately," she said. To my shock she seemed close to tears. It didn't look right on her somehow.

I stared at the hair twisting as mental clues shifted and fell into something recognizable. I remembered the last time I saw someone twist hair like that. Nicole Saber at the Gourmet Gala. Now I saw the same tilt of the eyes, the blond hair, the profile. *And she knew about the reclusive Richard Saber.*

"Oh my god," I breathed. "That's it. You're related to Nicole Saber somehow, aren't you."

Her posture shifted subtly, a feral look coming to her eyes. Before I could blink she vaulted from the bed, knocking me aside as she dove for the door.

Stumbling back, I cursed my not-very tanked state as I sprawled against the tray table, scattering origami animals. I expected her to tug vainly at the door handle, but to my shock she yanked it open.

What the hell? I scrambled up and out the door, made a wild snatch at the sleeve of her hospital gown, barely succeeding in getting enough of a hold to slow her as she tried to bolt down the hallway.

Behind me I heard a door burst open and running footsteps—Brian, no doubt. Heather spun and struck a hard punch at my forearm, loosening my grip enough for her to twist free.

"Would you chill?" I yelled, then jumped on her in a clumsy tackle before she could turn and run. She outweighed me by thirty pounds or so, and topped me by at least half a foot, she went down under my clinging assault. Didn't stop her from fighting, though. She clocked me in the side of the head with her good fist, and managed to knee me in the ribs hard enough to knock the wind out of me.

"Stop!" I wheezed. "You stubborn bitch!"

My eloquent plea had no effect, but Brian's arrival did. In about five seconds he had her face down, a knee between her shoulder blades, and was efficiently zip-tying her wrists behind her back.

Breathing hard, Heather continued to fight, though there was no budging Brian. Blood seeped through the bandage over the gunshot wound in her bicep, likely reopened by her struggles.

Brian finished securing the zip-ties. "Jacques!" he called, then looked up at me. "Let's get her back on the bed."

I helped him get Heather up to her feet. I expected her to go limp, but she continued to try and twist away, even though she had to know there was no possible way she was breaking free from two zombies, one of whom was no doubt tanked to the gills considering how quickly he made it down the length of the hall.

"Jesus Christ," I said to Heather, breathing a bit hard myself. "It's true, isn't it? What are you, her daughter or something?"

I might as well have been asking the wall. She kept her jaw clenched tight as we got her back into the room and onto the bed. Jacques arrived at a run, and Brian jerked his gaze to him. "Restraints."

I stepped back as the two men efficiently removed the zip-ties and secured her wrists and ankles to the bed with medical restraints. Heather pulled futilely at them, a look of wide-eyed panic on her face. "No. Please."

"What will you do now?" I asked Brian, worry rising.

"Make a phone call," he replied in a tight voice.

Jacques looked from the still-struggling Heather to Brian. "Sedative?"

"Wait! No, wait!" I said. "Don't sedate her yet and don't call yet." In reply, Brian stood back and folded his arms, face impassive as he regarded me.

Taking that as a temporary victory, I swung my attention to Heather. "It's out now. For fuck's sake, defend yourself! Are you related to Nicole Saber? Is that what this is all about?"

She gave one more useless tug on the restraints, then dropped her head back to the pillow. "Yes," she replied, voice breaking. "I was born Julia Saber. Nicole Saber is my mother."

I attempted to put it all together as Jacques unobtrusively replaced the bandage on the sluggishly bleeding wound on her arm, spread a blanket over her, and then quietly slipped from the room.

"You really were leaving town, weren't you?" I finally asked her. "Leaving Saberton."

A shiver went through her as she nodded, not meeting anyone's eyes.

"Oh, man," I breathed. "And so you figured if Pietro and Brian knew, they'd pretty much get everything you knew out of you, any way they could." Then I frowned. "But they were planning to do that anyway since you were holding back, and you had to know that. What gives?"

"Better than risking getting ransomed back," Heather said, voice breaking. She swung her gaze to Brian. "Please. Don't. Don't let them have me back."

An odd scent filled the air, thick and cloying, and it took me a few seconds to realize what it was. *Her fear. I can smell her fear. Oh my god.* My gaze fell on the pile of drawings. She hadn't wanted me to look too closely at them.

Narrowing my eyes, I scooped the pile up, pulled the bottom drawing out and peered at it. At first all I saw were the mesmerizing spirals. Then I took a closer look at the unfinished corner, fought to make sense of it. Tiny letters. I rotated the drawing and with much squinting made out "sc new orleans waterfront" followed by the word "key" and a series of numbers. *The key code for a Saberton Corporation building?* In the finished sections of the drawing, more hidden lettering, cleverly disguised as part of the picture.

"I don't understand," I said, dragging my eyes back to hers.

Sighing, she gave a half-hearted pull at the restraints. "That was for after I was dead . . . or escaped. It's all there. On the drawings." Her breath shuddered. "I wanted to help, no matter what happened to me."

My amazement increased as I flipped through the pages. In each of the dozen or so finished drawings, I picked out tiny lettering worked into the intricate and beautiful abstract designs, or curving around the edges of the figures. Without a magnifying glass, I couldn't get much from them other than the realization that she'd meticulously offered a shitload of information. More details. More confidential and proprietary information that I had no doubt would be damn useful to Pietro and his organization.

I looked over at Brian, passed the drawings to him. Expression grim, he took them while I returned my attention to Heather. "What would happen if you got ransomed back?"

"Best case scenario is they'd kill me," she said. The cloying scent of fear thickened. "Worst is they'd use me."

Brian tucked the drawings under his arm and exited the room, expression not shifting at all from *grim.*

I had a feeling I knew, but I had to ask it anyway. "Use you? How?"

"They need test subjects."

Zombie research. Yeah, I bet they did. "I'll tell you right now I won't let that happen," I assured her.

Heather's gaze went to the sprinkler above her, then dropped back to me. "No matter what it takes?" she asked, voice quiet but intense. "I can't go back there."

I knew exactly what she was asking me. I flicked my own glance at the sprinkler, which I realized probably housed a camera or something. "Whatever it takes," I said. Somehow. Shit. I'd worked in the morgue for long enough to know the human weak spots, and I was pretty sure I knew how to kill someone quickly. But damn, could I kill someone I actually *liked?* And yes, I did like her, despite everything.

I looked back to her. "Why did you leave?"

"It's a bit of a long story," she sighed.

"I'm not going anywhere."

She tried to lift a hand, but was brought up short by

the restraints. A mixture of annoyance and resignation passed over her face before she began to speak again. "Late last Friday my zombie friend Garrett got called in for a check up, but never came back." She exhaled. "I tend to not let things like that rest, and went looking for him early the next morning. I knew where he'd gone, so I figured that was the best place to start and got in without tripping the alarm, no problem."

"At first, I thought it was exactly what I was expecting—a medical station—but there was a gas chromatograph-mass spectrometer, microscope, fume hood, and other equipment that made me think more of some sort of lab," Heather explained. "I'd only been in a minute when I heard someone unlocking the door, and I ducked into a side room." She hesitated and a look of revulsion mixed with anger came over her. "The room wasn't empty. Garrett was there, strapped to an exam table, alive ... and vivisected, with all sorts of monitors and tubes connected to him. He had duct tape over his mouth, and ..." She swallowed. "And the look in his eyes. Oh my god."

Fury welled within me, but I stayed silent.

"The door opened, and I barely had time to press myself against the far side of a cabinet and pray whoever it was wouldn't look my way," she said. "A man came in, took some blood and direct organ samples, messed with the monitors, all the while talking shit to Garrett about how he'd be there a long time, so he better get used to it. Said he'd be back in a while for more samples, then headed out."

"Jesus," I breathed.

"The whole thing set off something I'd never felt before," she said with a shake of her head. "Beyond anger. It was still and focused and kind of scary. I fed Garrett brains until he, uh, could get himself back together and wouldn't kill me for my own, unhooked and unstrapped him, then went and found the guy who'd been cutting on him." She paused, mouth tightening. "By that time, I'd recognized him as Brent from research and development. But it didn't matter that I knew him." A haunted look came over her face. "I had every intention of killing him."

"Wait. Brent Stewart!" I exclaimed. The movie set victim. "I *knew* there was more to that."

She swallowed, nodded. "I followed him, looking for a place where I could make it seem like an accident. Once he got onto the school grounds and behind the trailers, I knew it wouldn't get much better. I hit him hard in the head with a two by four, then pulled the scaffold pipe down to mask the blow."

"You did a good job," I told her. "It's still classified as an accident."

She lifted her eyes to mine. "I know. Pretty coldblooded."

I shrugged. I sure as hell couldn't judge her. I'd have probably done the same damn thing if some asshole was torturing a friend. "What happened to Garrett?" I asked.

"He headed off with a bag of brain slices and a plan to go into hiding big time. Haven't seen him since." Sick anger flashed over her face. "Garrett worked hard as a driver. I know he didn't have any idea what he was getting into when he signed on with Saberton. They promised him a regular supply of brains. Didn't tell him what else they intended."

My gut was tight with horror over the whole scenario, but I simply nodded.

"So I'd gotten an up close and personal look at what Saberton was doing with zombies, and I'd killed one of the research guys," Heather continued, voice strained, "but they hadn't figured out it was me. I wasn't ready to jump ship yet, but I wanted to know more about my options. I went back to check out some Saberton confidentials on Mr. Ivanov's organization. I got into the security feeds without any problems," she said as if it was nothing. "But what I saw . . ." Her face paled.

"What was it?" I prompted.

Her eyes went to me. "The first video I pulled of any significance was of you, Angel," she said to my utter surprise. "I saw everything Kristi Charish's team did to you. Locking you in a cage, searching you." She swallowed. "And what they made you do to Philip and Aaron."

Numb, cold horror set in. *Videos of all that are out where people can see them.*

But Heather was still talking. "And there were more videos: with Philip, when he bit Tim Bell and Roland Westfeld, and with some other zombies later." Tears came to her eyes. "With my mother and brother right there. Condoning all of it."

I considered everything she'd told me. "What exactly did you *do* for Saberton?"

Heather twisted her head to wipe her eyes on her shoulder. "On the surface, I worked in the PR department and was a photographer for them," she said. "In reality, I did industrial espionage. And I was good at it." She said it as a statement of fact, no ego attached. "My grandfather had done espionage-type work for the military. He figured out early on that I *loved* it, so he taught me, doted on me, groomed me almost my whole life." An odd sadness touched her eyes. "My mother didn't seem to have any problem with it, encouraged it even. So at an early age, Nicole Saber's daughter dropped out of memory, presumed off at boarding school, and I got to do what I loved. Pretty lucky, huh?"

I made a noncommittal grunt. In light of recent developments, I didn't think she was feeling all that lucky.

"No one other than my grandfather, mother, brother, and a few insiders knew me as anything other than Heather Lucas, a nobody corporate photographer. And

I guess it was all just a big game for me until . . . Kang. And then Garrett. And the vids." Tears glimmered in her eyes again. "But it's not a game."

"No," I said quietly. "It really isn't."

She sighed, expression haunted. "Yeah, can't just call a do over. And now I know how dirty I am. Life really sucks sometimes."

I gave a soft snort. "I know 'suck.' Trust me."

"If I hadn't freaked the hell out when you IDed me as a Saber, I had the big plan of escaping tonight. I already had the door disabled. Not that I wanted to go, but I had to, y'know?" Heather took a deeper breath, glanced up at the sprinkler. "I swear, in those drawings I gave you everything I had that's of use."

I had no doubt Brian was making a *lot* of phone calls right now. "What happened after Brian caught you taking pics?"

Heather made a pained face. "I already knew I wanted out. No doubt about it. But getting out from under Saberton would take some time and planning. At the hospital after Brian," she lifted her splinted hand slightly, "I had the fantasy that I could just switch sides." She let out a low snort. "Like anything is that simple when dealing with this kind of thing. So I let that go and headed back to my hotel room to come up with an exit strategy." She grimaced.

I gave her a *Keep Going* nod.

"My brother was there," she said after a moment. "Andrew Saber. And everything went downhill after that."

I remembered him from the Gala. Tall, Blond, and Serious. "He knew?"

Her grimace deepened. "He knew I'd killed Brent Stewart. Put pressure on me about getting myself in line with the company philosophy. Threatened to let our mother know I'd killed the guy if I didn't." She let out a shuddering breath. "Mother can be . . . vicious, and I know my brother really well. I'd never be anything but his bitch for life if I agreed. I should have let it go. Should have agreed to anything just to get out of there, but I was exhausted, on edge and already doubting so much." A look of anguish came over her features.

"Did you kill him too?" I asked uncertainly.

"No!" she replied, eyes widening in shock. She shook her head in a firm motion. "No. God no. But I didn't let it go when I should have. I told him I was through with all of the Saberton crap." She winced. "Not a good thing to say to the next CEO. We argued and it turned ugly. Physical. He's stronger, but I'm quicker and I've had more training. I got in a lucky punch that laid him out, and left him hog-tied with the bed sheet." She looked at me. "That's when I knew it was over. They'd never trust me again. And so I had no choice but to run. Right then, with no plans or arrangements made."

"Okay. Wow." I fell silent for a moment while I processed it all. "I'm gonna help you any way I can," I finally said.

She gave me a weak smile. "You already did. The rest is gravy."

"I mean it," I said, frowning. "I'm real good at doing stupid shit. And I'm gonna bring it hard if Brian doesn't come in here with a goddamn welcome home fruit basket."

Her brow creased in worry. "Angel, it's okay. There won't be any welcome home fruit basket and it's okay. I don't want you getting yourself messed up over this. Really."

"No, it's not okay," I stated firmly. "And that's all there is to it."

"Damn it." She shifted in the restraints, tried unsuccessfully to sit up. "Don't. Please don't do anything stupid. And you know it would be. I mean, you have no idea how cool it is you have my back, but it would still end the same."

I gave a snort of amusement, smiled. "You really don't know me very well, do you?"

"Oh, man." She winced. "I'm afraid I do."

"I won't let them do bad shit to you," I said with a shake of my head. "I *can't*."

The door opened, and Brian entered with one of the drawings in his hand, face in *unreadable* mode.

Heather's gaze went to the drawing, and tears welled up in her eyes. "Yeah, no fruit basket."

"What's going on?" I demanded. "Brian?"

"She's the one who turned us over to Saberton four years ago," he said, voice even but carrying a dark undertone that sent a chill down my back. "It's why they know about zombies. Why they know so *much* about zombies."

My heart dropped into my stomach. "How?"

Brian opened his mouth to speak, but Heather beat him to it.

"Got into one of Mr. Ivanov's safes," she said. "I copied a bunch of research material. I didn't realize what it was until later." She grimaced. "After that I spent almost a year gathering more information on zombies. That's how I ended up with John Kang."

"Damn," I breathed, but then I shook my head. Lifting my chin, I looked back to Brian. "You can't lay all that at her feet. Charish was ready to sell us out to the highest bidder. It would've happened at some point."

Brian seemed unmoved. "Angel, I need to speak with Heather alone now."

"Yeah," I said tightly. "That's not gonna happen."

"It has to happen," he stated. "I give you my word that nothing will happen to Heather in that time."

I hesitated, but the memory of the hole in the office wall rose. He wouldn't have punched a wall in frustration if he was totally okay with treating her like the enemy.

"Okay," I said. "I'm trusting you." And with that I gave Heather's hand a squeeze and stepped out.

* * *

I obediently went off with the taciturn Jacques and allowed him to draw vials and vials of blood, after which I downed a fresh, warm puff pastry stuffed with brains and a to-die-for smoothie that Jacques called Dr. Nikas's Special Blend. It sure beat the hell out of juice and cookies. Yet then I had to wait—very impatiently—for what was close to half an hour before Brian returned. Didn't help that all I had to read was a decade-old issue of *Field & Stream*. Scriously, what the hell? Didn't zombies keep up their magazine subscriptions?

When Brian came to get me, his face was still utterly unreadable. I stood and set the magazine down, crossed my arms defiantly over my chest, and looked up at him with as much authority as a short and skinny high school dropout zombie could muster.

"I'm not much of a fighter, Brian," I warned him in a low voice, "but I'm mean, and I don't quit. So I sure as hell hope you have something good to tell me."

His expression turned grim, and dread curled into a tight knot in my gut as he approached.

"Goddammit, Brian," I said, unable to keep my voice from shaking in anger and stress. "Have you already done something awful to her?"

I caught a faint whiff of cherry, and then before I could react, the stoic Brian Archer took hold of my shoulders and planted a big brotherly Cherry ChapStick laden smooch right on my lips. He'd smeared it on extra thick too, the bastard.

"No." He pulled back, faint smile playing about his mouth.

A laugh of delirious relief burst out of me, even as I wiped the thick smudge of lip balm off my mouth with the back of my hand. "Oh my god, you must've used half a stick. So everything's okay? She's gonna be okay?"

He gave my shoulders a squeeze before dropping his hands back to his sides. "We're taking her in."

"As in . . . not fucking her up? And not ransoming her back?" I asked, still a bit wary. "You'll let her defect—or whatever it's called in the corporate world?"

"More than that," he said with a slight shake of his head. "Everything checked out. Andrew Saber was treated in private for a lacerated cheek on the night in question. She answered all—*all*—of my other questions correctly, even the personal and the hard ones." He took a deep breath, smiled. "And, well, she smells right. The fear is gone. She can't fake that. So, unless she does something incredibly stupid, she's one of us."

"Good," I said with a grin of relief. "I really didn't want to get ugly with y'all."

Brian chuckled. "Trust me, Angel. None of us want that."

Chapter 16

To my relief, my dad's truck wasn't in the driveway when Brian dropped me off. He waited politely until I unlocked my front door and gave him a wave before he pulled away and drove off.

As soon as I was inside, I pulled my phone out of my purse and called Marcus, excitement about the lab visit and relief about Heather's fate still shimmering through me.

"Hey, you," he answered, a smile in his voice.

"Oh my god, Marcus!" I said as I plopped onto the couch. "I got to see Kang's head! It was so . . . *eeew!*" I laughed.

"Really? That's . . ." He paused. "Wait. How did you see Kang's head?"

"I called Pietro this morning to ask him what was going on with the heads, and he said I could go see for myself, so he sent Brian to pick me up and so I went! So cool!"

"Brian picked you up, huh?" There was a strange catch in his voice, but I was too excited to want to stop and figure out why.

"Yeah, and *damn*, I've never ridden in an Escalade before," I continued to babble. "Sweet ride!"

"I've never been in Brian's Escalade," he said. "I imagine it is." He paused. "And he took you to the lab?"

"Sure did. Way out in the middle of bumfuck nowhere." I laughed. "I couldn't find it again if my life depended on it."

"I have no idea where it is either," Marcus said. "So, it was interesting?"

"It really was," I said. "I mean, I didn't understand half of what Dr. Nikas was saying, but he was really awesome and didn't talk down to me at all." I grinned. "Maybe after I get my GED I can go take some college classes. I mean I really love the Biology stuff."

"That's not a bad idea at all."

"And maybe I can even do some work with Dr. Nikas, help out at the lab or something. Marcus, he was sooo nice."

"Um, yeah. Sure," he said. "That would be great." Except that it didn't sound like he thought it would be great at all.

My smile slipped a bit. "Marcus? Is something wrong?"

He was silent for a few seconds—long enough for me to wonder if he had horrible news to share and was working up the courage to tell me—then said, "Angel, you can't *do* that."

"Do what?" I asked, baffled.

"You can't call up Pietro with stuff like that," he said to my utter shock. "I'm only telling you for your own good," he continued while I listened in numb silence. "Pietro said he'd let you know about the heads, and he would have. Annoying him isn't a good idea. And, well, taking up Dr. Nikas's time for nothing . . . hell, I've never even *been* to the lab."

Every speck of elation fled, and now I simply felt cold

and a little sick. Had I misread everything about my conversation with Pietro and my talk with Dr. Nikas?

"I . . . but Pietro didn't sound annoyed, Marcus," I managed. "And he's the one who suggested I come see the heads. I didn't ask for that."

"Look, babe, you could have called me first, talked about it," he said in a conciliatory tone. "Then I could have helped you with how to approach, or not approach it. I've known him a lot longer than you have."

The cold feeling tightened into a knot in my gut. "Oh. I see," I replied stiffly. "I obviously fucked it up even though Pietro seemed perfectly happy to talk to me and was the one to suggest that I come see the lab. But, y'know, this is *me*. So, yeah. I should check with you before I make a phone call." I sucked in a sharp breath. "Oh, wait, honey, I need to go take a shit. Should I wipe my ass or not? One ply or two ply? I know I desperately need your advice and guidance."

"Damn it, Angel!" he retorted, raising his voice slightly. "You're blowing this all out of proportion. We're talking about my uncle, not your normal everyday life crap."

"And you're the one telling me I need to check with you before making a goddamn phone call," I said, raising my voice right back at him. "I mean, Jesus Christ, Marcus. You're jumping my ass for fucking something up that wasn't fucked up!" At least I hoped it wasn't fucked up. A sharp barb of worry went through me. "Did Pietro say something to you? Is that what this is all about?"

He hesitated. "No," he finally said, exhaling. "I haven't talked to him since I called him last night after your attack."

"Uh huh. So once again this is you not trusting me to be able to handle myself." My jaw tightened. "Marcus, this is bullshit."

"You always jump to that conclusion, Angel!" he said,

frustration and annoyance thick in his voice. "I'm giving you advice—damn good advice—on *one* thing I know a helluva lot more about than you do and suddenly I'm the bad guy. *That's* bullshit."

"I didn't do anything wrong!" I insisted, fighting back tears. "He wasn't annoyed or mad or anything, and he wouldn't have invited me to the lab if I was wasting his time, would he?" I took a deep breath as the old buried anger returned. "And, goddammit, even if I did *annoy* him it's the least he could put up with after everything I went through."

He fell quiet. "All right, Angel," he said after a moment. "What's done is done. You've seen the heads and satisfied that curiosity, so we can just move on from here. I can't imagine that you'd have anything else to call him about, so it really is a moot point now."

I squeezed my eyes shut. "Marcus, I've been really nice and respectful to your uncle, even after everything that happened." I tried to keep my voice even and calm, but it still shook a bit despite my best efforts. "Pietro told me I could call him anytime I needed something, and y'know what? If I have another reason to call him, I fucking will." My hand tightened on the phone. "I was locked in an *animal cage* because of him. Strip searched by McKinney while four men stood and watched. So if I want to call him for the goddamn time and weather, I fucking will, and I'm not gonna worry about annoying him."

I heard him exhale. "I know," he said. "You had a horrible experience, and a lot of it was Uncle Pietro's fault. It's still crazy to push it. But never mind, you don't want my opinion, and this isn't getting us anywhere."

I was crying now. How could he still not understand? "No, it's not getting us anywhere. And you don't want to hear how bad it was. So forget it. I'll talk to you later."

I hung up before he could say anything else then buried my face in the couch pillow and gave in to a sob fest. For the first time I realized that I really didn't have anyone I could talk to about what happened to me. I sure as hell couldn't tell any non-zombie. Marcus had held me and listened to the whole story after my escape, but after that one time it was clear the subject upset him, and so I'd stopped saying anything about it.

My phone rang. It was Marcus, but I wasn't ready to talk to him yet. After a moment the ringing stopped and it dinged with the missed call alert. But he didn't leave a voicemail, and I didn't call him back.

Chapter 17

A sound woke me, a dull thumping, but without any particular rhythm or cadence. Early morning light filtered through the blinds, and I sat up, blinking away the remnants of uneasy sleep. The thumping sound repeated, and I looked down at the floor.

Water. Water everywhere. For a few precious seconds I thought that a water pipe had busted in the house. When I was about ten the pipe leading to the water heater had finally rotted through, and the entire back of the house ended up with an inch of water until my dad could shut it off.

But this was way more than an inch. At least a half foot of water covered the floor, lifting anything that could float. A shoebox rocked on its surface, bumping repeatedly into the dresser with a hollow thud.

Fear slashed through me as the implications sunk in. I jumped up out of bed and splashed through the ankle-deep water, then ran down the hall. "Dad! DAD!" *Oh, please don't let him be sleeping off a bender,* I silently prayed. He'd be damn near impossible to wake up.

"Dad!" I yelled. I shoved his door open, sending a wave rolling across the floor.

He jerked, blinked muzzily at me. "Wha . . . ?"

"Wake up!" I slogged to the bed, grabbed his arm. "The house is flooding!" The water was halfway up my shin now.

He came fully awake in an instant, jerked upright. "Shit!"

"It's rising fast," I told him, still tugging at him. "Something must've happened to the spillway."

"Hold on," he said. "Keep your head together now. Go grab anything you can't stand to lose."

"That would be you," I snarled.

He met my eyes, gaze clear and focused. Not sleeping off a bender at all, I realized. "I'm good, Angelkins." He stood and began to paw through his nightstand. "Gimme a minute. I gotta get some stuff."

I wanted to scream at him that we needed to go *now*, but I realized there was some stuff I needed to get, too. I splashed back to my bedroom, water up to my knees and halfway up the side of the mini-fridge in my room. Willing my hands not to shake, I spun the lock and put the combination in. Dad had been cool the past few months, but after the one horrible experience of him destroying my stash, I'd kept a lock on the fridge, just in case. But, damn, I hated it now.

On the second try I got the damn thing open, grabbed the five bottles of brain smoothie and tossed them onto the bed. Still at least a foot to go before that was underwater. My cargo pants were in the top drawer of my dresser, thankfully. Trying to pull on wet pants would've been a nightmare, and I didn't really want to try and escape the flood in my pink underwear. I snagged a pair of pants out of the drawer, jumped onto the bed to tug them on, then shoved two bottles into each side pocket and zipped them shut. The fifth I slugged down as fast as

I could. Best place to store brains right now was inside of me. Shoes were a lost cause though. I always dropped them on the floor, so who the hell knew where they were now. And the water had risen another half-foot at least in the two minutes I'd spent getting pants and brains. My phone was on top of the dresser, to my relief. I dumped out the contents of a Walmart bag and wrapped my phone in it as best I could, then shoved it in a front pocket. Finally I pulled on a jacket and headed out into the hallway.

"Dad!" I shoved my way through the now-thigh-high water. "We need to go!"

He was already by the door, pants on and also wearing a thin jacket. "C'mon," he said, motioning me toward him and the door, urgency thick in his voice. "Maybe we can—"

"Dad," I choked out, cutting him off, my eyes locked on the view out the window. He followed my gaze and sucked in a breath. The front yard and street beyond was a turbulent rush of water. If we went out there we'd be at the mercy of the vicious current. I was an okay swimmer and could most certainly survive drowning, but not my dad. No zombie parasite to get him through it, and he wasn't a good swimmer at all.

I seized his hand. "Attic," I told him, pulse racing a mile a minute. "We need to get to the roof."

We shoved through the still-rising water, and then he had to boost me up to reach the broken cord for the attic access. The fold-down ladder was a scary and rickety thing, and, after a brief screaming match about who should go first, my dad made it almost to the top before it gave way on one side. He managed to get up the rest of the way, then I used a bit of zombie power to haul myself up the broken ladder and into the attic.

I expected it to be pitch dark up there, but my dad had a flashlight he now shone around.

"There was a flashlight up here?" I asked.

"Grabbed it from the kitchen," he said. "Glad I did, but now I'm wishing I'd grabbed a crowbar or hatchet."

"Only crowbar is in the shed out back," I reminded him. Which was probably completely underwater at this point.

He scowled, but deep lines of worry framed his eyes. The water was still rising, steadily creeping up the ladder, and we both knew stories of people who'd drowned because they fled into their attics during Hurricane Katrina only to find themselves trapped. I knew people who lived in flood-prone areas who kept hatchets or axes in their attics so they could cut their way through the roof in a worst case scenario, but we'd never bothered to do anything like that. Why the hell would we? That sort of thing happened to other people. Not us.

Right.

My dad continued to sweep the flashlight beam around as if hoping a crowbar or hatchet would magically appear. "Damn flood coulda waited another couple of hours so I could get some damn sleep," he grumbled.

I snorted in agreement, then moved to the slope of the roof and rapped my knuckles against the wood. The house was at least fifty years old, and hadn't been re-roofed within my memory, so maybe there was some nice convenient weak spot I could bust through.

I moved a bit farther down the attic, then flicked a quick glance back at my dad. He was crouched, pawing through boxes that had probably been up here for decades. While his back was turned, I took a deep breath, braced myself with a grip on a rafter, and kicked the plywood of the roof as hard as I could.

I felt a snap in my foot, and pain flared, but I managed to make a splintery dent in the plywood. Gritting my teeth against the pain, I kicked again, and succeeded in breaking through enough to see daylight, though I had to stop and take several deep breaths while I waited for the pain to dull. The third kick didn't hurt nearly as much, though I felt something else break in my foot. Yet now a definite hole rewarded my efforts. I gave a feral smile of triumph and grabbed at the edge of the slight gap, pushing and ripping plywood and tar paper away. The sound of rushing water filtered through the hole, and a glance back at the attic entrance showed me that the water was almost to the top of the ladder.

It also showed my dad staring at me in shock. "Angel," he said with a distinct tremor in his voice. "What the hell are you doing?"

For a brief moment I considered coming up with a lie. *There was a hole in the roof already.* Or *It was a weak spot, super easy to get through. Aren't we lucky?* But instead I simply turned back to the hole. "Getting us out of here," I said. I took hold of the edge of the plywood, ripped a long section away and tossed it aside. Light streamed into the attic, and now I saw blood smeared along the wood.

"Your hands," he choked out.

I looked down. They were shredded and bleeding. A three-inch long splinter protruded from the edge of my left palm, and with a calm air I didn't really feel, I pulled it out and dropped it to the attic floor while I tried to ignore the fact that it had been embedded well over an inch deep.

"What the hell's going on, Angel?" he asked me, eyes meeting mine, silently pleading for a reasonable, sensible answer. Too bad I didn't have one for him.

"It's sort of a medical condition," I said. That was almost the truth, right? I unzipped a side pocket of my pants and pulled a bottle out, slugged the contents down. I didn't look at my dad, but I felt his eyes on me, watching, wary.

"That's the shit you keep locked up in your room," he stated. "What is it? Some kinda steroids?"

I tossed the empty bottle aside, then looked down at my hands. "I guess you could say it's a nutritional supplement," I said quietly, watching as the cuts closed up and the flesh became whole again.

My dad's flashlight clattered to the floor of the attic. "I . . . what . . . ?" He stared at me, confusion and shock battling it out on his face.

I gave him a sad look. "It's tough to explain." The fresh influx of brains sang within me. I reached for the plywood, ripped a large piece away as easily as tearing paper. "Come on," I said, hearing the catch in my voice. "We need to get out onto the roof."

"Christ," he breathed. He shot a look back at the attic opening and the rising water, then swallowed hard and moved toward me. I held a hand out to him. He paused before taking it, eyes on the blood that still clung to my hand even though the wounds were healed. Uncertainty filled his eyes as he lifted them to mine.

"Are you still . . . my Angelkins?"

I gave him an exasperated look. "Who the hell else would put up with your whiny bullshit?" I thrust my hand toward him. "Come on, Dad. Let's get on the damn roof already!"

To my intense relief, he reached out and took hold of my hand. I gave his a squeeze, flashed him as reassuring a smile as I could manage, then clambered out the hole I'd made and onto the roof. I used the grip on my dad's hand to steady him as much as myself as we scrabbled up to the peak of the roof and sat, straddling it.

For the first time I got a good look around. Water littered with plastic bottles, trash bags, branches, and other debris swirled a foot below the eaves. The familiar landscape of trees and houses and roads had been replaced by a seething unknown torrent.

I dug my fingers into the shingles. "Dad, we need to tie ourselves together somehow."

He stared, aghast, at the ongoing destruction. "All I got is my belt."

"Don't know how much good that'll do," I said. No way his belt was long enough to go around both of us. I fumbled another bottle of brains out of my pants pocket, gulped it down while I struggled to come up with a solution to our current situation. Whatever happened, I knew staying tanked up was a good idea.

"What are we gonna do?" he asked. "Current's too strong for us to do much of anything."

I took an unsteady breath and fought for calm. "Wait for help as long as we can." I abruptly sucked in a breath and slapped my hand over my front pocket. My phone! I pulled it out, carefully unwrapping it from the plastic. It appeared to be still dry, and miracle of miracles, I even had a signal.

I quickly dialed 911, then did my best to not sound as if I was completely freaked out and panicked, as I told the dispatcher that my dad and I were trapped on the roof of our house in the Sweet Bayou area.

"Rescue boats are being mobilized, ma'am," the woman told me, sounding frazzled. I had no doubt I wasn't the first person to beg for rescue. "They're having trouble with the current, though. The spillway collapsed, and I don't know how long it will take for them to get to you." I heard the apology in her voice, the knowledge that there was nothing more she could do for us. She was our lifeline, and all she could do was tell us to hold on and hope for the best. I almost felt sorry for her.

Numb, I thanked her, clinging to the niceties out of habit even as I clung to the roof, and then hung up and stared down at the phone. Now what? There were no boats in sight, no imminent rescue on the horizon. I should call Marcus. Especially after how our conversation ended last night. But then I looked over at my dad. His arms trembled as he gripped the shingles along the rooftop. As much as a make up call with my not-quite boyfriend might help my emotional state, Marcus wasn't the one who had the best chance of sending the help my dad needed.

"What did they say?" My dad asked.

I didn't try lying to him. He'd know. "Spillway collapsed," I told him. "May be a while before they can get boats to us." A shudder went through the house, a sensation so scarily unnatural that it set my heart pounding anew. There was only one option I could think of. I punched in Pietro's number, inwardly yelling at him to pick up the damn phone as it rang.

On the fourth ring he picked up. "Angel?"

"Pietro!" I had to shout a bit to be heard over the rushing water. It was up over the eaves now. "I need help, please. There's a flood, and I'm on the roof with my dad . . . and I know I'm okay but I'm real worried about him, and nine-one-one says they don't know when rescue boats can get to us, and the house keeps shaking."

"Hang on, Angel," he said. *Like I have a fucking choice right now?* I wanted to shriek, but I kept silent and waited. I heard a rustling and the beeps of another phone being dialed, then, *Brian, I've got an emergency. Angel and her father are on the roof of her house and . . . hold on.* "Angel? You're at your house, right? How high is the water?"

"Yes. My house. Water is over the eaves," I told him, then let out a small cry as the house shifted slightly beneath us. "Oh, man," I continued, voice shaking. "I don't think we have much time before it goes."

Pay whatever bonuses you need to get it up right now, I heard. A few seconds later Pietro said, "Angel, we're getting a helicopter to you." He had such absolute confidence and control in his tone that it was impossible not to feel reassured.

Of course then I looked at the raging water around us and went right back to being in *Oh shit!* mode.

"I'm going to connect you to Brian and leave the line open," he went on. "You let him know if anything changes. And hang on to your dad." I heard some clicks on the line.

"Angel?" That was Brian, calm and cool. "Can you hear me?"

"Y-yeah," I said, pulse slamming as the house trembled beneath me.

"I have a helicopter headed your way very shortly," he stated. "Should get to you in ten minutes, max. Has anything changed for you?"

"W-water's higher." Then I let out a squeal as the house shifted with a hard jerk. "I gotta go . . . house . . . ." I hung up and shoved the phone into the bag. I didn't expect it to survive this experience, but I had to at least try. Only lifeline I had at the moment.

"Dad! Put this in your jacket pocket." I thrust my phone at him, and as soon as he took it, I stripped off my windbreaker, then unbuttoned my pants and shimmied them off as quickly as I could.

He shoved the bagged phone into his pocket and zipped it again, then gave me a baffled look. "Angel, what the hell you doin'?"

"I need to tie us together!" I told him as I knotted a leg of the cargo pants to an arm of the jacket. "Turn around!" I waited for him to cautiously shift position, then I scooched as close as I could, wrapped the pants and jacket around the both of us and tied a double knot in the other arm and leg.

I put my arms around him, locked my hands together. God, he felt so damn frail. "Hold onto my arms tight, okay?" My breath caught as the house shifted again. No way was it going to hold for another ten minutes, or however long it would take to get a helicopter here. At this point I simply hoped it would stay upright. *And maybe a flock of seagulls will swoop down and pluck us off the roof and carry us to safety*, my cynical side snarled.

But right now, I felt my dad's heart hammering beneath my arms. He was as scared as I was, but he was doing his damndest not to show it, trying to be strong for me, doing what he could to protect me.

Dad's hands tightened over mine. "You hang on, you hear me?" he ordered. "You're gonna be okay, Angelkins."

I rested my head against his back, closed my eyes, and breathed in everything about him. The stubborn streak a mile wide, the prickly attitude, the times he'd come through for me when it really mattered.

"I love you, Dad."

I felt the vibration of a response, but his words were lost in a sudden loud snap and a horrible groaning creak as the house jerked hard to the right.

I clutched at him. "Here goes. Hold on!"

"What the hell d'ya think I'm doing?" he snapped back, and I damned near laughed with delight at his ornery spirit.

And then there was no more time for talk. With a final groan the house slid fully off its pilings, then tilted like a capsizing yacht. My dad reflexively scrabbled for purchase as we began to slide, but I kept my grip clamped around him. As we slid toward the water I tried to kick us away from the roof, suddenly filled with the image of us getting sucked under by the sinking house. Didn't make a difference. The roiling current snatched us and threw us right into the thick of the maelstrom. Water closed over our heads, and I kicked frantically, but I couldn't even tell which way was up. Something hard and heavy smacked into us, and I briefly lost my grip on my dad. Only the pants and jacket tied around us kept me from losing him entirely.

I got an arm around him again, broke the surface, coughing and sputtering. "Dad," I gasped. "Dad!"

His arms hung limp in the water, but he gave a weak cough and moan, reassuring me that he was still breathing at least. I clung to him with one arm while I fought to keep both our heads above water by kicking my feet and desperately paddling with my free arm. A grey-toned world, its sounds oddly flat, told me that my senses had faded—meaning I was either hurt or tired as all hell. Damn good chance it was both. The current flung us about, and I whimpered in barely controlled terror.

Something hit me hard in the back, driving the breath from me. I faltered in my frantic treading but somehow managed to get us back to the surface after only a couple of seconds. The raging water swept us past houses, light poles, trees, and who-the-hell-knew what else. I had absolutely no way to tell where we were or how far the flood had carried us.

I made a flailing grab at a tree as we swept by and managed to get my arm hooked around a branch. A *thup-thup* sound penetrated my dulled senses and the roar of the water. The helicopter! But how the hell would they find us? We were nowhere near where my house used to be. Though I thought I could see the chopper approaching, I didn't dare let go of my dad to wave for help. I didn't trust our makeshift safety belt to hold him, and I needed every ounce of strength to keep his head above water.

"An . . . gel . . . kins?" I barely heard the moan.

"Here, Dad!" I gasped out. "I . . . hear a helicopter. Can you wave your arms . . . or something?"

He floundered an arm out of the water in a weak wave. "If I . . . die . . ."

"You're not gonna die!" I yelled at him, though it came out as more of a strangled croak. Shit, my voice was going all raspy. I was going to start falling apart soon.

Without any warning, the branch I held gave way. I let

out a startled shout as the current sucked us away, but only a second later something punched me in the back, and I jerked to a hard stop. Oddly, I didn't have any problem staying afloat, but when I fumbled my free hand behind me to see what I was stuck on I realized why. I was wedged in the fork of a tree branch right below the surface. Except that one side of the fork was, well, *in* me.

Hunger flared hot and bright, telling me quite clearly that the branch had done some serious damage. Sudden worry gripped me, and I dragged a hand along the front of my torso, shuddering in relief once I confirmed that the branch hadn't penetrated and hurt my dad as well.

He still struggled to wave the approaching helicopter down. I tried to lift the arm that wasn't clamped around his waist, but my movements were too sluggish to be worth much. Instead I wrapped my legs around him and fought the intense rising hunger. I still had two bottles of brains in the side pocket of my pants, but there was zero way to get them out now without risking losing them or my grip on my dad.

The helicopter swept low toward us . . . and then over and past while I stifled a scream of frustration. *They didn't see us!*

My dad let his arm flop back into the water. "Now what?" he asked, voice weak and barely audible. Blood seeped through his hair on the back of his head, and I took in the scent of the brain beneath it.

Now what? I echoed, then inhaled deeply. Everything slowed down. The roaring rush of the water receded to a murmur. Peripheral vision dimmed as though all light gathered into that single mouthwatering focal point in front of me. Dad? *Brains.* My breath hissed as I looked for something to bash the head against. *Branch.* I snarled in deep satisfaction, shifted my grip to hold my meal between my hands. Rushing water tried to pull it from me, steal it, and I held tighter, twisted toward the branch.

"Angel?" The sound vibrated against my chest. "Angel, what—?" Stopped me. The smell called me. That voice . . . I screamed in frustration. An annoying *thup-thup* thundered overhead, wind whipping, water thrashing. I raked my gaze upward, ready to scream my defiance. Focused. *Helicopter?* Helicopter. I clung to the bizarre concept like a lifeline and expanded on it. *Flood. Dad. Hands on my dad's head.* No! I released it and wrapped my arms around his waist, breath whistling through my teeth with my conscious effort to hold off biting at the base of his skull.

I love you dad I love you dad I love you dad helicopter here I love you just a minute I can hold on just a minute I love you dad I love you dad I love you I love you I love you I love you

Someone tried to take my dad my meal my dad from me. I grabbed for what he cut, pants jacket brain bottles mine, wrapped it around my numb fist. *Mine.* I clawed at the man as he ripped my dad away, rose impossibly in the air. I screamed, reached for him. Nothing. *Nothing.*

I sank back, breath gurgling. Going still. Going quiet. Conserving. Waiting. An irresistible scent filling my senses, getting closer. *Brains.* I squinted against the wind as my prey descended toward me, my lips pulled back from my teeth in an eager snarl. I scrabbled against the tree branch, struggled to lunge and attack, rend and feast. He leaned toward me, and I threw my arm up, grabbed his ankle, pulled. Snapped at him. He reached, clamped my jaw in his hand, forced something between my teeth. My cry of rage died away as the leathery lump registered.

Brains. Chewy hunk of brains yes yes yes. My hand went to my mouth, held the chunk in place. Gnawed. Brains. Better, yes. Oh god. *Yes. I'm . . . Me. I'm Me.*

By the time I chewed and chewed and swallowed the brain-lump down, a hint of coherent thought returned to let me know I was almost up the cable with my rescuer. The desperate urge to rip his brain from his skull had eased to Gee, He Sure Smells Yummy, but . . .

Oh my god. *Dad?* Nausea and worry swept through me. *Dad.*

As soon as I neared the open side door of the helicopter, strong hands grabbed me and hauled me the rest of the way in. Someone else wrapped a blanket around me and shoved an already-opened packet of brains into my free hand. I greedily sucked it down and as soon as I finished that one, the empty was yanked from my grasp and replaced with a fresh one. My gut did a strange lurch, and I realized that my innards were still in the process of healing from the serious damage caused by the tree branch.

After finishing the second packet, I regained the ability to actually pay attention to something besides my own hunger. My left hand was locked in a death-grip around my pants with its two bottles of brains. Good ole parasite survival instinct must've kicked in to grab them when the rescuer cut the jacket sleeve to free my dad. I unclenched my fingers and finally took a look around.

I didn't know crap about helicopters, but this one looked military: utilitarian grey, with two seats for crew members up near the cabin; I was buckled into one of four fold-down seats at the back, though I didn't remember any of that happening. My dad was in the seat right beside me. He had a blanket around him and held a towel to the back of his head. He met my eyes, gave me a tremulous smile. I did my best to return it. I didn't know how much of my out-of-controlness he'd seen, but I sure as hell hoped not much. Thankfully, he'd been kinda out of it for the worst of the monster-mode. For that matter, so had I.

But I *had* been the monster for a while. If the helicopter hadn't returned, would I have been able to control myself? Would I have killed and eaten my own father? A shiver wracked me. I knew the truth, and it was a punch in the gut.

I almost ate my dad. The memory went through me like a knife. The scent, the drive to do whatever I had to do to get those brains—my *dad's* brains. No way could I have kept on living if I'd given in to the hunger and killed him. Or was suicide even an option? I had a feeling the survival responses of the parasite wouldn't make it easy.

But I didn't hurt him, I reminded myself. Yeah, the helicopter had returned in the nick of time, but I'd managed to hold on for those precious few minutes, even with a goddamn tree stuck through my back. Props to stubborn-bitch-willpower for saving the day.

I hugged the blanket around myself and accepted a third packet from the rescuer. Might as well eat their supply of brains instead of going into the two bottles in my pants, especially since I had no idea how long I'd need those bottles to last. Whoever these people were, they sure as hell knew how to deal with hungry zombies, right down to having chewy brain-cakes on hand to keep the hunger distracted.

Shifting, I moved to sit closer to my dad. The thwupping roar of the chopper made it impossible to have a conversation, but I mouthed *You okay?* and he nodded in response. He pulled the towel away from his head, looked at the blood staining it. Scowling, I turned his head so I could look at the wound. I saw his lips move, and I had no doubt he was cussing me, but he didn't resist. To my relief it didn't look too bad. Probably wouldn't need stitches, but I still intended to get someone with actual medical training to look at it once we got wherever we were going.

I released his head, gave him a quick hug, then made a comical effort to get my wet pants back on. I gave up after half a minute of contortions and simply tied the legs around my waist, wrapped the blanket around me best I could, and sighed. Looked like I was getting rescued in my undies after all. Thank god I wasn't in the habit of wearing a thong to bed.

My dad and I huddled close together for warmth and comfort as the helicopter circled the area. Two more times it descended to pluck people from the still-raging waters. The neighbors from across the street who'd called the cops on us more than once for domestic disputes. A single mom who lived nearby and her fourteen-year-old son who I suspected was responsible for the disappearance of tools from our shed. Petty neighborhood squabbles were forgotten as we helped each other get settled and offered comfort as we could.

Finally the pilot seemed to feel that either there were no others needing rescue, or there wasn't enough room for more. The doors closed, and I felt us gain altitude. I wrapped an arm around my dad, shut my eyes, and tried not to think of this as the end of our world.

I opened my eyes when we touched down with little more than a light jostling. Whoever the pilot was, he was damn good. The engines wound down, and the silence when they stopped seemed unnatural after the din of before.

When the doors opened, our rescuers efficiently offloaded us and passed us into the care of waiting emergency workers and Red Cross personnel. It took a few minutes for my surroundings to sink in, and then I registered that we were in a parking lot at Tucker Point High School. About twenty yards from the helicopter, several Red Cross vehicles clustered, one marked Disaster Relief. Tucker Point High was always used as a shelter during hurricanes, so it made sense for it to be used for this as well. A vague and misplaced worry wound through me about how the movie people would do their filming with flood victims sheltering here and getting in their way, but then I decided that the school was no doubt more than big enough to accommodate everyone, and I surely had more important things to worry about. But I didn't want to worry about the more important things. Not yet.

I kept the blanket wrapped around my waist and an arm around my dad, demanded that someone check out his head and snarled that I was fine. No one seemed to take any offense, and I dimly realized that I probably had an eyes-wide-in-shock look about me.

After asking a few pointed questions, I managed to learn that, earlier in the morning, engineers attempted to partially open the spillway in order to carefully bleed-off the overflowing Kreeger River down Cole Bayou and, eventually, out into the swamp. That would have been fine and dandy and would have caused a few extra feet of water at the most, except that minutes after the first bay opened, the entire aged structure gave way. In one gigantic rush, pretty much all the excess water in the Kreeger River diverted down Cole Bayou. The Army Corps of Engineers was already at work, though the general consensus seemed to be that, at this point, there wasn't much to do except wait for the river to drop below flood stage.

I hovered near my dad as a medic checked his head, and I listened to a relief worker comment in hushed tones about how the flooding had wiped out a small trailer park. I knew the place—a collection of six or seven trailers with almost exclusively elderly residents. I figured there had to be other casualties as well, but no one had any hard numbers. The only possible bright side was that the worst of the flooding had been on our side of the road since the bayou ran behind our property, which meant that, apart from the unfortunately located trailer park, probably less than a dozen houses had been affected. Moreover, at least half of those were fishing camps that weren't usually occupied during the week.

"You don't need stitches," the medic told my dad, and I yanked my attention back to him. "You probably have a mild concussion, though," he added.

"I ain't goin' to no fucking hospital," Dad snarled before the medic could even get the suggestion out.

The young man flicked his eyes up to me. I gave him a very slight shrug and shake of my head to let him know that arguing would get him nowhere.

"All right," he said to my dad. "But be sure to get as much rest as possible. And if you have any dizziness, headache, or blurred vision, let one of the volunteers know as soon as possible."

Dad grumbled something that sounded like an "Okay," and with that the medic moved on to treat the tool-stealing teen, who looked like a scared rabbit as he cradled his left arm to his chest.

The sun broke through thinning clouds for the first time in a week as another volunteer took us gently in hand and guided us toward the gym entrance.

Looked like it was going to be a damn beautiful day for the end of the world.

Chapter 18

It didn't seem right that it could only be ten a.m. Everything we owned was gone. Nothing left but the clothes on our backs, and in my case hardly that. My jacket had been shredded and my shirt had a tree-branch–sized hole in the back. Fortunately I still had my cargo pants with its two precious bottles of brain smoothie.

Surely it should take longer than a couple of hours to wipe out a lifetime of possessions and memories, right?

What the hell are we supposed to do now?

I wanted to fall apart and allow the magnitude of our loss to sink in, wallow and roll around in the grief and anger and unfairness of it. But I didn't. I had my dad to think of. I had to call work and start figuring out what steps to take. Figure out a place to live until we could rebuild. Or whatever the hell we were going to do.

Maybe that's what maturity was all about, I mused in a weird numb fog as I pawed through hastily donated clothing for something to wear instead of a blanket. Maybe being "mature" wasn't just holding down a job and starting a family and buying a house and paying taxes. Maybe it was about putting a hold on your own reactions and needs until after you took care of the people who trusted you.

Maturity sucked.

I found clothing for me and my dad, went into the bathroom to change, then came back out and put a pile of folded sweats on the end of his cot. "Dad, here's some dry clothes. You need to get out of those wet things."

"Sure thing, Angel," he replied, voice low and subdued. He didn't move for several seconds while the worry that he was broken clenched tight in my chest, but then he finally stood, gathered up the clothing and shuffled to the bathroom. A few minutes later he came back, wearing the slightly too-large sweats and looking even more haggard and vulnerable because of it. In silence, he sank to the cot and laid down, back to me.

Troubled, I left him there and went in search of a phone I could borrow, since the flimsy Walmart bag hadn't been enough to keep my own phone dry. I soon found a volunteer willing to let me use up her minutes.

Since I was actually scheduled to be at work, my first call was to Derrel. It went to voicemail which told me he was probably up to his eyeballs dealing with the people who hadn't been as lucky as my dad and me.

"Hey, Derrel," I said after the beep. "I . . . I'm not at work 'cause . . ." *Because I was clinging to my dad while impaled on a tree when I was supposed to clock in. My dad and I are only alive because I'm not quite human anymore.* "We got flooded. Bad. Lost my phone." *Everything we owned is gone.* "I'm at the shelter at the high school. Me and my dad."

I didn't know what else to say, didn't know how to put the magnitude of what-the-hell-do-I-do-now? into a voicemail. After a few seconds of my silence, the phone beeped again, and I disconnected. At least I hadn't had the Coroner's Office van parked at my house. Allen would have done his best to figure out a way to blame me for the collapse of the spillway so that he could legitimately fire me for losing the van.

I called Marcus, the ache of wanting him almost painful. So what if he tended to be overprotective? Right now that seemed pretty minor. But his cell phone, too, went to voicemail, and I left pretty much the same message for him as I had for Derrel.

After I returned the borrowed phone to its owner, I got a couple of slices of pizza that had been donated by a local restaurant and made my way back to where the cots were set up. Dad had shifted to lie on his back and stare at the metal beams and fluorescent lights of the gym ceiling.

"Hey, Dad. I got some pizza for us." I sank to the cot beside his, set the two paper plates down. "You want something to drink? They have cokes and stuff."

"Not hungry," he muttered. "You eat mine."

"You gotta eat," I said, worry pulling my mouth into a scowl.

He glanced over at me. "Yeah. Later." He muttered something I couldn't catch, then sighed.

I wasn't all that hungry either at the moment. "Maybe we can put a trailer on our lot," I suggested. "That wouldn't be so bad, right?"

Emotions flickered across his face. "Sure. A trailer."

It all hit me then. I mean, really hit me. The house I'd grown up in, lived my entire life in, was gone. Every picture, every scrapbook, every school paper from when I'd actually cared about school—gone.

I turned away, struggling to hold it together. Now wasn't the time to break down. I couldn't do that until I'd solved our problems and figured out how to care for my dad. I sure as hell didn't need to fall apart here and let my dad think he'd somehow let me down. That would be me letting *him* down.

Didn't matter. The tears came, and I grabbed for the blanket, pressed a corner of it to my eyes in a stupid and doomed effort to hide the fact I was crying. Damn it. We'd already been barely scraping by, and the only reason we were even doing that well was because the house was old and paid for, which meant we didn't have a mortgage or rent to deal with. Oh yeah, and because we hadn't shelled out for flood insurance since we'd never flooded so why the hell would we need anything like that? And what bank in hell would lend *me* money to buy a new trailer? And clothes and furniture and a car . . . *Fuuuuuuuuuuck*.

"Angel!"

I turned to see my dad looking around frantically. "Where's the jacket I had on?" He stood and began to dig through the blankets on the cot. "Where's my goddamn jacket?"

Sniffling, I gestured toward the foot of his cot. "In the trash bag on the floor there. Needs to be washed."

He grabbed the bag and yanked it open. I watched him, frowning.

"What's so important about your damn jacket?" I asked.

He muttered something about goddamn water as he pulled the sodden jacket out and fumbled through the pockets, anxiety visibly increasing.

"Dad? What's wrong?"

He abruptly pulled a soggy sock stuffed with something out of an inner pocket and heaved a thick sigh of relief. "Here, Angelkins," he said, voice shaking as he held it out to me. "You hold on to this."

Baffled, I took it from him and peered at the contents. Inside was a thick roll of bills.

I jerked my gaze back up to him. "Oh my god, Dad. Where did you get this? How much is in here?"

His shoulders twitched up in a shrug. "Not all that

much now with everything gone, I guess. 'Bout twelve hundred. You should hold onto it."

Holy shit. I carefully rolled it back up. "Where'd you get it?" I repeated. I'd never in a million years suspect my dad of doing anything illegal to get that money, but . . . damn, twelve hundred dollars was a solid chunk of cash for us.

"I been doing a little work in the last couple of months," he said, looking down at his hands, almost as if he was embarrassed to be telling me. "Carl Kaster's been letting me clean up the bar after closing and paying me cash under the table. I was saving it to buy new furniture, maybe a new stove that I'm not always worryin' is gonna burn the house down." Pain slashed across his face, then he let out a dry chuckle. "Can't burn the house down now, huh?"

"I think we're pretty safe from that," I said with a strained laugh. "That's why you've been out so late."

"Yeah," he said, then shrugged. "Mostly."

So he hasn't been going out drinking every night. The "mostly" part clued me in that he was still drinking some, but it sure as hell wasn't as much as before if he could actually hold a job. The relief that rushed through me allowed a few pesky tears to sneak out, and I pretended to rub my eyes to wipe them away. Didn't matter that he wasn't staying totally dry, not right now.

I shifted to sit on his cot and put my arms around him. He leaned into me and let out a low sigh.

"I wanted to make it better," he murmured.

"It'll be better," I assured him, forcing myself to believe it too. "We'll figure something out. I mean, it's corny, but we still got each other."

He pulled me into a hug, then straightened and peered at me. "Now tell me about this 'medical condition' that don't look like any kinda condition I ever heard of."

"Oh, man." I blew out my breath, then looked around to make absolutely sure no one was even remotely close enough to overhear. I'd known that someday I'd have to tell him, but, well, I'd sort of hoped that it would be fifty years from now or something. "Last year, right before I got the job at the morgue, I, uh, overdosed and nearly died."

He stiffened. "You never told me. How come you never told me?"

"Well, because I . . ." I shifted uncomfortably. "Things were real bad between us then. And also because, well, I kinda *did* die. Kinda."

His eyes widened in alarm. "What the hell does that mean? How do you *kinda* die?"

Shit. This was just as hard as I thought it would be. "Randy and me, we got into a fight." Randy, my piece-of-shit ex-boyfriend. "I got drunk and took some pills and was sorta flirting with another guy." I winced. "Turned out he put something in my drink. A date rape drug. Took me for a drive, but I was already so high I started having trouble breathing. The guy panicked and was gonna dump me out in the swamp, but he took a curve too fast and wrecked the car real bad . . ." I trailed off.

"God, Angel," he breathed, guilt and pain carved into his face. Things had been horrible between us back then. The bickering we did these days was nothing compared to the ugly and sometimes violent fights of before.

"I woke up in the ER," I continued after a moment. "Naked and not a scratch on me, even though I remembered being hurt bad." I shook my head in an attempt to dispel those nightmarish memories. "And there was a bag of clothing and a six pack of, well, drinks like I have now, and an anonymous note saying I had to take a job at the morgue or I'd go back to jail."

His eyebrows drew together in a frown. "That's like something out of a movie. What's in those drinks?"

My gut clenched. Of course he'd want to know. What "nutritional supplement" could give me super-healing ability and mega-strength? Throat tight, I shook my head. "I don't want to tell you. You . . . you'll never look at me the same."

"You're my Angelkins," he said, voice suddenly firm, and I nearly melted at the nickname. "When we were in the attic, *you* said that, no matter what, you're still my Angelkins. That's all that matters."

A shiver went through me, and when I spoke it was in a voice barely above a whisper. "Dad, I work in the morgue so that I can eat . . ." I couldn't say it. "I . . . I got made into something that night, and it saved my life." I gulped, blurted it out. "I'm a zombie."

"A *what?*" He shook his head.

My fingers dug into the canvas of the cot, and I stared down at the floor. "If I don't eat . . . *brains*," I nearly choked on the word, "I start to rot and fall apart and get real hungry for . . . more brains."

He stood, backed a step away, mouth working in what sure as hell looked like revulsion. *I shouldn't have told him*, I realized with sick dismay. Telling him had been a horrible mistake. I should've lied, come up with some other explanation. *Any* other explanation.

He rubbed a hand over his face, expression a painful mix of shock, disgust and, strangely, belief. He'd seen it, after all. Seen me heal up before his eyes. "All this time?" he finally asked, voice hoarse. "Almost a year?"

Throat tight, I nodded.

He fell silent again, eyes on the floor. The sick despair coiled into a thick lump in my gut, but I fought back the urge to start crying again.

His gaze came back to me, and there was a hint of desperation in his voice when he spoke. "You don't have to . . . *kill* people, do you?"

Shaking my head, I could only be grateful he'd

phrased the question the way he had. *Have* to? No. Not to eat at least. The unwelcome memory of a baseball bat crushing a skull rose, and I shoved it away. "No. That's why I work in the morgue," I told him. "I get the . . . I get what I need from there. From people who've already died."

Stark relief showed on his face. "Okay," he said, exhaling, tension visibly leaving his body. "Okay, that's good. We've had ups and downs." He paused. "A *lot* of ups and downs. And right now, you and me, we're on an up." He hesitated, and his eyes sought mine. "Aren't we?"

I took an unsteady breath. "You're okay with a zombie daughter?"

"Don't have much choice about it, right?" His head dipped in a nod. "You're my Angel. So, yeah. Guess I'm okay with it."

I managed a wan smile. "It really did save my life. I would've died in the car wreck for sure, even if the overdose didn't kill me."

He sighed and came back to sit beside me again, put an arm around me and pulled me close. "Then however it happened, I'm glad, 'cause you're here now, and I didn't have to bury my baby." His voice broke on that last part, and I had to wipe a few tears of my own away. "But you're not *dead*," he said, "so why d'ya call yourself a zombie?"

Frowning, I considered the question, then shrugged. "What the hell else would you call someone who has to eat brains?"

"Huh," he said, mouth pursing. "Okay, y'got me there."

I leaned my head on his shoulder. "There's, um, one more thing you should probably know," I said after a moment. "The little matter of who turned me."

"You mean the one who made you into a zombie?"

I shifted uncomfortably. "Yeah."

"You don't want to tell me."

I screwed my face into a grimace. "You won't like it," I told him. "But he saved my life, Dad."

He stiffened. "Not that no-account drug dealing Clive?"

"That asshole?" I gave a snort of humorless laughter. "Oh, hell no!" The last time I'd seen my former pill-provider was when the cops hauled him away for disturbing the peace and possession of drugs with intent to distribute. Truly a beautiful sight to behold. "No, it was Marcus."

"The *cop?*" he said, too loudly.

My shoulders hunched. "Uh, yeah. Him."

His mouth formed a dark scowl. "Well, shit, Angel. How am I supposed to hate him if he saved your life?"

I burst out laughing. "Oh my god. I guess you're fucked, Dad."

He gave a dry chuckle. "Story of my life, Angelkins."

"Well, you're stuck with me now."

He hugged me, kissed the top of my head. "Wouldn't have it any other way."

Chapter 19

The Tucker Point High School gym was one creepy-as-hell place at night. I lay on my cot, wide awake, soaking in the ambiance. Light from sodium lamps outside streaked in through the high windows, casting alternating patches of shadow and weak amber. Pipes near the locker rooms groaned periodically, and more than a couple of roaches the size of my hand—well, almost—had skittered across the floor in the last half hour.

Didn't seem to bother my dad. He lay on his back, snoring softly. A dozen or so other refugees either slept or did a good imitation of it, on cots grouped in family clusters around the gym. In the far corner, a few played a subdued game of cards, faces stricken and empty. A mix of men, women, and children, all homeless, all without anyone to take them in. Like my dad. Like me.

Like me. I didn't want to think about it, but there it was, staring me right in the face. Not only hadn't Marcus come to find me, he hadn't sent a message or anything. Sure, he was probably busy all day with the sheriff's office taking care of the shit end of flood stuff, but now it was after nine p.m. and nothing. I sighed. Who was I kidding? It was pretty obvious he'd decided *Fuck you, Angel* was his response to my hanging up on him.

I sat up on the stupid cot and pulled on the donated sneakers—after shaking them to be sure none of the members of Roach Explorer Troop 666 had made their way inside. Standing, I stretched out the kinks in my back left by the nonexistent cot padding, pulled the thin blanket a bit higher over my dad's shoulders, then crept out of the room.

The elderly security guard in the hallway looked up from his book and gave me a gently inquisitive look. "Everything okay?" With the white beard, jovial expression, and slight bulge in the middle, if this guy didn't already make extra money playing Santa every year, he sure as hell could.

"Yeah, just can't sleep," I told him, shrugging. "Figured I'd get some air."

He gave an understanding nod. "At least the rain stopped," he said. "It's a nice night for a walk. But be careful, okay?"

"Yes, sir," I said. "I'll be good." Wouldn't want to get on the naughty list.

He smiled warmly, returned his attention to the book. I slipped out the door.

The air was a touch cooler than I expected, but not enough to go back inside to scrounge a warmer shirt or jacket. I hugged my arms around myself and took a deep breath, looked up at the star-filled sky. *Now what?* I silently asked.

The problem was that it was too easy to focus on everything that was gone. There was so much of it—a giant cloud of loss. House, cars, clothing, furniture . . . Marcus. I knew I needed to take stock of what I still had and resist the overwhelming desire to slip into depression and self-pity.

But, damn, this was surely one of those situations where a little self-pity was allowed, right?

The sidewalk led to a practice field on the back side of the gym, not particularly scenic, but with fresh air and without skittering roaches or generalized creepiness. Off to my right loomed the dark football stadium where, only a few days ago, Marcus and I had spent a very enjoyable hour. Seemed like a dream now, with a hazy couldn't-possibly-be-real quality about it. I sat on a concrete bench in the shadow of the building and leaned back against the bricks. The darkness felt safe, a hidden vantage to watch over the minimally lit school grounds. Safe. What the hell did that mean anymore? After the attack and the flood, I didn't know if there really was such a thing.

I forced myself to consider the positives. The biggest was that my dad and I were alive and okay, of course. *And I still have a job. That's pretty damn good.* At least I sure as hell hoped I did. I had a hard time believing I'd get fired for not showing up to work on the day my house got washed away. Even Allen wasn't that much of a dick.

Not that I wanted to place any bets on that.

I also had every reason to believe that the freezer full of my stash of brains was safe and sound in my storage unit. That was on the other side of town, so it wouldn't have been affected by the spillway. Okay, so I currently had as assets: Life, Dad, Job, and Brains. Oh, and twelve hundred soggy dollars.

Yesterday Marcus would have been on the list. Damn it. Taking a deep breath, I pushed away the pain that tried to rise again.

A rasp of sound to my left cut my musings short. I froze, listening. *Labored breathing.* Grateful that the bench was in shadow and that by blind luck I'd chosen dark clothing, I willed myself to remain still. I knew that sound, one that could only come from lung tissue break-

ing down accompanied by a hint of fluid. This was a
zombie—and likely a very hungry one.

My pulse gave a weird double-thump as the figure
came around the corner of the gym and limped away
from me along the perimeter fence of the practice field.
Not just any zombie. This was *Philip.*

The asshole was obviously suffering and hungry.
Smug satisfaction with maybe a touch of gloating washed
through me but, a moment later, yielded to a rush of
dismay as Philip stumbled and nearly fell. Reflexively, I
threw out my hand as though I could reach him and offer
support.

Damn. There it was again, whatever parental instinct
my parasite had included in its total package. However,
this time, I was aware of it. If I hadn't felt the out-of-
place compassion for Philip during the extreme bullshit
at the boat launch, I probably wouldn't have given it a
second thought and chalked it up to natural compassion.
Both perspectives were alive and kicking and a genuine
part of me. I hated Philip, and he terrified me, but it also
twisted my guts to see him hurting.

Was *this* why Marcus was so overprotective? Because
he was my zombie-daddy? And if so, did he even realize
it was his parasite influencing him? Now there was some
serious food for thought. Not that it mattered anymore.

But for now I wanted—no, *needed*—to see what the
hell was going on with Philip. As silently as possible, I
stood and followed at enough of a distance that he
wouldn't be able to hear me. I was fairly sure there was
no risk of him scenting me; as hungry as he was, he'd be
keyed to brains that were actually edible, and wouldn't
be able to detect much of anything over his own decay.

He continued along the fence line, then slipped between two outbuildings to cut across a lot and onto a
dark residential street. I hung back before crossing the
empty lot, certain that he'd glance back at any moment

and bust me, but he seemed utterly focused on his destination, and I managed to follow without incident.

I almost missed it when he ducked off the sidewalk. He headed into the shaggy yard of a vacant Acadian single story house that outdid the creepiness of the gym by about a thousand percent. I drew back into the shadow of a tree and watched as he pulled a paper bag out of his jacket, went to the side of the steps, crouched, and . . . what the hell was he doing? His back to me, I could only wait and wonder what the fuck was going on. I heard a couple of soft clicks, a disturbing muffled noise, like a sob or moan, then the quiet rustling of the paper bag.

After about a minute, he stood, hands clenching and unclenching as his gaze swept the area, face twisted in . . . desperation? He didn't have the bag in his hands anymore. Had he tucked it back into his jacket? Left it under the steps? I remained still, watching and barely daring to breathe. He stood, returned to the sidewalk, and crossed back toward the lot, his breathing even more labored and noisy.

On the other side of the street, he paused, visibly shaking, head jerking to the side the way it had when he attacked me at the boat launch. I watched as he appeared to grapple with indecision, then he turned to the right and continued, near staggering, up the street.

After a brief internal debate, I hurried to the steps, crouched and peered under. Yeah, that did a lot of good. Since I didn't have a flashlight, my only option was to reach under and feel. Okay, I was a tough-ass zombie, but something about reaching blind under those haunted house steps made me question how badly I really wanted to know what was under there. After a brief struggle with my inner wimp, I put my hand into that darker darkness and groped for who-the-hell knew what. My fingers brushed something hard and moveable, and a second later I pulled out a shoebox-size black plastic container with a snap-lid.

Moving quickly, I flipped the catches and lifted it into the dim light to peer at the contents. Two zip-top baggies, one with a USB flash drive and the other with a bunch of two-inch-square papers, each with a number penciled in one corner and a dark splodge in the center that looked suspiciously like . . . blood?.

What the hell was going on? I snapped the box closed and shoved it back under the steps, then hurried to the street to see if I could locate Philip. He'd been moving slowly, probably to conserve his resources, and to my relief I caught a glimpse of him as he turned a corner about a block up the street. I broke into a jog to catch up and saw him ahead. I followed him a few more blocks to the parking lot of a small brick warehouse-like building that had seen better days, deserted except for two cars near me on the edge of the lot.

Philip's attention seemed to be completely focused on reaching the building, so I took the opportunity to duck behind one of the cars to watch him. He stopped about a dozen feet from the first of two doors—a dismal, solid thing with faded paint and a flush lock. He dropped into a crouch, wheezing so badly that I half-stood to go to him. I clamped down hard on that mama-zombie impulse and huddled down again, heart pounding from nearly revealing myself. I took a shaky breath and tried to figure out what he was doing. I had the feeling he was psyching himself up to go up to that door. But why hesitate? He was big and bad and tough even without being a zombie.

After about a minute he stood and staggered to the door, one hand on the wall for balance. The light above the door illuminated his face, and I had to bite back a noise of dismay. He looked awful. Yeah, he had some mild zombie-rot happening, but that wasn't what got to me. His eyes and features radiated a level of pain and despair that struck right to my core, even beyond any parasite-driven compassion.

Before Philip could knock or ring a bell or anything, the door opened and a Hispanic-featured man in a dark blue suit stepped out, a raised gun in his hand. His eyes narrowed as he took in Philip's appearance.

"Sir," I heard Philip rasp, "I . . . need sustenance and stabilizer. There was . . . none at the drop."

The suited man frowned. "Wait right there," he told Philip. "Don't move." He lowered his gun and pulled a phone off his belt, dialed a number. "Glenn," he said a few seconds later. "Reinhardt is on our doorstep." A pause as his gaze swept the parking lot. I shrank back in the shadow of the car. "No, no sign of anyone else."

Philip remained still as ordered, and then the sound of a female voice came from the open doorway. Though I couldn't see her, I *knew* that voice. Why couldn't I place it?

"Well, do you have them?"

The suited man looked back at the speaker and shook his head. "Not yet. Reinhardt's here. He says he needs brains and stabilizer."

What the hell was stabilizer? Did that have something to do with how messed up Philip seemed to be?

The woman stepped to the door, and I sucked in a breath as shock coursed through me. Slim and auburn-haired, and probably only a couple of inches taller than me. Of course the voice was familiar. Dr. Kristi Fucking Charish. I hadn't recognized it immediately since this time she wasn't using an intercom on the other side of a lab observation window while she forced me to do horrible things. Last time I saw her she was fleeing the about-to-blow-up factory with Philip and a handful of other guards. I'd figured she'd gone and set up shop somewhere else since she wasn't the sort to let one failure stop her. Ever since Philip tackled me on the movie set, I'd had the nagging worry that she was around.

She had on simple jeans and a sleeveless blue top, and didn't look much like a cold-as-ice crazy scientist, but I knew better than to let her lack of a lab coat this time fool me. The bitch had no heart.

The man at the door lifted his gun slightly, and Charish stepped back out of sight.

"Dr. Charish," Philip said, the ugly rasp in his voice even harsher than before. "Please, ma'am. I need brains and stabilizer."

Even though I couldn't see her, I definitely heard the condescending sneer in her voice when she spoke. "You were left more than enough a couple of nights ago," she snapped. "If you failed to ration them appropriately, it's not up to us to waste more resources on you. Get them from your handlers. Now leave before you're spotted."

"Required extra," Philip wheezed, desperation tingeing his rough voice. "God, please, ma'am. Please. I can't do this."

My hands curled into fists. Even as much as I hated Philip, I dearly wanted to slug Charish for being such an all-around heartless bitch. I already owed her quite a few hard punches. I knew what it was like to starve as a zombie, but this was something different, worse. Pieces started to fall into place. Philip. Tim Bell. Roland Westfeld. All three had been with her when she had me kidnapped. If she hadn't been fully working for Saberton then, it sure as hell looked like she'd signed on since.

The bitch in question gave an aggravated huff. "This one time only, and then you *leave* and don't come back here." A moment later she returned to the door and handed a paper bag to the suited man, who in turn gave it to Philip. "Now *go*," Charish ordered.

Philip clutched the bag to his chest and backed away.

"Thank you, ma'am," he rasped. "Thank you," he repeated, then turned and staggered off.

Charish turned to suit-man, mouth tight and eyes narrowed. "Get the items from the drop *now*," she ordered, before both returned inside and the door closed.

What the fuck? Could this be the place where Heather rescued the zombie Garrett from his vivisection hell? It was only a few blocks from the movie set where she'd followed Brent Stewart to kill him, so it was more than possible. After all, how many secret labs could one town hold? But any fantasies I might've had about breaking in and freeing zombie prisoners were gone now that I'd seen it would be pretty much impossible without getting shot a whole bunch. Or tranqed, which would be even worse, since it would probably land me right on my own vivisection table.

Suppressing a shudder of horror, I waited another minute or so in case the door opened again, then crept along the back of the parking lot and in the direction Philip went. I reached the street and froze as I saw him crouched not ten feet away, his focus on the paper bag as he tore into it. Heart pounding, I eased back into the bushes beside the warehouse sign and watched. Philip ripped open a packet, much like the ones that Brian and Rachel had given me, and downed it, near weeping in relief. *Must be standard zombie-issue in the corporate world*, I thought with a soft snort.

He downed a second packet and then went still as though waiting for the brains to take effect.

Behind me, I heard the warehouse door swing open, and I cast a cautious glance that way. The suited man stepped out, waited for the door to close fully behind him, then headed for the car I'd hidden behind earlier. I remained motionless as he cranked it and pulled out of the parking lot, then let out a soft breath of relief as he passed without looking my way.

For the millionth time I wondered what the hell was going on. Charish had told him to go get the stuff "from the drop spot." I grimaced. I probably should've pocketed the USB drive when I had the chance. Did the contents of that black box have anything to do with the attack on me? God, it felt like a century ago now, though I knew it had been only a couple of days. And what if they came after me again? Or my dad.

Worry clutched at my gut. I needed to get back to my dad. I turned and slowly worked my way behind the bushes, intending to emerge on the street a block or so down.

"Angel?" Philip said from behind me, voice ragged.

I sucked in a breath and spun to face him, my heart slamming as if it was about to burst out of my chest. He stood on the sidewalk no more than a few strides away, tatters of the bag in one hand and the empty packets in the other. His eyes met mine, intense and wild, his expression shifting with emotions I didn't have the time or inclination to identify. I tore my gaze away and broke into a run, sneakers slapping the pavement. Half a block away, I glanced back to see if he pursued, but he remained where he was, watching me go.

I controlled the urge to run the rest of the way back to the school, since doing so would be Stupid. I only had two bottles of brains left, and as long as I didn't do something clever like go for a midnight jog, they would hopefully last me until I could get to my stash. I compromised and walked at a quick pace, continuing to cast glances back over my shoulder to see if Philip or anyone else followed. Thankfully, the streets remained empty, and I made it back without incident.

The security guard stood waiting by the door when I returned. He smiled and gave a sigh of obvious relief.

"Thought something had happened to you," he said as he held the door for me.

I thought of telling him that I could take care of myself, that I'd taken care of myself for a long time. Instead I simply gave him a nod and a smile. "Thanks for worrying."

I headed down the hall to the gym, oddly comforted by the fact that someone I barely knew gave a shit.

Chapter 20

Hungry, I detoured to the small fridge in the coach's office where I'd stashed my bottles. Both were still there, to my relief, probably because I'd marked them in big black marker "Prescription! Do not drink!" After a brief internal debate I went ahead and got one out and chugged it down. With the ongoing zombie weirdness, I figured it'd be best if I wasn't hungry.

My dad was still snoring on his cot when I returned to the gym. I climbed onto mine and managed a couple of hours of horrible sleep before the sirens from a passing ambulance jerked me awake. One of the great things about living in the country was the quiet. Of course the drawback was that I hadn't learned to tune out the sounds of city traffic—even a city as small as Tucker Point.

Though exhausted, my mind whirled with worry. Getting back to sleep proved impossible, and I eventually gave up trying and stared at the damn ceiling until my bladder insisted I make my way to the bathroom. I did my business and was almost back to my cot when I spotted a figure standing by the wall on the other side of my dad's cot. At first I thought it was one of the other refugees. Then his head jerked.

I sucked in a sharp breath. Goddam Philip again. "You get the hell away from my dad," I told him, my voice low and shaking with intensity. How had he gotten past the guard? If he'd hurt Santa, I was going to be one pissed zombie-mama.

He spread his arms, hands open, palms toward me, the jerky shaking evident despite the gloom. "Come with me," he said, hoarse roughness in place of the ugly rasp of before.

"Get away from my dad," I repeated.

To my surprise he obliged by taking a step back toward the wall, keeping his hands in clear sight. "Please. Come with me."

I clearly heard the blend of intensity and desperation in his voice. He was dangerous and *so* not fooling around, but the "please" drew me. Shit. If he was about to do some nasty crap to me, I didn't want it to happen in here where someone else could get hurt or kids might see. "Outside."

To my relief he gave a single nod. "This way," he replied, barely audible, tilting his head toward the door at the far end of the gym, opposite the main entrance. My relief ratcheted up a smidge as he led me through the door and down a short flight of stairs to an exit. If he'd come in this way, hopefully it meant Santa was all right.

My pulse slammed as I followed him, and I breathed a silent prayer of thanks that I drank the bottle of brains only a few hours earlier. I was far from fully tanked, but at least I wasn't *hungry*.

He exited the building, then moved behind the hedge along the back wall and crouched, fisting his hands on his knees.

I stayed far enough back that he couldn't reach out and grab me. "What do you want?"

A shudder wracked him. "What did you see?"

"Yeah, right," I said with a snort. "Why should I tell you anything? So you know whether or not to kill me?" I smiled sweetly and spread my hands. "I didn't see anything at all. How's that?"

Even in the low light I could see the grimace that twisted his features. "You ... shouldn't ... tell me." He shook his head as though trying to clear confusion, then pulled two small glass vials from his pocket—one half-full of a milky-yellow liquid, the other full of a milky-blue one. His hands trembled as he uncapped the half-full vial and downed the contents.

"What the hell *is* that?" I asked, scowling. "What's going on?"

"Stabilizer." He held up a heavily tremoring hand. "For this."

I consciously resisted the urge to move to him, clasp his hand between mine to soothe him. Pursing my lips, I regarded him for a long, silent moment. "Dr. Charish did that to you?" I finally asked.

Giving a single nod, he leaned his head back against the wall and closed his eyes.

I took a very cautious step forward. "Do you need brains?" I asked quietly.

He didn't open his eyes. "Yes," he said in a cracked whisper, tinged with a desperation I didn't think he intended to reveal.

"Stay here," I told him. "I'll be right back." I didn't wait for a response, simply hurried back inside and to the little fridge and my last bottle. Holy crap, but I really hoped I wasn't making a godawful mistake. Every fiber of logic in me said to let him rot, literally. He'd been a complete ass to me since I'd turned him, and it was crazy to believe that as soon as I gave him the brains he wanted he wouldn't do something ugly.

I grabbed the bottle, then headed out again. Philip

had shifted to sit with his back against the wall, his head lowered, in that moment looking like anything but a badass zombie soldier. I unscrewed the bottle top and crouched by him.

"Here, drink this," I said.

He lifted his head, pain flickering over his face as if the simple movement cost him tremendous effort. "I shouldn't . . . be here," he croaked, making no move to take the bottle.

Scowling, I plopped my ass down beside him. "You're here now. *Drink*."

After another few seconds of hesitation, he finally took the bottle from me and slugged down half the contents. A wave of confusion passed over his face as he lowered the bottle.

I had plenty of my own confusion going. My zombie-baby had been a complete and utter asshole, but there was also no denying that something was seriously wrong with him. There was no damn way he could've faked the level of anxiety and despair I'd seen in him earlier when he begged Dr. Charish for assistance. The urge to help him kept hammering at me, no matter how hard I tried to focus on the bad things he'd done, and would likely still try to do to me.

"Drink the rest," I muttered.

His gaze skittered to mine, lines of pain deep in his face. "Have . . . more?"

I hesitated. No damn way was I telling him about my stash. "Not with me," I hedged. "But you can have the rest of this."

He remained still for another few seconds, as if running through his options, then lifted the bottle with both hands and drank another few gulps. He recapped it with a couple of inches of brain smoothie still in it and set it beside me. "Thank you."

Well, that was a whole lot nicer than the "Fuck you"

he'd given me down at the boat launch. "What's going on?" I asked. "Why did you come here?" I didn't think it was only to score some brains, even though he'd obviously needed them desperately.

"I shouldn't be here," he said again, then drew a breath that verged on a sob. "Angel, it hurts." A shudder wracked him. "Oh, god."

I put a hand on his arm. "Philip, I can get you help," I said quietly, suppressing a shiver at the stark pain in his voice. "Please. Let me—"

"No!" He drew in a sharp, noisy breath. "No," he said again, shaking his head. "I can't. You . . . no."

Annoyance at the stoic bullshit flared. "Great, so stay fucked up," I retorted. "You're a goddamn idiot."

Philip dropped his chin to his chest, shoulders shaking and breath coming as if weeping silently, though there were no tears.

"Damn it," I muttered. Sighing, I slipped an arm around him and pulled his head to my shoulder. Stooooooopid parasite. It felt right, but what the *hell* was I doing?

To my surprise he seemed to ease, breathing becoming a bit more regular. "Shouldn't be . . . here," he murmured.

"Yeah yeah yeah," I said with a roll of my eyes. "You said that already. Now shut up about it."

He closed his eyes, tremors easing more. I realized I was stroking his hair, though I didn't remember lifting my hand to do so.

"I'm sorry," he murmured after a moment.

For which part? I wanted to ask. There'd certainly been a lot of bad shit. But he was calm now, and I didn't want him upset and unstable again.

"Yeah, well, you owe me a new jacket," I muttered.

He lifted his head and looked into my face, eyes nowhere near as confused and pain-clouded as a few minutes earlier. "I have to go."

"Sure," I said. "But drink the rest of the bottle first."

Scrubbing a hand over his face, he shifted to sit fully back against the wall again. He picked up the bottle, looked at the remaining sludgy-brown liquid in it. "When can you get more?"

Was he asking because he wanted me to get him more? Or was he concerned that I'd have to go without?

I avoided a direct answer. "I'll be okay. My people will take care of me," I said, with the heavy implication that *his* people obviously didn't. "Drink the rest."

He gave a single tight nod, then nearly ripped the cap off before downing the remainder.

"Why were you dressed up as an extra for the movie?" I asked.

He rubbed at his eyes and set the bottle down. "Have to stay close to the subjects," he muttered. "Easiest way."

"Subjects? Of what?" I peered at him, eyes narrowed.

He blinked and looked over at me. "Shit," he murmured, as if suddenly realizing he'd said too much. He gave his head a sharp shake. "Nothing. Forget I said it." He paused. "I'm serious. You need to forget it."

Yeah, like that was going to happen. His shoulder was warm against mine, and I didn't want to lose the contact with him, but I also knew damn well he was super dangerous and working for people who didn't have warm fuzzies for me. Reluctantly, I pulled away from him and stood.

"You're better now," I made myself say. "You need to leave."

A barely audible moan escaped him as I moved away, but he pushed himself to his feet, gave a slight nod. "I'm going."

I slapped down the urge to tell him I'd find a way to give him more help. "You owe me," I told him instead. "I mean it. Don't come back around here."

A wave of what sure as hell looked like sadness

passed over his face before his expression hardened. He straightened, looked down his nose at me. "I got what I wanted," he said, then turned and headed off along the wall behind the hedge.

Confused, I watched him go, unable to shake the feeling I was missing something obvious.

Chapter 21

To my surprise, I managed to get back to sleep without any problem. Maybe my subconscious accepted that if Philip or any of his cronies were going to mess with me they'd had ample opportunity to do so when I followed him out. Or maybe I was simply tired as all hell. Either way, I slept like the dead until around eight in the morning, and only woke up then because another goddamn fire truck went by on the street outside.

A few more boxes of donated clothing had been brought by, and I managed to snag more stuff for my dad as well as a couple of t-shirts for myself. I even found cargo pants in my size, or rather in a teenage boy size that fit me well enough. After the clothing search I grabbed a quick shower in the girls' locker room, silently grateful that my parasite would take care of any godawful foot fungus I caught from the grungy tile floors.

My dad was peering at a newspaper when I came back out. "Have you eaten this morning?" I asked him as I dragged a comb through my wet hair.

"Yeah. Some fancy cinnamon roll thing."

"They have eggs and bacon too," I told him. "You should try and eat some protein." I tugged on shoes and socks. "I'm gonna see if I can get a ride in to work and then the phone store to get us new phones." *And the DMV. And probably the bank too*, I thought. I needed a new debit card, and wanted to deposit the money he'd given me. Holy crap, but there was a lot to do. Good thing most of it was in semi-reasonable walking distance from downtown. Sure, I wanted to find out more about why Philip was pretending to be an extra and who the hell the "subjects" were he was talking about, but taking care of my dad and me had to take priority right now.

"You need anything while I'm gone?" I asked.

Dad shook his head, turned the page in his newspaper. "Don't need shit."

That's when I saw it. A picture of Marcus at the bottom of the front page under all the stuff about the flood. And a headline that read, *Heroic Rescue Saves Family of Three*.

I snatched the paper away from my dad. "And when were you planning on telling me about this?" I asked, as I hurried to read the brief article.

"What? About that cop?"

"You should have said something," I said with a scowl. He muttered something I decided to ignore while I focused on reading.

The article praised Marcus for diving into a flooded drainage canal to save a young family from certain death after their car went off the road shortly after dark. Unfortunately, it continued, the officer sustained a broken leg and had to be transported to the hospital for treatment.

I silently cursed the lack of details, but exhaled in relief. A broken leg was nothing but an inconvenience for a zombie. And most importantly, it explained why he hadn't come by last night.

I hesitated, then thrust the paper back at my dad, gave him a hug. "It's all gonna be okay," I said. "We're still alive and that's what counts."

His eyes lifted to mine. "That's good, Angelkins. Everything's gonna be just fine. You and me."

"Damn straight," I said. "We're too mean to keep down for long."

"When you coming back?"

"I'll probably be a few hours, I figure," I told him. "Hope to be back by noon or so, though." My brow furrowed. "You gonna be okay? I heard someone say they're getting a TV in here to show movies."

"I know how to take care of myself," he said with a scowl. "You go do whatever you gotta do."

I scowled right back at him, but I couldn't help but be perversely glad that his orneriness was returning.

It didn't take long to find a volunteer who was more than happy to give me a ride to the Coroner's Office. Once there, she even gave me her number so that I could call when I needed a ride back.

It took me a few seconds and several brain cells to figure out why the front door of the office was locked, then I remembered it was a Saturday. *Crap. Guess I won't be going to the DMV today.* Since my keycard was at the bottom of the swamp by now, I used the number pad of the lock to gain entry.

My footsteps echoed through the quiet halls as I continued through the main building and into the morgue. I planned on finding a way to get to my storage unit, but if there were any available brains to be had here, I'd be stupid to pass them up. With all the weirdness going on with Philip and Saberton, I wanted to be *tanked*.

But when I pulled the cooler door open, I stopped in my tracks and stared in shock. Body bags—had to be over a dozen of them. All three stretchers were full, as were the shelves along the walls.

The flood. *Oh my god. These are people who died in the flood.*

My dad could have easily ended up in one of those. If I hadn't been able to call Pietro for a rescue, or if I hadn't been home, there was no way he'd have made it out. Goosebumps skimmed over me, and I quickly backed out of the cooler and shut the door. My gaze went to the whiteboard on the wall by the cutting room. Three had already been autopsied. Dr. Leblanc had probably worked late last night.

So far the only brains I'd refused to consume were children and friends—like when Marianne, Ed's girlfriend, had been murdered. I'd long ago lost my respect for the dead, at least that's what I tried to tell myself. But I still winced with a razor-sharp stab of regret as I went back into the cooler, found the body of Bern, Alfred B/M 78 YO, and feasted on his brain.

After I tanked up on both brains and guilt, I fired up the morgue computer and tried to decipher the instructions for applying for disaster aid. After a frustrating half hour, I decided that, for the sake of my own sanity, I needed to get someone to help me out. Since the flood had affected relatively few people, its victims didn't qualify for federal aid, which left only state agencies with their bizarre requirements and confusing instructions.

The search for a new trailer didn't go any better. Or rather, I had no trouble finding all sorts of trailers and dealers online, but the prices for anything that wasn't a roach-infested falling-down hovel were helluva lot more than I'd expected.

More than a little demoralized, I headed back into the main building.

"Angel?"

I looked up to see Derrel step out of the investigator's

office. He gave me a relieved smile. "Angel, so good to see you!"

I mustered a smile. "Hey, big guy."

"I'm sorry your area flooded," he said as he moved toward me, face clouded with concern. "It must really be a mess. I'll be happy to come help with some cleanup on my next day off." He tilted his head. "Hey, how'd the exam go?"

I blinked at him stupidly. Exam? Cleanup? What was there to clean up? "What exam?"

"The GED? Wasn't that this morning?"

A sick jolt went through me. "Oh my god," I breathed. "I totally forgot about that."

Derrel cringed. "Oh, sorry. Yeah, I guess you weren't able to make it." Then he flashed a smile. "But I know you'd have aced it."

"Yeah," I said, my throat constricting. The goddamn GED. All this time studying, and then I missed the test. One more thing the flood took away from me. "I guess so."

Behind Derrel, the front door opened and Nick came through. His eyes went straight to me, and then he walked right past Derrel and gathered me into a hug.

"I'm so *so* sorry," he murmured with such utter compassion and genuine sympathy that I did the only thing possible.

I fucking burst into tears. And then I couldn't stop. Nick held me and gently rubbed my back while I lost it on his shoulder. All this time I'd managed to be tough and strong and stoic and all full of positive thinking, and Nick's damn hug completely undid me.

"I was so worried," Nick said, still hugging me. And damn it, it wasn't creepy or grabby or anything. Simply supportive and comforting. "I just got back from . . . your place."

I sniffled. "You mean my empty lot? It's gone. All

gone." Behind him I saw Derrel standing there with an increasingly perplexed expression.

"I know. I saw." He gently released me and pulled back to look into my face.

"Wait, Angel," Derrel said, shock and disbelief heavy in his voice. "Your house? You lost your house? Oh my god. I didn't know. I thought you only had a foot of water or so." He shook his head. "I'm an idiot. I'm so sorry."

I wiped at my eyes and nodded. "Lost the whole damn thing. We had to climb onto the roof." I tried to smile. "But we got a helicopter ride out of it, so that was cool, y'know."

"Ah hell," he said, then moved up to smash me against his chest in his own massive hug.

I made an *oof* sound. "Can't ... breathe," I gasped dramatically. Derrel released me with a gruff snort and shaky smile.

"Is your dad all right?" Nick asked, expression serious.

"He's okay. Small bump on the head but nothing bad," I told them.

"What do you need?" he asked. "What can we do?"

I took a deep breath. "I'm not even sure where to begin. I guess I need a copy of my ID from my personnel file so I can get a new phone and debit card and, hell, new ID though that'll have to wait 'til Monday. And I need to go to my storage unit, and—"

Derrel held up a hand, stopping my babble. "You need a ride?"

"I'd love one," I replied, relieved.

"I may be slow on the uptake," Derrel said, "but I can at least play chauffeur."

Nick looked as if he wished he'd thought to offer a ride first, but he managed an encouraging smile anyway. "Angel, when you get your new phone, be sure to call and let me know what you need."

"I will," I said, moving to him and giving him a hug. "Thanks."

He gave a little shrug. "No biggie," he said, trying to be nonchalant and utterly failing. He headed to the investigator's office without another word. Derrel watched him go, slight frown puckering his wide forehead, then turned back to me.

"At your service, darlin'," he said with a slight bow.

I smacked him on the upper arm. "Don't make me start quoting *Driving Miss Daisy*."

He chuckled. "Y'know, if I squint you look a bit like Jessica Tandy."

"Oh my god." I laughed. "Shut up and help me break into the personnel files."

Chapter 22

Once again I found myself grateful that I lived in a small town. I expected to have to go through all sorts of hassle to get a replacement phone, since the DMV was closed and my only photo ID was a photocopy of my actual driver's license. But the guy at the phone store remembered me from when I'd been in a few weeks before, and I scored new phones for my dad and me with practically zero hassle. Unfortunately the brand new phone had barely any charge and, since I actually wanted to *use* my phone, I ended up buying a car charger as well so that I could give it some quick juice in Derrel's Durango.

The bank people were less accommodating and weren't keen to give me a new debit card without something vaguely official. However, they cheerfully accepted my dad's cash for deposit, though I remembered to hold back a couple hundred. Until I had an ID, I wouldn't be able to withdraw once it was officially deposited.

The storage unit was my last stop. I worried that Derrel would want to come in with me to help get stuff, which would have been awkward as hell since, well, y'know, freezer full of brains. I assured him I wasn't planning on taking anything out since I didn't have any place to put it, so there was nothing to lift or carry, and told him all I wanted to do was look for a scrapbook I thought I'd stored a couple of months ago. I spun a line about how it would ease my mind to know that something personal had survived the flood and, luckily, he bought my lie and waited in the car while I went inside. Of course then I got stupidly bummed out because there wasn't a damn thing in my storage unit but a goddamn freezer full of brains and some pork ribs, which meant that yeah, everything we'd owned really was gone.

Still have brains at least, I told myself. *Could be a helluva lot worse.*

I stuffed three bags of frozen brains into each of my side pockets, then instantly regretted the fact that I now had only the thin fabric of my cargo pants between me and frozen brains. Yeah, totally comfortable.

I returned to the Durango, gave Derrel a big smile. "It was there!" I lied.

"Awesome!" he said with a wide grin. Grief of loss swept through me again. Goddammit, but the next time I got some memorabilia I was going to make sure it was stored someplace safe.

"Can you spare me a few more minutes?" I asked as I unplugged the phone from the car charger. "I need to make a phone call now that I have a bit of charge."

"Take your time," Derrel said in his easygoing manner. I gave him a smile and walked a few steps away from the Durango.

I dialed Pietro's number, once again glad that it was so close to my ex-boyfriend's number and therefore easy to remember.

He picked up on the second ring. "Angel. I've been waiting to hear from you. How are you? I've been very concerned. I only recently found out that Marcus didn't pick you up from the shelter yesterday."

"Hey, Pietro," I said. "I've sure as hell been better. It's cool about Marcus. I saw the paper this morning." I shifted the phone to the other ear. "I can't thank you enough for sending the helicopter. I don't think my dad woulda made it if not for that."

"I was more than happy to help," he replied. "But I'm so very sorry you lost so much."

"Thanks," I said, then blew out my breath. "About Marcus. Brian told me not to say anything to anyone about the highway fight because of security. Does that include Marcus? We have enough crap between us without keeping something like that from him."

After only a second of hesitation, Pietro replied, "That situation is settling. Use your discretion and share what you feel you need to."

"Okay. Great," I said, more relief than I expected washing through me. "Look, I also called to tell you I saw Philip last night. Twice."

He fell quiet for a few seconds. I heard a click, and I had the strongest impression that he'd done something to record the call. "What happened?" he finally asked.

I told him about following Philip and what I found in the box under the steps, and about seeing him with Dr. Charish and how she gave him the paper bag with the packets of brains. Then I told him about how Philip came to find me and how I gave him my last bottle of brains.

"I don't know why I helped him," I confessed to Pietro. I wasn't quite ready to share my zombie-parent-compassion theory. "I mean, he's been nothing but a complete tool to me, but . . . god, he was so obviously hurting."

"Angel, you have no idea how thankful I am that you helped him," he said.

I blinked. "Um. You are?" I asked, baffled. "I don't understand. Isn't he working for Saberton?"

"Yes," he said. "But as an operative for me."

"Whoa," I breathed. I fell silent for a few seconds while I wrapped my head around that. "Wait," I said, anger flaring. "He was working for you this whole time? Even when he attacked me? Why the hell didn't you tell me?"

I heard him exhale. "Angel, I understand how you feel," he replied. "There was so much at stake. *Is* so much at stake. Everything has been on a need-to-know basis in order to protect Philip and his assignment. If the Saberton men with him ever witnessed anything from you other than your genuine reaction to him as one of them, he would be compromised . . . and so would you. However, as he is due to be extracted tomorrow, there's little harm in you knowing now."

"Oh." I scowled. I hated the answer, but I also understood it. Damn it. "Well, he's in really bad shape," I told him, then narrowed my eyes as another piece of the puzzle clicked into place, and I didn't like the picture that was forming. "Hang on," I said. "That drop he made . . ." Son of a bitch. If Philip was an operative for Pietro, that had to mean the stuff he left in the box under the steps was meant for Pietro's people. There wouldn't have been any reason for him to be skulking around to pass something to *Saberton* since he was openly working with them. And good ole Dr. Charish had been there waiting for the stuff . . .

A brand new anger flared. "Is Charish still working for *you?*" I walked a little farther away from the Durango. I had a feeling I was going to be raising my voice real soon.

He drew a deep breath and released it, and when he spoke his voice sounded heavy and tired. "I reacquired her a few days after she fled the factory lab incident with you," he told me. "She is contained and works under Ariston's supervision." He paused. "He needs her."

"Contained?" I spat the word. "Well no one contained her when she was a vicious cold bitch to Philip. He begged for brains, and she jumped his ass for not *rationing* properly. Then she only gave him two packets when he obviously needed a lot more." The plastic of my phone creaked, and I forced myself to relax my grip before I broke it.

"She and Dr. Nikas were temporarily at the Tucker Point lab location to monitor the data and samples from Saberton's zombie research that Philip left at the drop site," Pietro told me. "However, Ariston had to return to the main lab the night of your fight with the Saberton men out on Highway 1790. Heather needed medical attention, and he wanted to preserve the brain remnants for future use from the zombie she killed." His voice was a bit too calm and even, and I had a strong feeling he was more than a little pissed off himself. But whether it was because Philip had been wronged, or because the oh-so-secret mission had been jeopardized, I couldn't tell.

"Great, so he needs help from y'all and gets treated like dirt," I said, scowling.

"Philip has other means of signaling that he needs assistance," Pietro told me. "The lab itself was never a contact point, and he wouldn't have gone there if he'd been thinking clearly." He sounded oddly weary. "Ariston failed to foresee an interaction between Philip and Charish and so hadn't left any instructions. Charish knew him only as a Saberton informant working on the movie set."

My scowl deepened. "Well, y'all need to do something for him now. He's hurting bad and twitchy."

"Considering the current circumstances, I'll get word to him that we're going to move his extraction up for later today. You said he did get stabilizer?"

"Oh, the stuff that keeps him from shaking?"

"Right. That's Ariston's formulation to ease the pain somewhat and keep Philip functional."

"Yeah. He had two vials. One kinda yellow and the other a milky blue. He drank half of one when he was with me." I wanted to get pissed off again at the reminder of how Charish had fucked Philip up, but it was getting a bit tiring being so mad all the time.

I thought I heard a low intake of breath. "Angel, are you certain one was a milky blue?"

"Totally."

"And which one did he drink from last night?" The tension in his voice was palpable.

"The yellow." I frowned. "Why?"

"All right. There still might be time," he said, almost as if to himself.

"Pietro? What's going on?"

"The yellow vial is most likely stabilizer," he said. "The color varies with the batch as the formulation is improved. It's the milky blue one that concerns me since that's the color of the parasite stimulant that Ariston sometimes uses for testing. I'm no doctor, but I don't think it would react well with Philip's already unstable parasite."

Fucking hell. Had Charish given him the wrong thing on purpose? I knew in my bones that Dr. Nikas hadn't messed up the vials.

"It could simply be a coincidence, but I'm giving orders for his immediate extraction," he continued. "Thank you for calling me, Angel. This has been very helpful."

And with that he hung up. I stared down at the phone while I muttered a few nasty words, then headed back to the Durango.

"Where to now?" Derrel asked. "Back to the high school?"

I nodded. "My dad's probably wondering what's taking me so long."

It was a few miles. Longer than I would've wanted to walk, but only a couple of minutes to drive. "You can let me out by the gym door," I said as we got close.

"Sure thing." He glanced my way as he pulled to a stop. "Look, you guys are welcome to come stay at my place tonight if you want. It's not big but may be better than here."

I cocked an eyebrow at him. "I dunno. Do you have roving bands of roaches patrolling the halls? I'm kinda used to those now."

His face twisted into a mock grimace. "Unfortunately, I can't offer roach guards. But I do have a disdainful cat. Will that work?"

"Thanks, partner. I'll ask my dad what he wants to do," I said with a grateful smile. "I have your number if we decide to take you up on it."

"You're welcome, Angel," he said. "Give me a call later, or you'll get more texts than you know what to do with."

"I will!" I promised, laughing. I leaned over and gave him a hug, then slipped out of the car and headed inside.

There was no sign of my dad in the gym, and the plastic bag with his clothes and jacket was gone. My heart hammered as I jumped to the worst conclusion: Kidnapped by Saberton. Alarm rose as I swept my gaze around the room again, as if doing so would magically reveal that he'd been hiding. I took a breath and tried to convince myself that, with my dad, it could just as easily be that he left on his own through sheer bullheadedness.

The tool-stealing teenage refugee was flaked out on the floor in front of the TV.

"Hey, do you know where my dad is?" I asked.

His eyes flicked to me and then right back to the screen. "He left with someone."

My scowl deepened at the lack of useful information, and I moved between him and the TV. "What kind of someone?" I snarled.

He jerked his gaze up to mine, an outraged response on his lips, but it died when his eyes met mine. I was fairly well tanked up and oh-so-very-much not in the mood for bullshit, especially when it came to my dad.

His throat bobbed as he gulped. "A man. About thirty, I think. Short dark hair, on crutches. Your dad knew him."

Marcus. I bet he *loved* faking an injury. The tension drained out of me. "Oh, cool. Thanks!" Okay, so the thought of my dad and Marcus having guy-time together wasn't exactly comforting but it was better than the other theories I'd concocted. I yanked my phone from my pocket to call Marcus then scowled at the flashing battery symbol. Crap. Obviously five minutes on the car charger wasn't worth a whole lot.

"Angel!"

I spun to see the woman who'd given me the ride to the Coroner's Office striding toward me. "Your boyfriend was just here," she announced with a smile, and I had to bite down on the automatic denial that Marcus was my boyfriend. "I told him I didn't know when you'd be back," she continued, "but he wanted to go ahead and get your dad settled. He left a note for you." She thrust a folded piece of paper at me.

"Thanks," I said, taking it. She gave me another bright smile and then hurried off. I unfolded the paper and read.

Angel—
Your dad's safe with me. Please call when you get this note. You can both stay at my place as long as you want.
Marcus

I peered at a stray mark before his name. It looked as if he'd started to write an "L" and thought better of it. Love? Exhaling, I refolded the paper and stuffed it into a pocket. *Stay with Marcus.* It wasn't an ideal solution, especially considering our last conversation, but it was a lot better than remaining in the shelter. And I liked Derrel too much to inflict my dad's permanent company upon him. My mouth twitched in wry amusement. At least Marcus was already used to the ornery bastard.

As concern for my dad evaporated, worry for Philip flooded in. Now that I had a clue as to his real situation, I wanted to see for myself that Pietro's people got him out okay, and if they hadn't yet, to get some brains to him. I could call Marcus as soon as I did so. Pietro had said Philip was working on the movie, so now I just needed to figure out how to sneak into where they were filming.

Hurrying to the door, I almost ran smack into Jane Pennington as she came in, and it was only a quick maneuver by one of her staffers that kept us from all falling in a heap.

"Angel!" Her eyes widened in surprise as she recovered her balance and steadied herself on her cane. "I didn't know you were here," she said, genuine concern in her voice. "Pietro told me he got you out, so I thought you'd be somewhere besides in the shelter." Brow furrowed, she swept her gaze around the gym with its cots and motley inhabitants.

I winced. "Yeah, it's been pretty crazy," I said. "We spent last night here, but I think we're gonna be staying with Marcus. For a couple of days, at least." I could unpack my feelings about all of that later.

"I hope everything works out," she said. "I'm so sorry for your losses." She looked like she was going to say more, but one of her aides, a middle-aged man with sharp features and a serious expression touched her arm.

"I'm sorry, Jane," he said, "but they're about to start filming the crowd scene. We can come back here to speak to the refugees afterward."

Indecision swept over her face. It was clear she cared deeply about my situation, but it was also obvious that she *really* wanted to see the movie zombies. It was such a totally human and awesome and non-congresswomanly display that I had to choke back a laugh, and I sure as hell liked her even more for it.

"Hey, is it okay if I tag along?" I said, making the decision moot for her. Besides, this would get me behind the barricades so I could make sure Philip was being taken care of. And if Pietro's people hadn't yet reached him, I had two chunks of frostbite on my thighs—or rather, two pockets full of thawing brains—that might be of use.

Jane grinned. "Absolutely!"

We left the gym and headed toward the barricades across the gaps in the chain-link fence surrounding the football field. Beyond them, the movie crew positioned lighting and numerous cameras while a whole horde of zombies chilled out, waiting for the start of the filming. As I'd hoped, I had no trouble getting onto the set by following in Jane's wake. No questions asked.

The extras clustered around Jane in a strange meet-and-greet zombie fest. At first I wondered why they were so enthusiastic, then I remembered she'd been instrumental in assuring that laid off factory workers were given the jobs. The unaffected grin on her face told me she was in utter heaven as she peered at makeup and laughed at outrageous shambling. I sure as hell hoped Pietro was dating her because he actually liked her and not for some ulterior purpose.

The pace of activity increased as the crew members readied for filming. Makeup people touched up zombie rot and prosthetic gore, and other crew circulated through the crowd with water bottles and some of the white-wrapped bars. Apparently shambling was hard work, I thought with amusement.

A sudden shiver of unease ran through me for no reason that I could name, even as an odd noise like soft moaning rippled through the crowd of extras. Mildly weirded out, I surreptitiously palmed a handful of brains from a baggie in my side pocket and got it into my mouth without anyone seeing. At least I hoped not.

The *something's-wrong* feeling increased as I scanned

the area. Though filming hadn't started, extras began to stagger or flail their arms or sway in place. Definitely not normal. I downed another handful of brains as I slipped through the crowd, again glad that I was skinny enough to do so with ease.

However, I was less than thrilled by my lack of height since I couldn't see a damn thing. I went still and lifted my head, scenting the air and not caring how strange it looked. Hell, I was surrounded by a bunch of people pretending to be undead. I was the normal one in this crowd.

Yet my sniffing only confused me more. I caught hints of the distinctive zombie-rot odor, but it came from multiple sources. Not good.

Another weird ripple of unease passed through me, once again accompanied by a bizarre shift in behavior of the extras. Unnerving groans came from all around me, and a fake zombie nearby staggered and sank to the ground, hands clawing at her face and throat. My frown deepened as the latex peeled away, revealing a square stick-on patch on the side of her neck surrounded by faintly grey skin that didn't look made up. Baffled, I swung my gaze around, caught a glimpse of one of the makeup people holding a cardboard box in her hand with what looked like more of the strange patches in it along with some of the snack bars that had been handed out earlier.

I steadied my gaze on the makeup artist, and my heart skipped a beat. It was the petite black woman who'd stolen my blood at the boat launch. *A makeup artist who draws blood?*

Realization slammed in.

The subjects. Philip was undercover with Saberton, and he'd said he needed to stay close to the subjects. I stared around in shock and no small amount of horror as bits and pieces began to fall into place. The extras were being used as test subjects by the Saberton Corporation.

And now bits of the conversation with Dr. Nikas lit up.

Fake brains are the holy grail.

Dangerous to test them on zombies since it risks changing the parasite—like what ruined Philip.

A way to make temporary zombies . . .

Oh my god. The stick-on patches. The too-real looking grey skin. The snack bars. Some sort of research patch on a temporary zombie being fed fake brains? It made a horrible and sick sense. Saberton was temporarily zombifying the extras in order to test fake brains on them. No one would blink twice at zombie extras actually looking a little like zombies for a while.

Righteous anger flared—not only at the Saberton associates but at Pietro's team as well. Instead of putting a stop to it and trying to protect these people, they'd had Philip remain undercover so that he could steal whatever findings Saberton came up with and pass them over to Dr. Nikas to use in his own research. People didn't matter.

My gut tightened. Brenda Barnes, the cardiomyopathy victim, most likely died from this testing. The adhesive on her neck. It fit.

An extra staggered in circles nearby, confusion in his eyes turning sharp and feral. Something was going wrong with the temporary zombies, causing bizarre actions and actual zombie-like behavior. Then I felt it. With no obvious cause, a weird, twitchy unease touched with hunger permeated me. *Philip.* Call it a zombie-mama's intuition, but I had a bad feeling Philip was the source of the problem with the extras. He was somewhere in this crowd, going nuts and throwing off some sort of weird feeding frenzy pheromone. *Damn.*

Turning, I pushed through the crowd of temp zombies around Jane, elbowed one sharply out of the way as it reached for her. "Jane! You need to get out of here."

Her brow furrowed as she looked around for some
obvious source of danger. "What? Why?"

Crap. She probably thought the extras were still simply being in character, giving her a little demo. *Yeah, well
she's gonna get one hell of a demo if she doesn't get out of
here!* But what the hell was I supposed to tell her?

"Um, there's a labor dispute, and I think there's about
to be a riot!" I blurted, then fought back a cringe. Holy
crap, but that was without a doubt the dumbest thing I'd
ever said. "Look, you need to get off the set," I insisted.

A small frown of doubt touched her mouth as she took
in the increasingly erratic behavior of the extras. "Yes, I
suppose you're right."

I shot a look to her aide. "Get her out of here or . . . or
I'll tell Pietro you didn't get her out of here!" Too late I
realized the threat was pointless if he didn't know how
much power Pietro held.

Fortunately he at least seemed to understand that the
crowd was growing unruly for no discernible reason. He
nodded and slipped an arm around Jane's waist on the opposite side from her cane. "I've got her," he told me, then
looked to Jane. "Let's get you to the car, Dr. Pennington."
He shepherded her toward the barricades, and I stayed
long enough to make absolutely sure she was really getting
out of the crowd before I turned back to the mess.

Crew members and staff sought to regain order but
were losing the battle as the bizarre rowdiness increased.
Distantly I heard someone yell to get the cameras running. *What the hell?* I thought in outrage, though a sensible part of me totally understood that any director
worth a shit would want to film a crowd of zombies going
nuts. Besides, the director probably had *no* idea what the
real deal was.

I fought my way free from the thick of the crowd, continuing to scan and scent. My gaze passed over a black-
haired woman, then went right back to her. She stood

tall, scanning the crowd, and didn't seem at all disturbed by the craziness around her.

I shoved a stumbling extra out of my way as I got closer to her. "Heather?" I asked in disbelief as I peered at her, noting on closer inspection that she was wearing a dark wig over her blonde hair.

Her attention rested on me, and a smile touched her mouth. "Hey, Angel," she murmured, then went back to scanning the crowd. "I'm *in* with Mr. Ivanov. Can't thank you enough." She looked calm and oh-so-very ready for action.

"That's awesome," I said. I figured her minimal disguise was to help keep her off the Saberton radar. "You're looking for Philip too?" I mentally prayed for her to tell me they'd already found and extracted him, but she merely gave a sharp nod.

"Yep. Me and Kyle—my trainer—were nearby when the call came in," she told me. "Others are on their way."

Crap. Philip hadn't been extracted yet, adding confirmation to my gut feeling that he was the source of the problem with the berserk extras.

I felt his influence—a growing unnatural hunger accompanied by waves of unease, like insects crawling in my skull and sending twitches through my muscles. Unlike the poor extras who didn't have a clue what they were experiencing, I didn't have much trouble controlling the compulsion to feed, especially since I was fairly tanked. Yet along with the undesirable urge came something else—a strong sense of Philip, as though I *knew* where he was without knowing.

I lifted my head and scented the air again. There, to my left. I slipped through the increasingly wild crowd, surrounded by shouts and cries that were far too realistic to be part of a movie.

A fake zombie reached for me, confusion and anger warring it out on his makeup-covered features. I dodged the grab only to be forced to spin away from another who lunged toward me, lips pulled back from rotted teeth. For an instant I wondered if that was makeup or if the extra actually had poor oral hygiene. The latter, I decided as the few teeth in his head snapped together on nothing.

Baring my own—far better—teeth, I shoved the fake zombie back and continued moving toward where my newfound intuitive radar told me Philip was. Another zombie let out a gurgling moan, and a heavier waft of rot hit me like a fist. *Shit.* This wasn't one of the extras. This was Tim Bell of the broken nose, and he looked *bad*, eyes wild and desperate, and flesh shredding for real from his clawed hands. A young woman with only light zombie makeup stood beside him, eyes wide in confusion, but not acting erratically. Maybe not a test subject?

Tim let out a rasping snarl, then grabbed the woman's arm in a hard grip. She let out a shocked wail of pain, confusion shifting to a perfectly understandable fear. I could easily smell her brains, which meant it had to be driving Tim absolutely bonkers.

"Heather!" I yelled, hoping the woman was within earshot, even as I kicked Tim's knee as hard as I could. He staggered and let out a bellow, but to my relief he released the young woman. Snarling, he turned on me, a scary, dangerous expression coming over his face. In my peripheral vision I saw other extras grow more agitated as he focused his fury on me. Great. Goddamn pheromones all over the damn place.

The young woman fled through the crowd, but in her place Heather appeared. Her sharp gaze took in the situation and no doubt noted that this particular zombie was waaaay different from the other misbehaving extras.

"Whatcha got?" she asked calmly. Her eyes never left Tim as she pulled out a collapsible police baton and snapped it open.

"He's a real one," I told her quickly. "Philip made him, and he's all messed up." Tim was obviously hungry, and though I had pockets full of thawing brains, I wasn't about to waste them on this motherfucker unless absolutely necessary. "The other one Philip made might be somewhere in here too." Crap. And Philip. Like a nest of pissed off snakes in my belly, I sensed him escalating out of control.

"Oh, right," she said, brandishing the baton. "We're supposed to get those two as well as well as Philip."

I took a step back as she squared off against the very pissed-off Tim. "I need to find Philip," I said, feeling the urgency of it rise with every passing second. "You got this one?"

"Yep," she replied with an adrenaline-charged smile. "I got this."

I gave her one last dubious look, then continued to weave through the seething crowd. More extras grabbed at me, but thankfully, they only seemed to have a touch of the full zombie strength and speed, so a few well-placed kicks and elbows got me past them. I shoved an extra dressed as a rotting cheerleader out of the way, then breathed a curse as I caught sight of Roland, the other Philip-made real zombie. He didn't have any makeup on, and he didn't need it. His head swiveled from side to side, lips curled back and teeth snapping together repeatedly. Saliva strung from the corner of his mouth and his eyes shone with madness.

With a roar, he charged one of the camera crew who was trying vainly to restore some order in his little corner of the fiasco. I sucked in a breath. I knew there was no way I'd be able to intervene in time to save the crew member. Yet before Roland could close the distance, a stocky man wearing a shirt lettered "Security" lifted a gun and fired with a familiar *whuuush* sound.

A tranq gun.

A yellow tuft bloomed on Roland's chest. He took two more steps and then crumpled onto his face. The man with the tranq gun lowered it, and I got another start of surprise. This was the asshole who'd stepped on my hand out at the boat launch. Turning, I quickly lost myself in the crowd. I didn't want to get tranqed myself, and I was more than happy to leave him to deal with the neutralized Roland.

My zombie-mama heart lurched, and I froze as an inhuman, snarling bellow cut through the crowd noise. I ducked past another cluster of people and around the corner of the building that housed the concession stand, just in time to see Philip take a Saberton security man by the head and smash it into the cinderblock wall.

Well, shit, I thought. *This is bad.*

Chapter 23

As the body fell, Philip dropped into a crouch, tore the man's skull apart, and began to stuff chunks of brain into his mouth. His entire body jerked every few seconds as though jolted by electricity, and his dead-grey face was plenty horrifying without any movie makeup. He screamed in anguish through a gory mouthful, spattering the pavement with blood and brain bits.

Really, *really* bad. "Philip!" I yelled. "Philip, it's me, Angel!"

His hands curled like claws as his eyes snapped to mine, and to my dismay I saw nothing of Philip in them. Hell, he barely looked human. I felt my own lips pull back in an answering snarl. How the hell was I supposed to help him . . . or stop him?

"Angel, I have your back," said a calm male voice from behind me. "I'm Kyle Griffin, and Mr. Ivanov sent me."

Kyle—Heather's trainer. "Gotcha," I said without pulling my attention from Philip to glance back. I moved forward, then paused as Philip stood, breathing heavily, gore dripping from his hands and mouth. He tilted his

head back and let out an eerie wail that slid through me
like a blade of ice. The hair on my arms stood on end as
the zombie extras echoed the cry in poor, though equally
disturbing, imitation.

If I'd had any doubt that the temp zombies were reacting to Philip, it was gone in that moment. Hopefully
that meant if I could calm Philip, the rest of the commotion would settle down before anyone else got seriously
hurt or worse. Yeah, no problem. I drew a deep breath
and let it out, fixing my gaze on Philip as I shifted closer
to him. "Easy there, big guy," I murmured.

Philip let out a animal cry of torment, arching his
back and clenching his fists, and sending the extras into
an unnerving wailing frenzy. A tremor wracked him, and
he swung his head toward the source of the cries, a new
fever lighting his eyes. *Ah, hell, this is Not Good.*

Movement caught my eye. I flicked my gaze away
from Philip barely long enough to see the asshole Saberton dude who'd tranqed Roland come around the corner
of the building a few yards beyond Philip. His face set in
determination, he gripped the tranq gun in his right
hand.

Crap. I snapped my focus back to Philip and closed
half the distance between us, while somewhere on the
sidelines the sensible part of me wondered what the hell
I was doing. "Hey! Philip!" I called out, trusting that
Kyle would take care of Saberton Dude while I distracted Philip from the masses.

As though on cue, a tall and lanky black man strode
from behind me toward Saberton Dude, everything in
his attitude and posture announcing that he was going to
take this company man out of action and there wasn't a
damn thing anyone could do to stop him. Kyle Dangerous As Fuck.

"Stay back, asshole," Saberton Dude ordered Kyle,
raising the tranq gun. Kyle kept moving, apparently not

giving a shit about the tranq gun. The man fired, and
scored a hit in the shoulder, but Kyle didn't even slow.

Well, not for two steps anyway. Then he stopped and
stared down at the dart in his shoulder with an expression of shock and disbelief. It sure looked like he'd expected to have some resistance to the tranq. Realization
hit me. *The new tranq.* The same stuff that knocked me
out the other night rather than simply paralyzing me. I
couldn't help wondering how the hell Kyle could have a
resistance to normal tranqs, but now wasn't the time to
explore that little mystery.

Kyle crumpled to the ground, still looking surprised
and more than a little annoyed. A smirk of satisfaction
crossed Saberton Dude's face, but it quickly shifted to a
wide-eyed, holy-crap face as Philip screamed and turned
toward him, blood from the dead Saberton man still wet
on his face. He swung the gun around to point at Philip,
fired, and struck him low on his left side.

Oh, hell no! My zombie-mama-bitch protective instinct flared hot and bright. With a snarl I ran and dove
at the asshole. Saberton Dude's eyes widened as he
caught sight of me, and he tried to back pedal into a
position to fend off Philip and level the tranq gun in my
direction, but I slammed into him while he was still off
balance, all ninety-eight or so pounds of me driving him
back and over an equipment rack to land heavily on top
of him.

Philip gave another tortured scream that slashed
through my senses like a tumble of razor blades. Again,
the extras picked it up and echoed it.

With a harsh growl I ripped the gun out of Saberton
Dude's hand. "You don't touch him!" I yelled.

He seemed surprised by my strength. Maybe he
hadn't dealt with female zombies before? But he recovered quickly. "Get off me, you crazy bitch!"

"I'm not crazy!" I snarled. Baring my teeth, I drew my

hand back and punched him hard—backing it with plenty of zombie-strength.

His jaw broke with an extremely satisfying crunch followed by his gurgle of pain. Grinning with far too much satisfaction, I pushed up off him, then stomped hard on his hand.

"Okay, maybe a little crazy," I muttered. "And payback is definitely a bitch."

I turned away as Heather ran up, baton in her right hand dripping with what sure as hell looked like blood. For a second I almost felt sorry for Tim.

Nah, not even a second.

Her eyes flicked around, taking it all in: the dead guy with his head smashed open, Saberton Dude down and moaning, Kyle down and very still, and Philip with a dart protruding from his side—most certainly not down— looking even more pissed off and crazy, and now moving toward the extras.

"Here," I said, and tossed her the tranq gun. "But don't shoot Philip with it. It'll make him worse." I didn't wait for a reply. I yanked a bag from my pocket and gulped down some more brains, then ran after Philip and literally shoved the half-full bag into his face. He gave a weird hissing howl, grabbed the bag in hands still crooked like claws. He sucked the contents down and let the empty bag fall, but to my dismay the animal-crazed look still filled his eyes. He lurched toward the extras again and let out another scream-cry.

New fervor erupted in the crowd, and screams of non-zombies made my blood run cold. This was turning into total mayhem, and I knew I needed to do something to stop it, but what? My instinct shrieked at me to move, to act. Now.

Great! Sure! I snarled at it. *Tell me what to do and I will!*

Philip made a lunge toward the cheerleader zombie,

but I grabbed at his arm and used as much zombie-strength as I could to swing him toward me. Eyes wild, he raised a hand to strike me, tension in every fiber of his body. Yet to my surprise—and deep relief—he held the strike, face contorted and body quivering as though fighting with himself.

With an animal snarl of my own, I seized his shoulders, leaped up to wrap my arms and legs around him, and then sank my teeth into the big muscle at the juncture of his neck and shoulder.

That, my instinct crooned. *Do that.*

My breath hissed around my teeth as I latched onto him like a tick on a hound dog. I had no urge to tear or maul like when I'd turned him into a zombie. Just bite and hold. That was all.

Philip staggered back and made a strangled noise, but made no attempt to throw me off, though it would've been easy enough for him to do, strong as he was. He shook like a dog shedding water, and I bit harder. I heard a low growl and was surprised to realize I was the one making it.

Philip sank slowly to his knees, breath coming in low shuddering gasps. I kept my arms and legs wrapped tightly around him and teeth clamped down hard while I watched the movement around us.

Brian approached with a tranq gun in one hand and a regular gun in the other. He hesitated, indecision in his eyes as he took in what I was doing to Philip. Apparently this wasn't any sort of normal operating procedure when trying to subdue a crazed zombie. It was working though, no denying that. And Brian obviously came to the same conclusion, for in the next breath he turned away and began issuing quiet orders to the two people behind him—Rachel and Dan, the two zombies who'd cleaned up the mess after the highway fight with Heather.

The wails and cries of the fake zombies ceased, leaving a backdrop of shouts, crying, and general standard uproar from the normals. In my peripheral vision I saw the poor extras milling slowly about in confusion or sinking to sit or sprawl on the ground. Some frantically pulled at their prosthetic makeup while others spewed their lunch. Philip continued to calm in my bite-hold, though he still breathed in short, shuddering breaths.

"Heather, situation," Brian snapped, eyes returning to Philip and me, tranq gun pointed in our general direction. My eyes went to the gun. A low throbbing growl came from my throat as I snarled at Brian around the bite.

He blinked and lowered the gun, questions still crowding thick and close behind his eyes.

"Kyle got tranqed," Heather said from somewhere behind me. "One target zombie down, tranqed. The other down and injured." A touch of satisfaction tinged her voice. Roland was the first one, tranqed by Saberton Dude. But the "other" was Tim. I had no doubt she'd found a way to break him enough that he couldn't get up and cause trouble. "Got a dead Saberton man there and another down with broken face and hand, and the extras are still a bit crazy but more coherent now," she added.

Brian gave a sharp nod. "Good. Keep the Saberton man down until we're ready to withdraw," he said, then paused as though considering. "And make sure he gets a good look at you."

Now, that was interesting. Brian obviously wanted Heather's brother to know for sure she was working with us. I'd have to ponder the reasons for that later.

"Dan," Brian continued, "get Kyle to the van, and then you and Rachel see if you can secure the other two downed zombies. Minimal risk. Our priority is here." He gave a chin nod toward Philip and me, then frowned at the distant sound of sirens. "Quickly."

A shudder went through Philip, but I sensed that it

was from agony rather than the out-of-control frenzy state of earlier.

"Oh god . . . oh god . . . kill me." The words tumbled out of him in cracked and pain-filled sounds. "No more . . . please."

My low growl shifted to a trilling hum. Very carefully and cautiously, I eased the pressure on the bite. Brian took a step closer and crouched.

"Angel," he said quietly. "We need to leave before the authorities arrive. Do you think you can get him to my vehicle?"

I gave a slight nod, then released the bite completely and began to lick the wound. I knew it should have been weird and gross as all hell, but it wasn't. It was *right*. I tried not to think too much about that.

A moaning sob caught in Philip's throat. "Done . . . can't take it anymore . . . kill me."

"Trust me," I murmured, continuing to lick the bite, though totally ready to clamp down again if he started to freak out. "I'll take care of you."

He bowed his head and went still except for a heavy, generalized shaking. Taking that as consent, I slowly unwrapped my legs from him, though I still kept hold with my arms. "C'mon," I said as I gently tugged to get him to stand. "I won't leave you."

Brian straightened, swept his gaze around to check on the progress of his people. Apparently he was pleased with their results because he returned his attention to us. "All right, Angel," he said, still outwardly calm, but I heard a hint of an edge in his voice. "Everyone else is in the van, and we need to *go* before the police get here."

Philip stood, swayed slightly while I kept an arm around his waist. His gaze rested on Brian, and he growled, but subsided when I smacked him on the chest.

"Behave," I ordered. "You have to trust me."

A tremor shook him, and I bared my teeth up at him.

I knew we had to look pretty damn ridiculous. Philip was at least a foot taller and weighed about twice as much as me, but he allowed me to steer him in the direction Brian indicated, though he maintained an audible growl as we moved.

By the time we reached Brian's Escalade, Philip's growl had begun to develop the wet rasp that told me lung tissue was beginning to break down. I got him into the back seat, buckled him in like a kid, then slipped an arm around his waist and draped a leg over his, maintaining as much contact with him as possible. Then I fished another bag of slushy brains out of my pocket and held it for my great big zombie-kid to eat as Brian drove us away from the school.

I lost my virginity on the football field of East St. Edwards High School, and had been kidnapped from that same place years later. And now I'd just been in the thick of a crazed zombie mob on the Tucker Point High football field. Might be best for everyone if I avoided football in general from now on.

Chapter 24

I expected Brian to head to the same lab I'd visited the other day, where I'd seen Kang's head and met Dr. Nikas, but instead he stopped after about two minutes of driving and pulled up to a loading dock behind an old brick warehouse. It bugged me that the area looked familiar, and it wasn't until I caught sight of the battered sign by the street that I realized we were on the back end of the building I'd followed Philip to last night, where he'd begged Charish for brains. Damn good thing we'd come here instead of the other lab. I didn't think Philip could tolerate a long drive, and apparently Brian thought the same.

Brian parked and came around to open the rear passenger door as I finished stuffing the last of the brains into Philip's mouth.

"Let's go, Philip," I said. "We're going inside. We'll fix you up."

He managed a tight nod, pain flashing across his face from even that small movement. I quickly unbuckled him, then helped him out of the SUV with Brian's assistance. Philip didn't growl at him, which was damn good since I didn't know enough about the bite thing to be sure it would work again to calm him down.

As soon as Philip was somewhat steady Brian backed off and led the way to the back door. It was opened before he reached it by the door security guy from last night, so apparently we were expected.

"That's it," I murmured to the very unsteady Philip, keeping an arm around him. "Almost there."

Brian led the way inside and down a short hallway to a small room with lab equipment and a single computer workstation. Two narrow mattresses, obviously dragged in from elsewhere, dominated the floor space.

I glanced up at Philip's face as we walked. My gut clenched at the rigor of pain and concentration I saw there. Every movement was agonizing, yet he suffered in silence.

"Angel," Brian said, "if you can get him on a mattress, that would be ideal."

I gave him a quick nod to acknowledge I'd heard. "Okay, Philip, darlin'," I said, maneuvering him to the nearest mattress. "I need you to lie down now, and then you can be nice and still, okay?"

He sank to the mattress, knees buckling at the end and near-collapsing the last foot or so. A wrenching cry of despair that was echoed in his eyes nearly broke my heart. I lay down beside him, keeping as much contact along his side as I could without putting pressure on him that might cause more pain.

A few seconds later I heard low voices and footsteps from the hallway we'd entered through, and then Heather and Dan appeared, practically carrying Kyle between them. His head lolled but his eyes were open, and he seemed to be trying his damndest to make his legs work well enough to walk. Heather gave me a quick wink, then helped Dan get Kyle settled onto the other mattress.

"Do you need brains?" Dan asked Kyle, but the other man shook his head in a drunken gesture.

"Strange," Kyle slurred. "Not hungry. At all."

Dan's mouth pressed tight. "Not normal tranq, that's for sure."

"The mods did nothing," Kyle continued, obviously focusing heavily on speaking as clearly as possible, with only partial success. "Knocked me down in seconds."

Mods? That must have something to do with why he was surprised the tranq affected him. Some sort of antidote maybe? I turned my head toward them. "I got hit with that stuff the other night," I said quietly in order to not disturb Philip. "It takes some time to wear off. The non-hunger, that is. Brains'll be gross for a while."

Dan glanced at me. "Good to know." He looked back to Kyle. "You hear that? Just gotta wait it out."

"Got it," Kyle muttered. His hands and feet kept twitching, and it took me several seconds to realize he was consciously moving his fingers and toes in order to get his motor control back faster. The fact that he was awake but still without full motor control seemed odd to me. I'd been knocked out, yet as soon as I woke I was able to drive and move around with no trouble. Did it have something to do with the mods he'd mentioned? Perhaps he had an adverse reaction?

Philip tremored beside me, breath hissing between his teeth. I kept a hand on his shoulder while I let my gaze roam around the room, taking it all in. Heather sat beside Kyle's mattress with a hand on his arm. Dan stood by the wall, arms folded over his chest, watching, and I had the feeling he was primed and ready to respond to anything that came up. The door guard fiddled with a computer that showed the outside surveillance camera feeds, and Rachel checked out the monitor over his shoulder. With the mattresses taking up much of the floor space, the small room was downright crowded.

A soft intake of breath from the doorway drew my attention. Dr. Kristi Fucking Charish stood there, a look of slight surprise on her face as she registered my presence.

I felt my lips pull back from my teeth in a snarl of hatred. Pietro had told me he had this bitch under his control, but she looked pretty goddamn uncontrolled to me.

Slowly, I lifted my hand and gave her the finger. Her face instantly shifted from surprise to practiced coolness. Her gaze went from me to Philip. A flicker of distaste passed over her features, sliding to a smirk of satisfaction as she looked back to me. She held my gaze for several seconds, then turned away and moved out of sight.

What the hell did that bitch have to look satisfied about? Before I could wonder about it much more, Brian came back in, a frown tugging at his mouth.

"Dr. Nikas is on his way, and there are too many people in here," he announced. "Dan, Rachel, wait outside but stay close."

The two quickly complied. I gave Brian a puzzled look but held my questions. His gaze flicked to Heather and then to me. I half expected him to ask the two of us to leave, and I tensed for an argument since there was no damn way I was leaving Philip right now. But apparently Brian figured we were doing more good than harm. He moved to me and crouched.

"Dr. Nikas doesn't do well in crowds," he explained in a low voice. His eyes went to Philip, and sympathetic anger flared behind them, then he stood, turned, and went to one knee beside Kyle.

Heather looked up at Brian, gave Kyle's arm a little

squeeze. "He's still not able to move much, though it does seem to be wearing off."

Brian's head dipped in a small nod. "We don't know what was used or how it interacts with Kyle's mods," he said, "so it may simply take more time. I can't see Saberton using anything that would permanently harm a useful zombie."

Philip shuddered beside me. "Charish ... would ... did," he rasped out, voice thick with pain.

I looked back to him. "She's a fucking bitch," I muttered.

His nostrils suddenly flared, and he let out a low ominous growl. He shifted, pushing up on his arms, halftwisting to face the open doorway. He knew she was there. Could smell her or something. I felt the fury roiling through him and had no doubt that, despite the pain, he'd rip her to pieces if he could get his hands on her.

I wrapped my arms around him from behind and sank my teeth into his shoulder again, though there was a nasty part of me that wanted to leave him be and wish him good hunting. *Oops, couldn't control him. Sorry!* However, the practical side of me knew I might not be able to bring him back down after he rage-shredded Charish, and I didn't want to be responsible for anyone else getting hurt.

But Philip wasn't as easily subdued this time. He managed to push up to his knees while I clung to his back and bit harder. I sensed Brian near and ready to act in case I couldn't bring Philip under control, but to my relief, after a few seconds, Philip let out a low moan and sank down to lie on his belly.

"Was fine," he rasped, breathing harshly. "Was good. Strong after you turned me. She did this ... to me."

I let out a low growl of understanding, then released the bite and licked at the sluggishly bleeding wound. *Still not gross*, I thought idly. Too weird. I remained partially atop him—not that my piddling weight would slow him down if he went off again, but the physical contact seemed to keep him a bit calmer, though he still jerked and twitched.

Out of the corner of my eye I saw Dr. Nikas enter followed by Jacques, the pale tech who'd taken my blood at the other lab. Dr. Nikas paused as he took in the sights, and probably scents and sounds as well. He went to Kyle first, knelt by the mattress and placed a hand in the center of the stricken man's chest. "How is it?" he asked. "Movement returning?"

"Slowly," Kyle replied. "Very slowly."

Dr. Nikas gave a small nod. "I suspect they hit you with the new tranq, but if you feel stable, I'm going to go take care of Philip."

"I'm stable enough," Kyle said, to my relief. "Tend to him."

Dr. Nikas stood and moved to us, eyes going first to the deep bite marks on Philip's shoulder as he knelt. I shifted off to Philip's other side, and Dr. Nikas placed a hand in the center of his back. "Philip, can you hear me?" he asked.

"I can . . . hear you, Dr. Nikas," he gasped out, then squeezed his eyes shut. "Please. End this. Please." His voice cracked horribly on the last word.

"I will," Dr. Nikas replied, calmly and firmly. He met my eyes, and to my relief I saw full confidence that he could help Philip, and that he intended Philip's death to be an utter last resort. "Let's get you to your back first," he told Philip, and with my help we got him turned over on the mattress. Dr. Nikas looked at Jacques and rattled off some instructions that included words like "red-topped stabilizers" and "large bore eye-vee" and "five hundred mill normal saline."

Jacques hurried off to comply with the instructions,

and Dr. Nikas returned his gaze to me. "Angel, are you willing to stay with Philip for a short time?"

"Totally," I said. "But can someone call Marcus and let him and my dad know I'm okay and might be a while?"

Dr. Nikas glanced at Brian, who gave a nod.

"I'm on it," he said, pulling out his phone as he stepped into the hallway to make the call.

Jacques returned and set up an IV with several bags flowing into the tube thingy in Philip's arm.

I frowned. "How do you keep his body from healing up around the IV?"

Jacques didn't look up from his adjustments. "Needle and catheter have a camouflaging coating that keeps the parasite from reacting to it. Dr. Nikas's development." He stuck three patches on Philip's chest and switched on the heart monitor, then stood and retreated to the computer workstation.

Dr. Nikas filled a syringe from a vial and injected it into the saline bag. "Philip, as soon as this bag finishes, I'm going to set up a drip of a new formulation. It'll take a couple of hours, but let me know immediately if it makes anything worse."

"Yes, sir," Philip murmured, eyes already drifting closed. "Thank you." He already seemed to be better, and I had to hope it wasn't simply my wishful thinking.

Dr. Nikas stood and returned to Kyle. Carefully, he picked up the container holding the dart that had struck him. "Excellent, Kyle," he said. "This will give us a cleaner sample to analyze and hopefully a better idea of how this tranquilizer operates."

Heather's lips twitched. "Way to take one for the team, Kyle. We can tell everyone you got tranqed on purpose."

Kyle muttered something I couldn't hear, but I had no doubt the gist of it involved curse words.

Dr. Nikas gave Kyle's shoulder an absent pat, then

turned and headed toward the doorway, expression hardening.

I had no shame, and I quickly grabbed one of the packets of brains Dan had left for me and sucked it down. I was pretty sure Dr. Nikas was about to confront Charish, and I wanted some super zombie hearing right about now.

It kicked in barely in time.

"Tell me what happened to Philip," I heard Dr. Nikas say in a calm, even voice. Lucky for me, Charish had apparently been lurking just beyond the doorway. No wonder Philip had nearly lost it.

"I don't know. He's always been unstable," Charish replied, and even though I couldn't see her I had no trouble picturing the frown laced with the perfect amount of professional concern.

"What happened when he came here last night?" Dr. Nikas asked.

"Oh my god! Can you *believe* he showed up here?" she said, outrage thick in her voice. She huffed out a breath. "Begging, no less. He wasted all the supplies you'd left for him and claimed he was starving. I gave him some simply to get him to leave and keep from totally compromising us."

Dr. Nikas remained quiet for a few seconds before asking, "Why in god's name did you not *give him more?*" My zombie super-hearing picked up footfalls, and I easily pictured him stepping closer to her. "Did you think he was lying about being hungry? That perhaps he sold the brains I gave him on the street like pain meds?"

He didn't sound so calm anymore.

"No!" Charish said. "He obviously wasn't rationing properly. I gave him two, and Saberton fed him as well. He simply had to hold it together for a couple of days, that's all." She made an aggrieved sound. "Why would I waste valuable resources on a stupid zombie grunt, and an expendable one at that?"

Holy fucking shit, I thought, stunned, *She did NOT just say that!*

"Stupid . . . zombie . . . grunt?" Dr. Nikas bit the words out, and the anger in his voice sounded utterly foreign coming from him. "You call a highly skilled man who volunteered for extremely hazardous duty, suffered *your* botched efforts, and who managed to endure agony and extreme hunger without undue complaint a *stupid zombie grunt?*"

I heard a clatter, and I figured Dr. Nikas had backed her into a counter or something.

"I . . . I don't understand," Charish said, for the first time sounding a little afraid and genuinely perplexed. "You were going to terminate him tomorrow. And . . . volunteered? What do you mean? For what?"

"Terminate?" Utter astonishment laced the word. "I never had any intention of terminating him! You don't terminate your own people!" Dr. Nikas drew a shaking breath, obviously struggling for calm. "Why did you give the accelerant instead of stabilizer?"

"I didn't!" she cried.

"You are *lying*," he said through clenched teeth. "The two are kept in separate locations, look completely different from each other. Tell me *why* you sent an operative back into the field with a substance that could damage him and his mission."

"I thought he was just a mule," she replied, voice cracking in a way that told me she had tears going on now. Bitch. I glanced around the room to see that I wasn't the only one carefully eavesdropping. Brian stood by the wall, arms folded over his chest and eyes closed, but his jaw was clenched so tightly I thought he might break a tooth. Kyle's eyes were on the doorway, brow ever so slightly furrowed. He probably wasn't tanked up to where he could hear it all, but enough to get the gist.

"I didn't know he was an operative, I swear," Charish continued, crying now. "You said you were going to 'take care of him,' and I thought you meant kill him." She sniffled. "Ari, I was so tired that night, and upset that he'd come to the lab. Anyone could have followed him!"

Like me. Bitch.

"Because you thought him to be an expendable *grunt*, you chose to punish him. For a brilliant woman, you are remarkably stupid," Dr. Nikas said, voice tight. "Brian," he called.

Brian pushed off the wall, face instantly composed into a neutral mask that completely hid that he'd heard everything and how pissed he was. He moved to the doorway. "Yes, sir?"

"Remove Dr. Charish from these premises until a decision can be made as to her . . . disposition." He paused, and I heard Charish suck in a shocked breath. "And in the meantime," he continued, "she is to have no more than three hundred calories a day."

"Ari! No!" Charish gasped while I silently cheered. Three hundred calories a day? I knew damn well Dr. Nikas ordered that so Charish would get a hint of what real hunger felt like.

"Yes, sir," Brian replied evenly. "Secure cell, sir?" he added, emphasizing the word "cell" a bit, and I had no doubt he'd done so simply to fuck with her.

"Most definitely," Dr. Nikas replied.

"No, Ari . . . oh god. Please! You can't do this. Pietro will . . . oh, god." She was crying for real now, which surprised me. She struck me as the type to go cold and shut down. Maybe the thought of what Pietro would do scared the ice right out of her.

"I made the grievous error of trusting you with my

interests," Dr. Nikas said with undisguised reproach in his voice. "I will not do so again."

I heard a muffled whimper, and then Brian said, "This way, Dr. Charish." A few seconds later he came through the doorway, escorting her with a firm grip on her upper arm. Her hands had been secured behind her back with zip-ties, I noted as they passed. I didn't bother to hide the fact that I openly watched her be escorted out. No one in the room was hiding it, Philip included.

Halfway to the exit, she began to struggle and tried to pull away from Brian. "No. No! This isn't right!"

Brian visibly tightened his grip, fingers digging in. "Walk or be dragged."

She let out a low cry. "You're hurting me," she said, stumbling forward again. "Ari didn't say to hurt me."

"He didn't have to," was his utterly calm reply as they exited. A few seconds later the outer door clanged shut.

"Couldn't happen to a nicer person," I muttered.

Philip made a low noise. Shifting up onto one elbow, I peered down at him. "Is it getting any better?" I asked quietly.

"Really dizzy . . . all of a sudden," he said, voice definitely sounding more clear than earlier.

"Dr. Nikas?" I called.

He stepped into the doorway, and I was shocked to see that he looked anguished. He *liked* Dr. Charish, I realized with a start. Or at least he had before today.

I had a hard time wrapping my head around the kind and gentle Dr. Nikas finding anything at all appealing about that woman, but obviously there'd been something there. He'd called her brilliant. Had that been it?

Straightening his shoulders, he moved to Philip's side and crouched. "What is it?"

"He says he's really dizzy all of a sudden," I told him.

Dr. Nikas checked the IV and monitoring devices,

looked into Philip's eyes. "Other than the dizziness, better or worse overall?"

"Thinking clearer. Pain's easing some too, maybe," Philip said. "Hard to tell, but I don't think it hurts quite so much."

"All of your vitals look good," Dr. Nikas said with an encouraging smile. "I'm going to slow the drip down a bit, and I've started a mild sedative. If you can sleep, do so. It will be a few hours until you're back to your normal level of stability."

Philip managed a whisper of a smile. "I'm more than ready to sleep. Thanks for having my back." He took a deeper breath. "I'm sorry, Dr. Nikas. For all this. Two days ago, Saberton cut out all real brains for me ... and Tim and Roland. Only gave us their current alternative. I wouldn't eat them, didn't dare," he said. "I used up everything you'd left for me, then was starving. Should have signaled. Wasn't thinking straight and got desperate."

"Understandable," Dr. Nikas said. "We'll take good care of you now. I'm sorry you didn't get what you needed when you came here last night." He gave Philip's shoulder a light squeeze, then looked over at me. "Angel, may I speak with you a moment?"

I glanced down at Philip. The corner of his mouth twitched in a mild tic, but the general tremors had stopped, and he almost *almost* looked at peace. I checked in with my zombie-mama intuition, but it seemed to agree and didn't urge me to stay by his side. Giving a nod to Dr. Nikas, I pulled a blanket over Philip, then stood and followed him as he passed through the doorway, down the hall, and finally into a small office.

He closed the door behind us and opened his mouth to speak, but I beat him to it.

"Why didn't y'all put a stop to the testing Saberton was doing?" I asked, frowning. "Those people didn't volunteer. That fake zombie shit really fucked them up. A woman *died* because of it."

He let out a low sigh. "We were working on it, Angel. That was part of the reason Philip was undercover with them."

My eyes narrowed. "Working on it? Really?" I liked Dr. Nikas, but that didn't mean I was going to let this slide. "It looked more like Philip was undercover to steal their results and pass them to y'all."

Dr. Nikas exhaled and rubbed at his eyes. "Yes, but part of what he passed to us were details that we hoped would help us undermine their operation as a whole, not merely that small segment." He dropped his hand, expression pained. "The research was happening whether I liked it or not. To refuse to use the data for some misguided moral reason and leave it to Saberton exclusively would be . . . irresponsible."

I fell silent for a moment. The low tick of a clock on the wall seemed to reverberate through the small room while I tried to make everything fit into a pattern I could handle. "Was it useful?" I finally asked, voice low. "The data—was it worth it?"

He gave a grave nod. "Every bit of data, every sample helps. I know the direction they're going with their research and have projects underway based on it and to counter it. Invaluable." But then he shook his head, looking suddenly weary. "Was it worth the death of Brenda Barnes? No. She was an innocent."

Dr. Nikas knew the name of the woman who'd died as part of that horrible research. That, along with everything else I'd seen of him, convinced me that he actually did give a shit. I blew out my breath. "I guess Philip's meltdown put an end to that project anyway. At least for now."

A faint smile touched his mouth. "Yes. Not at all in the way I'd hoped to extract him, but they will be disrupted for a time." His eyes met mine. "He needs much care. You were kind enough to give me a small sample of blood at the main lab the other day," he said. "Would you consider giving a pint? It could be crucial in developing a more effective stabilizer for Philip."

He already had samples of my blood; I couldn't see any harm in giving him more. "Sure thing."

"I'm not *certain* yet if it will help," he cautioned, "but I'd prefer to have it on hand as I work with his issues."

"If there's a chance it'll help Philip, I'll do it," I replied, then frowned. "What about the two others—the ones Philip turned? Tim Bell and Roland Westfeld."

He exhaled. "I haven't had a chance to fully determine the nature of their condition," he explained. "How they were converted was . . . perverse, and I don't know yet if their damage can be reversed or even stabilized." His brow creased. "And they are Saberton men."

"They stood and watched me get strip searched," I said quietly, looking away. "Maybe it makes me an awful person, but I guess I don't have much sympathy for them right now." I sighed and looked back to him. "But I really do hope you can do something good for Philip."

Dr. Nikas nodded slowly. "Before those two were so poorly converted, their view of zombies was likely much in line with Dr. Charish's—occasionally useful second-class citizens." His mouth tightened, and he shook his head. "Pietro will make the final decision on what happens to them based on my assessment. As for Philip, yes, I can help him to at least not be in continuous pain, and to curb the unnatural hunger. In time, I may discover a way to fully reverse the damage. Your blood will help."

I considered all that in silence for a moment. The two men were seriously damaged. They didn't seem to have the same degree of pain issues that Philip had, but they were unstable and bitey as hell. I definitely saw how dangerous it was to have them roaming around with such screwed up parasites. Thankfully, it didn't seem like they'd converted any others into messed up zombies. Maybe the parasite was too damaged to spawn. *But isn't condemning them to death for being "too damaged" treating* them *like second class citizens and less than human?*

There were no easy answers, that much was for sure.

I tugged a hand through my hair, then looked up at Dr. Nikas, brow furrowed. "Why did Philip calm down when I bit him?"

It was his turn to go quiet for a moment. "Technically he shouldn't have," he finally said.

That only confused me more. "What does that mean? I don't even know why I did it. It just felt . . . right."

Dr. Nikas drew a breath, hesitated, then shook his head and spread his hands. "It is a characteristic that should not manifest in a *young* zombie."

I regarded him as steadily as I could. "And what does *that* mean?"

He met my eyes with one of those I'm-ancient-as-all-hell gazes that I'd received a time or two from Pietro. "It means that I have never seen a zombie less than five hundred years old with the instinct and ability to inflict a control bite."

I gaped as I tried to get the implications of this tidbit of info to fit into my world view. First off, that meant there were zombies over five hundred years old, likely including Dr. Nikas. And Pietro. I'd known zombies had the potential to live a long time, but having an actual number from someone who no doubt knew the truth blew my mind.

But even that seemed minor compared to the fact that, somehow, little ol' not-even-a-year-old zombie me was able to do some zombie judo hold that normally only Grand Poobah Zombies could do. What the hell did that mean for me?

Dr. Nikas pushed off the counter, gave me a sad little smile. "We can talk about this more later. If you're still

willing, I'll have Jacques take your blood, and then Brian
can drive you home."

Home. Right. Wherever the hell that was. "Sure
thing," I replied numbly.

He gave me a small nod, then turned and left me
alone with my roiling thoughts.

Chapter 25

I gave a pint of my blood to Jacques, accepted a packet of brains in return, then checked on Philip. He seemed to be sleeping comfortably, and the lines of pain in his face had smoothed out a bit. After twitching the blanket a bit higher over his shoulders, I looked over to the waiting Brian.

"Are you my ride?"

"Whenever you're ready," he replied. "No rush."

Kyle was resting quietly. Heather lay stretched out on the mattress beside him reading to him in a low voice from a book called *Abaddon's Gate* with a big spaceship on the cover. They weren't cuddling or anything, but I didn't think Brian was thrilled about it anyway. A whisper of an expression that might have been jealousy touched his face but disappeared the instant he realized I was looking at him.

Ooooh, Brian really does like Heather! My inner third-grader cheered. But then I had to mask a grin. It was only fair to leave open the possibility that it was *Kyle* who Brian liked. Either way it seemed there might be some zombie soap opera brewing.

Still hiding a smile, I exited the lab with Brian close behind, headed to his Escalade and allowed him to hold the passenger door open for me, but only because he beat me there.

"To Marcus's house?" Brian asked after he climbed into the driver's seat, and it took me a minute to remember why the heck he wanted to drive me there instead of my own house.

"Oh, yeah, right," I said. "My house is probably somewhere in the Gulf of Mexico by now." *And so now I'm gonna stay with Marcus.* I held back a grimace. This had the potential to be awkward. After the attack at the boat launch I'd spent the night with him, but that had been the first time in ages. And now I was about to basically move in, for who the hell knew how long.

"I'm sorry," Brian said. "You've had a devastating couple of days."

"It sure hasn't been the best week of my life," I said then shook my head. "No, actually it was a pretty decent week, even with all of the Saberton crap. It was only a few hours on Friday morning that sucked sweaty balls."

Brian let out a low snort. "That land you were living on, do you own it?"

"Well, my dad does, yeah," I replied. "So it'd be stupid not to stay there." I shook my head. "It was all right for ordinary flood levels. The spillway break was a once in a lifetime thing." I winced. "At least I sure as hell hope so. Anyway, I'm hoping I can buy a trailer or something and put it there."

"They have some pretty nice ones these days," Brian offered. "And modular housing that doesn't look like a trailer."

"Even if I want to get a shitty one, I'm gonna have to borrow money." I scowled. "Damn. This sucks. The only person in the world who might be willing to loan me money would maaaaaybe be Pietro, and . . ." I trailed off with a sigh.

Brian glanced over at me. "And?"

"I don't know if I want the strings that would come with it," I said quietly.

"Maybe find out what the strings will be before writing off the possibility," Brian replied. At least he wasn't denying that said strings would exist. "Can't hurt to talk to him. You don't have to commit to anything."

"Oh, I intend to talk to him. I don't really have a choice, do I?" I shook my head. "That's the worst part. I *don't* have a choice. Who the hell else would write me or my dad a loan to buy even a crappy used trailer at rates that aren't criminal?"

"I see what you mean," Brian said, exhaling. "But the alternative—having no resource at all—would be worse. And, yes, I know I'm biased." He gave me a slight smile.

"I know, I know," I replied, wrinkling my nose. "I'm lucky to even have this option. Don't mind me. I'm being stupid." I *was* lucky. I knew that. How did people without credit or collateral or other options go about rebuilding after a disaster?

"Not stupid," he said. "Simply wary of walking open-eyed into a trap. I get it."

"Right," I said. "I've done that kind of thing already and it wasn't fun." Like trading myself for my dad to end up as one of Dr. Charish's lab rats. I didn't regret doing so for a second, but damn, that had *not* been fun.

Brian cleared his throat softly. "I owe you an apology."

Frowning, I glanced over at him. "What do you mean?"

He kept his eyes on the road. "About what happened to you with Kristi Charish . . . and McKinney. I missed identifying McKinney as William Rook, an operative working for Saberton at the time." His hands tightened briefly on the steering wheel. "Charish hired him not knowing who he was," Brian continued. "McKinney got the info he needed and put her together with Saberton. The rest progressed from there."

I took that in, then shook my head. "Charish woulda still found a way to fuck Pietro over. You can't blame yourself for that."

"I don't dwell on it, but I damn sure haven't forgotten it," Brian said, jaw tight. "Rook was good, *really* good, at what he did." Sighing, he shook his head. "If I'd uncovered him at any point, it would have saved a lot of loss, and certainly would have kept you out of that situation. Maybe even cut off Charish before she gave too much to Saberton." He slanted a glance my way. "Only speculation now, though. Didn't have her under close enough supervision. I've tightened everything up since then."

"All of this corporate espionage shit is pretty crazy," I said. "Like the whole business with Philip."

Brian gave a slight nod. "He endured a great deal and gained us a tremendous advantage."

"Right," I said. "But, um, Pietro said something that I've been thinking about: Philip was undercover with Saberton before I got kidnapped, right?"

Apparently Brian knew exactly where I was going with this. "You want to know why Pietro left you in that lab if he knew what was going on."

I smiled tightly. "Something like that."

"Basically, he didn't know," Brian said. I gave him a dubious look, and he continued, "Philip managed to get onto the volunteer list for Charish's project by some devious sleight of hand and was only able to send a very terse message to that effect before he was taken to Charish's lab at that factory. And once there, he had no opportunity to get a message out with details or location." He looked over at me. "Angel, I give you my word on this."

I hesitated, then nodded slowly. I trusted Brian to tell

me the truth—at least as far as he knew it. "Okay." I fell
silent for the rest of the drive. I'd thought I'd known how
high the stakes were for Pietro and zombies in general,
but in reality they were higher than I could've ever imagined. It wasn't simply Pietro versus Saberton. The safety
of every zombie, as well as our ability to live relatively
normal lives and blend in with regular society, depended
on guarding our secrets and being the first to make the
advances such as fake brains and ways to modify the
parasite. Pietro had to be ruthless for a reason, and I
truly *did* understand it.

So maybe it was time for me to let go of some of my
grudges. Even if I could possibly live a couple hundred
years, life was still too damn short to cling to regrets or
old anger. Maybe that was maturity—understanding that
even the bad shit makes you who you are.

Maturity still sucked. And though I was ready to forgive Pietro, that didn't mean I had to trust him farther
than I could throw him. Maturity didn't have to equal
stupidity.

We pulled into Marcus's driveway, and Brian put the
Escalade into park.

"Thanks for the drive," I said. "And for listening to me
whine."

"You're welcome, Angel," he replied. "And you have
my number if you ever need anything."

"Um. No, I don't anymore, actually. Flood got it too."

He pulled out a new card, then wrote another number
on the back. "If it's an emergency, and you can't get me,
call that number and tell them 'one one three Archer.'
That will ensure you get assistance."

I took the card, nodded. Sometimes those strings-
attached could be lifelines as well.

Marcus barreled out of the house and rushed to me,
crutches and all, as I climbed out of the SUV. "Angel!"
He gave a quick nod of thanks to Brian but stopped be-

fore pulling me into a hug. Instead he simply took hold of my shoulders. "I've been so worried about you. Sarge was supposed to go by for you last night but got called to deal with looters." Uncertainty warred with relief in his eyes. I abruptly remembered that our last conversation had been oh-so less than pleasant, and because I'd hung up on him, he didn't know where we stood. All that seemed like a million years ago.

I slipped my arms around him and pulled him close. I felt a shudder of relief pass through him as he dropped the crutches and returned the embrace. "It's okay, hero," I murmured. "It's been a weird couple of days, for sure." I drew back to look into his face. "My dad is here, right? Is he okay?"

"He's watching TV in the guest room," Marcus told me. "He's fine. How about you?" His brow creased. "What happened to you today?"

Brian cleared his throat softly. "Angel, I'll be going now."

I glanced over, smiled. "Thanks, Brian."

He gave us a nod as I closed the passenger door, his professional mask in place while he backed out. Was the official air for Marcus's benefit? Brian had certainly been more relaxed with me alone. Or maybe it was simply habit. Who could tell with him?

After retrieving the crutches, Marcus and I headed inside where he immediately tossed the crutches into the corner and stumped along on his half cast.

"It must suck having to wear a cast," I said.

Marcus nodded. "Yeah. Everything went fine until the car shifted and caught my leg," he said as we settled onto the couch. "Fortunately Uncle Pietro has a doctor lined up for us to take care of hospital red tape. Can't get out of having an injury, but it keeps too many questions from being asked."

Now that was pretty damn useful. There was a lot I still

didn't know about the workings of the zombie subculture, but Pietro sure seemed to have his fingers in a lot of it. Then again, if he'd been around for centuries or so, it made sense that he'd have made plans for stuff like that.

"Well, I'm glad you're in one piece *and* saved that family," I told him with a kiss.

He returned it enthusiastically as we settled on the couch, but before we could get too distracted I paused the general naughtiness and proceeded to give him a rundown of the events of the past few days. The fire-fighter on Highway 1790, Philip undercover, Saberton and their shenanigans, the movie extras as test subjects, Philip freaking out and the resulting mayhem on the movie set, Dr. Charish and her fuckups. I didn't hold any-thing back, though I was well aware how outlandish some of it seemed. I figured that if Pietro didn't want Marcus to know *all* of it, that was his own damn problem, and he should have warned me.

"Shiiiiiiit," Marcus breathed when I finished. "Uncle Pietro had all of that going on?" To my relief he seemed to accept the whole thing without question, even the parts that sounded batshit crazy.

"Yeah, it was a mess." I rubbed at my eyes. The fatigue was starting to catch up with me. "I need to check on my dad."

Marcus nodded. "He's in the guest bedroom at the end of the hall."

I left Marcus on the couch and headed that way. The door was open, and my dad sat in a comfy-looking re-cliner watching TV.

"Hey, Dad, you doing okay?" I asked. I searched for any hint of anger or his usual orneriness, but apparently having a plush recliner and a flat screen went a long way toward pacifying him.

He looked over, gave me a slight smile. "Hey, Angel-kins. I'm doin' fine."

"So, um, everything's cool between you and Marcus?"

His bony shoulders lifted in a shrug. "We had a few words." He paused. "More than a few. But I'm sitting in his house, so that should tell you something."

"Yeah, I guess it does." I didn't even want to think of what words had been exchanged. "Look, I'm gonna ask Pietro Ivanov if he'll cosign a loan for me."

He frowned. "Why the hell would someone like that help you out with a loan?" The frown shifted to a familiar scowl. "And, dammit, I don't want to be sucking up to *any* Ivanovs."

I leaned against the doorframe, crossed my arms over my chest. "You think a bank will hand over enough to put our lives back together?" I asked.

A grimace deepened the lines in his face. "No, you're right. No chance with a bank."

"I'm hoping Pietro will help since he's, uh, like me and Marcus."

"Shit!" His jaw actually dropped a little. "You mean he's a—"

"Yeah," I said. "He's the one who made Marcus . . . like him. A zombie."

My dad let out a low whistle. "Jesus Christ." He narrowed his eyes at me. "How many of, er, you lot are there?"

I had to stop and think about that. "I don't really know, actually. I think there's maybe a dozen or so in this area," I hedged. I had a feeling there was a higher concentration around here because of Pietro's operation and support. It surely couldn't be as high everywhere. There simply wouldn't be enough brains to feed everyone. Plus, if there were a whole lot of zombies spread out everywhere, it would be impossible to keep it hidden from the general public.

"That's too damn weird," he muttered. "Y'all have meetings or anything?"

I let out a bark of laughter at the thought. *Zombies Anonymous? Hello, my name is Angel, and it's been three weeks since I've shambled.* "No," I said, grinning. "At least none that I've been invited to."

He merely snorted. "Don't let the bastards leave you out, Angel. You're better than any of them."

A sudden jolt of worry went through me. "Uh, Dad, you know you can't tell anyone about me being a zombie right? Or about Marcus or Pietro either." Shit. I'd outed both of them without even thinking, and there wasn't any good reason for doing it. I mean, I trusted my dad, but I needed to be more careful.

He laughed. "Like anyone would believe me?" But then he saw my anxious expression and sobered. "Won't tell a soul, Angel. Wouldn't do anything that might come back to bite you in the ass. Promise you that."

"Thanks, Dad." I moved to him, gave him a hug. He felt more solid than he had in a long time. He clung to me for a moment, then let me go. I quickly turned and left before either of us could get all weepy.

Marcus was still on the couch. I sat, then regarded him, brow furrowed. "So, how is this gonna work with me and my dad staying here?" I asked. "I mean, don't get me wrong, I'm really grateful, but . . ." I trailed off, not quite sure what else to say.

"Your dad is settled in the guest room just fine," Marcus told me. "I have plenty of space." He pushed a strand of hair back from my face. "This isn't us 'moving in together.' I know you aren't ready for that. *We* aren't ready for that."

Relief swept over me. I'd been dreading this conversation, totally uncertain how to lay out my misgivings without insulting him or screwing things up, and here he was being all understanding.

"I don't know how long it'll be before I can find me and my dad another place to live," I said.

"It's a three bedroom house." He gave me a soft smile. "I promise I won't pressure you." Then he shook his head. "Or rather, I promise I'll do my very best not to pressure you," he amended. "I'm crazy about you, Angel. I can't shut that down."

I kissed him, smiled. "I'm crazy about you too. And I think I know why you sometimes get too overprotective."

At his questioning look I proceeded to tell him about my theory of zombie-mama instinct with Philip. Marcus seemed a bit doubtful, and perhaps a teensy bit jealous when I spoke of Philip, but in the end he simply gave a serious nod.

"As much as I'd love to let the parasite take full responsibility, I'm not sure I can," he said to my surprise. He gave me an uneasy smile. "It couldn't have influenced my one-sided decision to turn you, since I wasn't your zombie-daddy yet. And the heavy-handed shit of black-mailing you into taking the job at the morgue? Yeah, the instinct might have had a role, but it was probably more just me being a superior dick and giving you a great Teaching Moment." Then he took a deep breath, met my eyes. "And even if all the stuff later was because of some kind of instinct . . . God, Angel, you've come so far in the past year. I know it's stupid and wrong to treat you like you don't know what the hell you're doing. You deserve better than that, and I promise I'll try my damndest to throttle it back, whether it's instinct or simple dickish-ness on my part."

I believed him. "And I promise I'll give you many chances to do so." I smiled, gave his hand a squeeze. "I need to meet with your uncle to ask him about cosigning a loan for me," I said, then extended a big horking olive branch by adding, "Would you call him for me?"

Marcus kissed me, a lovely, lingering kiss. "No. You should call him," he said, handing the entire olive tree back to me.

And so I did. Pietro seemed unsurprised by my desire for a meeting, and I suspected that Brian had already given him a heads up. After a polite inquiry about how I was doing post zombie-mayhem, he told me he'd send a car for me at ten the next morning.

With that taken care of, I snuggled up against Marcus. "I really like you a lot."

He slipped an arm around me. "Is there a 'but' coming?"

"Nope. No buts," I said. "I'm too exhausted to deal with buts." I frowned. "That sounds weird."

"Yes, it does," he said, laughing. "All you need to do right now is rest."

My eyes closed. Now that I'd stopped moving and knew my dad was all right, the fatigue swept in with crushing force. "Yeah," I mumbled. "Rest would be cool."

I heard Marcus ask me something, but I was already well on my way to sleep, and apparently he didn't need the answer badly enough to wake me up.

Sometime later, I woke in a bed that wasn't my own and wasn't Marcus's either. A clock nearby told me it was 1:14 in the morning, and a few more seconds of semi-coherent thinking informed me that I was on a futon in Marcus's office.

I smiled into the darkness. He wasn't pressuring me. I got up, headed down the hallway to Marcus's room and crawled under the covers to snuggle with him.

He woke, blinked at me. "Angel?" he asked in a voice thick with sleep. "You okay?"

"More than okay," I told him. "Now shut up and hold me."

And he did.

Chapter 26

I half expected some awkwardness in the morning, but Marcus was already cooking eggs when I woke up and shambled into the kitchen. He had on shorts, his cast, and nothing else, and he looked *seriously* hot.

He gave me a smile. "I'm making zombelets. Want one?"

"Uh, zombelets?" Then my brain kicked into gear. "Oh, zombie-omelet? Eggs and brains?"

"That's right!" he replied, chuckling. At my approving nod he pulled another plate out of the cabinet, then slid a portion of the contents of the pan onto it, and pushed the plate and a fork my way.

"And don't worry," he said as he served himself. "I'll wash the pan before your dad gets up."

Laughing, I dug into the "zombelet" with gusto. As I ate, Marcus pushed the newspaper toward me.

"Y'all hit the front page," he told me.

I peered at the headline over my plate. *Riot Halts Filming on Movie Set.* Tucking into my brains and eggs, I skimmed the article. No known reason for the fight that broke out between several of the zombie extras. Numerous injuries reported, several arrests. Filming to resume today.

I read to the end. No mention of a death, so apparently Saberton had taken care of the body of the guy Philip killed. I wondered if they would take care of any footage that was shot as well.

"Sucks for the extras who were arrested," I said with a slight grimace. "None of it was their fault."

Marcus gave a nod of agreement. "Uncle Pietro will probably take care of that. It's in everyone's best interest for this to die down as quickly as possible."

I finished my breakfast, then jumped into the shower to clean up for my meeting with Pietro. When I got out, Marcus produced jeans, underwear and a couple of shirts that I'd left at his place ages ago, which saved me from meeting Pietro while wearing the same donated clothing I'd worn the day before.

I made sure there was non-brain food available for my dad and, at ten a.m., a black Mercedes pulled into the driveway. The driver wasn't Brian, so I obediently sat in the back when he held that door open for me and, apart from a few polite pleasantries, rode in silence to Pietro's house.

To my surprise it wasn't the same house Marcus and I had gone to months ago for the barbecue but instead a very nice lakefront house only about ten minutes from Tucker Point. Even though it wasn't secluded in the sense of being far from other properties, it was surrounded on the non-lake sides by a couple of acres of woods, which added a strong feeling of privacy. Pietro was rolling in it, no doubt about that. No telling what he had for resources if he really was hundreds of years old.

We pulled up in front of the house, and I managed to remember to wait for the driver to come around and open the door for me instead of barreling out on my own. I even followed politely as he went up to the house and rang the doorbell for me, though to my relief he stood back once he did so. Apparently I was allowed to speak and act for myself now that the hard part had been done.

I listened to the frogs' chorus from the lake as I tried to go over what I had to say to Pietro. Dread twisted my gut. I knew damn well Pietro held all the cards, but I needed to make sure I didn't sell myself out completely.

A tall brunette answered the door, slim and stylish, wearing dark maroon slacks and a conservative white silk blouse, with her hair in a soft updo. She gave me a warm smile. "Ms. Crawford, I'm Alicia Dane, Mr. Ivanov's personal assistant. It's so nice to meet you."

Personal assistant? Yeesh, definitely out of my depth here. I took a deep breath and plastered a smile on for Ms. Dane, reminding myself that I'd survived kidnapping, firefight, and zombie mayhem, so there was no need to be intimidated by the insistent reminders of Pietro's wealth and power.

Yeah, right.

I managed to respond with a polite greeting and then allowed Ms. Dane to escort me to a room with a huge antique-looking desk, a couple of big wingback chairs, and one wall lined with shelves of old books. A huge window commanded a stunning view of the lake, and French doors led out onto a broad deck.

Pietro sat in one of the wingbacks by the window and stood as I entered. "Angel, good morning."

"Hi," I said. "Sorry to bother you."

"You're not," he assured me, then looked past me to Ms. Dane. "That will be all for now, thank you."

She nodded and withdrew, closing the door behind her. Pietro gestured to the other wingback chair.

"Would you like something to drink?" he asked.

"Oh, no thanks, I'm cool," I said as I settled into the

chair. I expected it to be uncomfortable, but it was far from it. "You probably know why I'm here, right?"

He sat back down, picked up a cup of coffee from the table beside him and took a sip. "I suspect it concerns assistance in your current situation."

"Right." I took a deep breath. "Well, I came here to ask if you'd be willing to cosign a loan for me."

To my shock he didn't even pretend to consider it before he shook his head. "No, I won't do a cosign."

Dismay tightened my chest. "You . . . won't?" I fought to keep my voice even, even though it felt a bit as if I'd been kicked in the teeth. *Guess all those worries about strings were pointless.* What the hell was I supposed to do now? "Look, I know I don't have anything resembling credit, but I swear I'll pay it back and won't miss any payments. I could handle being homeless if it was only me, but I can't put my dad through that—" I stopped as he held up his hand.

"Angel, I don't want to go through a bank," Pietro told me calmly. "I'll work out a loan for you myself. Cleaner to draft it directly to you."

I blinked, sat back. "You will?" The dismay receded, replaced by wariness.

He took another placid sip of coffee. "Of course I will," he said. "How much do you earn a month?"

I had a feeling he knew exactly how much I earned, but I told him anyway. After that came some questions about my expenses and my dad's disability income—and again, I couldn't shake the sense he knew it already but was being polite enough to actually let me volunteer the information.

Unfortunately, by the time we hashed out how much I needed to borrow and what I could afford to pay, even with more than reasonable financing terms, it came down to a loan that would take me over fifteen years to repay, and that was only if I got a shitty trailer, a very used car, and shopped at Goodwill for the next decade and a half. No eating out. Definitely no college classes.

"You need additional income," Pietro stated, echoing the thoughts that churned in my own head.

I couldn't hold back the sigh. With my education and skill-set, about all I could hope for would be to pick up some shifts at convenience stores.

"There aren't many part time jobs that will be worth the effort for the compensation," he pointed out, then surprised me by adding, "I'd much rather you work for me on occasion, or for Dr. Nikas. I guarantee the pay would be much better."

Hello, Strings, I thought. I gave him as unwary a look as I could manage. "What kind of work?"

"Dr. Nikas told me you found the lab interesting," he said, "and also mentioned that he wouldn't mind your help with some of his projects."

Okay, now that wouldn't be a bad string at all. In fact, that would actually kinda rock.

"As for me," he continued, "though I have nothing definitive in mind at this time, I know that having a smart female zombie can be useful on certain assignments, and you've certainly proven more than capable in stress situations." He set his coffee cup down with a soft *clink*. "Apart from Alicia and Rachel, I don't have many who are."

Now *that* was the sort of string I'd been braced for. Yet even as he said it, I couldn't help but think *why not?* So far I'd been "capable in stress situations" for free. I also couldn't deny the little glow of pleasure that he thought I was smart.

Yet along with the glow came a creeping apprehension. Pietro operated in a moral grey area. Very *dark* grey at times. If I took a paycheck from him, I'd basically be saying that I was okay with some of the "less clean" aspects of his operation.

I could walk away right now. It would suck, but I'd find some way to survive.

However, I had my dad to consider. If I stayed on my rickety moral high horse, he'd be homeless.

"Can I say no to assignments I don't like?"

"Absolutely."

I didn't know whether I believed him, but I also knew damn well that working for him would pay a shitload better than working the night shift at the XpressMart. I could give my dad a better life, and right now that was what mattered.

After that we hashed out the details of exactly how much I figured I needed. Pietro gave me the name of someone he knew at Harbor Homes who he said could give me a good deal on some cosmetically damaged properties, as well as the name of a guy who he promised would offer cost pricing on cars for me and my dad. After that he called Ms. Dane back in to have paperwork drawn up, and within half an hour I had a copy of the papers in my hand, and a confirmation that the entire sum would be transferred into my account as soon as the banks opened for business Monday morning.

Pietro stood and moved to the desk, opened a drawer and removed an envelope, then returned to me and held it out. "This isn't part of the loan," he said. "Use this to get some necessities—clothing and such. And don't argue. I'm making small contributions to many of those affected by the flooding."

He was crazy if he thought I was going to argue over a cash gift. Any pride that might have had me doing so had been destroyed along with my house. But when I peered into the envelope I still felt a jolt of surprise at the sight of what looked like about two grand.

Glancing up, I cocked an eyebrow at Pietro. "I'll consider this retroactive pay for any assistance I've given you over the past week."

His lips twitched. "Fair enough. But please don't expect to always be paid at that rate."

And with that he escorted me to the door, gave me a light kiss on the cheek, and sent me on my way to begin rebuilding my life.

Chapter 27

"You sure this is a good idea?" my dad muttered. He peered into the oven at the fancy hors d'oeuvres which I'd carefully selected from the frozen food aisle of the local warehouse store.

"Nope!" I replied cheerfully. I dumped a bag of chips into a large bowl and set it on the table with the various other foodstuffs. "But I figure we might as well let people see the place while it's still kinda decent, and then we never have to let anyone in ever again."

He barked out something close to a laugh, poked at one of the tidbits with a fork. "I guess you have a point. Let 'em get it out of their system."

"Or we could keep the place kinda decent," I said, grinning. "That'd be wild."

"Now you're talking crazy," he said, closing the oven.

It had been six weeks since my conversation with Pietro, and two weeks since my dad and I moved into our new ever-so-slightly cosmetically damaged house. We'd scored a decent two bedroom prefabricated house with patched siding damage on the back. Sure, it wasn't as solid as a house of standard construction, but it had been installed well and included a great additional front porch. Once I paid Pietro off—in a decade or so—and maybe got some extra money, we could replace that siding, but for now I didn't give much of a crap. The damage was on the back, so the only people who'd see it were people who were welcome here and wouldn't care.

And now here we were, throwing a frickin' housewarming party. I checked that the beer keg for the non-zombies was tapped and that there were plenty of non-alcoholic beverages set out. The parasite considered alcohol a toxin and burned up brains to clear the body of it—a waste of brains without even a buzz to show for it.

My phone rang as I checked to see if we had any more big bowls. I dug it out of my pocket, peered at the caller ID. I didn't recognize the number, but I answered it anyway.

"Hello, Angel. It's Ariston Nikas."

"Hi, Dr. Nikas!" I said brightly. "How's it going?" I'd only been back to the lab once in the past six weeks, but he'd let me help with the monthly examination of the heads and changing the medium in their vats. Totally gross, and I'd loved every second of it.

"Good. It's going good," he said. "I, ah, wanted to thank you for the invitation and let you know that I won't be able to make it."

"I'm sorry to hear that," I replied quite truthfully, "but I understand."

"Yes, I don't do well in crowds," he said, "so best to see me in the lab. Have a lovely evening, and I'll see you soon."

"Sure thing, Dr. Nikas," I said. I couldn't help but smile. I really liked Dr. Nikas, and it warmed my silly little heart that he'd bothered to call.

Marcus called out from the door as I hung up. "Anyone home?"

"In the dining room!" I hollered back. My house had a dining room. How cool was that? Sure, the place would never be mistaken for one of Pietro's houses, but I still enjoyed a nice twinge of pride.

Laden with grocery bags, Marcus entered the dining room. He'd shed the cast only a few days ago, finally able to let go of faking his broken leg which had now "healed." That had been weeks of torture for the poor guy, and stuck on desk duty as an added torment.

"Evening, Mr. Crawford," he said right before I draped my arms around his neck and gave him a very nice kiss. I heard my dad mutter something in response to Marcus's greeting, but we both ignored him as Marcus kissed me right back. The last couple of weeks of living with Marcus had sorely tested the abilities of both men to remain civil, and all three of us were seriously glad when the house was ready.

I broke the kiss, then glanced back at my dad to see him poking at the hors d'oeuvres again. "Those are done, Dad," I told him. "You're not used to an oven that works."

Smiling, Marcus set the bags on the table. "What do you need help with?"

If he thought I'd give him a polite "Oh don't worry, I have it" he was sorely mistaken. I proceeded to weigh him down with a list of tasks, and then I did my best to keep my dad from burning the finger food.

People began to trickle in, and before I knew it we had an honest-to-god party going on. Among others, I'd invited everyone from the Coroner's Office, as well as Detectives Roth and Abadie, since I worked with them on so many scenes. Ben Roth arrived with his boyfriend, Neil, a rugged blond with a carefree smile and a great sense of humor. And, to my utter shock, Mike Abadie showed up too, though he claimed he was only there to soak up my food and beer in payback for having to put

up with me. To absolutely no one's surprise, Allen
Prejean didn't stop by, for which I was more than a little
relieved. My animosity with Abadie was entertaining.
Not so much with Allen. Plus, while the thin "scar" on
my thumb looked real enough at a casual glance, it
wouldn't hold up to any close inspection since it was little more than a temporary tattoo. Brian had helped me
out with that. Apparently I wasn't the first zombie who
found it necessary to accessorize with a fake scar.

"Not bad," Nick said to me after the party was in full
swing. He took a sip of his beer and cast his gaze around
the living room.

"Thanks," I said. "I got a really good deal on the
place."

"You're settling in all right?"

I nodded. "It's weird. I mean, I lived in that other
house my whole life. But this one's pretty nice."

"I guess after what you went through, having a place
of your own again has to feel good."

"It does," I admitted. Through the back window I
could see people sitting in lawn chairs, laughing and talking. It was still a bit of a *holy crap* for me to realize I
actually had a lawn. Pietro had thrown in all new landscaping as a housewarming gift. Grass, bushes, trees, even
a frickin' gazebo. "I mean, Marcus and I are doing great
now," I continued, "but I'm still not ready to move in for
real or anything. And besides, my dad still needed a
place to live."

A combined expression of disappointment and hope
passed briefly over his face before being controlled and
replaced with a typical Nick disinterested expression.
"Sure. Great that your dad can have that now."

Sometimes I could be a little slow on the uptake, but
I was starting to figure out that Nick liked me. And while
I liked him well enough as a friend, I wasn't sure I'd ever
feel anything more—even if I wasn't already involved

with Marcus. However, this was the first time I'd ever been in this position, and I didn't have the faintest clue how to handle it.

"So, um, I rescheduled my GED," I said, scrambling to neutral ground. "Two months from now. You still up for pounding knowledge into my skull?"

He gave a diffident shrug. "If you still need it, I can make myself available," he said casually.

"Hell yeah, I still need it." I smiled. "And I'm also gonna get tested to see if there's a reason I'm so darn thick-headed."

"That's a good idea," he said, then abruptly looked discomfited. "I didn't mean that you're thick-headed. It's just good to find out about the possibility of dyslexia."

I laughed softly. "I know. It's cool." I actually already knew the answer. I intended to get tested to make it official, but delving into my school records had uncovered preliminary screening suggesting dyslexia with further testing recommended—testing that my mother had flatly refused to pursue. There was even a note in the records about repeated inquiries to Mrs. Crawford that had been rebuffed. Had my mother known the hell I went through because of that? And if so, had she cared?

I doubted it. Made me all the more grateful to have people around me now who cared for real.

I gave Nick a smile. "GED, here I come." Over his shoulder I saw more people come in. "Oh, there's Dr. Leblanc . . . Good god, and the coroner. I'd better go say hi." I gave Nick a hug. "Thanks for everything."

He returned the hug, then released me with only a trace of reluctance. "No problem," he said gruffly.

Smiling, I moved off and greeted the new arrivals, then found myself drawn into a bizarre conversation with Dr. Leblanc, Derrel, Dr. Duplessis, and Mike Abadie about the usefulness of the examination of stomach contents in solving murder cases. I finally excused myself

to check on drinks, only to be surprised as all hell when
I saw Pietro and Jane Pennington enter—followed by
Brian in his black suit and looking every inch the per-
sonal security guard.

I gave Brian a smile and wave. He responded with a
slight nod and then returned to checking out exits and
possible threats and whatever the hell else someone in
his position did.

"Pietro! Jane!" I said, grinning. "I didn't think y'all
would come. Thanks!"

"We almost didn't," Jane admitted after giving me a
quick but warm hug of greeting. "My flight was delayed
an hour, and we literally came straight from the airport."

"I'm really glad you could make it," I said fervently. I
hadn't spent much time with the woman, but she was
already one of my favorite people. "It's not a mansion,"
I continued, gesturing around me, "but it's definitely a
step up from the old place."

"It's a nice house," Pietro said with an approving
smile. "And the landscaping turned out well."

"Yes, thanks so much for that. I have a lawn! And an
actual driveway!" Grinning, I looked to Jane. "Not even
a year ago, the driveway was paved with crushed beer
cans. I had quite the trashy look going on."

She wrinkled her nose, chuckled. "Yes, I can see the
appeal of pavement."

I gave a mock shudder. "I'm almost respectable!"

"Angel, I'm sorry, but we can't stay," Pietro said. "Jane
has a heavy schedule. However, we wanted to at least
stop by."

"That's cool," I said. "I appreciate that you came at
all."

We made our goodbyes, with Pietro surprising the
hell out of me by giving me an honest-to-god hug and a
kiss on the cheek before heading to the door with Jane.

Brian stepped up to me before they exited. "I'm with

them, so I can't stay, but I wanted to congratulate you on your new home." He smiled, and I had the sense he was referring to more than just the physical house.

"Thanks," I said automatically, but I couldn't help but feel another twinge of worry and angst about being so much deeper into the Pietro "home" now. "I hope it all works out for the best."

Brian was sharp enough to catch my slight hesitancy. "That's pretty much what we're all shooting for in the end," he said, then gave me a smile. "Enjoy the party."

I watched him go, then frowned slightly when a woman I didn't know came in. At least I thought I didn't know her until I caught her eye and she gave me a bright smile and cheery wave. I smiled back in delight.

"Heather!" I cried out. She had hazel contact lenses in, and her once loose, blond hair was now a deep chest-nut pulled back in a flattering twist. Her face was subtly different as well, and after a few seconds of peering I decided, at the very least, she'd had cheek implants and a nose job. She was still quite pretty, but she'd be able to blend into a crowd easily.

"Angel!" she cried. "This is so great!"

"I'm so glad you made it," I told her.

"Wouldn't miss it," she said, "even though my social calendar is sooo jam packed." She rolled her eyes.

I laughed. "You're way too busy kicking ass and taking names."

"I can't help myself," she said with a snort, then glanced back, frowned. "Dammit, I lost Kyle. Where the hell did he go? He was right behind me."

"He's probably scouting the perimeter," I pointed out.

Her mouth curved into a fierce scowl. "This is a parrrrrty. He isn't supposed to be working."

"I think he's always worrrrrking," I replied.

She laughed. "True. Not even going to try to argue that one."

"How's everything going for you?"

"Pretty damn good," she said with a smile, then cocked her head toward a quiet corner and headed that way.

I got the idea she wanted a private word and followed. "What's up, chick?"

"I'm dead!" she said with a mischievous glint in her eye.

"Yes, I know," I replied with a grin. "I even went out on the scene, though there wasn't much body to recover."

Two days after Philip's meltdown on the movie set, the burnt-out shell of Heather's Jeep had been found at the end of Shore Road. When the sheriff's office investigated, they discovered a body—or rather they discovered teeth from a body, since the fire had been hot enough to burn the bones to ash. Between dental records that convinced authorities the teeth belonged to Heather, and a significant amount of blood near the burned car that matched her DNA, there was no doubt in the eyes of the law that she was quite dead.

Heather hooked a finger into her cheek and pulled it away to show three molars that looked a little too perfect to be real. "New teef!"

I shuddered. "Oh my god. I can't believe you let them pull your teeth."

She dropped her hand, winked. "That's what anesthesia and Percocet are for!" But then she grimaced. "It was the best way, short of chopping off a body part, to convince everyone I'm dead."

"I guess it's worth it if it helps keep you safe from Saberton."

A wince flashed across her face. "And my brother."

"Do you think he'll believe you're really dead?" I asked.

She gave a slow nod. "I've thought about it a lot, and I'm fairly positive he will. After all, I can't imagine he'd believe that Pietro Ivanov would actually welcome Julia Saber into his fold." She shrugged. "The story that was leaked is that I tried to come over to your side, and that when Mr. Ivanov found out who I really was," she smiled and spread her hands, "shit got ugly."

"Well, you look damn good for a dead chick," I told her, smiling. And now I understood why Brian had wanted the Saberton man to get a good look at her on the movie set. Had to let them believe she'd been brought on board.

"Thanks! Oh, and I have a new name. Naomi Comtesse."

"And a new hair color too. Looks great," I said with a grin.

"All part of the new identity, thanks to Mr. Ivanov," she said. Then she shook her head. "He sure has a lot more connections than I knew, and I'm pretty sure I'm only seeing the tip of the iceberg even now."

I doubted she knew that iceberg was likely over five hundred years old. "Yeah, he seems to know everybody," I said in a noncommittal tone.

"I'm not complaining," she said fervently, then looked past me toward the door. "There's Kyle. I'll go check in with him and catch up with you later." With a cheerful wave she headed off.

Musing, I watched Heather-Naomi go. There was no denying the look in her eyes when she saw Kyle. She definitely had a thing for him. I let out a soft sigh. I'd had every indication that Brian really liked her and couldn't help but feel a twinge of regret that the no-nonsense head of security had apparently missed out.

I turned back to the party, mingled, and did my best to spend time with everyone who'd shown up. Satisfaction wound through me as I made the rounds and checked on food and drinks. I had honest-to-god *friends*, and it felt damn cool. Okay, so most of them had no idea I was a brain-eating monster, but they all seemed to be more than okay with the non-zombie side of Angel. And that was a helluva lot more than I had before I was turned.

The party slowly wound down until it was clusters of people sitting and talking both inside and out in the backyard. I went to the kitchen to get a head start on clean up, surprised to find that one or more of the guests had taken out the trash and loaded the dishwasher. For about the thousandth time that evening I smiled and basked in the knowledge that there were people who had my back, even for little stuff like tossing empty cups and wiping the counter for me.

A subtle butterflies-in-the-stomach feeling passed through me as I went back out to the living room. I looked around, surprised and pleased to see Philip standing unobtrusively by the door, gaze roving over the remaining people. He looked a helluva lot better than the last time I'd seen him—the day of all the mayhem. Obviously Dr. Nikas had done a lot of work to fix or control the damage to him.

I moved to him, smiling. "You made it," I said softly.

He returned the smile. "I did." He looked up to scan the room, then back down at me. "Step outside with me for a minute?"

"Sure," I replied. I swept a quick glance around to make sure everything was going all right, then followed him out to the front porch. The night was warm though not oppressively so. A nearly full moon hung above the trees, and the muted sound of laughter and conversation drifted from the backyard. Mosquitos buzzed, but they had no taste for zombie blood and left us both alone.

Philip moved down to the far end of the porch before turning to face me. "It's been too long," he said. "I should have found a way to come and talk to you sooner. It took me a while to reconcile everything, the actions I took while undercover." His eyes met mine. "And I did. I know I did what I had to do, and . . . and that it was worth it." He exhaled. "But for the parts that involved you, I don't expect you to hold that same view. All I can do is say I'm sorry for hurting you in any way. And, thank you for all that you did for me."

I touched his arm gently. "It's okay," I said. "I mean, once I knew you were undercover I was able to look back and see that you really did everything possible to keep me from getting hurt worse." I gave him a smile. "It sure wasn't easy being your zombie-mama, but I'm really glad you seem to be doing better."

"I *am* doing better," he said. "Dr. Nikas has worked wonders. I still have periods of pain, but not continuous like it was before, and it doesn't get intense." Remembered agony shimmered briefly in his eyes, and my heart clenched in sympathy for what he'd endured. "I've even been able to cut my excess brain consumption back considerably." He shook his head. "My first six months as a zombie were a nightmare on so many levels."

"I know," I said, mouth tightening. "It pisses me off. It shouldn't have been like that at all."

But Philip shook his head again. "It wasn't only what Dr. Charish did. It was the first-hand experience of being a second-class citizen with Saberton. An eye opener, to be sure." He met my eyes again. "I went from being one of the guys and a valued member of a team, to being . . . less than human. *Worth* less than a human."

An involuntary shiver went through me. I'd spent the last year pulling myself up from being a second-class citizen, doing my damndest to turn my life around and make something of myself. And yet there were still people who would see me as less than human. *This* was why Pietro's damn zombie mafia needed to exist. I sure as hell didn't always agree with the methods, but without it or something similar, we were all on our own, waiting to be exploited or killed.

"I'm sorry you had to go through that," I told him.

He gave a nod of acknowledgment. "Of course, the instability crap emphasized my difference, but it was *disturbing* to note the change in attitude, when nothing else about me had shifted."

I gave him a sad smile. "I'm glad you're not under-cover anymore."

"As am I," he replied. "I suppose I have Dr. Charish to thank for that, both for the original debilitation, and for fucking me up so badly that last day." A grimace swept over his features. "I'd have been with Saberton much longer if I'd been, well, normal. And, on a personal level, I'm very glad I'm not."

My brow furrowed. "You're glad you're not normal?"

Philip chuckled. "Ah, no. I'm glad I'm not with Saberton anymore." He smiled wryly. "I wouldn't mind being a 'normal' zombie at all."

"Oh, right. Of course," I said, wrinkling my nose at my obtuseness. I tilted my head and regarded him. "Y'know, this is gonna sound weird, but if anyone had to make you a zombie, I'm glad it was me."

His smile widened. "I'm glad it was you too. You rock." Then he bent and picked up a largish flat rectangular box that had been leaning against the wall. "Here, I have something for you."

"Oh?" I said, raising an eyebrow as I took the box from him. "I kinda like presents." I opened the box, then grinned as I pulled out a brand new jacket in the exact size and style of the one I'd worn to the Gourmet Gala. "No, *you* rock!"

His eyes crinkled in a smile. "Had to cut the other one to make sure Bell didn't break your skin when he bit you. No idea what effect his truly screwed up parasite could have on a normal one." He shrugged. "Maybe nothing, but if he'd drawn blood I'd have found a way to get word to Dr. Nikas, just in case."

"Thanks," I said. "You didn't have to get me a new one." Then I grinned. "But I also won't let you take it back now."

He let out a bark of laughter. "A scuffle on the front porch could be entertainment for your party."

"It would give the neighbors something to call the cops on us for," I said with amusement. "They don't know what to make of the new, outwardly-respectable Crawfords."

Philip lifted a hand to my cheek and looked into my eyes, smiled gently as he leaned down. For an instant I was absolutely positive that he intended to kiss me—and almost absolutely positive that I wouldn't do a damn thing to stop him.

But he simply laid a gentle kiss on my forehead and straightened, though his hand lingered on my cheek.

"I don't know about them," he said, voice soft, "but I'm pretty impressed by the inward respectability of Ms. Angel Crawford."

My heart thudded erratically as I struggled to come up with something to say in response to *all* of that. "Um. Thanks," I managed.

Smiling still, he withdrew his hand. "Come on, Zombie-Mama," he said. "You have a house to warm, and I have beer to look at longingly."

Chuckling, I tucked the box and jacket under my arm. "Best zombie-kid ever."

Diana Rowland

The Kara Gillian Novels

"Rowland's hot streak continues as she gives her fans another big helping of urban fantasy goodness! The plot twists are plentiful and the action is hard-edged. Another great entry in this compelling series." —*RT Book Review*

"Rowland's world of arcane magic and demons is fresh and original [and her] characters are well-developed and distinct.... Dark, fast-paced, and gripping." —*SciFiChick*

Secrets of the Demon
978-0-7564-0652-3

Sins of the Demon
978-0-7564-0705-6

Touch of the Demon
978-0-7564-0775-9

To Order Call: 1-800-788-6262
www.dawbooks.com

DAW 176